"*Passages*, the third and final novel in Evie Yoder Miller's sweeping Civil War era trilogy, is a masterful insight into individual lives and consciences struggling to discover where their political, familial, and spiritual allegiances lie. The multiple perspectives of her characters reveal not only the differences inherent in families, churches, and towns, but also the uniqueness and preciousness of each individual life. Set in an era of shocking loss of life, this brings an enormous humanity and poignancy to Miller's novels. Her characters are our kin; we know them and participate in their lives. There is no better reading experience than this."

—Suzanne Wolfe
Author of *The Confessions of X*

"This powerful last volume of Evie Yoder Miller's epic trilogy draws us deeply into the heartbreaks, losses, struggles, and persistence of its characters—Anabaptists caught up in the last bitter year of the Civil War. With evocative prose and skillful use of multiple narrators, Miller creates a vivid, poignant portrait of women, children, and others often left out of conventional war stories. Whether trapped in the path of predatory armies or in the relative safety of the North, the plain people in this taut, compelling novel find their values challenged and their lives disrupted by a war where, as one puts it, 'Maybe no one counts as civilians anymore.'"

—Jeff Gundy
Author of *Without a Plea* and *Songs from an Empty Cage*

"Evie Yoder Miller explores the moral horizon of the Civil War as it is reflected on the inner spiritual and emotional landscapes of historical figures [illegible]haped by the peace-church heritage of Amish, Mennonite, and Old Ger- [illegible]tist communities. In Miller's complex and convincing narrative, [illegible]sist amidst disaster and death, and the ordinary routines of [illegible]iety supply the momentum to carry both characters [illegible]olding national catastrophe."

Gerald J. Mast
[illegible]sor of Communication, Bluffton University

"In the third and final installment of Evie Miller's Scruples on the Line series, the characters do not flinch from the hard choices faced by Anabaptists who lived through the final years of the Civil War. Set in the thick of unfolding, true-life events whose outcomes were not yet known, the Amish, Mennonites, and German Baptists in *Passages* stay true to their pacifist calling. Drawn from a varied cast—young and aged, loyal and questioning, staunch and humble—these voices have much to offer anyone seeking to discern the way of peace in an increasingly divisive time."

—Sara Phillips
Editor, *Wisconsin Magazine of History*

PASSAGES

Passages

—Book III—

SCRUPLES ON THE LINE:
A Fictional Series Set During the American Civil War

Evie Yoder Miller

RESOURCE *Publications* • Eugene, Oregon

PASSAGES
Book III

Scruples on the Line: A Fictional Series Set During the American Civil War

Resource Publications
An Imprint of Wipf and Stock Publishers
199 W. 8th Ave., Suite 3
Eugene, OR 97401

www.wipfandstock.com

PAPERBACK ISBN: 978-1-6667-0478-5
HARDCOVER ISBN: 978-1-6667-0479-2
EBOOK ISBN: 978-1-6667-0480-8

08/26/21

Contents

List of Illustrations

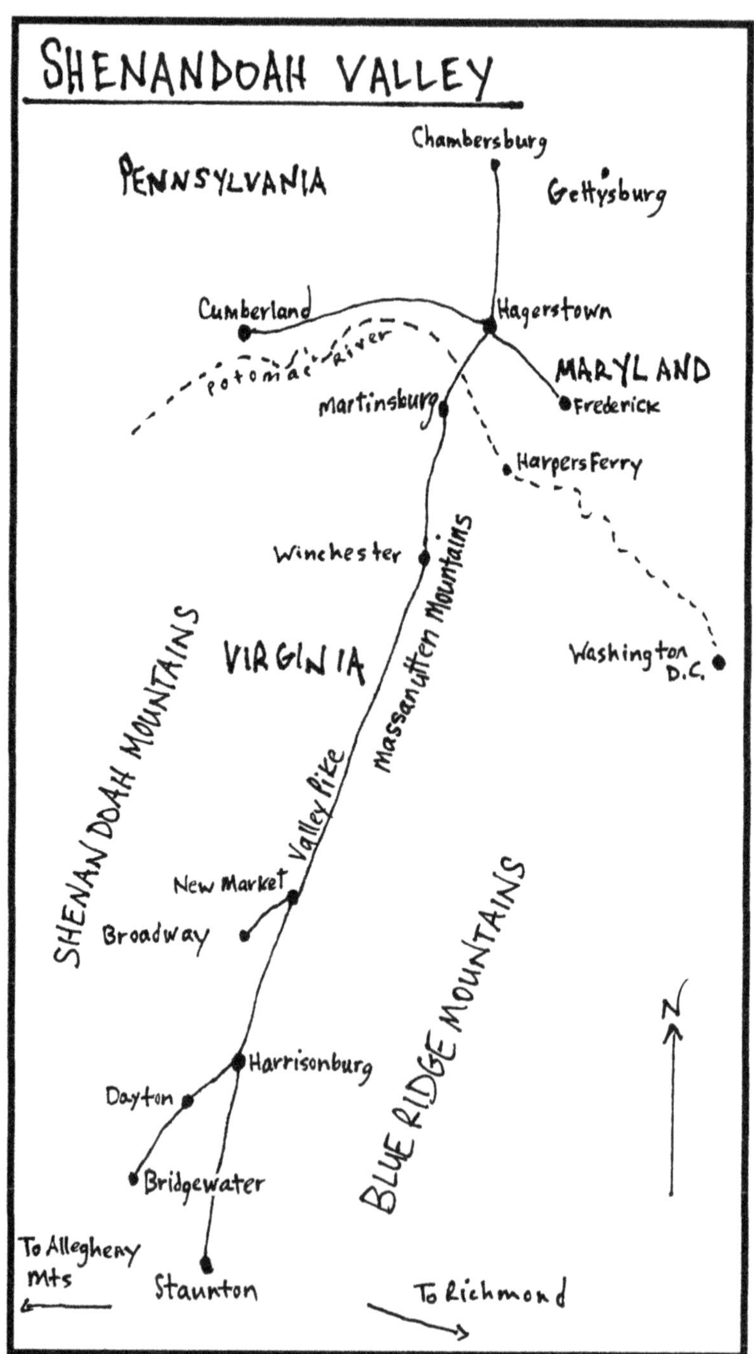
SHENANDOAH VALLEY
PENNSYLVANIA
Chambersburg
Gettysburg
Cumberland
Hagerstown
Potomac River
MARYLAND
Martinsburg
Frederick
Harpers Ferry
Winchester
Massanutten Mountains
Washington D.C.
SHENANDOAH MOUNTAINS
VIRGINIA
Valley Pike
New Market
Broadway
BLUE RIDGE MOUNTAINS
N
Harrisonburg
Dayton
Bridgewater
To Allegheny Mts
Staunton
To Richmond

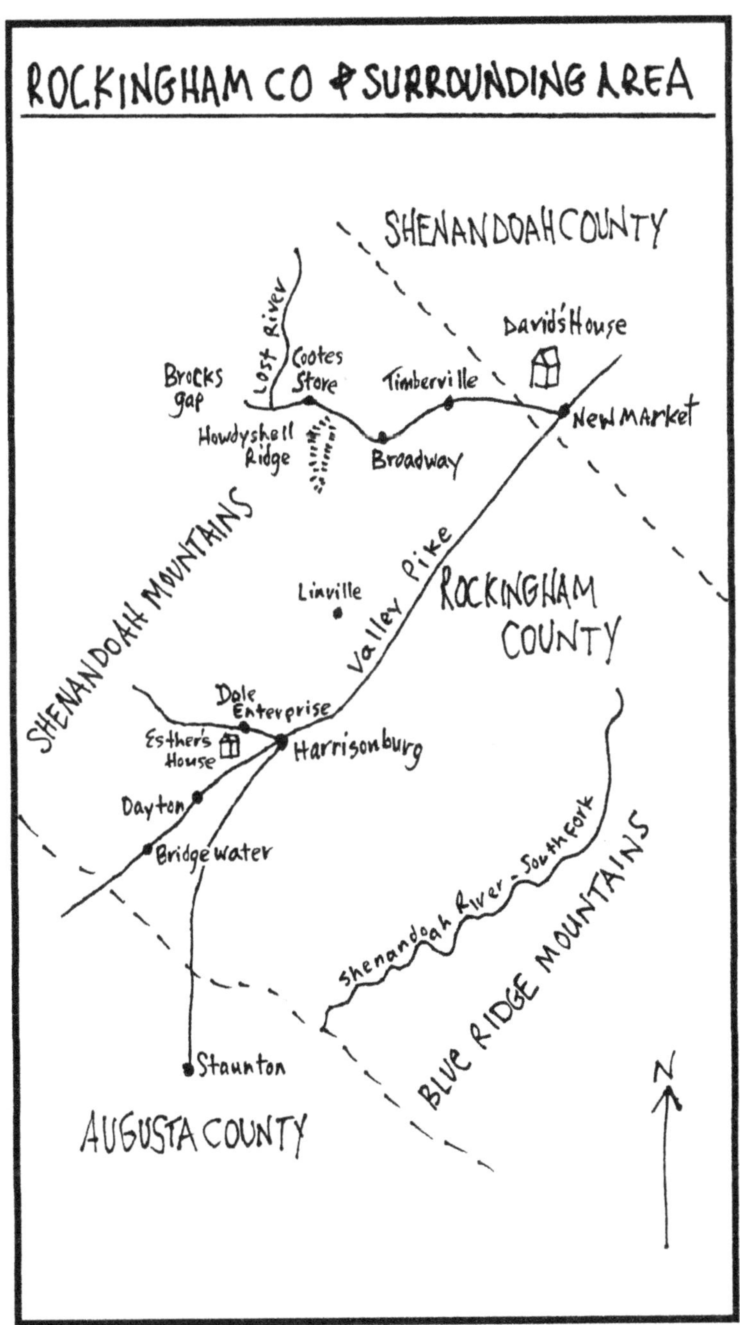
ROCKINGHAM CO & SURROUNDING AREA
SHENANDOAH COUNTY
Lost River
David's House
Brocks gap
Cootes Store
Timberville
New Market
Howdyshell Ridge
Broadway
SHENANDOAH MOUNTAINS
Valley Pike
Linville
ROCKINGHAM COUNTY
Dale Enterprise
Esther's House
Harrisonburg
Dayton
Bridgewater
Shenandoah River - South Fork
BLUE RIDGE MOUNTAINS
Staunton
AUGUSTA COUNTY
N

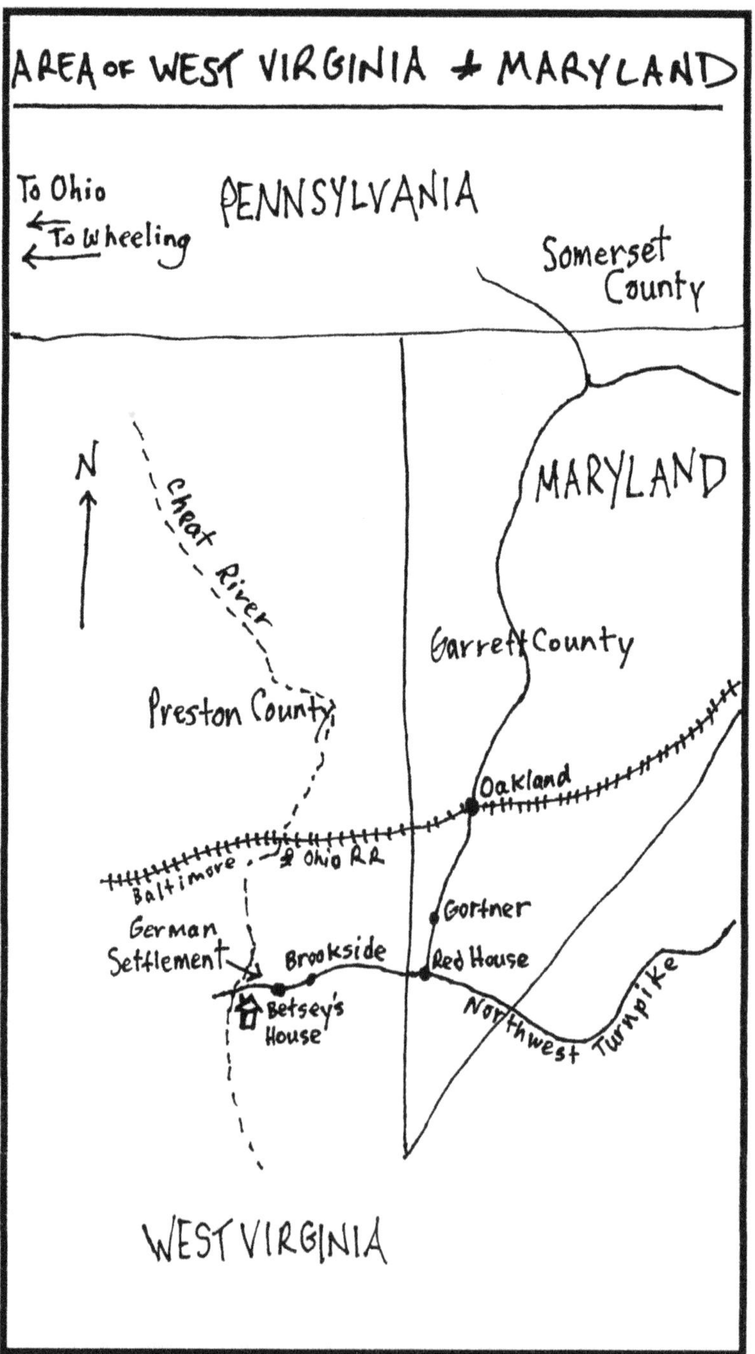
AREA OF WEST VIRGINIA & MARYLAND
To Ohio
To Wheeling
PENNSYLVANIA
Somerset County
N
Cheat River
MARYLAND
Garrett County
Preston County
Oakland
Baltimore & Ohio RR
Gortner
German Settlement
Brookside
Red House
Betsey's House
Northwest Turnpike
WEST VIRGINIA

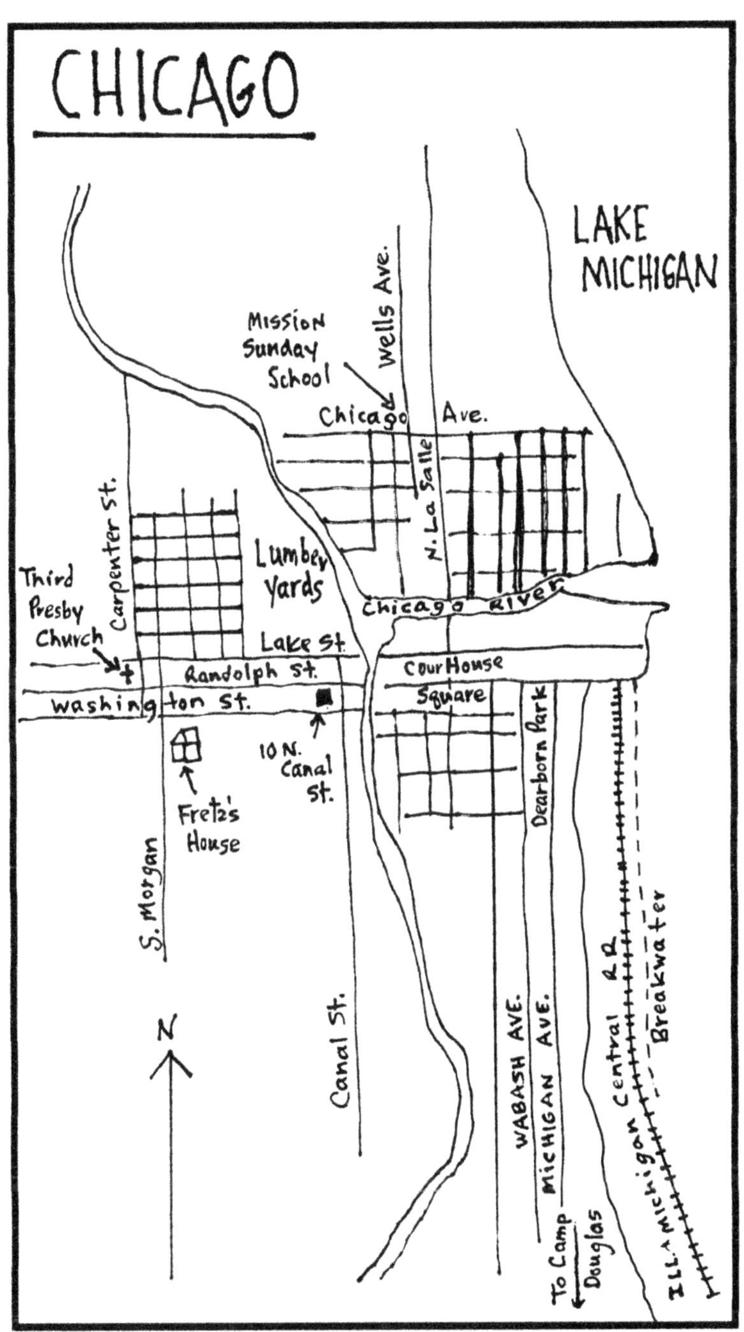
CHICAGO
LAKE MICHIGAN
Mission Sunday School
Wells Ave.
Chicago Ave.
N. La Salle
Carpenter St.
Lumber Yards
Third Presby Church
Chicago River
Lake St.
Randolph St.
Washington St.
Court House Square
10 N. Canal St.
Fretz's House
Dearborn Park
S. Morgan
N
Canal St.
WABASH AVE.
MICHIGAN AVE.
To Camp Douglas
ILL. MICHIGAN Central RR
Breakwater

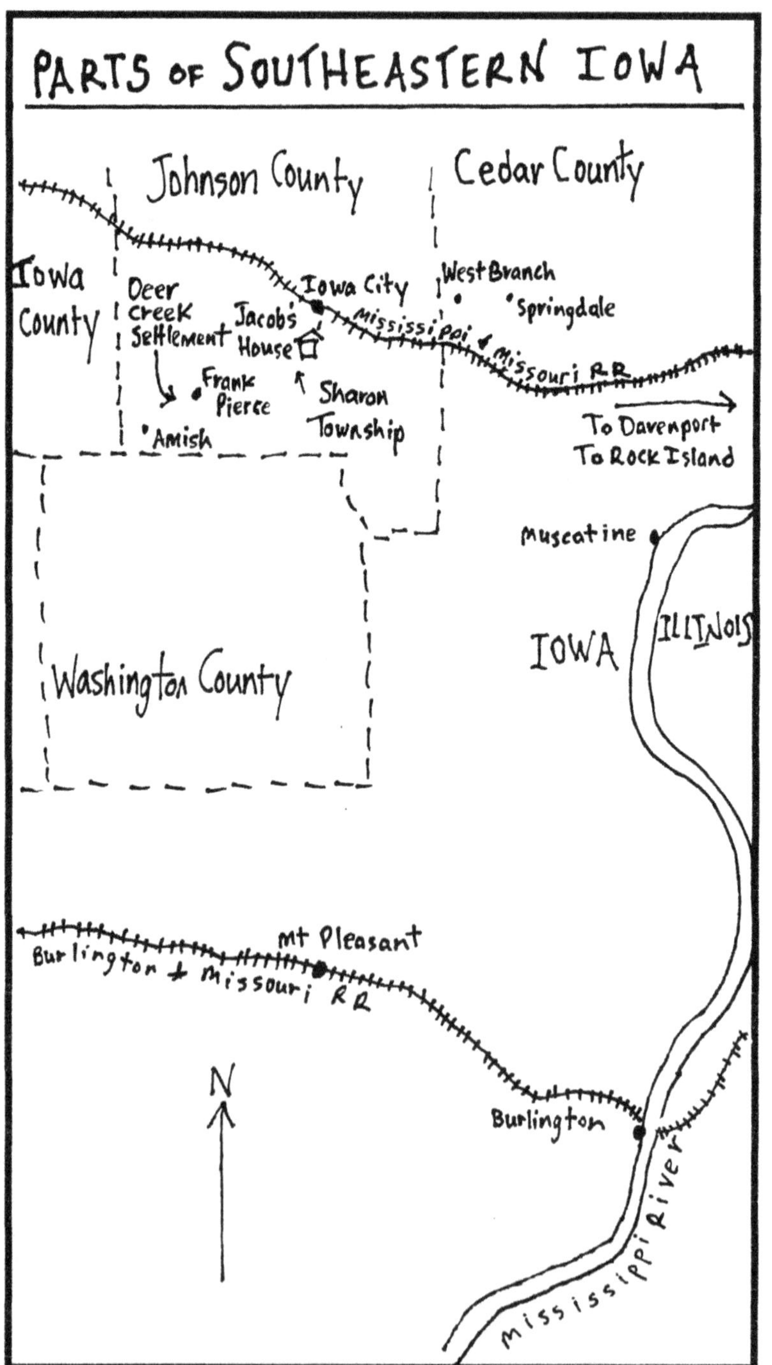
PARTS OF SOUTHEASTERN IOWA
Johnson County
Cedar County
Iowa County
Deer Creek Settlement
Iowa City
Jacob's House
West Branch
Springdale
Mississippi & Missouri RR
Frank Pierce
Sharon Township
Amish
To Davenport
To Rock Island
Muscatine
IOWA
ILLINOIS
Washington County
Mt Pleasant
Burlington & Missouri RR
N
Burlington
Mississippi River

Jacob Schwartzendruber Family

(Select characters in novel)

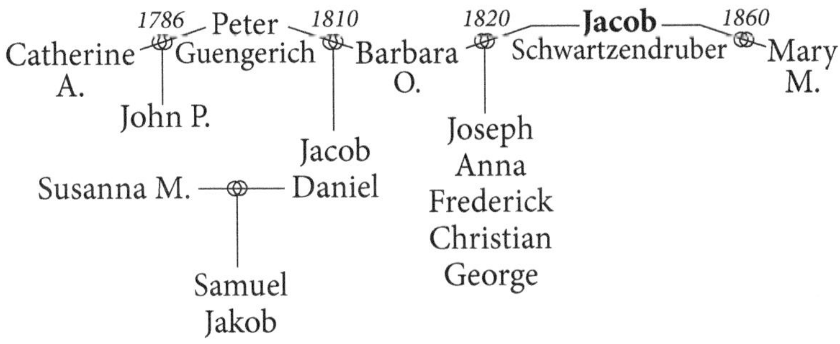

Fretz (John) Funk Family

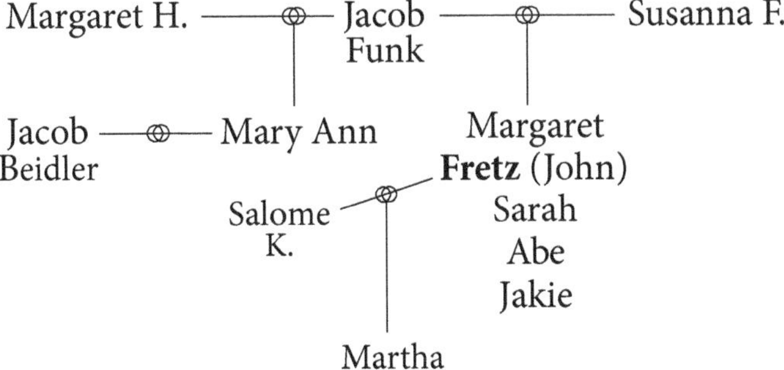

Betsey Petersheim Family

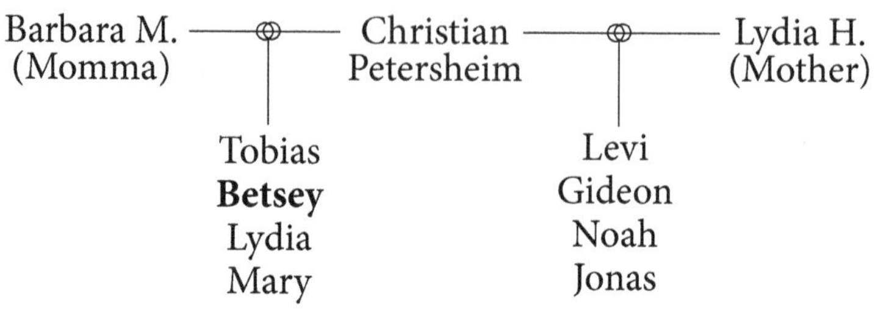

David Bowman Family

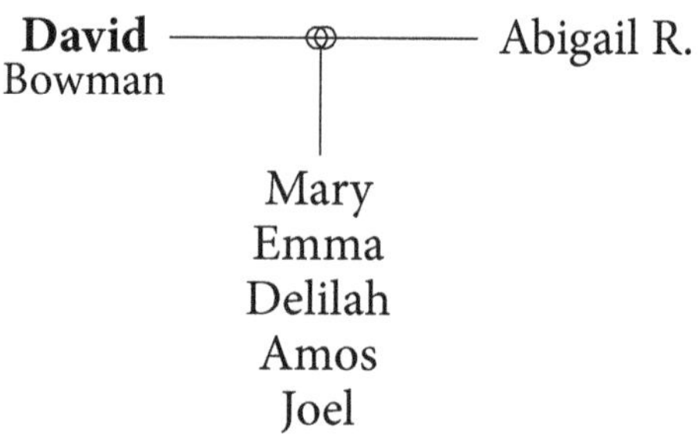

Esther Shank Family

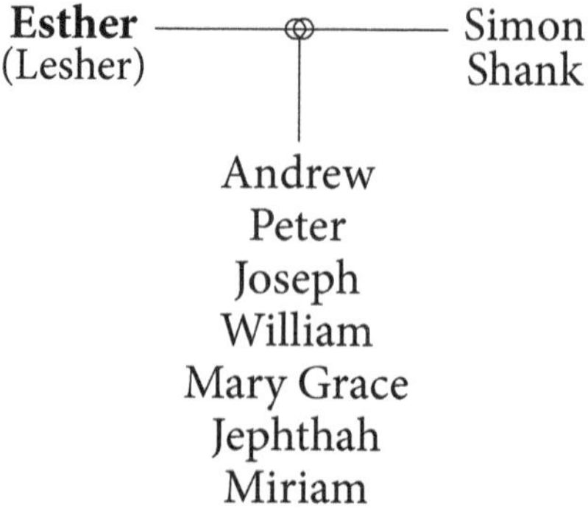

dedicated to all who
stand for human rights
across race, culture, and creed;
live interdependently as neighbors
not as rivals;
balance the weight of sorrow,
the treasure of joy;
give voice to dreams
while calling out courage in others

If there is no struggle there is no progress . . . Power concedes nothing without a demand. It never did and it never will.

—Frederick Douglass,
West Indies Emancipation speech, 1857

Yea, though I walk through the valley of the shadow of death,
I will fear no evil: for thou art with me; thy rod and thy staff
they comfort me.

—Psalms 23:4 (KJV)

Esther Shank — Shenandoah Valley, February 1864

My breath is short. Words and thoughts come out choppy. Most everything seems scrambled. Prayers on the loose. Little protection.

My men, gone again. A third time for my man Simon and our oldest, Andrew. No word from Peter. Our next, Joseph, on the brink. A month ago I couldn't bear to send him with Andrew. I needed a big one to stay and help put in crops; we can't be entirely alone. But now we don't know if we'll plant, come spring. William and Mary Grace will help, but . . . How much longer, this not knowing? This waiting for all to be safe again? I barely remember how that was.

Nor can I say half of what races through my mind, not when another babe pushes to burst forth, perhaps soon. I don't seek to hide my bulge; I never lost gain from Jephthah's nesting. If I ever need to wear the black—it won't fit; I've become *flotchety*.

Mary Grace—what would I do without her? How little she knows what may lie ahead, far beyond what any thirteen-year-old should face. Far more than rustling up food. I will need to give instruction. Oh, we can't be alone! I go through the steps. *Heat the water, but not to scalding.* If the baby is a girl, Mary Grace may do the naming. I know she'll pick Miriam.

One change after another, forced upon us. Back in December we heard stirrings about losing our men's exemption. Governor Letcher called an extra session of the lawmakers in Richmond. Simon came back from town, the dark of winter already upon us; he brought word: no more substitutes. It's said to bring the Army discouragement. From then on, no more smacking of lips from Simon. His talk of the Almighty's protection, a thing of the past. He jumped at every noise; our spoons rattled. Brother Samuel stayed calm but said, "Be a step ahead, if need be."

Simon cogitated on several counts. The first surprise came at Christmas. Gabriel's Harriet has a comb like this: long and creamy white, a swirl of gold in the center. Simon wouldn't say the what or wherefore.

"Not one of those peddlers," I said.

He shrugged.

"Frequenting the mill?"

"I want you to have it," he said.

He wouldn't spend excess when we don't know the future, would he? I thanked him—the comb, solid to the grip—but some mornings it feels like a weight in my hand. Another sudden purchase as marks the past: Midnight, the cookstove. I don't mean to be ungrateful, but I would rather have affection than splashes. I gave Mary Grace my old comb with the missing teeth. This new one pulls better through long strands to get the kinks out. By day, I still wind my hair into a tight bun at the back. But I can't let go the thought: *he shouldn't have.* We know so little.

When Samuel, our bishop, passed along official word—all men, seventeen to fifty, told to report—that's when Simon and Andrew, and others of our church, skedaddled. We women fell to weeping, like on the day officers first entered our church and barked orders. This time, younger and older ones included in the call-up. Oh, not my Joseph! He, like the three other young boys at Weavers who recently turned seventeen, hasn't sealed his vow to God with baptism.

Oh, I should have sent him with Andrew; I kept him for myself. Risky now; he could easily pass for older—a good six feet. Of no use in our cellar. The haymow offers scant hiding. He'll have to flee, knowing scouts wait to snatch. Yet he keeps mum, not saying exactly. I don't think he'll deviate, but the Rebel Army would swallow him if they could. He's listened to Peter, our enlisted one, heard reply from Simon. Brother Samuel tells us to trust, but he agreed: Joseph must flee when conditions are ready. All those that age must go. But not alone. Some older one must accompany the lads.

This morning she came again: Mama stepping from the shadows of the lantern as I went to milk the cows. I stopped dead, as if accosted. She came dressed in black, bouncing on lightened feet. In one second, she appeared, out of a puff of my warm breath. I reached with my bucket, whether to fend or not. The next, she vanished. I peered far. The lantern of no help. Gone, as on other visitations. Not even a rustling in the brush. I hurried to the milk shed and leaned on the entryway to catch my breath, scarce daring to look back. My heart pounded; inner kicks set active.

Simon always said, "The Devil's work, to see sights. Don't allow yourself to dwell unhinged." He scorned Mama's knowing twixt beautiful and bad when it came to deaths.

Two weeks ago, Simon left; it seemed for the best. He hadn't slept solid, hadn't been himself, talked as a daft one. "I can't be hunted as an animal anymore."

I grabbed his arm. "What do you mean?"

"I can't stay close. No more coming back for cheese. The cave, too cold; dry firewood, scarce." He railed at our unfit weather. The snow, the short days even shorter when swallowed by heavy fog.

What could I say to dispute, when my own upside down of a cow's cluck, a rooster's neigh, flitted within?

Simon spewed family tales, the likes of which I'd never heard before. He'd always acted uninterested when asked. But now: whippings from his father, and a mother, given to sourness. Picked on by his big brothers, except for Gabriel, his only protector. Simon wanted to seek him out; insisted he must. He promised to take the back ways to reach his brother's place, walk backwards in snow, if need be. He should be there long over a week already, depending how far out of the way he went to deceive.

I said, "Go," but now it settles: he's gone. Everything seems exaggerated this time, like unseen forces conspire. Omens of another spring with another round of hassles such as we went through two years ago. My own taste of bile, when I bend to a cow. My walk back to the house, cautious over slippery paths. I daresn't spill. How will I hand over a ham again? Soldiers will help themselves to flour. But how, give of my cloak? Brother Samuel says seventy times seven. Are not two sons, my man, enough? This week's *Rockingham Register* charges that we Mennonites and Dunkers don't plan to raise as much grain this summer, only what's necessary for ourselves. Those so quick to criticize don't think straight. How can we grow the same, if no men here, not even to get a start?

Neither Simon nor Andrew wanted to flee with a group. "Easier to give slip alone," Simon said. So far as I know, he made no arrangements with Zigler. He wouldn't take the rifle, but wouldn't say if he'd bought a pistol. He only spoke of Gabriel this and Gabriel that.

Andrew said, "Hard to go undetected with others. Someone turns an ankle—slows everyone."

"But lost in the forest," I said. "Where do you mean to go?"

"I've done this before, Ma. I know the shortcuts to Chambersburg. Easy to find Uncle Matthias's place."

"But Army men won't be where you expect. You can't count on the same."

"Best not to worry, Ma." He shrugged like his father.

Simon boasted. "I know these mountains; fool a scout as quick as flick a wrist. Gabriel will protect. Like old times."

I grabbed his arm as if he were William, made him look at me. "You don't know your brother's circumstances. It could be worse, those parts."

"Maybe by March," he said.

"Maybe what?"

"No more snow then. Maybe back to the cave, if warmer."

What consolation was that? My man and Andrew left, loaded with provisions.

"Only together a short distance," Simon said. "Help with his start, but soon to part." Simon must have bought a pistol.

What does Andrew know of a mother's worry? I carry him, heavy as the babe to come, a hot lump beside my burning for Peter. I insist that William and Joseph sleep on pallets by the fire; the loft, too far away for my liking. I let Mary Grace snuggle. What other comforts are there? She gets up some nights to quiet Jephthah.

My friend Frances knows of my coming need. But roads can't be counted on; snow falls near to every other day. I've gone over duties with William. He must fetch, come day or night. He must stay on Rawley Springs Turnpike. If only I'd kept in touch with Genevieve, despite differences over war. How long ago, when she and Frances and I talked freely, had a nose for need from one or the other. Not bothered by barriers back then.

Before each meal we hold hands at our table. Jephthah, too. Mary Grace asks why I whisper. "Because I can't say loud," I reply. My eyes droop with shame. "God hears pleadings." I turn to Joseph. "Hears mumbles, too."

When I sag into bed, my sighs come unheeded. My legs swollen from their day's load. Mary Grace says I groan when I settle at the loom also. But lining up threads—that I can do. A respite from standing or bending to other tasks. My girl does the spinning and saves me long hours of standing at the Big Wheel. I must speed up to finish this carpet of rags.

* * *

He came back, but only a night. As fleeting as Mama's comings and goings, but in body. Not Simon, but Peter, this time—his beard shorter again, but shaggy elsewhere, like a woodsman. His looks are different every time. Wearing a long heavy coat like an old man, his haversack kept close, like always. Jephthah clapped, remembering. We shared our pot of beans with bacon, half the meat of other years. He showed no surprise at Simon's and Andrew's absence. He must have noticed my heavy walk but said naught.

His talk was about Jubal Early—like a trumpet calling. There must have been switching around of men, for he used to speak of a Ewell man. Peter looked long at Joseph and reminded him again of greater choice if volunteering. All last month the Confederate Army hadn't wanted Peter or others; too many mouths to feed while idle. Last fall, typhoid fever and measles raced through the ranks. Peter went with Benjamin to that Hildebrand family! My boy doesn't know his home. Only here for a night.

They're gearing up again. Benjamin received a call-up for the 52nd; that means Peter, too. He tried to make a joke: "Soon we won't need to stuff rags and newspaper in our boots to keep our feet warm." I had no kraut left to protect against colds.

He showed me the rip in his shirt and asked Joseph to stay up late and cut his hair, the back and sides. William turned the lamp higher, and Peter sat on a tall stool while I mended. I snatched glances—his bare back and frame, his lame arm. Locks of hair fell softly to the floor like feathers of a molting duck. My ears stayed tuned for any troubling sign from Joseph. He couldn't up and slip away—not that I know. He'd have to report in town, not just tag along with his brother.

Peter said his usual about keeping the Valley safe, stopping Yankees from Richmond. But now and again, a weariness crept in. He spoke of how people clamor for war news, how folks want action. But his other news: "Benjamin's brother, Gideon, has joined."

"Tall like his brother?" Joseph asked. He held a clump of Peter's hair taut in one hand, cut straight across.

"Medium-build, but strong like me," Peter said. "One day we had a snowball fight, though not wet enough to pack good. Ended up wrestling. Gideon's been with the Home Guard, but the father didn't approve. Some of their methods don't sit well." He paused, as if I might question. "Gideon's transferring to the 1st Virginia Cavalry, rewarded by his father with a handsome black horse. Not their best, but very nearly so."

"Why not the 52nd?" Joseph kept cutting, as if he meant no special import.

"Brothers don't fight in the same unit," Peter said softly, "not anymore. Not if it can be helped. Blood brothers don't. Gideon's choosing more risk, astride a horse. Watch it! My ear."

"What sort of family, these Hildebrands?" I asked.

"Very religious," Peter said, straightening on the stool. I couldn't see any scar on his smooth back. "They made the old man a deacon in their Mennonite church, back on Christmas Day. Eight nominees in all, and Jacob drew the right slip." Peter half-turned to me, against Joseph's protests to hold still. "The man keeps abreast like always, knows everything. Very godly, mind you, but goes into Staunton—wants whatever news can be had. 'I'll always follow my boys,' he says." Peter brushed loose hairs from one shoulder, then the other. "Knows where we're sent." His voice quieter to add, "Wants results, though."

"A letter would be nice," I said. "William could write back, if you tell us where. Your pa was the one, thought it best not to know what might befall."

Peter seemed not to hear. "Old Man Hildebrand's a rare one, all right. All he's seen, but still not deterred. Yankee bodies, rooted out of graves by hogs." The scissors' clip halted. "Near Port Republic, where he saw bones scattered."

The babe leaped within; Mary Grace stirred, restless in bed. William's back turned away on the pallet—deathly still.

"Yanks don't dig deep," Peter said. "Too much hurry with us on their tails."

"Nothing to boast," I said, closing my eyes and resting a hand on my belly. "The spirit of a man may linger."

"Easy, man," Peter said. "Not *too* short in front; only short enough to see the panther coming." Joseph stood stiff, but Peter's voice softened again. "That day when Gideon left, it was Benjamin's twenty-first birthday. The old man's words: 'Stay close to God.' Tears shed all around. Never forget that."

I couldn't bring myself to commend the man.

"The three of us made a pact before Gideon headed off," Peter said. He held up his good hand for Joseph to stop cutting and swiveled toward me. "Anything happens, Ma—you'll hear from Benjamin. All right?" My needle stopped—the same that had made zigzag stitches over initials inside his haversack. I fixed on the floor. "I do the same for Benjamin. Make sure he gets proper burial—need be. We've seen too much of guts mixed with mud and ashes. Trampling of carts and horses. I only mean to settle you, Ma, not disturb—"

I made effort to lift the shirt closer. Blurry to see where I'd left off.

Peter's voice stayed tender. "No one wants to die unknown. The worst. Benjamin and I—if it comes—make certain of whereabouts for next of kin. Hard to keep track of Gideon—cavalry and all. But die a good man. I want you to know, Ma."

"Thank you," I whispered back. I couldn't ask whether his other shirt still had his name pinned.

Peter's sudden anger. "Bunch a' butchers! Those hypocrites—the North. Not gonna come here like invaders and spoil our Valley. Pretending they care about dark ones."

"Good—good of you to see to each other," I said. My fingers fumbled to make a loop. The knot ended far from the cloth.

A few more clips of the scissors, and Joseph said quietly, "Done."

"Wish you'd believe me, Ma. Just once. Jacob Hildebrand understands. Rights of Southerners. Oh, he gets impatient, like everyone; it's gone on a long time. But Ma, we do it for you, all of us. Keep things square. *Our* Valley."

Joseph banged the broom against the fireplace wall; clumps of hair sizzled in the fire.

Peter slid partway off the stool, brushed loose hair off his chest. “President Davis wrote to us last fall. Very inspiring. We will *not* submit to a despotic government. He told us never to give up. Fight hard to get out from under. Lincoln’s big proclamation—pfft! No man’ll tell us what to do. *Our* property. Live the way we know to be right.”

He took the shirt from my outstretched hand but squatted in front of me. His eyes brimmed, like mine. “I love you, Ma.”

I reached to touch his face, tucked a wayward tuft of hair behind his ear. “My big boy.” He stumbled to stand before I could catch his eye and hold.

In the morning he left when Joseph and William went out to chore. Peter was last, his haversack secure. I grabbed his arm. “The Lord be with you,” I said.

Peter took a quick breath and looked to the rafters. Then he straightened and nodded, strode out the door.

I turned to Mary Grace, peeling potatoes nearby, and wept on her shoulder. I know of Lincoln’s promise. But I know that freeing slaves won’t change men’s hearts. Soldiers will come again, as determined as Peter not to change direction. They’ll stomp on my porch—expect kindness, leave without thanks. As resolute as my boy.

I don’t want another round. My heart stays cold, save for my youngsters. Joseph, still waiting until conditions improve. My man, safe with his brother; he should be there. We dare not lose our *milch* cow, our cream and butter. I can’t say what we’ll plant. Or whether.

Oh, Peter, my son, to go thus, willingly.

J. Fretz Funk — Chicago, March 1864

Who can describe the joy? Poets have tried. Wise men, reduced to babbling about the mysteries of love. Lesser men, descended into crime and corruption for love of a woman.

Long ago, I memorized Elizabeth Barrett Browning's sonnet: "*How do I love thee? Let me count the ways.*" I didn't understand the half; maybe I still don't. All I know: my new double bed is warm with my mate nestled by my side. Her softness! Tiny at the waist—twenty inches, she says—but such tenderness she affords. The ecstasy! No wonder, men grow attached.

Salome has shed tears for her family and all the folks at Nace's Corner, especially her best friend, Ann Libb Bryan. I can't stop thanking her for coming my way. She's held her tongue, for the most part, about Chicago. She doesn't go out alone, and I've seen her turn her face from filth in the streets. She can't stomach the sight of blood, not even matted on a mongrel dog. She goes with Mary Ann to the market and is learning which merchants to trust for an honest pound of beef. For the time being she's content living in the Beidlers' house—we're boarders in my room on the second floor. But it won't be for long. When our muddy streets dry out—much rain in February—we'll take the carriage to investigate options.

Salome had never met Mary Ann and Jacob; she was only five in 1844 when my sister and brother-in-law moved to Illinois. She says Mary Ann looks like my father, a high forehead and wide, but not as stern through the eyes. Salome reminds me to wipe my shoes when we come inside so we don't track on the wooden floors. Her tidiness is welcome, and she helps Mary Ann keep things picked up. So far as I know, they've had no disagreements over food, although Salome favors cornmeal mush, something Mary Ann says she ate too much of as a child.

The day before we arrived, I sent a telegram giving our approximate arrival. But trains aren't known for punctuality, and we pulled into Chicago late on Saturday. I had checked my inner pocket several times to secure my key for Jacob's house. Salome smiled wanly at her first sight of the city and commented on the late night "hubbub" in the station.

Mary Ann wanted to hear about our time in Pennsylvania—a full two weeks, including the wedding and visits to relatives—so on the first Sunday evening of February, we three sat in the warm kitchen. Jacob was nursing a cold and had retired early.

"We were married by Isaac F. Meyer at my church, Deep Run," Salome said to Mary Ann. "A Tuesday at ten in the morning." She still had that limp look, like an uprooted plant.

"A rainy spell from the day before into that Tuesday," I added.

"You went from bitter cold here," Mary Ann said.

"I haven't forgotten," I said with a shake of my head. I was trying to make my piece of cherry pie last as long as possible—Mary Ann's Saturday baking—so I wouldn't be tempted by seconds. "Thirty below to start the new year here. Everything on hold for three days. Railroads blocked by blowing and drifting."

"Your frozen fingers," Mary Ann said, "from shoveling a path to the animals."

Salome turned to me quickly. "You didn't tell me that." She's slowly coming to understand how much I dislike being cold. At first she tried not to notice when I put on two sets of underwear, two pair of heavy woolen socks.

"Only my fingertips," I said, grinning sheepishly. I held up my hands for inspection. "I barely made it to Pennsylvania in time for us to be published."

"What happened?" Mary Ann asked. "You must have been worried," she said to Salome.

My wife—what pleasure to say that!—blushed and smoothed her hair. "I didn't realize—" She hesitated. "I didn't know he had so many people to see along the way."

"More than John M. Brenneman?" Mary Ann asked, like a mother. "That's all you said."

"Others like Peter Nissley. Well, John's younger brother, Daniel, was the problem. The man pays no attention to time, insisted on introducing me to some brethren in western Pennsylvania; Peter Risser for one." I waved a hand but savored my last bite of sour cherry. "I didn't get to Philadelphia until January thirteenth."

Mary Ann's eyebrows shot up. "You left here on the fourth!"

"No need to tell me. Delayed by everything from train collisions to an ox that weighed 3,700 pounds."

"The timing was tight," Salome said, "but we had all day together on the fourteenth and were published at Line Lexington the next day."

Mary Ann kept looking back and forth between Salome and me. "A train wreck?"

"Delayed by such, three or four times," I said. "Two trains, both ordered forward, collided. Not the train I was on, but I was *behind* the wrecked one going East. So we were delayed getting to Cincinnati; I spent the night freezing on a freight train, going ten miles per hour. Poor coal, a bad stove, careless conductors, a smoky caboose car!"

"That makes my first ride here seem better," Salome said. "He had warned me about excess noise and dirt from smoke. But we had only traveled five hours from Philadelphia before the cars came to a stop. Pitch dark and we didn't know where we were."

Mary Ann glared, as if it were my fault.

"A landslide, some distance ahead," I said. "Fortunately, a freight train ran into it before we got there— But still, very unpleasant waiting. Eight hours to clear the mess of large rock and earth that had rolled down the mountainside and rested on the track."

"Some other train always reached trouble before ours," Salome said.

"Oh, you poor dear," Mary Ann said to her. She pushed the pie plate toward us. "You must have been dreadfully cold."

Salome shook her head at the offer of more pie. "Delicious, though." She looked at me cautiously. "He's the cold one. One time I took his pulse to see if he was alive."

"I've always had a slow heart rate. Fifty-seven isn't unusual." I held up my hand at the offer of more pie. "But a worse train accident had made me late arriving in Philadelphia—two killed and two others injured. That delayed my transfer train."

"Oh," Mary Ann said, her fingertips tapping her lips. "So this Daniel—why was he the problem?"

"Unusual by all counts. A narrow face, but bushy hair. He seems to enjoy saying strange things like 'savage as a meat ax.'" I shrugged. "He took me to see a man's natural spring filled with fish. That's where we found this 3,700-pound beauty."

"One of the brethren in the water?" Mary Ann asked.

At that we had a good laugh, and Salome covered her mouth like she does. "The ox sighting came after Daniel and I had spent most of a Sunday in Pittsburgh. I tried to tell him that I'd spent a whole day in Pittsburgh on an earlier trip, waiting for a second train when my first train going East broke down. He brushed it off, that I'd walked down to the river once before and had gone to the top of a mountain to look down on the city. I mentioned a bookstore I'd found; I described the laziest barber ever—a very poor shave. None of that made any difference to Daniel. He wanted me to see a Presbyterian church, then a Catholic church, as if those were unheard-of sights in Chicago. People speak poorly of our city, but my impression of

Pittsburgh hasn't changed; it always seems dingy and dirty. I suppose it's the dark mountains surrounding."

"You said, though—worthwhile to meet people in Pennsylvania," Salome said.

"True," I said. "Mostly around Mount Joy—but I had other things on my mind." I reached for her hand. "Tell Mary Ann about our adventures finding your relatives after the wedding. Rushing streams from two days of solid rain."

"Some of it was treacherous, but Fretz is very good with horses," Salome said.

"I didn't always know where I was going," I said. "Some of Salome's aunts and uncles live at out-of-the-way places." I shook my head; Salome might not realize: I shouldn't have attempted that fast-moving water, two feet high. "But we found everyone," I said quickly.

"Wonderful gifts, too," Salome said, "very generous. My father gathered all the boxes we had packed, household goods and such, and took them to Doylestown. They've been shipped, but we don't know when—"

"Could be a month," I said. "We hope there's a little extra room for storage."

"We don't want to impose," Salome said quickly. She's said that more times in a week than I can count. "Only until we find our own place."

"Plenty of empty space in the attic," Mary Ann said. "Don't worry."

"And Fretz's mother—very tender in her farewell," Salome said.

I don't know why Salome said that, but yes, my mother's parting advice lingers: "Look to your sweet woman now." I shouldn't feel embarrassed to know I'm a lucky man. "We stayed overnight with Benjamin Frick and his son in Philadelphia, the night before starting here," I said. "Everything's different, of course, with Ben remarried. Six and a half years already since our sister Margaret— Ben's as warm as ever; said to come back anytime." I looked to Salome, her head down. "I don't know that we will."

So it is that our married life in Chicago has taken its start. I've always worn socks to bed in the winter. And the bed covers—that's another story. I like them considerably heavier than Salome does. The first time we finally settled to sleep, I put the top cover over my head. She thought I was still playing some kind of game.

The joy that filled us on our wedding day stays strong, even though it seems surprisingly long ago. I'm determined not to let the unity of marriage be marred by a war that wreaks division. Salome says both realities are true, not one or the other. I had told Mary Ann earlier about Salome's beautiful brown wedding dress; she made it herself. Now I worry more than she: it may never get to Chicago. She called the material taffeta and had fashioned it with a small red-and-green checked scarf worn at the neck. We don't know when there will be occasion for her to wear it again, but I insisted we put it in a specially lined box for shipping. But now with this war and uncertain train schedules . . .

Our first difficult decision had to be taken care of right away. We had talked about it at length on the train ride, and Salome has helped me stay firm. I turned in my resignation as superintendent of the Milwaukee Depot Mission school; some days I still can't believe it.

We were received with such warmth on our first Sunday there! My boys greeted Salome with respect, although we heard one lad whisper, "Why does she pin her hair back so tight?"

Afterwards, she only allowed herself to say: "Some of the children are hard-looking."

Now, a month later, it still feels strange—like I'm missing an arm—not to go to one school or another on Sunday afternoons. But Salome has turned that time into catching up on rest; she insists I must make time to be without obligation. Her blue eyes scold if she catches me looking through unanswered correspondence.

Yes, after all my agonizing last fall, we officially started a religious newspaper at the beginning of this year. It's been a whirlwind! The first issue went out already on December thirtieth before I left for Pennsylvania. That's partly why I had more people to meet on my train trip. So far, Salome has pitched in like this newspaper was her idea. When she's not busy making another pie, she reads and copies manuscripts for *Herald of Truth*. Her handwriting for mailings is much better than mine.

Of course, I had much to catch up with at the lumber yard, after being gone most of a month. At first, I spent ten-hour days with lumber and then came home to work on the next issue of the periodical. When I'm writing articles, I can get up at four in the morning; that's stimulating. But Salome's complexion darkens when she asks how long I can keep that up. I reassure her: the work will lessen as it becomes more customary. The hard part, though, is when I have to get up early to translate the English edition into the German language edition of *Herold der Wahrheit*. Especially when I've put it off until the last minute—then I have to rush and my meanings don't come across clearly.

Sometimes Salome chides, "You're dawdling. Your wording is good enough."

I've explained before: I enjoy rolling words around; that's nothing new. As long as we have subscribers in Europe, and some here in the States among the Amish who only know German, I'm determined to keep both versions.

While our life has had hectic moments with deadlines, it's also been sweet. Salome mends my clothes and does extra sewing for Mary Ann's children. Her stitches—well, Salome does everything with exactness. She should not scold me for wanting a better phrase. I've never seen her dress pleats not neatly tucked. She'll hold up a piece of cloth for me to touch or inspect, but I'm not sure what she's pointing to. "You think *I'm* particular," I say. I take her in my arms, but she pulls away so as not to wrinkle the material between us.

I would never have guessed at her fondness for our butter. She declares she's eaten more of quality here than in all her life previously. I wouldn't have thought she'd find Bucks County grass inferior, but her eyes brightened when she first saw the Beidlers's cow in the back yard. She practically begged to do the milking and said it was like being at home.

She's put her foot down, though, about certain habits of mine. I didn't know so much would need to change, but she happily reminds me I'm not a bachelor anymore. I knew my habit of grinding at night might bother her; on that score she's been sympathetic, knowing my history with dentists. But she abhors cigar smoke on my clothes or person. "Why taint yourself?" she asks. At first, I thought she was teasing, but that is not the case. That's curtailed my evenings of after-dinner conversation in the parlor with Jacob, but I wouldn't trade a hundred boxes of cigars for her enthusiasm about the newspaper.

I admit I made a foolish decision on my way home from work recently. I blame it on the unexpected warmth in our early springlike air; I wanted to show my old friends how contented I am as a newly married man. Much as I have turned from the Wide-Awakes, I'll never forget the camaraderie, the way they helped me feel I belonged as a Lincoln supporter. So one evening I walked with them again and came home late, with two new holes in my only decent coat.

Salome put a stop to that—the holes and the attendance—with her muffled "One mending and that's all." Pins protruded from her mouth. No sympathy whatsoever, when I said it's almost impossible *not* to catch a spark from someone's torchlight. "Pfft!"

I've learned to be careful with my language, too. I've always joked that this is the place—meaning Chicago—to get good for nothing. But when Salome asked, "Why do you say that?" her face had turned red all out of proportion to my comment.

"I don't know," I hedged. "I thought it amusing."

"It alarms me. It's not a thing to be lighthearted about."

When her chin gets rigid like that, I know to give it up; there are far more important things. And when I cut my fingernails on the right hand,

I'm extra careful, so as not to provoke myself. I'm sure her father never tolerated an oath if one of his boys cut too close with a knife. It's good Salome doesn't see me at work, for I'm still careless there on occasion. I've shown her around the premises, of course. She likes Jim, and she likes the setup in the lumber yard. But it wouldn't be wise for her to hear me when I tell an employee, "You'd best get ready to ride the rail—a no-count job like that!"

The only time I've heard Salome exclaim was when she stepped into bath water that was hotter than she expected. I came at once at her shout: "Mighty Oceans!" Then I wanted to linger—so lovely!—but she waved a towel and shooed me away.

Worst of all, it's a comeuppance for someone to point out parts of my behavior that don't fit with my attempts to be newly clothed with religious understanding. She sniffs out any words of exhortation on paper that don't ring true. Of course, my everyday walk must be in compliance; I want it to be. But who doesn't say one thing and do another on occasion? She knows I get irritated with Ross; my behavior has never been perfect with him. But one time I imitated him again by pounding a fist into my cupped hand. She wasn't amused when I pounced on certain words repeatedly, wanting to get an indignant response from her.

Later, when she was proofing sheets I'd written about the way of peace, she brought it up by saying sweetly enough, "Have you thought about—?"

Easy for her to say. She doesn't have to work with Ross.

Now he says, "Battles are nearly over. They say some parts of the South are threatened by starvation."

I nod but I don't look up from my work; it's easier that way.

He'll add, "Some places don't have enough food for citizens, let alone for their fighting men."

I don't contest his statements, but I don't have solutions to the shortages. Nor do I have as much time to follow war developments. I know, though, that President Lincoln has called for more troops, last month and again this one. But if I say, "People in North Carolina are resisting the demands for more men," he'll question that. I'll have to explain that it's primarily the ones who bought substitutes in the past and now are being forced into the ranks. That will open the gates between us.

My brother Abe and I don't talk as much, either, since Salome's here. But after a Sunday noon meal when Mary Ann invited him to join all of us, Jacob and I lingered at the door with him when he was leaving. Abe said, "There's much I don't know—the draft situation and all. But better to be here than back home."

"Illinois men have stayed willing," Jacob said, slapping Abe on the back.

That's when I said, "Overall, though, men aren't responding as readily to Lincoln's call. More complaints about the senselessness of the effort. Incompetence in some of the commanders, too."

"Some folks will never accept emancipation as a war aim," Jacob said quickly. "It's understandable if they don't want to fight alongside Negroes. Well, that's what I've heard."

"As long as I can pay a commutation fee"—Abe reached inside his jacket to scratch—"it will be better than being dragged."

"Have to remember, though, that's a privilege for some of us," I said. "Many can't afford it. Like last summer when immigrants and Catholics made clear how rigged the system was. If they don't show up, they're forced to be illegal evaders."

"That's the catch," Abe said, slowly stroking his beard. "They have to report."

"No one's forced," Jacob said.

"Oh, yes!" I said. I slowed myself. "Ten days to report to the draft board and be examined, if drafted."

"Law sees you as a deserter if you don't show up," Abe said. "A criminal."

"But your neighbor"—Jacob paused longer than needed—"sees you as un-American."

"Exactly," I said, not to be upstaged. "A common view. But think about a man with a family to support and no money to spare. He came to this country wanting a better living. Why would he willingly put his neck on the chopping block?"

"He should have thought of that before he came," Jacob said, as matter-of-factly as when dealing with a customer whose account was in arrears. "Too many make up some preposterous disability: show up faking a limp, or say they've had a hernia for twenty years."

I leaned my arms on the pedestal at the bottom of the staircase, regretting I'd amplified this argument. "Maybe so. But there's fraud *within* the system, too, especially with substitution. It's demoralizing, full of corruption."

"Always relied on it, though." Abe twirled his hat in his hands. "Father said the pattern was brought from Europe and thought of like a tax owed Caesar."

"That doesn't make it right," I said, "not necessarily. But yes, difficult to change, once established. I don't believe in buying a slave and using him for labor. But how is buying a substitute any different? Using someone else to do my dirty work."

At that, Jacob burst out with a loud laugh. "That beats all, Fretz. You *pay* a substitute to fight. That becomes *his* work. He gets paid. Money! How your mind can distort!" The rattle of dishes in the kitchen had stopped.

"Who's distorting?" I asked. "Maybe it's not exactly the same, not in *every* way. But if I buy a substitute—like *property*—I'm saying his life doesn't mean as much as mine. *Go ahead and kill. Get killed.*"

"What in blazes! The substitute agrees to it; he chooses to fight," Jacob said. "If he comes out on the short end, that's life. Full of risks. You don't *own* the man." Jacob kept his gaze on me.

I took a deep breath; I couldn't stop. "That poor white—say an Irish Democrat in New York City—has no alternative. No extra money to buy his way out. Right? He's a slave of the war system. But what will his family live on while he's at war? He's treated as if he has no rights in this country—second-class. Isn't that slavery? Not in shackles, but still—"

"A crapshoot," Jacob said. "That's what life is. He should know when he comes here—when he *decides* to come here. Not my fault he came. Maybe things'll work out, maybe not. I make choices, too; take chances. Investments may or may not pan out. You know how that is, Fretz." With that, Jacob turned to open the front door like a ceremony and nodded to Abe.

My brother hesitated only briefly before donning his hat and leaving.

I had no desire to pursue the debate. I found Salome cleaning up dishes in the kitchen; Mary Ann had gone to put Augustus down for a nap. My cheeks must have given me away, for Salome asked right away when we got upstairs, what we'd been talking about. I shook my head. "Time to rest."

I was in a foul mood. Salome hasn't had the advantage of talking about politics in her childhood home, but now she's catching up by reading some of the newspapers I bring home. But that Sunday afternoon I didn't want to discuss the background for why the anti-immigrant and anti-Catholic sentiment of established whites is no better than the attitudes of secretive Know-Nothings who flourished back in the '40s and '50s. That motley group, partly old Whigs, but mostly made up of men, filled with religious bigotry and suspicions about foreigners. They turned their venom—caught in the middle of their own conflict—against the hated migrants who came as a result of the potato famine in Ireland. Of course, those Know-Nothings hated the elites, too, but they knew better than to contest *them.*

I also didn't want to hear Salome call me out if she thought I'd been inconsistent. She's heard me fuss sometimes about men on our company's payroll—the same ones I defended downstairs. I've told her often enough: it's nothing new for one group or another to pile their grievances on yet another innocent group.

But there've been many more times when I've been grateful to talk problems through with Salome. Recently, we tried to imagine what it would be like to serve the needs of strangers in a hospital. I couldn't keep the rumors from her—no one knows for sure—that the latest draft law includes an option to care for wounded men instead of armed soldiering. That's the same idea John M. talked about almost a year ago. And it's what Walt Whitman has done voluntarily for almost two years.

Salome didn't know anything about Whitman, the poet. I kept it simple, telling her "He lives his beliefs—not afraid to say unpopular things that make the papers. One time he was quoted: 'The people who like wars should be compelled to fight them.'"

Her eyes had a glint in them. "That didn't go over."

"Exactly. Some folks criticize his loose lifestyle or call him immoral. Some say his poetry has too much self-importance."

"And you?"

"I overlook the flamboyant parts that some ridicule, because, well, he speaks the truth about war. His critics attack him personally to distract from what he says. Politicians certainly don't want anyone thinking *they* should be required to speak to the men with broken bodies and spirits that this war produces. No personal responsibility for them."

"And you?"

I looked at her a second time, but she didn't blink. "I try to imagine . . . I don't know if I could hold up, meeting torn men day after day." I shook my head. "Not that I *ordered* the war. But I've told you about my friend Joe, the way he came back—his future limited. Plus, it would grieve me to the bone to part with you—if I had to go to a field hospital. Be gone several nights in a row. I didn't bring you to Chicago for us to live separated lives! My mother would think I abandoned you."

"Thousands suffer far worse," Salome said. "All while we're caught up in the joys of marriage!" We ended up holding each other—such welcome respite. Who wants to talk about thorny issues after that?

And yet, she never fully lets unpleasant things go. The next day, she brought it up again. She said if I were absent awhile, she could be of more help to Mary Ann. I suppose she was trying to put on a good front. But our newspaper—surely she knows it would die! Oh, I know, it's better to care for the needs of freedmen and those injured in the war, than to pay a commutation fee that likely buys more guns. But hands-on care?

Of course, we don't know if this option of tending the wounded will materialize. It's like much of the information we're given: subject to exaggeration and constant revision. The idea might be put forward to gum up the works. That was Joe's interpretation of military strategy sometimes. If you can't win, gum up the works and hope to wiggle your way out.

What's clear, though, from the war front: General Grant's been promoted to Lieutenant General by the North. Such high esteem! After successes in Tennessee last November—Chattanooga, Lookout Mountain, wherever else—someone wrote a song, "All Hail to Ulysses." As best I can tell, his military plan is straightforward: "Get Lee." Everything points to a spring campaign. And here we are, the month of March with early winter thawing. I've read nothing about conciliation—not from him, not from Lincoln.

One other conversation with Salome sticks in my head, too. She brought cheese and cold chicken up to our room so we could talk without being interrupted by children. I like Mary Ann and Jacob's older ones—Salome prefers babies, even Augustus—but it's not restful to come home to wiggles and spills at the table. During our meal by ourselves, I passed along Ross's latest view of the long-talked-about march to Richmond. "'The prospect of a *final* engagement from which there will be *no* possible *retreat* for the South.'"

Salome heard my irritated emphasis, but she latched on to the fuller import. "More casualties? Armies passing through areas where common people live?"

I nodded. "Not a word gets said about that. Except that the Union insists there won't be any mass murder or rape of innocent civilians." I chewed slowly on a bite of chicken. "The ultimate goal: destroy the wealth the Rebels have based their survival on."

"That means, innocent farmers will be affected along the way? Southern civilians?"

"Exactly. It could be as disastrous as the current state of the prison system, where neither side follows accepted rules anymore."

"That news article you brought home yesterday"—she clicked her teeth. "Tensions over prisoners worsened when Negro soldiers joined the battle."

"Apparently that's true. The Confederacy won't recognize dark-skinned prisoners as equal to whites. So if they recapture slaves-turned-prisoners, they return them to their masters. Or"—I hesitated—"put them back on the battlefield as shields for white soldiers."

"Oh, Fretz." Her voice trailed off. "Still seen as property."

"No question. The South's usual line: property can't be exchanged. And Jefferson Davis? He says compromise is weakness."

"So Lincoln won't exchange prisoners either."

"That's how it works. The North thinks they're putting more stress on the South, but prisons on both sides are overcrowded with terrible conditions." Salome sat rigid at my words; she hadn't eaten for minutes. I reached for her hand. "Union forces don't offer Negroes fair treatment either, the slaves who've escaped to the north and want to join the fight. They're tormented and treated like laborers, assigned menial tasks like digging ditches.

That's what I read. This General Banks is said to be one of the worst; he won't pay cash for their labor."

"Still slaves?'

"No better. Or barely."

Our small room closes in on us. Our silence, heavy. Only when the weather cooperates can we bundle up and go for an evening walk. I've retraced routes I used to take alone on my restless nights. At first, Salome thought it odd, walking on city streets. But I've told her how I used to need to walk—*to get there.* She smiled, as if she understood.

On one of those recent walks, I had figured out how to avoid the worst mud puddles. In some places, the city has replaced old planks with firmer ones. Salome followed up again, as if no days had intervened. "So why *does* the Negro fight?"

I looked at her, startled, but said, "Hard to figure, isn't it? Could be: they don't want any question. This war for union is a war for *freedom*. They'll work for it, die for it. They don't want it simply *given*."

"Will it make things better? In the end—for them? To fight?"

"Who knows? Many will die; their lives are considered less valuable. But Frederick Douglass supports his two sons who've enlisted in New York; they don't get paid as much as white soldiers of the same rank. But somewhere I read their father's words: 'Enlisting is the best way to overcome prejudice.'" I lifted my hands; let them fall. "Maybe he means: *best* to show the men aren't lazy or cowards. Another time he wrote, 'Take a little . . . the better to get more.'"

"Like doing menial tasks at the lumber yard to gain respect?"

"Hnnh. Could be. But Douglass's sons will *never* be appointed to officer's rank. He surely knows that, but he still says things like 'a half loaf is better than no bread.'"

"*Killing* to earn respect," Salome said, "with *half* the pay."

"All because of prejudice. People say those with dark skin aren't as smart. Or I've heard folks claim, 'those poor ones—they're *content* to be slaves.' Completely misunderstand. Whether inequality will ever be overturned—whether this war can be the means to an end . . . The methods seem like mass foolishness to us, but some see heroism." I shrugged. "Baffling that freedmen and slaves who've escaped are willing to fight and die for the North."

"All to be accepted by those who admire fierceness."

"And who see it as manliness," I said quietly. "So many ambiguities."

It's also been impossible to hide from Salome my mixed feelings about our country's leadership, not that I've needed to cover them up. But one night I was relaxing after we'd finished preparing another article. Again, we had followed our usual roles: I write; she plays the questioning reader. At rest, we propped our backs against the bed's headboard and stretched our legs.

"Now if only I could make sense of President Lincoln," I said.

"Something new?" she asked.

"No, I'm still thinking about his speech at Gettysburg last year when they dedicated the cemetery. He wasn't even supposed to be the main speaker."

"Something inspiring?"

"Of sorts. The good parts were his words and their impact; I marvel at that. If I could ever come *close*. He's a master at sending a strong message in the fewest possible words. Not just *any* words, but ones that stick! 'Government of, by, and for the people.' That's *unforgettable*, whereas I'm too wordy. But what's confusing—how am I to blend his conduct of the war with his lofty speech? I'm supposed to respect him—my president."

She shifted on the bed but said nothing.

"I know it's not always the length of an editorial that matters. But he has a knack for finding the *exact words* to carry the sentiment. 'Four score and seven years'—he sounds noble from the start. Everyone knows we're a young country, but who would have thought of saying it that way?"

"What impressed me about that new cemetery"—she turned on her side to me, propping her head with a hand—"they buried bodies in semicircular rows."

"All connected—unending circles. But—only united as one side against the other."

"Why didn't they think of that *before* either side started firing? Now I've read that they'll leave corpses unattended." She shuddered as if physical pain ran through her body.

"That's what I mean. How is that noble?" I scootched and wrapped an arm about her. Finally, I let go and lay with only my head raised. "My brother Jakie used to say that I was naive to be horrified at warfare. Well, I'm still shocked. They use that idea of comradeship in fighting and death. The sentiment is likely genuine, but for states to exhume bodies and rebury their own sons at that huge new cemetery . . ."

"A kind of reward," Salome asked, "intended to wipe out pain?"

I moved my hands up and down as if shifting a weight on a scale. "So much I can't judge, not having been there. But I never want to forget the evil that's underneath this: the awful treatment of the Negro."

"Nothing can be justified there."

"But here's the rest of it." I sat up again. "Right when I think Lincoln might be serious about establishing a nation that builds equality into its core, he ends that impressive speech with the same worn-out idea. 'We need to continue fighting so those who died won't have died in vain!'" I slumped and slowly relaxed my fists. "That's another never-ending circle. Justification. I suppose it drew hearty praise. I can't; I can't."

"Everyone's exhausted, too," she said.

"Maybe that's a good sign: waning appetite, desertion still going up. I can't help but ask: what *is* a lasting contribution? For *me*."

Salome snuggled closer. "Your calling is none the lesser."

"There's nothing heroic-sounding about a religious newspaper. Some would call it an escape. What *am* I doing that will make a difference?"

Her reply was swift, as if I were the pupil. She sat up and said, "You'll do what's been given. And do it the very best you know how, Fretz Funk."

I pulled her to my side, warmed again. But I couldn't voice other troublesome thoughts. I'm not equal to the task. I may have taken on too much.

Esther — Shenandoah Valley, March 1864

He came with such stealth—no warning! Gabriel led his horse through the bent stubble of weeds beside our lane. Not so much as a clop-clop; only rustling. He had taken the back ways to get here, so as not to attract attention. At first, my heart leaped with gladness. Some news! But he stayed only a short while, refilling his canteen before retracing to his home place near Broadway. Now I catch myself—*not so!* How could—? Not Simon's brother as messenger!

His face stayed tight. No idle greeting; only straightforward. "Such sorrow, Esther. Cursed by venom, your man." And softer to my children: "A good man—"

"No!" I said. "What do you mean?"

I pulled Mary Grace to me; Joseph turned abruptly on his heels toward the barn.

Gabriel handed William the harness so he could dismount and put a stiff arm about me.

"He sought protection," I said, muffled. I searched Gabriel's face, the same black eyes as my Simon. "Not so!"

His tale, choppy, after Joseph had stalked back and stood aloof.

"Broken-hearted, we all—" Gabriel's voice broke again.

Inside, Jephthah banged on the door. Our new babe may have cried out.

Mary Grace tugged on Gabriel's coat, her voice a shriek. "Tell us what!"

"Your father came some weeks ago. Seeking safety. We took care in all things; he burrowed in the cellar with blankets aplenty. He wanted to outwait the North's move southward before attempting passage farther north." Gabriel licked and bit at his lips. "We thought it wise that he only went outside for short periods. That fateful day, our warmest yet, my boys and I had gone out to saw up logs, fallen from winter storms in the timber. One thick one in particular, entangled with gnarly wood. We stopped for our noon meal—gave our arms a rest—and Simon kept saying it wasn't right, not to lend a hand.

Gabriel's voice turned brisk. "Not out with us—not even a full hour. He took the opposite saw end from me. None of us— That viper must have nestled 'neath dry leaves. None of us saw— Not till after." Gabriel's eyes tormented. "A rotten log nearby—likely its winter home. To this day, I don't know why he reached, as if to strike first."

At that I swooned and nearly toppled Mary Grace as well. Gabriel grabbed to steady, walked us to the back step.

"No, no, no!" I cried. "Not so. Mama always said—"

Gabriel waited to take up his tale again, while Mary Grace went inside and returned with Jephthah. "He lived yet a week, Esther. We thought him better. 'Making recovery,' he said. We had cleaned the wound as best we knew how, though it stayed red and swollen. Harriet applied sour milk, too." Gabriel turned sharply—a ruckus in the barnyard, but no two-legged intruder appeared.

"One night Simon tapped with a stick on the cellar ceiling. I went down at once. He scarce could catch his breath. Said he kept falling off a deep stairway. Stretched out his good arm, told me to come closer so he could see. I was right next. He could scarce lift the bad arm. Clammy skin. Harriet insisted that we try fire, too."

"Simon, oh my man," I cried. "'Look it in the eye,' Mama always said. 'It can't hurt you.'"

"None of us, not one, saw nor heard before the instant," Gabriel said. "Harriet—all send condolences." He whirled his head to look beyond the well. A flapping of crow's wings.

"Where is he?" William whispered. "My pa! I want my pa."

"The body," I said. "Whereabouts?"

"The best burial possible," Gabriel said, still jumpy. "The very best. I couldn't tow him here for fear of attention; roadways give uncertain clearance. His body rests now—the family cemetery, near to Mother and Father. Friends helped dig. Come summer, we can exhume. Bring the remains— If the war, over and done. The first opportunity."

"Did you kill?" Joseph asked, his face aflame.

Gabriel tensed, then relaxed his fists. "The viper? Yes! Destroyed! No more from that one!" Gabriel's face crumbled into muffled sobs in his coat sleeve.

He stayed agitated. But partly—the need to get back before dark. So little time. What could we offer but bread and questions? The same questions. To hear another time would not change anything. My poor man's gone. No way to know if Gabriel was given safety on his return.

After he left, William yelled, "Why couldn't uncle save my pa?"

"Not for us," I said. "The Lord's ways—here but for a span."

"I hate this war!" William shouted, his face fiery from coughs that turned to barks and wheezing.

No one could give comfort. What more could be said?

We went through the motions. My milk, poor for Miriam, our babe. Never to see her poor pa's face. Simon—his flight turned to a dark grave. Why, oh why? They had taken precautions.

The night for us, given to tossing. We all looked rocked about the next morning. Joseph asked if he should ride to Brother Samuel's to take word.

I gripped him with a fierceness. "You will do no such thing."

* * *

Time passes, but nothing further of import has transpired. My nerves afire. My man, gone and buried. How am I to do? Gone for protection, when he couldn't stay put here. Gabriel said nothing of Simon's possessions. Perhaps Simon had given his brother the coins for safekeeping. My weeping hands shake to tend Miriam's cries. She's a good one and sweet, not like Jephthah when first born. But still, born to cry. Some days I don't do my hair; I go about—a straggly braid. I can't pick up the comb—Simon's last gift—full teeth and soft to the scalp. More men may come. My children and I must do the best we can.

Samuel and Frances know now; Frances wept with me. But no way to mourn proper, without the body. No warning.

No word from Andrew, nor Peter. How much longer dare Joseph delay? All my boys. No word if Brother Samuel might flee also. Or someone else. Frances said a man named Riley—for twenty Confederate dollars—will take a refugee to another pilot, a Mitchell by name. That one takes men to Petersburg. The state of West Virginia. Passage westward through New Creek Station. Said to be all the way to the Baltimore and Ohio. She repeated the route for Joseph; I may have jumbled it. We have no Confederate money; Simon wouldn't touch. But gold. He had stowed in two places. I don't know how much to spare. But I will, for safe passage. A son. No man to tell me what for what. Which way.

Our cold stays. Fog and dampness. Winter's grip again, after things had warmed. Far from planting now. I put my boys to chopping. They know to watch and never to reach! Our lime kiln—no use at all.

My children must eat! But our potatoes shrivel, our milk cow reduced. Poor, frightened soul. An owl calls in the middle of the day.

Jacob Schwartzendruber — Iowa, March 1864

The long winter drags, but without mishap. How well I remember the exact words of the four brethren who came from out-of-state: "Mend what is broken." Now for three months I have used a kinder voice, even when preaching of perils.

The sermon fell to me for two Sundays in February. I could not shy away from reminding: severe consequences if trying to serve two masters—Matthew's words in chapter six. But I hastened to add promise: we are not to worry. Our heavenly Father knows what we need! Mary vouched for my effort, saying I did not bristle or pound, as was once my habit. "Still resolute, but a trifle dull," she added. No malice flickered in her eyes, so I did not take offense.

So far as I know, Joseph Keim has kept his part these months also, not snaring John Mishler or others to hold additional church meetings. It is true: we had to silence Mishler when it became clear he could not be counted on to administer the poor fund as intended. But others concurred, and throughout that ordeal, I never once raised my voice, speaking only of disappointment at his poor judgment. That money was intended for those most in need. Since then, no one has seemed aggrieved that he no longer reads Scripture; it was at times burdensome, waiting out his hacking spells.

Since the time of my reckoning last year, I have learned of another dispute, this one back in Pennsylvania between Solomon Beiler and Abraham Peachey and their congregations. Contentions over stream baptism and preaching deacons had turned into unseemly personality clashes. How easily a difference over Amish practice can deteriorate into naked dislike for a brother! While I fell into error with Keim, I am now determined to uphold God's Word and the discipline, as understood by our forefathers in the Amish church. I can preach with kindness, the truth of *Nachfolge*, following after. When we claim as ours, the way of Jesus and the disciples as shown in Holy Writ, we find contentment, not rancor.

There are still times, though, when I need to forbear with women in the church who see nothing wrong with house decoration or personal adornment of the hair. Surely the Lord will provide unity yet. That is what we strive for: agreement in all things, not clinging to obstinate hearts. Then it is, we may again partake of Communion.

This ugly war between North and South still looms as another threat that could set our church teetering. The work of mending may prevent further breakage among us. Those of my generation thought we had left forced militia service behind when we came from the Old Country. How well my stepsons, Daniel and Jacob, knew that strain before we came here. But now with these increasing drafts by the Union, our young men are the ones who feel the pressure to volunteer; unfortunately, they are not always prepared.

For more than sixty years on this earth, I have devoted much study to Scriptures that pertain to our Amish church's refusal to kill humans with our own hands. Along with the commandment "*Thou shalt not kill*," Romans 13 remains my fortress; we are to be subject to government, but *only* when it *refrains* from activities contrary to the Word of God. Our church body has sometimes practiced sharing the financial burden that comes to a member who may not be able to pay the entire fine the government levels in lieu of military service.

This is all good, but we must not become complacent—nor allow inconsistency. I pay attention to whether any of the alternatives to warfare amount to paying protection money, as some have whispered. We hear that our men in the East, more subject to the draft, continue to use the provision for a drafted man to hire a substitute. But increasingly, that is not a sure thing, because a man cannot always be found to go in another's place. Or if he does, sometimes only at a very high monetary cost.

I include my grandsons among those I must watch and exhort. Not an easy task, when Samuel has gone back East to live. After Emanuel Hochstetler enlisted from our midst, I thought of him as the *one* lost sheep from here in Iowa—an exception. Since then, no one else from our settlement has joined the 22nd unit; enough volunteers continue to spare Iowa from needing a draft. But still, it can be tempting for young men to align with the ruling powers of this world. This Philip E. Shaver, a captain of the First Iowa Cavalry, F Company, has been hailed in the community ever since he returned home after two years. A wealthy farmer before he left, he feared he might lose all his livestock and property when his wife became seriously ill.

But those others in that 22nd where Emanuel served, have traveled farther away. Last summer we heard that they maintained guard duty and siege operations in the area of Vicksburg until the fortress finally fell in July. But one report said they chased a Confederate general by the name of Johnston all the way to Jackson, Mississippi. Now their exact whereabouts are more of a mystery; we hear that they could be as far away as Louisiana or Texas.

I am sorry for their fathers and brothers who need them to return to their families for farm work this summer; surely, that will come to pass soon.

While burdened with these heavy matters over the winter months, I have been blessed to see my way lightened with Mary. Relations were never broken between us, but over the three years we have lived as man and wife, our lines sometimes felt the strain of opposite pulls, especially when restricted to staying inside because of snow and bitter cold. I believe her youthfulness has accounted for some of her applying the sharp needle of question from time to time. Yet I will never forget her kind spirit in pulling me out of the depths of December's reprimand.

Because of all that swirled that month, I missed Mary's birthday; I did not want to wait another year to show my gratitude. I am not given to showering gifts; she will attest to that. But given that she has had to adjust to Iowa's wilderness—occasionally a barb still slips from her about our backwardness compared with Indiana's—I wanted to brighten and make her life easier.

I turned to my daughter Anna and asked if she might have some canna bulbs to spare. She raised both eyebrows but said, "Of course." I mentioned the need for secrecy, and she broke into a smile.

As I had hoped, Mary clapped her hands with joy—"oh, you found some!"—when presented with the box of large bulbs, spread out in dampened soil.

"Your hands will turn them into magnificent red flowers, come summer," I said.

But the bigger task came when I set about to acquire a new flax wheel. I almost agonized too long: *What will others think? Word might get out. Can I justify the expense?* Finally, I turned to my son Frederick to give a hand in plotting. He knew the best place in Davenport to place the order, handled the correspondence, and promised to deliver by wagon when word came of arrival nearby. I did not need to make up a farfetched excuse about meeting a train in Iowa City in the winter! Everything worked without a hitch, especially when Frederick needed to replace some parts on his threshing machine from the same merchant.

I pretended innocence when Mary heard Frederick's team and wagon crunching on our snow-packed driveway. "What now?" she asked, taking quick steps to the window.

In truth, I was surprised she had not commented earlier that morning, for my jitters had led to spilled milk. "What now?" I repeated. "Perhaps Frederick—"

"His boy, Jacob, too. Unloading a crate of sorts," she said.

"A crate?" I came to the window to oblige.

"It looks to be heavy. Cumbersome."

"Hmm."

She took a swift look at me. "Jacob, you play the mouse!"

I could not stifle a slight smile. "Well then—we will see shortly. Uhmm. Lugging—" I hurried to open the door.

Mary stood with hands on her hips.

"Do not be distressed," I said in my most soothing voice.

She hurried to extricate a carpet at the door. "Careful! Do not scuff, nor trip, whatever your affair."

"To the hearth," Frederick said, jerking his head to his son. Their puffs of cold air and heavy breathing filled our cabin.

Some jostling ensued as they set the box on two corners and lowered it slowly so as not to ding floorboards or pinch fingers. I had thought to bring tools to the porch that morning for the time of revelation.

"Jacob!" Mary said, clutching her hands to her chest. "Jacob! What is the meaning? We gave away—"

Frederick and his son made short work of unpacking.

"It never suited you," I said. "This will fit better—my fervent prayer. Exceedingly late for your birthday. Or dare we call it early?"

"A double-drive!" she said. "A double treadle!" Her eyes fairly popped with glee.

"It may not satisfy," I said, "but your quick movements—"

"It better satisfy," Frederick said, slapping the metal frame. "Or I know another home."

Young Jacob and I laughed. I have rarely surprised Mary; I am usually the one gasping. "The Lord be gracious," I said with fervor.

Mary had never liked Barbara's single-drive flax wheel. Oh, at first, it was acceptable, but it soon became an object of scorn. I could not get the tension right to suit Mary's hold. And the treadle, jerky—not a match for Mary's short legs and quick moves. When she complained of the small bobbin, I obediently half-lugged and walked the wheel to the corner where it sat reprimanded. Mary made do with Barbara's Great Wheel. For that, her hands were accustomed to the feel—much like what she left behind in Indiana—although sore tiring to stand for hours, producing woolens enough for my pants.

"Linen!" she said. "I will make myself a new dress! Flax enough, too—a shirt for you. Oh, Jacob, how did you know?"

"It was not hard," I said, pulling on my suspender.

In truth, I had stubbornly thought that what was good enough for Barbara was good enough for Mary. I cannot remember if we bought that first flax wheel when living in Somerset County or after we moved to Maryland.

But when my stepson Daniel's daughter Barbara married David Kauffman, I welcomed the opportunity to pass on my first wife's wheel. The younger Barbara's joy at receiving her grandmother's sewing chair also sealed that effort.

This new wheel includes parts cut by a machine—uniform, and a smoother fit. I credit my experience with the pulley systems of water wheels—not the same but on the same order—as giving me some mechanical knowhow. The double drive band goes around the wheel twice and turns the flyer. That horseshoe-shaped flyer surrounds the bigger bobbin—the better to hold sufficient yarn. Frederick was taken with the distaff that holds unspun fibers. "Not so easily entangled," he said. Plus, the knob that allows the tension of the drive bands is much smoother, rather like a screw, moving the spindle forward and backward. Mary has become a quick study, learning to make adjustments herself.

"Would you rather have had a vertical spindle, above or below?" I asked.

"Oh, no. This is perfect, Jacob. Always choose the horizontal."

A frown may have escaped at the thought of her expecting *another* replacement. She knows my age; this will surely have to do. But the Lord provided mercy, and I thought to say, "Along with your Great Wheel—many good years left—this addition will allow you to do more and faster."

After all the excitement—it is *only* a machine—I felt a trifle foolish. But the gift suits her well, and she is pleased with me. I trust I have not become lax. For certain, the wheel does not glitter like a comb in someone's hair on a church bench. Nor does it carry any bright colors—no gawdy paint added. Surely the Lord approves of my bringing harmony to our hearth, and perhaps I will not need to hear complaint again about her heirloom dishes from the Old Country still needing to stay in their box. How well I know: I may need Mary's help once more, if the women persist in their murmurs.

I saved the other surprise—yes, another!—for much later, when the new wheel was well-established and working smoothly as if it had grown up through the floorboards. After much prayer, I have determined it is the Lord's will for me to attend the *Dieners-Versammlung* in June. Mary hesitated not one second to say she will go with me to Indiana on the train.

For her, it will be longed-for time with her daughters and other family members. But for me, my throat tightens at the thought of dissenting church brethren. Too many contrary winds blow among our Amish churches. I had been writing a letter to be read at the meeting, but now I will be able to deliver my message in person, not send by mail or use Frederick as the courier. He plans to attend, but only for a few days—what with the usual farm work. Mary and I may stay some months. And depending on the war, I might go on East to see with my own eyes how my grandson, Samuel, fares. Mary frowns at the thought of me traveling farther, and she may be right. I only say, “We must stay well, so the Lord may bestow further blessing.”

David Bowman — Shenandoah Valley, April 1864

Two men came to my door at dusk, bent and huddled over. Their bedraggled outerwear, soaked from heavy rain. They looked to have come some distance. Coats, pulled up to cover their ears. I never got a clear look. Our cold wind unabated.

"A morsel," the one said, holding out his hand. The other man, unable to steady his shivering.

"Come in," I said. "The wife has leftover stew." In truth, we had finished our carrots and beef for supper, but we had been blessed with plentiful eggs that morning.

"Something stout," the shivering one said, his head down, arms crossed in front.

"Out here," the first one said, taking a seat on the porch steps with a thud, as if he had misjudged the distance. He bent his forehead to his hands, cupping a walking stick. The other man turned his back also, leaned against a pillar, and raised his head to the mountains. The outline of his face showed a beak-like nose, a chin jutting. His hat was smashed on one side.

I went inside to fill mugs. Abigail called from the bedroom, but I ignored her. When Delilah started to rise, I motioned for her to stay. Then I thought better of it and pointed in the direction of the bedroom. She rose at once to be with her mother.

The men grunted at the ale, but neither looked me in the eye. I waited to see if the first would ask again for bread. He slurped at his drink, so I perched atop one of my barrels.

The sitting one half-turned and whispered loudly, "We need passage."

"That I cannot provide," I said.

"The closest gap. Now." He cocked his head slightly and showed himself to be younger than I first thought. "Take us."

"Must a' done thirty miles today," his companion said.

"Twenty." The first one tipped his head and mug to drain.

"I do not do that," I said.

At that, the one sitting, shifted his weight toward me again and said, "But you know."

"Not the closest; not certain." I stretched my legs straight in front, flexed my hands.

He spat, then spat again with more force.

The man standing had stopped his shaking. "Another," he said, extending his mug sideways without looking.

I hesitated, head down. *How was I to extricate?* Two no-goods. At my moment of inattention, the first man pounced like a cat and knocked me off my perch. I offered no resistance, but toppled like a nearly empty sack of flour. The man kicked at my groin and placed his boot on my chest to shove. I feared to scoot; he might press harder. Delilah's voice called, but I had no breath.

"Asswipe! Get you next time." The boot lifted; the man stumbled off the porch.

I barely raised my head, watched blurred figures as they retreated, one of them walking halfway backward. The older one muttered, "Could a' got me another one."

"Shut up," the first one said. "I'm the one, handles things."

My head sank, eyes blinking fast to clear. *Slow your breathing.* I rolled to my side and staggered to my feet, leaning my weight on a porch post to steady, crouching and peering for any sound of return.

Delilah cautiously opened the door and stepped out. I dabbed at my cheek; something sharp had snagged under the eye. Delilah guided me inside and applied cold cloths. Abigail wailed her questions.

"They acted the part," I said. "As if refugees."

"Your eye—" Delilah said—"stormy. Open, Father. Hold still, so I can look."

"Tears will wash it clean." How often have I heard Johnny say that. Delilah touched the sudden puffiness of my cheek; I flinched. My stomach askew. "They asked regarding a nearby gap, wanted me to guide. Tricksters. Doubtless, knew the way."

"Did you recognize?" Delilah asked.

I shook my head. "Bad-looking, the both. Could have walked into a band of their ilk."

The Partisan Rangers in Linville are said to be better organized again. My friend J. M. says they pay a man three dollars a day as a scout, plus a dollar for his horse. Some of them train to use blasting powder; others tap telegraph lines.

Since then, my scrambled brain has jumped to William E. Coffman, charged with escorting deserters. So far as I know, his outcome remains uncertain all these months. Would that the man could escape West! But disputes continue about whether he should be hanged for his work as a pilot. The same haggling prevails for Joseph Beery and his son Solomon: threats of a trial, but no conclusion. They were arrested and accused of aiding and advising deserters—*aiding and abetting*—forced to spend four weeks in a Richmond prison. But then nothing. Left dangling. This older Beery—the same Mennonite as in trouble two years ago. Someone may have snitched to authorities again. People roam, intent on making our walk difficult. What good—? My puny efforts of refuge for those escaping.

* * *

My recovery stays slow. My eye keeps its blur, but the cheek has lost its swelling. Delilah wanted to go with me in the carriage to get Brother Kline's assessment, but I had no stomach for such a trip. When bright sun finally blessed us, I stayed inside, my eyes closed in a dark corner. "Time will heal," I say. Much outdoor work needs to be done, but even on overcast days, I would rather linger at the fragrance of cherry blossoms, squint at dogwood petals. Will any good come from planting seeds? My sons—lost to us almost three years. Will Amos and Joel ever give us help again? Do they have steady work in that Iowa? Do they ever think on us?

Two Sundays after the incident, I attempted the opening Scripture at our Flat Rock church, but my eye soon clouded. I skipped a line and lost the sense. I have never been a smooth reader, but now this . . . I had to begin again, using my finger to steady on the page. Our attendance is erratic—Brother Wine was absent, too—because of the lawless element. Some of the women have no man to bring them. I cannot blame them for staying home to protect what is left. I would not want Abigail and Delilah to venture out alone with Ruby and the carriage. Unsavory ones, quick to take advantage.

Next weekend is the planned alternate meeting for us German Baptists. We will need to journey south to Franklin County, a temporary adjustment made to avoid the hazards of traveling all the way north to the Annual Meeting. If only we can convince Johnny to be content with this taste of fellowship among a larger circle. Those from eastern Tennessee have promised to be in attendance. An equal distance for us, but to travel south of Roanoke seems exceedingly far. My choice is between poor and poor: tell my women to stay alone for two days, or take them by carriage and hire a lame man to do our chores.

First, we had a mix-up over dates; Abigail says I get too het up. In the end we obliged and postponed our church business at Flat Rock to accommodate this regional gathering on the Saturday before Easter. But the graver problem: Brother Kline seems determined to *also* go to Indiana next month. He admits to receiving threats about his proposed travel, but that does not provide impediment enough to deter him from going to *both* meetings.

Every spring—this is the third year—we have hassled with this same disagreement. I want to spout: "You will get yourself killed, trying to prevent division in the church." But I settle for a more reasonable: "Crossing military lines is *not* the only way to show forth unity."

As is John's custom, he is gracious. "Do what the Lord requires of you."

But I hear the strain in his voice. I am tired of his line: "They can take my life, but they cannot kill my soul." Of course, he is right, but there are other points to consider. What reassures him and others in planning these holy times of thanksgiving to God, leaves me with eyebrows raised.

If I try to continue the argument, "Fear is a natural protection from rashness when danger lurks," he sighs, as if I am a troublesome gnat.

But he studies awhile, as if humoring me, and then says, "Fear of God means reverence and obedience to his commands."

I remind him, "Uncertainty remains—the law that secures our religious liberty."

He nods. No one is immune to the rumors that fly: the Confederate Army is desperate for recruits. But he says, "Both Colonel John B. Baldwin and Judge John T. Harris have promised that Congress will stand firm on the exemption."

There is no value in saying what is common knowledge: a large number of Union men have come into the northern part of the Valley, perhaps as close as Winchester. Some say as many as 8,000 on foot, plus horses and artillery. Others point out that both sides are at a low ebb. How does that reassure anyone? Those in the know say the Rebels' goal is to outlast the North—not necessarily to win outright, but to force the other side to quit. How does that produce a thankful heart?

Equally troubling, those of us in the Valley with scruples against warfare keep adding to our own disarray. We do not give consistent witness to peace. Rather than a clear explanation as to our principles, confusion abounds! The *Rockingham Register* increasingly directs venom toward us German Baptists and Mennonites. They mistake to call us Mennonists and Tunkers or Dunkers. That is minor compared with the way they parade us out for attention. I can say without equivocation: no one has joined us at Flat Rock purely to take advantage of the religious exemption. We do not allow that sort of fabrication.

But several weeks ago, a vicious writer charged in the newspaper that people like us should be put in the front ranks of the army, if we do not contribute to the great cause as farmers. Delilah reread the exact wording: "Be made food for gunpowder." That same person said the names of anyone who makes unpatriotic statements should be forwarded to the Confederate Secretary of War. Someone with those views will never understand Brother Kline's thinking: "The highest form of patriotism is found when people love God first of all, and secondly, love their neighbors as much as themselves." On that, I firmly agree. No one can fault John's devotion to building up our country, unless they are determined to misunderstand.

We shake our heads at other printed voices also. Last week an unnamed writer said those of us with scruples would do all we could to raise grain for the Confederacy. This person even promised to excommunicate any member who refused to raise more bread and meat than what he and his family need. Where did that voice come from? Johnny would never make that claim categorically by himself. If a Mennonite, by what authority did he write for all? Now this week another article goes yet another direction, praising us for being loyal citizens who respond to the needy wherever possible, including those harmed by Yankees.

Mischief. It is all mischief. No wonder our nerves rattle when ink adds to the disputes. We are tossed about. With detectives and spies converging—even women masquerading!—my trust all but disappears. No wonder my eye loses its place. Confederate spies work for both sides! A local man was caught smuggling and also accused of acting as an informant to the Detective Police—the North!

I look to the right and to the left, but no step seems safe. Even answering a rap on my door may bring repercussions.

Esther — Shenandoah Valley, April 1864

Right when the ground was beginning to dry out and mud balls not stick, he came to me, head down. "Ma, I have to go."

I'd tried to prepare. But this timing—all by my lonesome. Not that William and Mary Grace don't help, but they lack strong muscle. Yet there's no dispute: Joseph dare not wait longer. Springtime or not. Henry and another older one will lead these young ones whenever we get word. Soon, when the coast is clear.

No tears came. Dried up and gone for Simon. No proper way to put my man to rest. Now my last big boy. Scouts on the loose. All my men—one risk or another. Joseph's bag is packed, except for cheese that must stay cold.

This Henry Brunk has been hiding most of two years; everyone tight-lipped about him. Before that, captured and forced to haul provisions for the Confederacy. But he came to conviction: hauling hay for cavalry horses was part of the war effort. These months since, the man lives here and not here. Refusing to flee, but hiding in one attic or another, providing what he can for his wife and children—a pittance making willow baskets. When his little boy was buried in the cemetery at the Bank church, Henry hid—hat pulled down—in the shadow of a tree. Southern scouts there, looking.

Maryland—that's where my boy and others will head. But not for certain. Joseph might misinform to spare me, if questioned. Deception knows no end, when safety is all. He will throw in his lot—these others walking. Near to a dozen from our church and elsewhere. Simon wouldn't approve. I try to warn: the difficulties of staying as a group. But where else to turn?

Yielding my boy to this Henry's care . . . doubtless a good man, living with a price on his head these years. Now forced to leave—the hounds circling; the smell of blood in the air. More deaths likely, whether beautiful or other. How does anyone know? Oh, Mama, does anyone get to choose . . . what kind of death?

Henry's remaining children said to be riddled with illness. His wife, Susanna—what must she think? The man and boys plan to walk the ridges, stay away from roads. Simon never said about ridges, but Joseph's eyes are clear to follow. His mind, made up. Strong in body. He doesn't know: trust isn't all. I daresn't cast doubt. Frances seemed certain: they'll cross the mountain at Dawley's Springs, go to Clarksburg—another place to take the oath of allegiance to the North. She shrugged when I said the story keeps changing, how they'll go.

My mind keeps its flutter. No more need to wait for Simon's tap on the window. No protection, no funeral. But near to his mother's bones. No more "maybe later"; the cave would be warmer now. If Simon were here—no, not to pretend. It's Gabriel who came, but only a brief time. No thought to ask whether Simon carried a pistol. I wear the dark blue—near enough to black.

But never a peek for Simon—his baby girl! Such a sweet one, our Miriam. Over a month and rid of her birth scratches. If she were a fusser like Jephthah, my prickling rash would be worse.

William stares at a crow that pecks on a possum carcass. He says what no one else dares: "I need a man." He forgets his hassles with his pa.

I grab William's smooth chin; his red eyes watery. "We'll do what we can. Don't go looking for bad signs. Look at you: a year bigger." We both know: his arms stay skinny. All these years he's taken orders, mostly from one brother or another. "We'll take turns managing the field horses," I say.

His voice wheezes from springtime misery. "Don't let Joseph go."

"We must be strong for Joseph. Now is not the time to fear. We don't have to plant both fields. We'll start where the ground does best."

"But Brother Samuel says—"

I put a finger to his lips. "Joseph and the others know to outsmart the fox."

William turns away, shoulders drooping like Simon's when weighed down.

I know when William's fears took a turn. This past Sunday Bishop Samuel departed from the usual, swayed by his own grief. Every spring we hear about the sower: some seeds fell on good ground, others on stones or thorns, even by the wayside. Samuel read the proper verses but said, "Our planting days are fraught with peril. Many of you women, you lads, doing the work of two or three times your number." He put a fist to cover his mouth. "Bear with me."

Brother Coffman stands a tall one—not overly, but seeming to look from a height, as if reading from a high beam. But that Sunday, he stood reduced. "Tragedy has struck my family. A second message pushes to the fore this morning, rising out of marching boots and demands to obey mortal men. Animosity among neighbors." He paused again, shoulders sagging. "I don't mean to frighten, only to encourage readiness. I pray—there may be edification, despite . . ."

A restless child cried with a fierceness, and a young mother hurried to the cloak room.

Samuel lifted his Bible with two hands, as if a weight. "We know not when the wicked one may rip out that which has been sown in the hearts of our young. The enemy plants tares amidst wheat. That we know from Scripture." He squinted from under thick eyebrows, his gaze to the back of the room where the young boys sat—his own among them—not that there was rustling. He shook his head and put down the Bible.

As if in conversation, he folded his arms. "Forgive me. Most of you know, I grew up in the mountains of Greenbrier County. That is part of West Virginia now. The North," he added, as if begrudging. "My grandparents, Isaac and Esther Kauffman; late in the eighteenth century they started a church there. My parents, Christian and Anna, produced ten of us. Even so, the church stayed small. Our former bishop here, Martin—his grandparents, you may recall, are the same as mine. He traveled to us in the Greenbrier area on occasion, maintaining concern." Samuel paused, blowing his cheeks wide. "Most of my siblings still live there, but many have joined the Methodists. My walk kept safe, when I came to Rockingham County as a young man seeking labor, finding Frances. I ramble."

Samuel idly turned the pages of his Bible, as if seeking direction. "The crux: late last fall the North captured two sons of my Greenbrier first cousin David, a Whanger and deceased. Both boys were wearing Confederate garb when captured; both events happened less than ten days apart, near a big bridge called the Gauley in the Kanawha Valley, fifty-some miles west and north of their home. You likely know, the two sides no longer exchange prisoners."

Again, he lifted his head, peering to the back of the room. "My sons . . . I look on all our young boys anew, as sons . . . It strikes the heart." He paused before adding, "All of you young ones in this church, closer to me than distant family."

I sat taut, but settled Jephthah farther from my bosom, his mouth pursed as if to suck. Miriam's eyelids stayed shut, her rosy cheeks and black hair held secure in Mary Grace's arm.

Samuel's voice brought me back. "We don't place faith in all reports. Some certainty, though, the two boys were taken farther north." He wiped his brow. "Perhaps a place called Charleston; perhaps farther by riverboat to Wheeling. The Ohio River. No word, regarding survival this past winter—most likely, cold barracks or tents—a hostile northern climate."

My mind leaped to Simon; he had talked often of the pull of flowing water. The Potomac, that same place that Peter had sung about: the sentry keeping guard by his lonesome. Oh, my boy. He never promised any word would come from Benjamin about captures. Where goes that Jubal man? Oh, to stay my wild imaginings! How am I to make room for another goodbye? Not Joseph! Given to moods, but always a hard worker.

I jumped back to Brother Coffman; he mentioned other places: a Camp Chase in Ohio, an overcrowded prison farther west on a Rock Island. That one, said to be Illinois, near the Mississippi. I didn't catch all. My mind darted. Snatches of words: ". . . powers and principalities . . . in Lewisburg a year . . . different companies . . . The Lord desires prudence . . . not tarry unduly."

I knew then, it wouldn't be long. Samuel was changed.

But of a sudden, he turned to the few middle-aged men: the one, exempt because of pleurisy; another burdened with a lame shoulder; still another, unsound lungs from birth. "Union thievery may have played a part for my cousin, the father of these captured boys." Samuel gripped the edge of the long preacher's table. "This David Whanger, a farmer and blacksmith, had been called as a Mennonite minister in that struggling settlement. His death came after the sudden appearance two years ago of Union men on his farm. That was 1862; they took his horses. Soon after, he died."

Frances had never breathed a word to me about this death, but she told about a family that lost three girls to scarlet fever in a short stretch of days. Might this be the same? That was back when our own troubles started—Simon and Andrew in prison, Midnight taken.

Samuel spoke trance-like, his eyes half-closed. "The times are such—give heed. Signs and more to come. If I have erred, not holding forth regarding seedtime—things may darken—if thinking to be elsewhere, do not delay." Of a sudden, he walked halting to a seat on the front bench, bent forward and placed his head in his hands.

No wonder William pulls out clumps of hair. We didn't sing "Blest Be." We wobbled to our conveyances. No one said a word on that Sunday, riding home. Joseph guided the horses but sat wooden-like. Drastic, for Samuel to be so shaken. Barely a benediction. Those captured cousins may not be the only story. Before we stepped down from the wagon, Joseph reminded William once more, not to pull the harness with too much tightness.

I can't fall to my knees. I sit staring between one son's fear and another's readiness. My mind flits like a bat again. *Banging hard at the window pane.* One of the captured boys, named Joseph. *Darting to the darkness of the rafters.* Why didn't I say better words to Peter? *Soaring high to the loft.* I could have said, "Stay near to God," like that Hildebrand. *Hiding behind barrels of flour.* No prisoner exchange; no safe return. Whether 'tis worse to die in battle or uncared for by the enemy. *Flying on the silent wings of evil.*

We're Union, William. Joseph must go. Soldiers don't ask about loyalty; they want food. Andrew? Can you hear—? *Beware the viper's stealth.*

We have no recourse. I keep watch with Joseph for the lantern.

* * *

Days pass. Another siege of chilly damp weather. The time, still not come. Joseph waits silently. His calm, a blessing. My restless sleep: I can't let him go; we'll find a way to stow. But when light creeps up, I fear he's missed the signal. What if we both slept through the flickering! I *must* release him.

Brother Samuel rides here in broad daylight, making the rounds. "No meeting for worship tomorrow," he says. "Perhaps not next Sunday either. The roads clogged with soldiers."

Joseph is to remain in readiness, but we aren't to venture out. Only exercise extreme care: the mountains crawling. At the first opportunity, the lantern will come. Samuel promises. When signaled, Joseph is to meet others at our Weavers church. *John* Brunk, not Henry, will greet the boys and give instruction as to their next step.

The shakes return; the pans rattle. William wheezes. How can I think to send another?

Samuel's face, strained when here, speaking in low tones of Maryland. Joseph was right about a place called Hagerstown, where they'll set their sights. But under no circumstance is Joseph to separate and strike out on his own. Not depart from the group or take a chance to find Andrew.

Samuel assured me before he left: "People in the North know of our difficulties. They will provide shelter if called upon. Not necessary to be blood brothers."

I must be strong—four young ones entrusted. But my brood and I will not sing tomorrow. At most, a verse. Joseph could carry the low part, the rest of us on melody.

"We don't know the Lord's designs," Samuel said. His eyelids closed. "God's promise is to be with us." He pressed my arm at leaving. Tenderness from my friend's man.

I'm to be of good cheer, even when hope for a lantern withers. Come summer, Joseph could be someone else's farmhand, an extra.

Betsey Petersheim — West Virginia, May 1864

Mother says everything happened at once, but Poppa says, we have no troubles like the state of Virginia.

First, a new calf surprised us. Mother is right: we expected it, but we did not know how early. Nor how weak—falling and falling. Tobias checks the mother extra, too. Then right when Poppa wanted to get an early start with the oats, his nerves took a bad turn. He had dizzy spells and bumped into doorways. One time he spun around and crumbled on the floor. Tobias says I mean "crumpled."

I ran to him. "Poppa, Poppa!" He did not move for long minutes. Then he lifted his head a whisker before dropping again slowly. I tapped him on the shoulder, for fear.

Mother came from separating the boys and their squabbles. "What happened? Crist. Christian!" She knelt and shook his arm. "Open your eyes! Speak!"

He mumbled and rolled onto his side, covering his face with his arms.

All the little boys came running, and I had to shoo them away with my apron like chickens. "Poppa needs rest," I said, my finger to my lips. I am a big eleven years. "We must not bother."

We children had to go outside; we hunted for violets and counted to see who had the most. Poppa did not sit at the table to eat with us, but kept to his rocker or even the bed.

The next day Tobias rode Frank to fetch Auntie Mommie. She hitches her skirts and rides like a man, but Mother always sits sidesaddle when she rides.

Auntie Mommie clicked her tongue when she held her hand to Poppa's heart. "No field work," she said to Mother, as if Poppa were nowhere to be had.

"Weak is all," Poppa said, but placed a hand to shade his eyes.

"No man is weak in the spring," Mother said. "Come fall, we understand. But now, your blood must be off; your sister will get to the bottom."

"Did you try sparrows' broth?" Auntie Mommie asked.

"That is for a severe case, and long," Poppa said. "Nothing of that."

Levi began to whimper. He is the oldest of the little ones at four years but the quickest to cry and slowest to keep up. Even Noah can run faster, and he is barely two. Gideon is the in-between stairstep of the three little boys. We girls helped the boys weave strands for straw baskets; we made a big one for Poppa. Mother let me make popcorn, even though it was not Sunday, so we could put fresh violets and popped corn in the baskets.

"Your poor poppa is worn out," Auntie Mommie said at the supper table. "Too much worry. Gideon, you do not need to chew like a hungry horse, nor provoke to the left or right. Soon, your Mother's nerves will fray, too." Auntie's mouth hung way down.

She gave more orders before she left. She is not a doctor, but she told Poppa she would come back when she found something stronger. "It may be the bile—your humors not working." She turned to Mother. "Sassafras tea will thin his blood." She put both hands on her hips and looked stern at Poppa. "Whatever the case, eat your rhubarb, Mister; that will remove poison."

My friend Sarah Beachy told me once that her poppa had to let go his blood because it was dark and corrupt. Now when he preaches, I see gaps where he should have teeth.

All the rest of that week, Poppa walked slowly to the table like his legs were new. He said the Lord's Prayer with us, but stopped eating if he tasted a second time. We did not go anywhere on our visiting Sunday.

Back in January, when Poppa had had his birthday three days after mine, he said he was thirty-eight. All was jolly then, even with cold nights. But now Poppa drinks Mother's special tea; he is quick to snap his thumb and finger loud when the boys make too much noise.

Tobias and I have had extra chores to make up for Poppa, even though church men like Auntie Mommie's Christian came. The rains have made for a slow start in everyone's fields. When I took Gideon along to feed the chickens and hunt eggs, he chased the old hen, Gertie, until she turned on him and made him run to the far end. He thought it was a fun game and came toward her again, half-running on his hands and toes. But I caught him and squeezed him so tight, he stood straight up. "Look at how you've soiled yourself!" I scolded.

When we came back inside, shivering after washing at the well, Mother was crying over moths in a new bag of flour. Lydia and I could not find where they hid.

The very next morning Mary was sent with the little boys to play in the barn. It felt warmer like spring, and the boys had been bucking like colts in the house. Lydia and I were hoeing to break up hard clods in the garden, but we ran to the barn when we heard shrieking.

"Gideon jumped too close," Mary said, louder than his cries.

He would not stretch out his arm for me, but Levi pointed to the haymow. "He smashed his head!"

I picked straw out of Gideon's hair but saw no blood. Mary kept hopping, her eyes bulging and her lips tight.

Tobias helped us carry Gideon inside—I had to hold his dirty bare feet—and laid him on the day bed.

"Merciful heavens!" Mother wailed at the bump on his arm. "No doctor to be had—this war! Only that dirty blacksmith of a bonesetter."

"A man of many trades," Poppa said, but when he stood, as if to make ready for a trip, he sank again to his rocker.

"You dare not," Mother said. "Tobias must fetch your sister again. Where has she been? She promised."

"No one has opium," Poppa said.

"She could rustle something," Mother said.

By afternoon, Auntie Mommie had come with a satchel and bag. She was all business and set to work. "Prepare the table," she said to me, as if I knew. I brought a big bucket and guessed to bring old towels and rags. Mary was still hopping about, as if she had the leaks.

"Lydia and Mary!" Auntie Mommie commanded like a man. "Keep Noah and Levi outside. Shoo! No mischief this time." She had brought two thin pieces of board and clapped them together. "Out with you!" Then she turned again. "Water! Tobias, you smell like the hogs. Too much time with that fool calf again. Fetch us more water! Someone, bring Gideon; his arm must not sag."

Gideon commenced screaming, and Mother put her hand over his mouth. She motioned for me. Poppa whimpered.

At last, Gideon's body stilled but for jerks on the table, his lips pressed tight.

"Good boy." Mother purred the way the Beachy's cat hums when I pet her. "Hold still for Auntie. She will make a splint, only for you."

Between loud sniffles, Gideon allowed Auntie to take a better look. Mother motioned to me again. "Hold firm, Betsey—his hand—so Auntie Mommie can make certain—his bones."

"You are fearfully and wonderfully made, Child," Auntie said in her regular voice. "Never forget that. Make a fist now for Auntie. Uh-hum. Listen!" She moved to hover directly above his head. "We will get a good result, if you cooperate. You dare not bang. Do you hear? What did I say?"

Gideon's voice trembled. "Be good."

"*Ja*," Auntie Mommie said, "not one lick of a wiggle. No more *nixnutzich*!" Spit flew from her mouth. "You bumped hard, but no blood to speak of. Swelling is for natural." Her voice came soothing again. "No dirt, a dab of ointment. Then we wrap your arm in this soft cloth. You may watch; it will not hurt. See—a bandage, Gideon. Then we affix these boards. Gentle but firm. This is how you heal. Wrap another cloth and tie with cords. Like a blanket. Awkward, I know. Do not say aught. Tight, but you will become accustomed." Her voice grew louder; her eyes sizzled. "What did I say? You dare not move. Your bones will go splat." Her voice cracked like a whip.

"It hurts," Gideon whimpered.

Poppa groaned and sat with a handkerchief to his face.

Auntie was back to soothing. "Your poppa will tell you stories from the olden days when he was a boy. Little boy bones are the best for healing, like my Valentine's when he fell from a horse. The elbow—" Her eyes crossed and her forehead had furrows. "No one can know. I do my best. Betsey will make your favorite pudding. Ice! Why did someone not . . . Tobias! Only a small block—dull the pain. You will need to bring more tomorrow," she called to him.

Her hair set loose and eyes trained on Gideon, Auntie Mommie grimaced like Poppa does when he lifts something heavy. She gave more orders mixed with sweets. "No running for a week. No bumps! One time will undo everything. *Verschtehscht?*" She clapped her hands. "Your Poppa will keep track of the weeks until Tobias can give you a horse ride again." She patted Gideon's knee. "Good boy. Honey on your bread. But if you roughhouse, I will have to come and do over. Do you want that?" She pinched his cheek. "Sugar will make you sweeter."

Of a sudden, she grabbed her satchel and turned to Poppa. "Now then, Mister—" She held up a bottle. "Hostetter's Celebrated Stomach Bitters." As quickly, she held up her other hand. "Do not debate! I know what you will say. I bought from a Dunker of good repute for stomach, liver, and bowels—whatever ails. We must quiet your dyspepsia—the man agreed. You will get stronger when you stop emptying yourself every time you eat. What good is food, if your innards reject?"

"Bitters do not work," Poppa said. "Years ago, I tried Dr. Flint's Quaker remedy. Quackery. You did not give good money, did you?"

"Do not trouble yourself," she said. "This is different. A man cannot live with poisons; you must rid yourself. How hard is that?" She whirled back to Gideon. "Are you remembering?"

Gideon whispered, "Yes, Auntie."

"Your son, three years old, understands. For you, Mister Petersheim, three times a day—a stout spoonful. Highly recommended. No skimping. I know how you are. The Dunker man said your organs have taken the lazy boat. That's why, those nervous headaches. Like the bottle says. Read it!"

Poppa kept his chin on his chest, but he did not pull out his handkerchief this time.

"If you doubt the efficacy, it will not work," Auntie Mommie said. "Is that what you want—affix a jinx? No castor oil anywhere to be had," she muttered.

"Wishing does not make things so," Poppa said softly.

Ever since, Mother sees to his daily portions as Auntie instructed. Poppa holds a hand to his stomach when he slurps. His body shudders. "Bitters," he says. But already, he walks better; sometimes he rocks Noah and hums. I smile for him when I catch his eye.

We had barely gotten used to new ways when more surprise came—two big men, strangers and bedraggled. One turned out to be a very tall boy, but he ate like a man. His name was Joseph and he had thick brown hair; it did not go on the fritz like Tobias's. Mother said Joseph's face was sweet. The older man, Isaac, had to stoop also when he entered our house.

At first, Poppa had stayed at the door to talk with the men.

"We will not falsify," this Isaac said. "We flee from Virginia. Our church does not believe in killing people."

"Nor do we!" Poppa nearly shouted. He clutched Noah to him, and we all followed out the door. "You are safe here." But then he looked to Mother.

She moaned softly and seemed to have lost her bearings. Levi tugged on her skirts.

"We're headed to Maryland. A place called Hagerstown," Joseph said. "The two of us had to split from the rest." He licked his lips. "Would it be a bother—a cup of water?" He held up his canteen.

"Mercy!" Mother said. "Forgive, forgive. Betsey, hurry! Bring fresh."

Joseph followed me to the well, and that was the start. We made a good team; he pulled the rope and did not tease when I spilled to pour. After they had drunk their fill, Poppa invited them inside. "I need to sit. Dyspepsia and nerves," he said, "but getting better. What is your story?"

The big folks and Tobias sat at the kitchen table with the strangers; Noah climbed onto Mother's lap. We girls huddled on the hearth, and Levi got to perch on the day bed with Gideon.

"We signed allegiance to the North at New Creek," Isaac said, "but after that, our group couldn't agree." His shoulders slumped. "Several times of splitting, though strongly instructed from the start not to do so. Very sad. Some wanted to go straight north to Somerset County, claiming to avoid Oakland."

"That could not be good," Joseph interrupted.

"Still others insisted on heading to Cumberland—a relative there or some such. Very set in their ways for young ones; I didn't know such was the case when we started. Only Joseph and I"—Isaac paused to look at his companion—"saw the wisdom, retracing a short distance, before coming this way. Our plan: around Oakland far enough on the west side, before going north, and then back east."

Joseph scratched at his chin whiskers. "Some were homesick and forgetting the dangers of any direction."

Poppa clicked his teeth, as if he understood. "Too much rigor?"

"Not certain," this Joseph went on. "But the mountains can be heavy cloaks, and nighttime animals appear suddenly. Even lizards give shivers in the dark."

"Whatever the case, the indecision—" Isaac said. "We tired of it. There may be blame. But the more tired and hungry, the more entrenched."

"We all started out as friends," Joseph said. "But Henry Brunk stayed with the restless ones, determined to still proceed directly to Hagerstown. Some thought this Pike too public."

"Since then, we've heard of Cumberland's troubles. We happened upon a Quaker family, once heading westward. The Lord kept us—" Isaac stopped a long time. "We don't know—the Quaker man said, for certain we would have walked into Union snares to the north." He shook his head. "We don't know—which way they ended up." Noah squirmed to get down from Mother and went to Lydia. "Brambles may have clogged their minds. Doubts instead of trust. But home folks—I fear to think. We pray—the Lord's mercy."

"One good thing," Joseph added, "easier for just the two of us. Better time. But sad."

"We have been distressed also," Poppa said. "Afflicted these weeks—unsteady in my weakened state, but following a regimen. I hesitate"—he looked to Mother—"but it comes to me—the Lord's good timing may have sent answer. Your burden much heavier." Poppa shook his head but sat straighter. "I do not—your timeline. But perchance, if you could help Tobias—yes, and Betsey—with flax, perhaps some oats. Not privy, of course, your urgency. Only know—a great help to us." He paused, his lips trembling. "Is that not so, Mother?"

"Where do you mean?" she asked, looking about and speaking fast. "Gideon must have the day bed, so Levi does not bump him in the trundle. A broken arm," she said, as if the new ones could not make sense of the bundle he carried.

"Surely, Lydia, we can make do," Poppa said to Mother. "A floor bed for Gideon with an extra tick brought down from the loft. Our big little boy has been learning new ways. Gideon would be safe beside this nice young man." Poppa looked under the table. "Right under here. You do not thrash, do you, Joseph?"

Joseph smiled at Gideon but shook his head solemnly for Poppa. "Not that I know. Nor flail."

Poppa nodded. "Isaac, if perchance—you must have the day bed." Poppa's eyes turned to Mother again. "All could be commodious. Not so?"

She stood and turned this way and that; her mouth opened and closed. I held my breath, tightening my grip on Mary. Suddenly, Mother commenced with orders: "Fetch the ticks, Tobias. And Betsey, we must make fresh cornbread. Cakes. We will add corn cakes to our supper."

It was soon agreed: the two from afar would stay for most of a week and work for their keep.

"One thing yet," Poppa said. "We have not seen soldiers lately, but you know to be on the lookout. In a flash, they can appear, even here. Johnny Reb or Billy Yank. You must exercise care and be alert."

"We know," Isaac said. "We have passes, but some northerners aren't friendly. We won't bring dishonor or troubling questions to you or your family." He nodded at Joseph. "Safe shelter a few nights—a blessing, even though longer. A brother, this family, in need."

"Show them the set-up for animals, Tobias," Poppa said.

Mother and I fried our shriveled potatoes with the jackets on to go with the cakes, and Lydia found dandelion to make a salad. I fetched cheese from the milk house, too. "We will do better tomorrow," Mother promised the new men. "We had meat this noon."

Isaac looked at Joseph as if to laugh or cry. "We can make do—a banquet." I wish I could meet his children sometime; he said two of them have dimples.

"Survivors all . . ." Poppa said. "The Lord blesses."

That is how we made room for two extra big ones at our bulging table. We all went to bed before dark that first night. Gideon's little-boy eyes looked like he wanted to giggle when he bedded beside one so big. "I will beat you to dropping off," Joseph said.

Before we could plant the next day, our two new friends sharpened the plow as best they could and hooked it to Tom and Frank. Poppa had fresh tears.

Some nights Joseph washed out his dark blue shirt and wore a light brown one instead—or the other way around—to go with his britches. Tobias has two pairs of pants, but the one is more for church.

When Joseph did not need to help Isaac with the plow, he sowed flax seed next to me. The second day I still felt shy, but I asked, "Do you have sisters?"

"A tiny baby, Miriam, and another sister, Mary Grace, taller than you." He looked at me carefully. "Two brothers stay at home, too—one is older than Mary Grace and the other is about the size of Noah." His lips turned sad. "My big brothers scattered early, one side or the other. One went north like this; I want to find him. But Ma . . ." He brushed the backside of his hand over his forehead. "I miss them. Everyone. Pa, too." He turned away and I could only see his back side where his straight hair cut across above his shirt. "I wasn't always a good son. I kept to myself. Ma said I had moods like Pa. I didn't know—not till I ran." He turned back. "You're good to help your mother. One day your pa could be gone."

I nodded and told how Poppa had hauled for one army or the other.

"He hauled?" Joseph asked and frowned again, like when he told of the ones who split. "Your pa doesn't seem . . ."

"What?"

"Like he would give in. You're Amish, right?"

"Poppa had to answer," I said.

Joseph jerked his head to me but then looked down. "Maybe different . . . I run because I won't yield, either side. Not be for either cause. Our bishop teaches us not to assist or take up the sword. Isaac says the same. He hauled supplies awhile but learned his lesson. Now the South thinks he's a deserter for running."

I did not know what to say. Poppa teaches us right from wrong. But Joseph seemed sadder than a boy should be, only a few years older than Tobias.

Finally, Joseph said, "Your pa's a good man. I don't mean . . . he feeds us well."

"My mother is not my momma," I blurted.

"Oh!" he said. "I didn't . . . you mean—a step?"

I nodded. "From Somerset County. Five years already. All is different. Most everything."

"Oh," he said again. "My ma, alone now with four. Pa . . ." His Adam's apple looked big when he swallowed long. "A viper took—a month ago or so. Why Pa reached—"

"No! Were you there?"

"He was on the run, staying at his brother's place. An accident. When I told Isaac, he said, 'No more innocence for you.' Plans don't always work, when there's warfare."

Tobias whistled from a distant row. "Hey, you two—" I turned to see him grinning.

I moved quickly to make up for lost time. I did not want to stop talking, but Tobias might tell Poppa, and I did not want Joseph to hear Mother scold.

We never talked again by ourselves, but I still think about Joseph. I wish I could meet his sister with the two names. I did not tell him I had another name once.

Sometimes during our suppers, Poppa and Isaac talked about differences for Mennonites and Amish. "More alike than not," they always said and nodded their heads. I kept quiet like Mother and listened. Sometimes Gideon needed help cutting his meat. I did not want extra commotion. Never once did the men talk about hauling.

One evening, Isaac and Joseph taught us a new prayer before our supper meal. Mother and Poppa looked at each other but showed no alarm. I peeked when our new friends prayed together. Once I saw them open their eyes when they said the part "*Steh' uns bei in aller Not, Und verlass uns nicht im Tod.*" Then their eyes closed tight again. It was like they shared a secret promise: *leave us not in death*! I wish I could ask Poppa, but I do not want to say I opened an eye.

The men often helped Mother clean up after supper. "Why should we take our ease?" Isaac asked. "We're not the only ones who worked today." Sometimes the men played I Spy with us children before we readied for bed. One of us girls or Tobias took turns being a partner with one of the little boys. No one was allowed to run to find an object; that way Gideon could play, too.

Other times, after Mother and I had readied the boys for bed, Poppa asked the men to tell stories about Virginia before we said our prayers. Isaac said, "Things are tighter here. Your mountains squeeze, except for this open meadow. You found the right spot." Then he put his head down and tapped his chest. "I carry my home mountains." He tapped again. "My dear wife and children, our beautiful spot."

Joseph said his favorite place to play when little was in their barn. "My pa attached a swing to a rafter above the haymow—higher than yours here." Gideon's eyes opened wide. "After a summer day's work, we could swing until the bats came out." He paused. "I made a hiding place in that same haymow. Scouts about—this spring."

"Were they thick on trails coming here?" Poppa asked.

"Only certain places," Isaac said.

Mother stood and said, "Time for bed, Gideon."

That meant the end for us girls, too; everyone had to go to bed at the same time, so the lamp would not bother. But Joseph answered, "Good travelers, too. A man named Josiah."

Tobias asked quick, "One of your friends?"

Mother folded her arms in front to listen.

"No, not from home," Isaac said. "Josiah was of the Negro race. Coming this way, too."

"On the run?" Poppa asked.

"A very nice man," Joseph said. "We almost missed seeing him; he blended in." He paused and looked at Mother, but she made no move with the boys. "We had stopped at a clearing where this man pressed against a tree—near where we stopped with the Quakers. Isaac spotted him first. I had to hold my hand in cold stream water to stop the itching. We passed along bread and cheese to Josiah—from what we'd been given. Not all is danger."

"That's so," Isaac said, "once certain of each other. Tell how it was, Joseph."

"He saw my swollen hand—red and itchy of a sudden—and walked with us awhile; he didn't want us to miss the fork. Along the way he pointed out more plants to stay away from. Different leaves for different kinds of poison ivy and oak. Most of it I knew, but I must have been careless. Josiah wanted to make sure."

"Were you scared?" Tobias asked.

"My hand throbbed." Joseph turned his hand over to inspect. "But with Josiah? No, not after the first startle. We had food; he knew the way. Easy friends."

Mother beckoned to Gideon, but he looked half asleep. I slumped between my sisters on the hearth to stay low.

"On the run?" Poppa asked again.

"We all were," Isaac said. "We all are. But he was in more danger. More consequences, if caught. Joseph and I had passes—something he will never get unless freed. Not fair, but we carry hope for all Negroes." He nodded to Joseph, as if passing another secret promise. "We pray he makes it safely. Once past the hidden turn, Josiah took off through brush. No goodbye, only 'Could be mean ones—up that way. Soon as not—'" Isaac stopped. "I can't say all. Except he said, 'Mean fellers could take me straight to a nest of graybacks.' Never forget that Josiah."

"A far sight better than the smugglers we met," Joseph said. "Trinkets cover up their rifles—probably outlandish prices. They watch for runaways, too. Smugglers might get extra pay for a man like Josiah. Grab him and find his owner. Nothing fair. Our passes, our white skin."

The talks that night finally ended. We girls hurried to the loft without being told and said our prayers quietly. I had never heard stories like that, not even when someone whispered loud after a church meeting. Only once, after Mister stopped with us long ago, Mother had clicked her teeth that there was not always fairness. Now Isaac and Joseph said the same.

On the very last day when we were helping Isaac with a start of oats, Poppa walked all the way out to the field that afternoon and said we should stop work early. "A grateful heart," he said, "overflowing. You must not leave here exhausted, Isaac."

Before we milked the cows, Tobias and I rested by the well with Joseph and took long drinks of fresh water. He said their well at his house is a trifle bigger and has red bricks mixed with brown. We each said what our favorite spring flower was. I said hepatica right away. I knew Tobias would say, spring beauty. Joseph's was blood root, because it is one of the first after winter. He also favors bluebells over blue phlox and said they'd seen huge patches on the way.

"I do not want to ever travel," I said. "Not far away to Iowa. Or anywhere."

"Ohio would not be far," Tobias said.

"Ohio is a nest!" Joseph said. "Not safe. Maryland will be better. For sure, Hagerstown. I want to find my brother in Pennsylvania."

"But you will have to sleep again with owls and bears." I could not hide my shiver. "Are you never afraid? One time you said lizards."

Joseph shrugged. "Isaac's very smart; he knows smells and what to watch for. He taught me whenever I was hungry or thirsty, to chew the bark of dried slippery elm. He's told me things I would never have learned at home—serious things, even about death. 'Nothing to fear,' Isaac says, 'if you live right.' But he misses his family terribly. And the ones who started out with us. We don't know whether we'll ever see them again."

I was going to tell about when Jacob and Elizabeth had to move back to Somerset County, but Joseph had more to say.

"Isaac and Henry both taught us young ones about how to be kind to a woman." Joseph looked right at Tobias. "'Never be cross, even under duress,' he said. Everyone wants respect: my ma, Josiah. That was back when our group was all together. An old woman saw us and ran away from fear. It turns out, Henry was an orphan when young; his cousin John became like a father to him. That same John had helped us back at our start; he's very kind, too. Almost every day he walks twenty miles, if need be, to help someone. Even when our country is at war, there are good people. Like your family."

I wish the men could have stayed longer. I got to hear more of grown-ups' talks without needing to sneak like with Mack and Muck. Everybody thanked everybody—Mother, too, and we sent all the provisions they could carry. After the men trudged off, we were all sad. Almost every day, Mary wonders where they are. Tobias and I have to finish planting the oats by ourselves, but I remember what Joseph said about his ma. And his pa. And about good people on trails.

Poppa says, "The men were our angels." His head keeps getting better and he can stand long times now to graft our apple trees. So far, Mother lets Gideon sleep under the table at night. He says he whispers secrets to Joseph. I have a new secret, too, but I will not tell anyone, not even Sarah. I never thought of Gideon having secrets, but maybe we all do.

Soon we will plant corn, and Poppa wants to help. He says he can work mornings and rest in the afternoons. He says there is enough seed for three to a hill.

David — Shenandoah Valley, May 1864

Death interrupts my thoughts; I cannot stay my mind.

It happened again when I told Abigail and Delilah of our latest deed. I paused in the middle: "We came upon a man lying by the side of the road." It sounded like a Bible story, but was not. What else had I intended to say? A sudden disappearance, not uncommon.

All about us waits in confusion—more than some can bear. This is springtime; we should not dwell in disarray. But where are we heading? Seven precious souls lost already this year from Flat Rock. The latest bereft mother for me to visit: her child had succumbed to illness, her husband hiding, their supply of food dwindling. She boiled oats in water to make a gruel, a replacement for coffee. Once home, I said to my women, "I will not drink gruel ever again, no matter what."

But yes, the runaway—we were near Johnny's house, planning to dig crowfoot and lady's slipper along the way. Earlier we had made another house call; one of our brothers is quite low. But our digging was interrupted. We came upon a man—a path, leafed out anew—with a leg that could bear little weight. Last year around this same time, Johnny had set the broken leg of a deserter near to Broadway.

This time we tied our horses to trees and, like Good Samaritans helped the man, short in stature, to Johnny's house; he hopped on his good leg, one arm around each of us at the shoulder. Perhaps stocky at one time, but now a hollowness prevailed. Once he was stretched out diagonally on Brother Kline's long wooden kitchen table, his head propped on a pillow, I hurried to retrieve our horses while Johnny assessed the man's injury.

The man runs from the Confederate Army. He had misstepped in the dark from a barn loft ladder where he hid, thinking he had reached the bottom rung. But it was a longer step. He dragged himself more than a mile, but his wrenched knee kept giving out. Difficult enough, the stealth required to escape on two strong legs. But one alone? That is the nature of our days: delivering ourselves up in search of some slim line of escape, a morsel of food, surcease from sorrow.

Before returning inside Johnny's house, I dug dandelion roots to make a strong batch of tea. Some army hospitals use such as a substitute for opium. John refuses to pay the prices asked for chloroform; a one-pint tin has gone from fifty cents to fifty dollars or more in three years' time. The man cried out at Johnny's repeated attempts to rotate the knee. When the man's color improved, Johnny compelled him to drink of the tea as a relaxant.

The man never gave his name, so far as I know. I learned later: he stayed at Brother Kline's two days—the day bed in the front room—taking nourishment and making certain no complications set in. The merciful choice, not to let a fellow human being suffer when we have resources to lessen the pain. But any binding of wounds sets us up for condemnation. Even so, John will not shy away from unwanted attention.

Before I left that first day, I wanted to say to the young man: *Tell no one.* I thought to yell or whisper, to convey the gravity. Jesus said, "*See that no man know it*," when he healed another and feared the news would stir enemies to greater rage. How can this be any different? If the Linville Partisan Rangers hear of our medical assistance, they will take on greater wrath.

While tending the man, I became nervous on another count: Anna's face peered from behind the curtain. Anyone in the house would have heard our talk and stirring about—to say nothing of the man's moanings. But no questioning voice came from the face—only emotionless eyes watched steadily.

"All will be well," Johnny said to his beloved. "Rest at your ease." The curtain swung shut and I heard footsteps retreating. John has not given updates on his wife's condition for a long time, nor have I asked.

In late afternoon, when I rode home unsettled, I urged Ruby to uncommon haste. Our trees offer their tender green leaves, but the same canopy affords avengers a place to lurk.

I had not seen Winfield all spring, nor had I noticed much evidence of trapping efforts during the winter months. But two weeks later he came to my farm on horseback. We stood outside the sheep pen; my newly sheared ones were skinny and skittish, as if they knew a strange voice or heavy step could signal that one of their number would soon be gathered up in a rush.

"This friend of yours, the Kline man, we know what he's up to. His snooping. That story about rescuing a lamb stuck in brambles close to the road—a likely tale! How stupid does he think we are?"

I stared at Winfield; we have been chilly neighbors now several years. No civil greeting had been offered by either of us. "I know not whereof you speak," I said.

"Poppycock! You talk with him. Am I not right? You and your religious ilk. In cahoots, the bunch of you. Everyone knows, you Drunkards—or is it

Dunkards?" He guffawed and stepped closer. "You let the rest of us down!" I took a ragged step back. "Your duty to the Confederacy. You benefit from living here, don't you?"

"We believe in religious liberty to follow—"

"I know what you say." He stretched his wide face and squirrelly sideburns toward me. "I swan, a bunch of Nancys!" Then he pulled back in a mirthless grin. "Nasty scar you have there."

I shrank further and prayed Delilah would not come.

"Tell that man, that pudgy friend of yours, if he goes north, he'd better stay there." Winfield suddenly stuck a finger in my scarred cheek. "Tell him if he leaves and comes back, we'll get him. You hear? We know he carries information to the enemy."

"He travels empty-handed," I said, my voice thin as a sheep's bleat in the far corner.

Winfield pressed harder with his finger. "I believe that, like I believe he was rescuing a lamb. The man's a spy! We know. Let me tell you—every time I see a casualty list, I think of the likes of you. Missing."

"I know nothing of a lamb."

"Saturday afternoon, you numbskull!" he yelled. "Snooping around on Howdyshell Ridge. Lucky someone didn't take care of him right then. He's probably the one who set fire to our guns and supplies, too. Someone prowled around the root cellar that day we lost the shed."

"Not the man I know."

At that, Winfield clamped a rough hand to my throat. I was forced to stare at his sandy red sideburns. "Shut your trap! I hate idiocy. If the fat preacher plans to cause trouble, pass on names . . ." He towered over me, his hand like a vice, his breath like cloves. "Remind him: we have authority. As good as the military, every last one of us. We get our pay."

My face must have turned ashen, for he released his grip. I staggered backward and sucked in hard. I bent, hands on knees; then, gasping, straightened with my head back.

He went on. "No trouble, replacing our supplies. We've got Spencer repeating carbines; like to see one of you outrun that. Henry rifles, too—16-shot, breech-loading, if you don't know. Lots a' men willing—seized weapons from the North."

Hands on my bent knees again, I tried to lengthen incoming air. My coughs, gone from weak to loud and wracking.

"We'll wipe out your sappy smiles. You and your serene friends. My men—listen to me!" He jerked my arm, and my head snapped back. "*My men* speak *last*."

Another coughing spasm hit; I hunched again. He left suddenly. My sheep stayed huddled at my barking.

When able, I walked slowly toward the creek where my walnut trees flourish. I could not let Abigail see me yet, nor hear my raw thin voice. I studied the furrows in the black bark, ran my hand over its roughness. Tent caterpillars show up sometimes in the spring and eat foliage, but last fall I pruned carefully, removing branches where larvae had spread their webs. My beloved trees—my beautiful ones. I rested my good cheek on one, patted the tenderness on my scarred one. I ate no solid food that evening; I made no pretense of fasting.

Disaster lurks everywhere. Southerners in a rage, fighting to waylay the aggressor. Spies and detectives from both sides, swarming. The Home Guard, a military police force, keeps order for slave owners. Partisan Rangers spread their shadowy intent.

In our midst, an elderly brother from our church carries a basket into the mountains each evening and leaves food. The appointed place for his sons hiding.

Johnny has already left for the Nettle Creek church in Wayne County, Indiana. Winfield's warning for my departed friend carries no more weight than my own earlier pleas: "It is not safe to attend the Annual Meeting. You may never return. Why abandon us? Why forsake *our* need?"

As always, John looked pained in the eyes, studied his clean fingernails. "It may seem foolish. But for the sake of the gospel—" As if Scripture requires us to take *unwise* risks. As if the rest of us know nothing of loss, of counting the cost.

Johnny's plan was to ride by horseback, take several days to get to a friend's place close to Oakland, Maryland, where he would leave his beloved Nell, as he did two years ago. Following that, he would board a train for Ohio and on to Indiana.

No way to know his location now. We may never see Brother Kline again, certainly not any more this month. I am not being overly dramatic. How many times can he take this risk and expect a positive outcome? And if he returns? No one would think Winfield's threats, idle.

Before John left, he maintained his usual line: "I will die when and where the Lord wills." But his watery eyes betrayed him. People at Linville Creek said his recent sermons were overwrought with emotion. No one could lay a hand to stop him.

* * *

Grant's men roamed everywhere last week, o'ertaking our Valley. Loud crashes and booms came from soldiers amassed on the turnpike. I surmised to my women, "They will go on by, to Staunton or farther south." All of this month it has felt unsafe to venture out beyond necessity, tending our animals and such. Two more sheep gone in three days. Why am I surprised each time? The men have to eat. But how do they know to come all the way out here from the main road? I have continued giving the required ten percent of my produce to the Confederacy. Now these hungry foragers from the North side ransack my leftover corn.

"Did you forget to add a smidgen?" I ask, fully aware that Abigail hoards salt.

She knows what I miss but says, "Bad spots spread through the potatoes."

"Put a touch of bacon atop," Delilah says to me.

I do not like being ignored or chided. I drum my thumbs on the table.

We stayed put during the loud fighting, our quarrels rendered silly. Three days of hard rain, yet the noises persisted. At last J. M., like a son, brought us report through ongoing drizzle, our wet garments still spread about inside to dry. We maintained a fire against the damp air, even though summer should be near. J. M. took off his boots outside the door; his wet socks left wet spots on the floor with each step.

He stood by the fireplace, turning from side to side. "My spring wheat trampled, but worse—empty boots stuck in rows of mud on my property."

My women gasped. I clutched the top of a chair back.

"David against Goliath," he said.

"The North? But where the worst?"

"Fighters stayed in the open valley," J. M. said. "Bushong's farm, one place of battle. You would never guess the extent."

We gaped.

"Men slogged through fields." J. M. turned his back to the fire. "The North had endless reinforcements. The South, desperate, allowed 200 students—young boys!—from Virginia Military Institute to join the fight."

We could only look from one to the other, Delilah with a hand covering her mouth. Finally, I said, "Like unto using a colt to pull a plow—frisky and eager. Impossible to harness."

"That is so." J. M. turned sideways again. "A man by the name of Breckinridge led Rebels on the charge. This Northern general, a German-sounding name of Franz Sigel, led the counterattack with twice as many men. But the gray ones and their lads pushed harder, capturing a Union cannon, other supplies."

"Young boys," Delilah said in a whisper.

"Young boys," J. M. repeated. "By middle of the afternoon, Sigel and his men turned tail and headed north for Strasburg. Rebels gave chase; rain still poured down. So much smoke hung over the fields afterwards, I could scarce see."

I had to ask. "You said 'empty boots.'"

J. M. sat heavily on the edge of the hearth. His voice took on a reverence. "The North abandoned their wounded. No evidence of their new ambulance service here. Night fell; men covered in rain and mud. The next day citizens of New Market helped Confederate soldiers bury the dead. They carried the wounded to farmsteads—makeshift hospitals."

I shivered, remembering past scenes of barefoot men in rows on barn floors. "You went?"

"Yes, a call for straw," J. M. said. "A slight softening of beds. Word is, General Sigel has been replaced. Men still fleeing when Grant ordered Hunter to take over."

"Hunter," I said softly. "We know of him, his hard men."

My women and I said little after J. M. left. No one made effort to set out food for supper. We do not go to war, but the war comes to our door, besmirching our Valley.

Before bedtime I said, "The North will return; this General Grant will not be deterred. My losing sheep—a small matter."

"Young boys," Delilah said, "shaming the Union."

"No one knows to make a stop," Abigail said.

* * *

Two days later our lives took another turn. Making my rounds, I walked from my walnut trees to the pine grove at the front end of our lane. From a distance, it appeared that nettles had been piled on rock in a manner different than I remembered. Approaching, I stopped suddenly. Inching closer, a bare foot stuck out. Not a rock, but a rounded back—a body curled. I tapped and dug at the soaked earth with the toe of my boot. A mangled hand. I could not do more alone.

I found Delilah inside and motioned for her to join me on the porch. Abigail saw my spooked eyes and followed. We are past hiding or protecting. "We have a Visitor. Not the best." I grabbed a burlap bag hanging from a porch nail and retraced slowly, my women following, wordless. We stood, breathless, surrounding the still body.

Delilah took the bag from me and gently brushed off pine needles. "Must have come in search."

"No sign of scuffle," I said. "How he got this far . . ." We stood silent. No way to know—only conjecture. A ripped coat, soaked with dried blood, blended into dirt and needles.

"What are we to do?" Abigail asked, looking about, as if an attacker lurked.

"Appears—Union," Delilah said. "But how can we contact officials?"

"Only bury and leave a marker," I said. "One of the many. Unknown. Left to die, far from home. This foreign place. Wandered away, probably from fighting. Ours—to care for."

"Like a son," Abigail whispered.

"Yes," I whispered back.

"But . . ." Delilah began, only to swallow her thought.

"Not boards enough to fashion a coffin," I said.

"The earth will cradle," Abigail said.

Delilah and I set about to dig a grave in the pine grove. We took turns opening clay ground, sticky from heavy rains.

Abigail used a broken limb to measure the needed length and width. The man had not been tall. I asked Delilah to fetch water and the shovel, my mouth dry; Abigail brought my long-handled knife, found an old piece of muslin from years ago, when we had tried to raise tobacco.

While alone, I poked in vain for identification, the chest too caved to molest.

When my women returned, we rolled the body, face up, onto muslin—enough cloth to grab the ends. We scarce talked. I cut off two buttons from the man's coat; Delilah pointed to a patch from the jacket arm as well, but I shook my head. I nodded for my women to take the foot end, and I grabbed at muslin beyond the man's head. Together we lifted the body into the grave, covered the dark eyeballs with last year's oak leaves. We stood, arms linked along one side, silent in prayers.

"All who die, die in the Lord," Delilah said.

I was even more startled when Abigail said, "All is well with those who believe."

I could not stay silent. "In the name of the Father, the Son, and the Holy Ghost."

Again, Delilah and I took turns, tentative in covering the body with light scoops of packed dirt. Abigail made trips to the closest field and returned with stones we had removed to the edge years ago. In the end, we all carried rock and stone to place atop the mounded dirt. "There may be caving," I said.

We marked the head end—flat stone piled atop stone—until Delilah said, "Enough."

"Enough," I agreed, rubbing caked dirt off my hands, scraping mud from our tools.

Every day since, we go back, together or alone, making certain no critter has molested. We repile the marker, add daily blessing. The two buttons sit on our mantel.

J. Fretz — Chicago, May 1864

These constant swings from despair to near-ecstasy. Where is the balance, the even keel? Humdrum would be welcome.

On the up, we'll soon be in our own house at 42 South Morgan Street! Salome thinks it's more house than we need—four good-sized rooms upstairs also—but I smile and say we'll fill it as time passes. It ended up, easier to buy from Jacob than build our own; we'll be practically across the street from him and Mary Ann. Still the same pleasant neighborhood, not bothered with bad smells and the smoke of other locations. The lot I bought over a year ago will have to wait. Too much else occupies my thinking; not the time to oversee building a house.

The downward drift: Lincoln keeps putting more men on the battlefield. He drafted 200,000 more in *both* February and March. Many who signed up for three-year terms back in 1861—the ones who survived!—don't want to re-enlist. But the war effort doesn't stop. And conditions for prisoners—decidedly worse.

Late in the winter, reports had leaked into local papers that prisoners held by Confederates—Andersonville in Georgia was often mentioned—were killing and eating rats. I considered that another exaggeration intended to make the South sound completely evil. In my mind, their refusal to negotiate over dark-skinned Union prisoners was guilt enough.

But it's not only the South. Our same local papers have called Camp Douglas unfit for use—right here!—because of swampy land and lack of latrines. Still, I excused myself of responsibility to investigate. What good would that do? Final steps for purchasing the house took time, along with long nighttime hours on the *Herald*. Even my irritation with muddy streets and their cycles of freezing and thawing counted in my mind as absolution—all that *I* had to endure. But I'd not forgotten my trip to Camp Douglas with Phil two years ago when the camp was mostly a training ground for Union soldiers. That ominous atmosphere lingered.

Finally, my discomfort forced me; I was putting out a church newspaper but didn't know exactly what conditions prevailed for prisoners at Camp

Douglas—four miles from downtown Chicago and close to Lake Michigan. When something besides our publication wakes me early in the morning, I can't ignore it. For over a week, Abe had come up with excuses. Finally, when the weather warmed, he came around.

Nothing could have prepared us. Before long, Abe slumped to the ground and put his head between his knees. The stench was ten times worse than from any accumulation of hog manure we'd ever forked from the shed as boys. I could understand why men would try to escape and end up frozen near the lake. If I were stuck in a prison, it wouldn't take long before I'd cross any marked dead-line. Death on a battlefield sounded better.

I'm surprised they let us in. For a while, only physicians and ministers were allowed to visit the men. But this new Colonel Sweet is said to be a better commander—more organized and a disciplinarian. When we were stopped at the entrance—I'm embarrassed to admit—we offered to write a few letters for prisoners. I'd brought along sheets of foolscap, a pen, and ink. I had in mind Walt Whitman's example of visiting men in hospitals. The guard all but laughed in our faces. "I suggest you look around first. Let me know if you still want to do that."

What we saw—rundown barracks, poor rations, unruly prisoners. Probably corrupt guards. Abe nearly swooned a second time. He pressed his bowed head against the wall of a building. They've increased the hospital beds but still don't have enough space for the sick. The place isn't fit for a healthy man, let alone an ill prisoner.

They wouldn't let us see the White Oak Dungeon—not that we begged. Men who've tried to escape get stuck there. Punishments like reduced rations sounded like standard treatment. But made to sit on the thin edge of a sawhorse-type device, with weights tied to your feet? *Lord have mercy!*

We stumbled back to my carriage. Abe was furious—with me. "Your crazy ideas! What a waste of time."

I could barely raise a hand to the guard when leaving. I was sorry to have exposed Phoebe. I'm not a Southern sympathizer, but I'm a human sympathizer. *Shameful!* I couldn't begin to tell half to Salome. The smell of urine and feces clung to my clothes.

For the next days and nights I slept fitfully, ate almost nothing. I'd never seen men emaciated like that. Sharply angled bones; sitting with sunken eyes. Human beings! I tried to imagine a photographer—or picture a victorious headline: "Spirits Crushed." That prison couldn't possibly be within a deity's will. Gross inhumanity—no other words. How could my country allow . . .

Gradually, I've emerged from numbness. It's helped to throw myself into our anticipated move. Salome stays busy sewing curtains for upstairs windows. We want garden space, so I spaded a small plot and worked in horse manure. Barely an odor. We planted string beans and decided where our grapevines and currant bushes will go. There's not yard enough to keep a cow, but Salome will still help Mary Ann make cream and butter. We're assured of our share.

Salome pulled me out of my doldrums, too, by reminding me: when it snows again, we may have additional responsibilities. I don't want her going outside to milk the cow next winter. A baby on the way!

"For certain?" I asked.

"I feel a tenderness and haven't seen blood for several months." Her blue eyes stayed steady and bright—a shyness couched in her smile.

I looked at her in amazement. Something better than our own house to be excited about! But fatherhood—I don't know how to take in that part of it.

"We should wait awhile before we write to our folks back home," Salome said. "Unless I tell Ann Libb; she'll seal her lips."

New life coming in the middle of wartime, while men starve in prisons! The swings of agony and joy never far away. I can't say anything to Salome about the long Battle of the Wilderness. Hand-to-hand combat with clubbed pistols. The ground, slippery from excess blood.

I can't . . .

Esther — Shenandoah Valley, June 1864

The man stumbled in our house last week like a drunk one. My butcher knife at the ready on the chopping block. I only meant to keep him at bay. Other soldiers shouted outside. Was it so wrong to hide a loaf for my children? How many loaves have I given away? Plus, my man and three big boys given, one way or another. Taken! On the day the soldiers came again, I sent William outside with orders: "Give each man one loaf to his lonesome." I kept one loaf for my children to share.

I said to Mary Grace afterwards: "I'm not a bad person. I don't want anyone to starve." I said it again; she nodded. Now she reminds *me* to eat—our Miriam, four months, needs nourishment. She came long before this latest infestation of soldiers. Some days, I hardly remember her birth, so much has happened since.

The men at our place—ravenous and lacking manners—shouted outside, until this wild one staggered in, his eyes glazed. I shook in my bones. What did he intend? The last loaf at the far end of Miriam's cradle, back in the back room, under bedding. Others tell of hiding eggs, too. The smell of bread lingered, but that man wasn't going near my babe. I waved my knife like a sword. I meant no harm. Mary Grace says I shouted. She kept Jephthah turned away in the back room, tried to make a game of rocking Miriam—one hand on the cradle, one eye turned back to me.

A man outside had yelled for someone to milk the cow; he'd dragged one toward the house, banged with a knife on the bands of the bucket. My tender William put on a brave face, standing at the door, sneezing and stammering, "Not time yet."

"Milk the blame cow!" The man roared his bad words. "What the devil, youngster! Grab her teats!" Something flashed, as I heard heavy steps of another on the porch. A second man's body pushed past William, inside. My head awhirl between him and the voice outside.

William clattered down the steps, out of sight. He says he knelt, one knee, but could squeeze little more than a cupful.

Mary Grace had to wrest the knife away. She wrapped her thin arms around my waist—the man backed out. She talked quietly. "They're gone, Ma." I couldn't let go—like a frightened sheep. "They're gone, Ma," she said again. The shakes came; my grip stayed clenched. I never meant to use. Slowly, she pried the handle from my fingers, said soothingly, "It's over, Ma." I didn't know she could muster. Jephthah wrapped his arms and tugged on my leg.

My man, Simon, gone and buried, abed for good, amidst his kin. It seems a year these months. I bang a fist against my forehead when I catch myself thinking he'll return—it can't be. Otherwise, how—?

This week, while Mary Grace stayed inside with the little ones, William and I hoed at starts of corn. We never planted clover or timothy seed, but we must have corn. Frances came—she looks out for me—wanting to see how Miriam fares. I felt shame; I hardly spend time with my babe, except for feeding. We walked in the door, and I said, "No trouble from her. Only a runny nose. Mary Grace answers her coos and sings with her and Jephthah."

We took a quick peek at Miriam sleeping; I slid her thumb from her mouth. I told Mary Grace to trade places and take my hoe with William. Frances sat on the hearth and watched Jephthah with his fence of blocks surrounding empty spools—his animals. He mooed and stretched out long baas for his pretend cows and sheep.

Frances brought news of Hunter.

"Here in these parts?" I asked. "Again?"

"His men here. This Grant fellow is said to have ordered Hunter to move up the Valley. Supposed to go past here, bothering citizens, and destroying railroads—all the way to Lynchburg. There to make ruin of the supply depot and scout the route to Richmond. Hunter, seeking redemption for two years ago."

"Not so loud," I told Jephthah, but turned again to Frances. "Orders, you say?"

"Samuel thought—well, someone at the mill. Speculation that Hunter's men around these parts might have been separated from their supply lines. Left to fend. Foot soldiers going house to house, drinking their fill, downing bread. Snatching a horse, if possible."

"That sounds like those—"

"Rebels here, too," she interrupted.

I held my voice.

"In and out of the area, late last month. Hard to know. Some say, fires to the north." Frances stopped as Jephthah made crashing noises—his play sheep and cows jumping and trampling fences.

"Jephthah!" I said. "Build again; keep your animals safe this time." We watched him recapture spools and scold bad ones.

Frances got up to retrieve one last stray sheep before she continued. "Now folks here turning against Union," she said. "Halfway to Staunton—Hunter's larger batch met up with Rebels. He prevailed, but then ran into guerillas."

"Southerners—but not soldiers?" I asked, my eyes on Jephthah.

"Regular folks, yes, but working for the Confederacy. Might have been Imboden leading. Turned the tables when they came upon *Hunter's* supply wagons and caused havoc *for him*." Frances's voice, softer than usual; hard to catch everything.

"Still going south, though?"

"So thought; still heading for Richmond. Might have crisscrossed the Blue Ridge a time or two to deceive. Some thought also: Rebels might have sent Hunter back. Or he may have slipped away to West Virginia. No one certain—his whereabouts."

"But local folks turning against Union?"

"Folks never took to this Hunter." Frances stood, gathering her bag and patting Jephthah on the head. But before she left, she half-whispered, "Some think Lee might send Early. Give Feds a taste of what the North gives."

Not Early! My eyes met Frances's silently, pleading for it not to be true. She turned to the door, but I put a hand on her arm and said, "Don't forget us."

She nodded and slipped silently out of sight.

I sat again, dismayed. All these comings and goings—the Pike, in and out of mountains. Our woods could be next. Miriam stirred soon, and I clutched her to me. How can she be content, born into this house of disarray? No pa, no big brothers—unbothered.

I sat with her yet awhile; Jephthah showed how the blocks stand higher than the spools, end to end. "Uh-hum," I said. My precious little ones. Their stormy world. I must gather all that scatters within; they can't fend for themselves.

Frances had no word of the boys and men going to Hagerstown. I didn't think to ask if she knew how Genevieve fared. Our friend always knew when to give a womanly hug.

Nor did Frances ask about more goings on here—full of her own stories and guesses. I didn't tell about the butcher knife. Didn't have to say. We all carry the load—what must be shared, what can't be told.

I settled Miriam in the crook of one arm, reaching under the bottom of my skirts with the other hand to claw at my ankles. The mosquitoes stay quiet, but welts come on their own. I must stir more elder bark with water and lard. A little resin, too, for itch.

David — Shenandoah Valley, June 1864

I wept when I saw him. I had feared I would never lay eyes on Brother Kline again. I knew not whether there would be opportunity to pass along Winfield's warning. But there he was on that bright summer day, unharmed at his untarnished house, back from the Annual Meeting in Indiana. As I tied Ruby, he approached and we gave each other the Kiss of Peace.

But all is not sunshine. Johnny goes about with quietness. How could anyone *not* be sobered, when destruction flares around us?

"The burning—when did it commence?" he asked. "What is *your* story?"

"Ever since Hunter. This General David Hunter came in late May; his men burned houses and stores of those *not* loyal to the North."

"The same as what my hired man says," he mused.

"Hunter pretended to protect, but he made us targets."

"Five of my neighbors suffer greatly. I cannot shelter them all," John said.

"The burning started between Newtown and Middletown; 'working its way up,' the general said. He promised to take possession of our Valley." I could not avoid my shudder. "His men boasted of heading for Lexington and the Virginia Military Institute. Those Feds have not forgotten the young boys—the rout at New Market when you were gone."

"Two of my neighbors lost their out buildings," John said.

He seemed preoccupied only with what had already transpired. "The danger has not passed," I said. "Hunter has set us up for retaliation from those with burned properties. *Your* untouched house and barn stand like a sore thumb. Friendly to the North."

"That will come as no surprise," he said.

I sighed. "So says my Delilah. 'Our neighbors had already reached their conclusions,' she said. But, John, it worsened tensions; no man's situation remains clouded now."

"The Lord will prevail. We cannot do now what we have left undone in the past."

Johnny must not have heard about the killing pit—the Battle of the Wilderness last month. He must not know the enormity: the blood thirst at Spotsylvania Court House with eye-to-eye combat and something called the "Corner." Men gone mad for twenty-three hours of clawing, stabbing, throwing bayonets like spears, beating with rifles like clubs. The stories have dug wedges in my mind. But I said nothing of the fifteen-hundred-yard pit, of biting like animals.

Instead, John invited me to his porch and motioned to the wooden bench. He bent to tighten the leather ties on his shoes. He had not let go being Brother Kline. I tried to pay attention as he told of meetings and places where he had stopped on his travels. Yes, I could picture Nelly Henkel's place; I know how vines cover her front porch late in the summer, so fully as to hide the entry. I am acquainted with the Cosner families but know less about churches in the Eglon area, now West Virginia. I can understand how handing out small vials of cinnamon or peppermint drops—pretend medicine for children—must have brought him joy. But greeting an Amish family with seven youngsters—his highest honor?

On he went. More than one hundred miles on horseback over four days to get to Oakland and board the train on the night of the tenth of May. More stops on his return: another night with Henry Yost in Dayton, Ohio. All of this, worth the danger?

He paused in his recital and looked around in wonder. "It is good to be home—my heart's ease. These mountains that cradle. Anna has stayed well."

I could wait no longer. "What do you know about a sheep caught in brambles?"

He could not hide his eyes opening wide. He quickly looked down to stare at the laces he had retied. "How—what do you know?"

"My neighbor, Winfield, told me. Trespassing, or snooping, he called it. They plan to harm you." I had to be clear. "'If you return from the North,' he said."

"I only sought to return a stuck lamb to a farmer's pen. I did not know it would be a lion's den." He started to say more but closed his mouth and shifted his weight toward me. "Tell no man." He looked straight through me until I nodded. "I have gone to see Algernon Gray since returning. I told him of a plot to kill. You must not speak of it, David."

Surprise and relief swept through me. Algernon Gray, the respected attorney in Harrisonburg, has continued to befriend us German Baptists, in spite of the turbulence. He must have heard of threats also, for when John was in Indiana, stories circulated that Algernon had gone to the Partisan Rangers and tried to convince them of Johnny's innocence. As with most tales, I had dismissed half of it. But now— "You say a definite plot?" My voice trembled.

He hesitated so long, I squirmed on the bench. "While returning from Indiana, I was followed on the train and asked to identify myself." He studied me, as if meeting for the first time and taking the measure of my trustworthiness. "Later in Oakland, before going to get Nell, I stayed overnight as is my custom at Rogan White's Tavern. There it was . . ." He stopped, his thumbnail pressed to his lips. He started to rise.

I seized his elbow. "What was?"

A cow's sudden movement compelled his eyes to the pasture before he settled back. "A plan against my person. Told to stay in the North." He spoke softly into the warming air; I dared not move for fear his words might stop. "That the war was almost over. That I could return home safely, later." He puckered his lips, as if a taste of vinegar lingered. "I thanked the men for their concern. But I said if I did not come back to Virginia, those who sought to harm would turn their wrath on my brothers."

"What men?" I asked.

Ruby's loud snort distracted me, but John continued, his body hunched, arms folded, like with stomach pain. "That would not be acceptable, to put my safety above others. There may be no way out. The Lord knows—what is best."

I bent also and covered my face. Winfield's words: *My men will—* As bad as I had feared. I had to convince John. When I straightened, though, he sat stiff, looking away. "You must stay inside," I hissed.

His answer came swiftly—always two steps ahead. "People need me. I will not let a few, consumed by dangerous intent, rob me of my ministry."

We sat thus, my soul consumed. Sorrow, then anger. I have never been able to change Johnny's mind. I blew my nose and cleared my throat. "Did Algernon offer protection?"

"Nothing can be promised. Men will do what they are going to do." His voice turned to scolding. "You know the tenor of our times. There is no stopping." He turned wistful. "Only if God shows mercy. Puts a stop . . ." His head jerked. "Even then—a miracle. As of now, a boulder rushes downhill, seeking to crush. Sorrow for those misguided ones. Even if they succeed, they will not find the satisfaction they seek. Vengeance offers only fleeting pleasure."

"My closet—come stay with us. Please." I grabbed his arm.

"I will not hide, but thank you. Do not speak of what I have told you, David."

I had to look once more into his clear blue eyes, nod again solemnly.

Abruptly, John returned to details about the Annual Meeting. He reminded me, as if I cared: the Nettle Creek church was being built when he first visited there in 1844. This year, though, the church building was used for sleeping quarters. Good crowds in a large grove of trees for three days. Committees formed; queries brought forward. I fidgeted. His every word was intended to justify. Stops at Columbus, Ohio; Richmond, Indiana; back to Dayton, Ohio; other places, too. Finally, back to Oakland.

Even after warned, he took five days to return home. More house calls. His litany of visits—a blur. I would have come with haste; more likely, not come at all. I fight bitterness—Winfield and these others, provoking my anger. Now my shame, lacking interest toward widows, the blind, the handicapped.

Before I departed, we shook hands. I said once more, "Stay home! Please, John." But I knew my words would make no difference. He views my advice as human understanding; he stays attuned elsewhere.

Since that conversation, we have heard more tales of Hunter and his men, many on horseback, on south to Harrisonburg, even all the way to Staunton and beyond. Selectively burning classrooms, laboratories, the library at Virginia Military Institute. These Yanks will not be deterred; they seek to end anything that smells of sympathy for Rebels.

* * *

It is over—the long agony of waiting. No more calling on Providence to keep him safe. He is gone. Nearly sixty-seven full years on this earth. Taken in the most cruel of ways, but said to have been found with a smile on his face. He might have been singing—"*Rock of Ages, cleft for me*"—when the first minie ball hit. "*Let me hide myself in Thee.*" Three young lads found his body; they had heard shots and went to investigate—abandoned their play on stick horses. Soon, they came upon Nell, his bridle rein dangling, the saddle empty. The body. The boys ran for help.

Somewhere, some man hides—perhaps more than one—cowering from this vile deed. The news spreads. Abigail makes no pretense of work; Delilah stays inside also, except to help with animals. I should not be in shock, but I did not check our Visitor's grave today. A small portion of relief slips in. Not that the dastardly deed is done, but that we can put off wondering when or if. Cursed with doubt. How can we count ourselves among the loved, when the Lord allows evil hands to prevail?

* * *

We have put our beloved brother's body to rest along the stone wall at Linville Creek cemetery. The second day after John's demise, dirt sits freshly mounded to cover the remains of his earthly tent. A good death to be among his own, not dying an unknown like our Visitor. But I took no pleasure when our Brother Miller from Greenmount deemed it necessary to recount John's mighty deeds: thousands of miles of travel by horseback and on the cars, attendance at twenty-eight Annual Meetings, more than 4,000 sermons in a matter of thirty years. Who kept track?

My friend, the one I sometimes argued with, is gone—his spirit freed. I looked to him for wisdom, even when I protested his recklessness. Is his path carved for the rest of us as well? Three shots from behind, enough to knock him off his horse. A minie ball to his back, another in his hip, yet another lodged in his upper arm. A final shot into the chest—what human could do that?—a pistol at close range.

We know some of the lead-up that day, though contested. He had stayed home the day before. Why did he not do the same on Wednesday, June 15th? Did he feel pressed toward martyrdom? His twisting route. Uncertain, how many stops. Towards Brocks Gap, some say. Along Turley Creek, others insist. To the blacksmith. About that, there is much disagreement. To the Emsweilers is definite: he repaired their clock.

I say to my women, "He knew to stay away from that ridge. The rough element." I do not say: the same vicinity where he found the stuck lamb.

The Emsweilers tell anyone who will listen: they entreated him to stay with them, not go home by way of Howdyshell Ridge. But instead, he made known his plans. Even told a not-so-innocent inquirer of the route by which he would be home for lunch! Why? Everyone knows the woods on the ridge are dense, the spots for ambush plentiful. Did he need to prove his lack of fear? Was he compelled? A pawn of the Almighty?

I cannot dwell on it, but it is all I think on. The three lads saw smoke rising after the shots. Men gathered in the intersection, a grove of pines. Still later, folks piled field stones, marking the exact spot. I do not care to see it. A nephew hitched his team to his spring wagon, conveyed the body, covered by leafy branches, to Johnny's home two miles away.

His good wife, Anna. How she must be rent. Her vision from years ago brought to pass. Was not her life wasted? No healing. Johnny, the one who helped many, unable to spare her.

Brother Jacob Wine took the lead in the service, reading parts from Brother Kline's diary. On the way home from Indiana, John had written down what he likely had said along the way, "Possibly you may never see my face or hear my voice again." That sounds like him. "I am now on my way back to Virginia, not knowing the things that shall befall me there." When that part was read to those gathered, the weeping turned to sobs.

My own voice shook when I read from the eighth chapter of Acts, the great persecution against the church at Jerusalem. How Stephen, a Christian martyr, took on the face of an angel. I could not follow with my planned comments regarding the disciples' boldness on behalf of the Gospel. I sat with a thud on the bench, forgetting the part: we are all commanded to take up the ministry.

It is not for me. All these years I have lived in the shadow of Brother Kline's ministry, quaking at Winfield's voice.

Delilah repeats other words that were assigned to Brother Kline: "Neither count I my life dear unto myself, so that I may finish my course with joy . . ."

I flinch, but Abigail says, "He never gave concern—the perishable things of this earth. *Good* will come."

I mumble what may pass for assent. I dare not speak from inside. A stillness pervades our area. Some say Johnny's forgiveness has stifled bitterness, his blood has quenched thirst. I doubt it. For one thing, threats continue. Even on the way to the funeral, some reported passing Confederate cavalrymen. No words were exchanged, but soldiers pulled to the side, staring. When will this enmity ever cease? Hatred squeezes out any impulse for goodness.

Betsey — West Virginia, June 1864

Our friend from afar is gone! More gone than far away in Virginia. Not Joseph or Isaac, but the preacher who visited us twice from that same area. Poppa came home from Brookside and said, "Johnny made it safely to his home—long travels." But then Poppa said, "*O, nee, nee,*" like a cry. "A bad thing for us: his passing on. But for him, the Lord's reward."

This is worse than Frank. Worse than losing Jakie and Elizabeth to Somerset County. It reminds me of Joseph telling about losing his pa of a sudden; he never gave in to tears. I could not be that grown up, if needed. But for Johnny, Poppa and Mother went out to the porch to talk. I wanted to hear more, but I knew to stay inside. Mary boo-hooed, but she had not even remembered this John from the first time. I count him my special friend because of before, when Momma died. I wonder now if Momma knew when her time was nigh.

When Johnny first saw me this spring, he said, "My, how you have grown!" Tobias got to shake hands with him like a man, but I stood close to the little boys and kept them quiet because I am Mother's biggest helper.

Johnny was on his way to a state called Indiana when he came this second time. It was the first time Mother had met him; she said he walked on tottery legs. Poppa said, "Only at first, when he got off his Nell."

Lydia claimed she remembered him, but I am not sure. Mary ran and hid. The little boys were not even born back when Momma died. This time Gideon, Levi, and Noah, all got to sit on Johnny's lap. He called them little lambs and asked how Gideon had broken his arm. Gideon hung his head, but Poppa said Gideon knew now not to jump close to the edge in the haymow. He has let go his splint, but Mother still tells him not to stretch out his arm too fast.

Mostly, Johnny came to visit his people in Brookside and other places nearby. He said the white dogwoods were still abloom along the way, but in Virginia they were done for. Like before, he and Poppa said names back and forth, like Beeghly and Fike. Poppa told him about our latest visitors from Virginia. He did not know of a Mennonite lad named Joseph Shank, but Johnny thought he had heard good things about an Isaac Blossom. "Big build and tall?" he asked.

Poppa nodded and Gideon said, "Joseph is tall, too—my best friend."

When Johnny asked all of us children to sing for him, it was easy to choose. At our church service we sing the same song nearly every time. But with Johnny we started out shaky. Tobias gets crackly in his voice, so Mother and Poppa helped with, "*If one ill treat you for My sake . . . Be joyful, your reward is nigh . . .*" Johnny said he knew the tune but not our words. By the end he wiped at tears. "*Of such a man fear not the will, / The body only he can kill . . .*" Maybe everyone gets to know, but not family or friends.

Before Johnny left, we all ate rhubarb. Early that morning Mother had chopped a big batch. While I tended the boys, I had kept an eye on the rhubarb to make sure it did not scorch over the fire. We squeak by on sugar, but before we sat to eat, I saw Mother add extra pinches. It was not even mealtime, but we all sat at the table. Lydia and I shared a bowl so Johnny could have one for himself. He smacked his lips and said, "There is not a better springtime treat." Poppa nodded but did not say about eating it all spring for healing.

Johnny had another surprise for us: he pulled new starts of a plant he called hosta from his saddlebag. He said it will grow leafy with white or lavender flowers late in the summer. Mother put me in charge, and I was allowed to dig a patch of ground in the shade. I made the space extra wide, as Johnny had instructed, and Poppa added horse manure. Now that the rains have slackened, I give the plants a drink every day, for we do not want to lose our friend's gift. Especially not now!

That whole day, after Poppa brought the sad news home, everyone stayed quieter. Sometimes Mary still sniffled, and Poppa walked more slowly again when he went out to the barley and peas. They are finally perking up from all our rainy days. When Mother and I stemmed strawberries, we did not sing like usual. All Lydia could think to do with the little boys was have them draw stick people and barns in the dirt. Then she had to scrub the boys extra before they could come inside.

"Why does everyone have to die?" I asked Mother.

"That is how we are made," she said. "God made everything good."

"But this is worse than Frank," I said, "for Johnny to be gone."

"Frank was old age," she said. "Think how wobbly he would be, if he got older and older and never expired."

"But Poppa said it is hard for Tom to do all the plowing and pull our wagon by himself. He and Frank made a good team."

"Remember, though, your poppa only had to buy new shoes for *one* horse."

"But why is it us? We lost Jack, too, and now Johnny."

"It is part of life, Betsey. It changes nothing to question."

I did not want to be disagreeable, but Poppa had blinked his eyes extra, back when Frank died. I never saw twitching, but he breathed so hard that sometimes his nose hairs whistled. Even when he said the usual to Mother, "*Mir kumme aus*," his voice was quivery. Big folks do not always say everything. I wonder if it is more of that wild inflation; Poppa said we did not have money to buy another horse.

That night when we knew about Johnny, I did not forgive Noah for slobbering on his bread at supper. He gave me half, but it was already ruined. Nor did I sing loud with the boys when we gathered at bedtime. Poppa took the lead, but it was no good. We all had our sad lumps.

Poppa looked right at me and said slowly, "We are not to go about glum, Betsey. We feel sad, but we are not to be sour. Do not make a rooster; it spoils your face. Even if the times spread *harm*, we are not to let bitterness wrack. Only be ready."

"But did Johnny know?" I asked. "When he was here? He shed tears at our song."

Poppa blew loud into his handkerchief. "We cannot know another's thoughts."

"He should not have gone to Oakland," I said. Poppa and Mother looked at each other with big eyes. "You said that, Mother. You picked at nubbins on your shawl. After Johnny left."

Poppa said, "He made it home to Virginia safely." Then Poppa clamped his mouth.

I could not stop. "When Mother told you that Johnny looked subdued, you said that he carried burdens."

Poppa stroked his beard long. "You have sharp ears and a good memory. But we are not ever to be angry with God. We cannot always understand why things have to be. But always remember: we are to love everybody. Now none of us will sleep, if you keep on like this."

Lydia and Mary trailed me up the ladder to the loft, but I am almost for certain: this war is to blame. It makes for all the bad we have. We have had more soldiers again, but not like a year ago when all was helter-skelter from both directions. This time, only men in blue asked for food. Sometimes when our rains pounded, they came to our porch and talked loud. Mother called them boisterous, but Poppa did not start twitching because of that either. We are still allowed to play outside extra when we finish our work—Lydia and I like to catch monarchs—as long as we follow the rule and come inside at the first sign. One time a lone soldier trudged in the lane, and I had to shout a second time for Gideon and Noah to obey.

The grown-ups at church do not sound like trouble has ceased. The Sunday we met at Joseph Slabach's house, a belly ache came over me. While the women and other children finished their eating, Mother made me stay in the cold room. The old day bed had a bad smell, but Mother fixed special pennyroyal tea for me to sip; the mint helped my tummy even before I tasted. I lay down and pulled the blankets tight but kept the bucket close to catch my *Kotze*. I turned away from the low rumble of men's voices interrupted by a woman's loud laugh in the kitchen. But of a sudden, I perked up at the men in the next room.

"Those of ours at the Glades—given to degradation, laxness."

"Drafters are said to carry grudges. Called some of our men twice."

"We already sent over $15,000 to help with their fees." Poppa's voice!

"I can vouch"—Peter Schrock's deep voice—"safely stowed near the foot of Negro Mountain. Under a ledge and hidden by thickets of tall rhododendron, the appointed place."

Dishes clattered in pans, and I could only make out bits and snatches—"slaveholders . . . southern part, Somerset . . . that rough element" before the door to the cold room closed.

I held my body stiff. The men might have been talking about my home-home. I slowly turned back to the door, my feet touched the cold floor, and I tiptoed to open a crack again. But by then the men must have gone outside—empty benches in disarray. My stomach lurched and I shivered to hop under blankets again. I could not go out to see what Sarah and others might be playing in the warm air. And I did not dare ask Poppa later if Peter Schrock had, in truth, hidden money. Joseph had never said about secret deeds like that in the woods.

J. Fretz — Chicago, July 1864

"That much we can agree with," Salome said, as she got up to refill the serving dish with boiled potatoes and pour more water for Moses.

I looked up quickly. We've had few serious disagreements in our six months of marriage. One of us usually defers to the other's wisdom or stronger preference. Or sees that nothing can be gained from continuing the argument. For one thing, we don't see horses the same way. Salome thinks they're good for pulling a buggy or plow; she says I dote on Phoebe. When I fed hot mash to Jacob's horse and mine on cold mornings last winter, or even warmed Phoebe's bit to keep her from a sore tongue, Salome teased about my pampering. But I ignored her, and now she says nothing when I take a morsel from the table as a treat.

We've lived in our own place for over a month already. We don't often use our dining room—only the table and six chairs with embroidered seats. But Salome chose to overlook the sparseness this time. Abe joins us for a meal at least once a week, and we've had a boarder for two weeks—my cousin, Moses Rittenhouse from Ontario, the one who asked endless questions about Chicago at age ten. When Aunt Betsy and Uncle John inquired recently whether there'd be a place for him, I couldn't refuse. They wouldn't let him come unless he could live with us.

Mary Ann and Jacob took me in for seven years, so there was no question about Moses. I won't take rent money until he has a decent job, and then, not more than ten dollars a month. Such eagerness: no task is beneath him. He sweeps floors and cleans spittoons in a print shop, but I hope we can offer him something steadier at the lumber yard soon.

On this particular evening, though, Salome's sharp comment came after I had mentioned the book she'd given me for my April birthday: *Non-Resistance Asserted.* At the table I had said, "Musser thinks money belongs to the realm of the world. He also says that government has the right to spend the money due it, our taxes or commutation fees, as it wishes. But he makes one distinction: the government doesn't own *our person.*"

Moses looked at me with a slight smile. "I came here—Chicago, the place to get ahead."

"Same here," Abe said. "I didn't come all these miles to live on the street."

"I'm the only one of us," Salome said, "who didn't come here for money."

"And I'm much the better for it," I said, as Abe murmured assent.

He waved a fly from his plate. "Who is this fellow? This book?"

"A Reformed Mennonite," I said. "Daniel Musser got his start in eastern Pennsylvania, more educated than most in the church. A strong vocabulary, distinct style, but given to repetition."

Moses helped himself to more dandelion salad. "Never heard of *Reformed* Mennonites."

"Some have moved up to Canada," I said. "More like the Amish, but not entirely; they shun fallen church members over unconfessed sin."

"Nothing I want part in," Abe mumbled.

"He doesn't call attention to being Reformed," I said, "and says little about his work as a doctor. But his book tests my ideas, same as this war. He allows *no* place for overthrowing government; we're to obey laws if they don't conflict with God's higher law of love." I brushed bread crumbs off my vest. "But—we may have to suffer."

"I'd heard so much about this man," Salome explained to Abe. "I knew Fretz would want to read for himself."

"No more eye for an eye," I said. "But always this reminder: God never promised we *wouldn't* be inconvenienced." Salome had been clever enough to purchase the book with Jacob's assistance, after John M. had mentioned it so often. I had no inkling what she was up to.

"So are you with him?" Abe asked.

"Some of it seems extreme," I said. "He follows the truth to its very limit; I'm more a follower of Aristotle's via media—a philosophy of the middle way."

"Like what?" Moses asked, helping himself to another chunk of pork roast.

I marvel at all the food that disappears in Moses—seventeen and still skinny, with a start of whiskers—but I like talking with him. "One example, my desire for courage—a preferred path between cowardice and rashness. Or friendship—a better choice than either extreme of flattery or quarrelsomeness."

"But what's extreme?" Abe asked. "Besides shunning." He pointed to the gravy bowl.

"Overall, he's very critical of Christianity," I said, sending the gravy Abe's way, "at least as it's practiced. Oh, I know, you think I'm critical, too. But I'm not so blunt."

"Hnnh," Abe grunted, catching a drip of gravy with his finger.

I waved at the pesky fly. We have to keep the windows open to allow a cross breeze on hot evenings. "Musser's motivation for avoiding participation in *any* level of government seems to be: avoid unwanted questions. For example, stay away from someone asking: *Why can some of you be exempt from warfare but still receive the advantages of living under our government?*"

"Some people criticize most everything," Abe said. "You can't please everyone."

"Government's supposed to keep order," Moses said.

"And Musser agrees," I said. "But he holds a very low view of human nature."

"Nothing wrong, holding office," Abe said. "Folks back East—nothing new to be a county commissioner or township trustee."

"You're right; Father liked to talk about our relatives in local or state politics," I said. "But Musser thinks office-holding muddies the waters. Same goes for courts of law settling disputes among Christians. Even police providing protection, he questions. But then he gets more pointed: *Would you deter an intruder by pointing a gun?* Hard to know."

"I always thought those Reformeds a strange lot," Abe said. "Never knew what exactly."

"What about voting?" Moses asked. He emptied the last of the potatoes onto his plate, scraped the last dab of gravy.

"Musser says no. That's my turmoil; I'm struggling, writing an editorial. Can I vote to re-elect Lincoln when I don't support *all* his efforts? He's more on the side of freeing Negroes, but using all-out war to force the issue? A worthy goal; a terrible method."

"I don't trust *anyone* but Lincoln," Abe said. "If I don't vote, that helps the other side."

I nodded. "Far better than Fremont. And Lincoln's smart to have Andrew Johnson, a Tennessean, on the ticket. But calling the party National Union to pull in Democrats? That's suspect. Still, both Lincoln and Johnson understand the value of hard work. Like you, Moses."

"A rail splitter, Lincoln. But Johnson?" he asked.

"A tailor before he became a public man," I said. "But Johnson disagrees with candidates who favor slavery and who think manual labor should be done by an inferior caste."

"Some people object to Lincoln's rumpled suit or coarse humor," Abe said. "Think he's too common."

"You have to overlook minor drawbacks in any candidate. But these reports about the Army of the Potomac getting to Richmond—" I paused while Abe tiptoed up to the fly, sitting on the sill. "Our troops lost 7,000 men in thirty minutes! Eight miles from Richmond. What was Grant thinking, telling our men to charge over open ground right in front of entrenched Rebels? No wonder he's been called 'a fumbling butcher.'"

"But should we criticize?" Salome asked. She knows that is John M.'s main question.

"And what about paying taxes?" Abe asked, sitting again. "I've heard Quakers want complete exemption without needing to pay anything for equivalency."

"Musser says yes to paying taxes as tribute. But that's not correct about Quakers's position." I glanced at Salome. She's cautioned me with Abe; says some things are better left unsaid. "The key for Quakers: a willingness to suffer. Same with Musser. But Quakers don't petition for permission to live their beliefs; they do what they think is right and take the consequences."

"That's better than saying belief, or willingness, doesn't cost anything," Salome added. "I don't *want* to suffer, but the road may take me places I don't want to go."

"Like coming to Chicago," I said gently.

Moses started to laugh but stopped.

"I'm grateful every day, Salome," I said and turned to Moses. "I can mull things over for days, while she spots the essence like a bee flies to clover. She reminds me that Abraham in the Old Testament had uncertainties, too. I'm learning—slowly—when to go ahead and act, even with limited understanding."

"No different for Abraham Lincoln," Abe said. "I'll bet he follows a path he doesn't fully comprehend."

Salome murmured assent, but asked, "One more thing—what does Musser say about fleeing?"

"Another distinction." I stopped. "That fly!" Everyone but Abe laughed. "Your question, Salome—Musser says if drafted against your belief, use natural wit and reason. Try to escape by fleeing or hiding. But—*if* captured, be harmless; don't make any effort to defend or resist."

"Do good to those who ridicule?" Salome asked.

"Yes. . ." I looked her in the eye. "But here's something John M. wouldn't like. Musser says a nonresistant *shouldn't* help pay the commutation fee for another person. I disagree. Jesus taught his disciples to bear each other's burdens. I'm going to write about that." Salome knows I work through questions by writing about them.

"This war would be fought even more exclusively by the poor," Abe said, "if wealthy ones didn't help those who struggle. I don't much care for this man."

"What's worse, John M. told us of church people—some of our own—giving money to a bounty and encouraging *enlistment*—for others," Salome said.

"So why not just pray and go about your business?" Moses asked, sopping a mix of potato and gravy juice with his last corner of bread.

"Musser says not to pray for the success of either side," I said.

"Whoa!" Moses squinted and frowned. "I always pray for the North. That's justice."

"Same here." Abe pushed his chair from the table, folding his arms across his chest.

"Both sides have done terrible things," I said. "People who favor the South are equally sincere; they believe just as strongly that their cause is just."

"Both sides can't be right," Moses said.

Salome had disappeared into the kitchen but returned before I could answer.

"Is that what I think it is?" Abe asked. "How I miss Mother's shoo fly."

"Keeping the flies dizzy," I said.

We all relaxed, anticipating the sweet molasses pie with crumb topping. Our conversation slipped into talking about annoying Funk family traits like cracking knuckles. Salome brought more coffee and we showered her with thanks for the sweet ending.

But I couldn't resist. "Another thing—Mennonites in Pennsylvania willingly vote for Governor Curtin, even though he supports a vigorous war effort. Outsiders see that and feel disgust. Nonresistance takes on disrepute."

Salome folded and refolded her napkin as if putting a period on a sentence. "You'll have to decide for yourself, Fretz, whether or not to vote this fall."

"Not easy, though. If I may, Salome?" She gave no indication one way or the other. "Take Congressman Thaddeus Stevens, a Radical Republican and very forceful; he strongly favors the war. So my question: Is it dishonorable for Mennonites in his district to vote for him, but refuse to honor the draft? Stevens supports their right—the Amish also—to hold scruples. But are they voting for their own protection?"

"A shrewd man, that Stevens," Abe said. He split the extra piece of pie with Moses. "You told me he's defended runaway slaves and doesn't charge them for his service."

"True," I said. "The man has good points, but it looks like a cozy relationship. The favor of our people—and their wealth—on his side. Money, Moses, drives everything."

"Wrongs don't cross out the good. Anybody votes to protect his interests. I do," Abe said.

"Don't we want someone who *represents* our values, especially honoring human life?" I countered. "Isn't that more important? Maybe Musser and traditional Amish are right. No one in government thinks completely like we do, so we shouldn't vote."

Without further ado, Salome asked Moses to help her clean up in the kitchen. He gulped his last bite and followed her. Abe and I soon switched to talking about where to stack extra lumber coming in. With a year's experience managing the yard, he's become much more confident.

So yes, I'm the one stewing on my own until the election. When I voted for Lincoln four years ago, I knew he'd be commander of the Army if elected. I knew he might use methods I couldn't fully support in a crisis, but I counted on him to use solid reasoning. Now I'm stuck. I'm not the same person I was in 1860. I've read Philemon 3:20 too often: "*Our citizenship is in heaven.*" Is that to be taken literally? But whatever verse snags me on any given day, it's still the president's *duty* to put a stop to any attempt at insurrection. Lincoln took the oath of office; he has authority. *But* this awful inhumanity we've been put through. I go around and around.

My questions about money don't go away either. What haunts me most—Macbeth's dagger!—I should never have taken anyone to court for not paying his bill! That's been over two years, and I can't forget *my* use of force with Norton. I didn't want to hurt him—I delayed—but still I went along. Salome gets tired of hearing me rehash that, too. I stay unsettled. Business partners have to work together; Jim wouldn't trust me if I weren't willing to sue a debtor. *Never let someone take advantage.* And I can hear Beidler shout, "Preposterous!" if I suggested giving a debtor *extra* credit *and* wiping out his debt.

Perhaps I ruined our meal by talking too long—another Funk trait—but Musser's words have worked their way inside. John M. probably knew they would. If we're *literally* to follow Jesus's command to turn the other cheek—if we're pilgrims and strangers in this world and we accept *Nachfolge* like the early Anabaptists—what rights do we have? We can't seek redress for a grievance. And this thing of primary loyalty—why do I still debate, as if I don't understand?

When Salome finally convinces me to put aside internal debates, we reminisce about the goodness of our married life. I always bring up our first meal in this house; Salome made the best potato soup. And the next morning she surprised me with fish for breakfast! When Moses first arrived, Salome worried about feeding a growing lad, but she accepts his appetite better than I. He's very fond of her puddings, while I squeeze in hints for her pies—any kind but dried apple schnitz, Mother's standby. Salome relishes doing her own cooking, while I'm relieved she doesn't mind going to the market by herself now. Nor has she complained about the delay in buying more furniture; we've ordered a hutch, but the factory is far behind.

At first, though, this house was so quiet, it bothered me. Not having the Beidler children underfoot suddenly became as loud as a noise. No cries during the night from Augustus! I was grateful, but everything seemed strange. Our voices echoed in these high ceilings until we found a carpet for our bedroom. Now Moses has added his commotion—not *klutzich* exactly, but given to scraping chair legs excessively. Salome's thankful that we added shelves in the pantry and bought an icebox to keep our food safe, since there's no cellar. I wonder, though, if she might have been happier with only a sitting room; we rarely use the parlor.

But now—a baby to look forward to! It seems certain. Salome still hasn't been doctoring, but those unpleasant mornings—mostly before Moses came—convinced her. She couldn't keep her corn mush down when her head was spinning. I worried about smallpox sweeping our city, but there's no indication her upset portends a case of that.

Salome's only been unreasonably cross one time since moving here. Oh, she tells me I don't drink enough water, but that's a good-natured concern. When I explained I don't like cold on my teeth, she switched to serving coffee or tea more of the time. But her big upset—in truth, a piffle—came over envelopes! I kept forgetting to bring the ones she likes from the office. I knew she'd written to her folks and to Ann Libb soon after we moved; she had the letters ready. I'd promised, but for some reason it kept slipping my mind. Three times. Finally, she gave me the silent treatment, and I realized how much I'd disappointed her. I could only beg forgiveness and try to mend my ways. If only I could wipe out some of Daniel Musser's ideas so easily.

Jacob — Iowa, July 1864

I sit with my head in my hands. The steady ticking begs me to follow these other hands—our solid oak wall clock with its mellow tones and painted flowers at the four corners. Fleeting minutes add up to hours. Beyond that—day after day. Each one governed by faithful movement from darkness to light, fading again to dark. No way to know the end. Ours or mine. I turn my hands, palm to back. I rub the thin skin, press it smooth, and watch it fall back, wrinkled. Time has been kind and cruel, from birth to bruises. All the years of my life.

That passenger who died on our ship crossing the ocean—his hour came on our stalled journey. He ended up wrapped in a piece of sailcloth with bricks tied to his feet. His corpse laid on a board and dropped, feet first. Our Captain Hermann Grau gave a nice speech. All these years I still remember: "We would all be lost, if God punished us for our misdeeds as we deserve to be punished." Very nice, indeed. We sang a hymn, and then the solemn affair was done. So it will be.

But for now, my bones ache from weariness. Mary, too, has slept extra hours since our return. I have never been so glad to be home again, here where our land supports hills. I had forgotten how flat that Indiana land is, miles on end. Rolling Iowa suits me better, while not nearly so steep as our former places of residence: Somerset County, Pennsylvania or Garrett County, Maryland. Certainly not Waldeck in the Old Country. We have more balance here, mostly a gentle rise and fall, along with the sometimes bluffy lay of the land.

In my absence the boys were busy, mowing and raking prairie grasses. That sweet smell of summer, freshly cut hay, surrounds us. Frederick does not want me wielding the heavy wooden rake anymore; he has recently purchased a new table rake. With two large wheels, a horse can pull this hay rake and cut down on our manual labor. Frederick's sod corn looks promising. Always a surprise, how our brush sod can yield more bushels than prairie sod, all because it holds moisture better.

Mary is glad to be back with her new flax wheel also, but I may have muffed. After almost four years of marriage, short when compared with Barbara and me, I am not always certain where things stand. During the winter months I had been diligent at working for betterment with Mary. But now upon our return, she has expressed dismay at a family of raccoons claiming residence in the crawl space under the side porch. The babies manifest a cuteness with their dark rings about the eyes, but Mary jumps at the sight. I have not pointed out where rats chewed while we were gone.

Of course, we are late with planting our garden—Frederick's Sarah gives us extra of their early greens. We spent nearly three months with Mary's relatives in Indiana—one daughter or another, plus a sister. I did not much care for the one son by marriage. He is coarse and given to boorish behavior. It was not safe to step anywhere in the house without first looking for his tobacco spit. I do not see how Mary's daughter could have chosen so poorly, but what is done is done. Two of the boys show signs of following their father's lead; they did not even offer to shake hands when first greeting. Indiana is not the frontier, but you would never know it from that man.

And Mary's daughter Nancy, taken with everything from fancy window coverings to bows and lace on her little girl's dresses. Why can she not think ahead to what will happen when her little Judith becomes a woman? If given license now, she will have difficulty submitting her individual desires to the church's precepts.

One day Nancy started to leave their house to help the menfolks in the fields—right and proper when more hands are needed. But Nancy had perched a man's hat on her head. I stopped her and asked regarding her thought on the matter of apparel.

Her response was swift. "The hat brim protects me from the sun better than a kerchief." With that, she strode through the door and went her willful way.

Caught by surprise, I spoke with Mary at once and said we would no longer partake of food in that household. Ornamentation had troubled me enough, but I could not tolerate back talk. Seeking to be the same with her man! From that day on, we stayed with Mary's sister. But larger church matters and our country's ongoing unrest weigh even more heavily.

When first embarking on our trip, my hope had been to continue by train to visit my grandson Samuel in Somerset County. He intends to teach again during the winter term, even though he would not need to stay in Pennsylvania. I had already written to remind him that he could use his *McGuffeys Readers* and *Spellers* just as well in Iowa. But once we arrived in Indiana, conflicting reports of battles farther east led me to give up that extra part of the journey. Even civilians have been used as targets, as we learned from sad reports of a man in Virginia, an elder for the German Baptists and about my age, ambushed by Rebels. I had to pay heed.

Some days I still wonder if we should have made the trip to Indiana at all. But I had promised Mary in the dark of winter; back then, I expected more ready obedience to the *Ordnung* as a result of my exercising less harshness among our people. But that did not result; even before we left for Indiana, we still could not have Communion. I hated to be considered derelict to duty by leaving our settlement for travel, but I also feared a letter from me might not be taken seriously at the *Dieners-Versammlung.*

Whenever I had expressed misgivings about the trip, Mary immediately spoke of traveling to Indiana with Frederick, even though he was only going for the time of the meetings. And when I asked, she had been vague about her return. I decided it was of more importance to go *with* my letter and see for myself. My cane helped me manage the times of standing during this third meeting of its kind, but I doubt I will ever make a trip like that again.

Since returning, I have said to Frederick, "We may need to separate ourselves from the more radical faction if we want to stay true to the Amish faith."

When he did not dispute my assessment, I was sobered even more. "Dissension remains strong," he said.

"Schisms used to crop up only in certain areas," I said. "Ohio, or sometimes back in Pennsylvania. But now—"

"Yes, whispers of widespread division have become as loud as a rackety train."

I still need to learn details of who preached what during my absence from Iowa. I had told Frederick to keep an ear out for developments in Moses Kauffman's land transactions and to pay close heed to any other murmurings. But the talk in Indiana last month has left me with enough to digest. They spoke of bridging the gulf *next* year, but it is hard to find comfort.

As before, the change-minded element planned most of the conference—Sunday to Wednesday in Samuel D. Miller's barn in Elkhart County. Bishop John K. Yoder took the reins with Grose Mose Miller as his assistant. This Yoder maintained the *Ordnung* is very important, but I fear that is lip service. Too often he manifested a spirit of toleration. What do we stand for, if we stand for any number of positions? My soul was blessed with the singing, admonition, and prayer, but the contentious spirit of our country has infected our church body as well.

Such indecision among the sixty to seventy of us Amish bishops, ministers, and deacons gathered to draw up rulings during the proceedings. Some are so afraid of legalism. Back and forth, regarding inside and out.

How is it not clear? If God instructed Israel to marry *within* the tribe, it must be an unholy alliance for a person to marry *outside* the Amish church. That would include Dunkards and Mennonites. But a brother from Illinois asked that we *not judge* those on the outside. Another went so far as to suggest that those who belong to another nonresistant denomination are not *fully* on the outside. I am not against safe mingling—hundreds of laymen and others of like faith were welcome as attendees at our meetings. I am glad for all the new ones I met. But we members must stay true.

Twice I called on my courage and rose to speak. "We *are* to discern the sheep from the goats, even among like defenseless groups." My hands shook on my cane. As I looked about, I saw only a few heads nod.

Questions came up also pertaining to this war that divides our country. We could not agree on whether to allow voting in public elections. Grose Mose spoke in favor of letting a person's conscience be his guide. Such fear of anything hard and fast. There was more agreement to *only* provide admonition. John K.'s concern: if we make a ruling, it might cause a disturbance, even division, among us. Baffling, that he cannot see: *not* making a ruling disturbs. Where is his second eye?

During the gathering Frederick and I safely mingled with many strangers. One day I was introduced to an Emanuel Hostetler. I shrank back. Of course, it was not the young Iowa man we had lost at Vicksburg. But when I explained my surprise, this man from the Goschen congregation produced another jolt: "Nearly every Amish group has had to deal with a similar tragedy."

"Nearly every Amish group has lost a son?"

The man insisted. "Not able to hold our own." He paused. "There was a Zug—goes back to Hans Zaugg, I believe. Perhaps you know—?"

"Banished from Switzerland long years ago?"

"The very one," he said. "A descendant of Christian, as I recall, in the eighteenth century, seeking religious freedom."

"Of course, of course, although the spellings vary today."

"So it is. Whatever this forty-year-old man's exact lineage—perhaps Moritz—he went by the name of Samuel Zug. Sadly, he had risen to prominence in the Northern Army but was killed by a Rebel ball that ricocheted off a rock and deflected back into his upper torso."

"Surely not."

"*Aber ja.* Mortally wounded at Gettysburg. Internal injuries so severe, he was not taken to a hospital."

"And you say nearly every Amish group stricken?" I repeated. The man's answer did not change. When I saw him yet again, he still seemed entirely sober.

And another man, a John Funk from Chicago, left a mark on my thinking. He is younger and Mennonite—parts his hair on the side—but earnest. Frederick and I came upon him, tapping the clapper of the dinner bell against its inner wall. “The mellow sound makes me homesick,” he said.

We shook hands, and Frederick asked about his whereabouts.

“A circuitous path for me, from eastern Pennsylvania to Chicago and work in the lumber business. But now I've started a church newspaper; you may have heard of *Der Herold der Wahrheit.*” We nodded and he continued. “We share a concern: how to keep our young men faithful in spite of pressures to enlist.”

At that I shook his hand again—refreshing and forthright in his fellowship. I told him of my grandsons, his age and younger, who must resist the lure of the national cause. My Samuel would like this Funk; both are teachers at heart.

We had a wholesome chat over our beef and potatoes, but for his disturbing news of bounty jumpers. “These men collect a bounty, join the Army in one locale, report to camp, and then disappear,” he said. “Next thing anyone knows, they sign up in another county or state and collect another bounty there.”

“Jump from Ohio all the way to Iowa and swell our volunteer ranks?” Frederick asked. “Only to disappear and go to Missouri?”

“The sad truth, how it can be.”

“Perverse,” I said. “A false kind of soldiering, getting rich quick.”

“Much corruption,” he said. “Some places offer a bounty as high as $400 and add that to a soldier's regular pay.” He leaned toward us. “Some of *ours* contribute. Yours, ours—we are brothers, equally tempted.”

My hand stopped at cutting beef. This John did not seem a slick one, not bent on false accusation.

But Frederick questioned. “You say our Amish folks pay to keep enlistments up?”

“That is so,” Funk said. “Some do. As do some Mennonites.”

At that, I lowered my head and glanced around the room. Did others know of these betrayals? Has there been no teaching? My hand squeezed into a fist against my thumping chest. “Fathers paying extra to hasten others toward killing and death? In their sons' stead?”

Again, John stretched toward us. “We are more alike than we think.”

But Frederick's next question caused me to jerk. “Other disparities to speak of?”

The young Mennonite did not flinch. “Cases where monetary excess occurs with payment of the commutation fee.”

I searched his face again. Not one flutter of his eyelids or other sign of prevarication, only steady concern. "How so—this excess?" I cupped my ear to block out distracting voices. Did he know I have encouraged payment of the tax?

"There's no consistency when putting down money in exchange for exemption," he said. "Some men are forced to pay $300 with *each new draft.* Should we participate?"

"Where does all that go?" Frederick asked. "Is it only paper? Those greenbacks?"

John's brow wrinkled. "Yes, where? As I say, corruption. Paying extra to stay out?" He raised an empty hand. These brokers want to make money. Vast disparities also, among those buying a substitute. No uniformity. A purchase might last nine months—or three years. Some agree to substitute only until the next draft."

"Such confusion," I said. "Can nothing be counted on?"

Again, our new friend raised a limp hand. "Many drafts add to the disarray."

Since then, the long rocking and jerking of the train ride back to Iowa did to my body what those revelations did to my mind and soul. I can no longer claim ignorance; our hands, contaminated. I believe that young man. When I had asked several other brethren, no one could give solid evidence that our commutation money had bought food for hungry men. My concern grows on the same ugly question: is there difference—buying a substitute or paying $300 so the militia can follow a general's command to attack?

Yet one more jolt came while I was in Indiana. A brother from Pennsylvania reported that half the men drafted in Elklick Township—where Samuel lives—claim to be conscientious objectors. But then he whispered to me, "In truth, they are not all constituted thus."

I grabbed his arm—a Hertzler, as I recall. "What say you? Our preachers allow such? Going along with subterfuge and evasion? *Harboring falsehood?*"

He looked on me, his eyes watery like mine. "Deviation will ruin the name of us all—including those of us sincere in not doing battle."

Since home, restlessness interrupts my sleep. I cannot stay my mind, whether regarding troubles here or far away. Coyotes bark in the distance; my church brethren, near to my heart, carry widely different understandings. I rise at odd hours, only to doze on my rocker. But then my neck aches. Other times, I make myself stay abed, but solid sleep eludes. When the dogs quiet, the clock's ticking takes over. All that has been brought to my attention. Forces pushing relentlessly for adaptation. Mary's relatives. A young

Mennonite's words. Much as I wish to hide my face, I may need once more to resort to what appears harsh for some, if we are to remain true.

And while I do not want to go to Ohio next year, I may need to send another letter. I am convicted, even in hot July, to wrestle and write what the Lord is showing. Old age dare not be an excuse if *more* is required. And if Frederick becomes a full deacon, he also dare not spurn the call to additional preaching. When filled with wisdom from above, he can still be a progressive farmer and a faithful shepherd, all at the same time.

Esther — Shenandoah Valley, August 1864

I saw sudden movement out the window last week: Frances and a companion approaching on foot. It turned out as I first thought: the same woman, Margaret Rhodes, who had ridden here at dusk almost a month ago. Tall and erect on the saddle that night, a postmistress known for carrying messages. That time, she had brought welcome news that Henry Brunk had made it to Hagerstown safely, and that he and others were finding field work among church folks. Rumors have circulated that some of those seventeen-year-olds who fled had separated or even returned home. That was not the plan, but when I asked, Frances only shook her head.

But of the two, walking here in daylight last week, Frances cast only fleeting glances my way. My house was steamy from sauce, but she undid her shawl, only to wrap it about her again.

I motioned for them to sit at the table. The gist is, there's been trouble—that area where Joseph fled, this Hagerstown. Andrew's safety may be in jeopardy, too. Peter could be marching near either of them. *Oh, my sons.* For everything told, there is much we don't know.

Margaret's narrow face sagged; skin puffed under her eyes. "Some of our refugees have fled to escape the Cumberland Valley. Gone on to Illinois."

"Oh?" My breath quickened. "Battles? You say, Illinois?"

The women looked with surprise at William, come in from weeding cabbages. Mary Grace sat down also beside Frances but sometimes turned to Jephthah, playing nearby. I could have sent my youngsters from the table, but I made no move.

"Not thought to be battles, but Rebels in that area," Margaret said.

"We think the ruckus at Frederick happened first," Frances said, her voice low. "This can't be true, but Jubal Early is said to have demanded $200,000."

Jubal *Early!* "I don't . . ." I motioned for William to look to Jephthah, banging on the wood box, but William wouldn't budge, his red eyes stark.

"No one believes $200,000." Margaret's black dress sat on her like an empty sack. "Likely a large amount, though; they threatened to burn there, too."

"Burn buildings?" William asked.

"Jephthah!" I scolded. "Cease!"

"Demands in Hagerstown, too," Frances said. "Clothes or money for ransom."

"Men—for ransom also?' I asked.

"Oh, not that we know," Frances said.

"It seemed that folks from Hagerstown may have abandoned their property and gone to Shippensburg. But then, moved back." Margaret's hand swept one way, then the other. "Not for sure. But horses—"

William sat sniffling. He wiped an eye with a fist, smudged with his dirty knuckles.

"Set fire with torches was said about Chambersburg." Frances fidgeted with tassels. "Furniture broken into pieces and used to start fire in the town hall." She grabbed at her shawl, slipping off her shoulder.

"Chambersburg?" I asked. "Matthias is to the north, his farm. A Mennonite church nearby."

Mary Grace reached across, cupped her hands over mine on the table. She looked to Margaret. "What had they done?"

Margaret raised empty hands again. "We're in the dark, Child. But hatred—a mighty fire. The North's been burning here in Virginia, and Rebels are said to be desperate for supplies."

Jephthah's tower of blocks fell; he clapped with glee.

"Samuel thinks it retaliation," Frances said, "for last year."

Margaret nodded. "Gettysburg. An eye for an eye."

"Soldiers went through those same parts last summer," I said. "Andrew said. No word from him this round, though. But Joseph?"

William strode to the fireplace and commenced jabbing at stone with the poker. Miriam cried out from the cradle.

The women tried to ignore the clatter. Margaret leaned forward. "We don't mean alarm. Which ones, if boys. Nor do we want you in the dark."

"Peter had told us of strict orders not to harm property. No plundering," I said. Mary Grace brought Miriam to me, and I gave her to suck.

"Yes, the case a year ago," Margaret said. She sat tall, severe again.

"This brother-in-law of Lincoln's," Frances said, "he's the one who led at Chambersburg."

"President Lincoln?" William asked, the poker wavering in the air.

"Goes by Major Todd," Margaret said. "Orders to burn, if the town didn't supply demands. Horseshoes, nails, coffee—a long list. Vast amounts, impossible to fill demands. Sole leather, flour. One report"—she looked to Frances—"$500,000 ransom for there."

"No townspeople could round up that much," Frances said. "Only a fool would ask. Short notice—three hours." She leaned across, fingers to her mouth like a fort. "Liquor!" Her teeth clicked. "Women mistreated."

Startled, I saw Margaret's head shake, her lips squeeze tight.

"You don't know where though—exactly." I adjusted Miriam.

"That's right," Margaret said quickly. "We don't know the extent. Whether anyone—"

"Matthias, a mile north of town," I said again.

Margaret nodded. "Good, very good. Not all Rebels disposed to wreck or given to vengeance. We know that."

"But Joseph?" I asked. "Did you say fleeing west?

"No, only Henry Brunk was known to have gone on to Illinois," Margaret said.

Frances wrapped her hands inside the ends of her dark blue shawl. "That one report, though: 'Others might follow.'"

The women's voices mingled. "Maybe not your Joseph. Nor Andrew—nothing about him. We thought it best—"

My mind flitted. If Joseph were at work, hoeing—Peter would be merciful, if he saw—oh, I don't know—this Jubal. Such wrath, when laughed at by Northerners. If Peter camped on church grounds again, and Andrew hauled wood—

"Houses built tight together in town, but not so, on a farm," Frances said. "You know how spread out, Esther. Flames—not so fast."

"Matthias would know how to forestall," I said. "Did you say this just happened?"

Margaret shook her head. "No, the end of July. Saturday, July 30, the worst day. Word came only yesterday. Much as we shrink from conjecture, we must pass on what news we have—anyone with family."

Miriam cried out and I moved her to the other side. My milk gone slack. "If you hear names—" I couldn't stop the quiver of my lips.

Frances jerked at Miriam's loud sucking. "Prayers for mercy. For all."

I had to ask. "You don't—you didn't hear of captures?"

"No, no word," Margaret said. She reached a thin arm toward me.

I offered a taste of peaches, our first of the season, on the wooden sink to ripen.

"You keep," Frances insisted. "Put away your extra."

When the women left, my big ones and I took on the mope. Only Jephthah kept playing, but he patted Miriam on the head so much, she cried out again. I gave no thought to the kraut I had planned to make—not enough salt anyway. William refused to go back to the garden, but I made him wash his face and hands and bring more water from the well. Earlier in the summer, we had all worked outside together, the little ones in tow, because Jephthah had needed to run his legs awhile. But that only made more problems; he'd wander off in a blink, stub his toe on a big rock or stir up a nest of yellow jackets.

"Why would they burn?" William asked. "What good is that?"

"Andrew said he was always at the wrong place at the wrong time," Mary Grace said.

"Why would they send false reports?" William asked.

"Joseph runs very fast," Mary Grace said. "He practiced hiding in the haymow."

Finally, I begged my youngsters to stop their talk. "We can't know until the boys—any of them—come back. '*Pray for mercy*,' Frances said."

But William persisted, his face stony. "How can a president have a brother-in-law fight against the North? Frances said—"

"No sense," I said. "But the president has family in Virginia—now and in the past. Men turned opposite." I saw no softening in my boy. Like a whisper, I added, "Families divided—"

Nothing comes easily, not for any of us. No way to know how things can go every-which-way. Back in May already, I should have paid better attention. We'd heard of how this Samuel Rhodes had fled two years ago—that awful spring. He was barely more than twenty, strong in heart and body, leaving his mother Anna behind. He made it to this same part of Maryland where he found work on a farm. *Oh, I never thought—* But then winter came and Rhodes had to go to Pennsylvania to find work in railroad shops. The next summer, he fled again when Rebels caused turmoil where he was living. This time, he went all the way to Iowa, farther than Illinois. *It can happen.* By all counts, he did well at first, making wagons and cabinets. But dealt another terrible blow during the winter, when frightfully cold weather brought illness and more trouble. He became weak, then weaker. Hacking and vomiting possessed his body. His final desire: to see his godly mother once more.

I can scarce review the next part. This Rhodes found fortitude enough to travel to Indiana, where he boarded a train filled with soldiers and proceeded back to Frederick, Maryland. Alas—here is the part again—once hearty, but suddenly reduced. Ill health took him over. Never to see his beloved mother's face again. Oh, Simon—did my man ever think . . . Ever take a notion to start back from Gabriel's? Is anyone spared? My three big boys . . .

Not so for Margaret Rhodes. Her invalid husband died earlier this summer; now she's left with debt and five children. But she keeps going, keeps delivering messages; her mother-in-law helps with the youngsters.

That doesn't help my William and Mary Grace. They know: all is precarious. They ride our conveyance; they see our spotty crops. The wheat might do well, but I won't let William take grain to the mill alone. Some man will need to give help. I don't know who; all the able ones have fled. Samuel has too much to tend; I dare not ask. Up in the air, like most everything. Our boys' whereabouts—one more thing.

* * *

They came again yesterday: a half dozen hungry ones in blue. I sent Mary Grace outside with two loaves of bread. I prayed for a mighty hand to quell their hunger. She dashed out and returned quickly, but the men made themselves at home in our orchard. They acted like they'd found the Garden of Eden. We took turns watching from the window. One man headed for peaches. Another shook apples; I had to turn away. The red ones not nearly ready. One burly fellow helped hoist a smaller one, so he could grab onto a limb, snatch his knapsack full, toss more to his comrades.

That burly one banged on our door. "A basket," he yelled, craning to peer inside.

I motioned to William—peach pie, his favorite. "Fetch what the man needs."

Our three sturdiest picking baskets, gone now. One man twisted a clump of grapes, gave up, and yanked. Spat them out with a vengeance. I didn't go out to direct him to the sunny side where grapes have turned better. We'd made juice the day before—not fully anticipating, but stowing jars in the cellar. The taste not the best, lacking sugar. For one batch I tried molasses; sorghum, the other. Better than nothing.

Those same men, plus one more, came back today; this time they walked right inside, claiming to thank us for the fruit. I backed up and stared from one to the next. Mary Grace scurried to the bedroom with Miriam, but Jephthah had no fear. He ran to the men before I could stop him.

"Hey there, little feller," the burly man boomed. "Saw you the other day." With one quick motion he gathered Jephthah in his arms and swung him in the air. William came in an instant but stood back, biting his fingers. Jephthah yelled, "Whee!" and raised his arms to touch the upper beams. He's not had roughhouse since Joseph left.

"Stop!" I said, half stumbling toward my littlest boy.

"No trouble, Lady," the man said, swinging Jephthah away from me. "No trouble at all." Jephthah let out another shriek.

A man with dark eyes ready to pop out of their sockets, barred my path. "We miss our little fellers at home." His kind voice made me look again. "No harm, Ma'am, no harm."

They passed Jephthah among them. The small man half-danced around the kitchen table, swinging Jephthah with a wildness; the boy's bare feet bumped the tops of table chairs and rattled a kettle, empty on the hearth. I stood in the corner, clutching my broom. I would have swung and given chase, like with bats, if need be.

When the last shaggy one took his turn, he sat Jephthah on his shoulders and marched about the table, singing "*Oh, we'll rally round the flag, boys, we'll rally once again*." Then he headed for the bedroom but turned back smartly; the others joined in the chorus:

> The Union forever, hurrah! Boys, hurrah!
> Down with the traitors, up with the stars;
> While we rally round the flag, boys, we rally once again,
> Shouting the battle cry of freedom!

The man sang yet another verse; then all of them sang the chorus, louder—Jephthah tried to join or clapped his hands—as they marched about. At last, the men tired of their cavorting and spoke their farewell, calling Jephthah "little man" and giving him a swat on the behind. The burly one gave him a big smooch.

We fell to sobbing, except for Jephthah. He went to the window and slapped at it, as if to call the men back. I made him sit on the wood box, but he banged his heels and sang, "—rah, boys, rah."

"Jephthah, stop at once," I said. "No more singing or banging your feet."

Mary Grace came with Miriam. "Did they mean us?" Mary Grace asked. "That ugly word."

"Peter," William said quietly.

"They don't know who or what," I said. "They only sing their song; it makes them feel strong."

"But we're not traitors, not theirs," Mary Grace said.

"I don't care; Peter's my brother," William said.

"He's our boy," I said, "but those would see him otherwise, if they knew."

"Not an enemy," Mary Grace said. "Not Peter."

"Never," I said, hugging her to me, squishing Miriam. "Blood runs deep. But war takes sides; tries to label who's for, who's against. As if simple.

They thought us South. But no better for us to be North—the way they see it—if we don't take up rifles."

"Rah, rah," Jephthah said quietly.

I picked him up and sat him on my lap. "Only words and a tune for you," I said. "But listen." I swiveled his chin, so he had to look at me. "We *don't* sing that song. Not you. *Not ever*." I looked to my older ones. "No one's innocent—your brothers. None of us. Not the noisy men either. All of us, someone's enemy. But remember: family's stronger."

"It feels bad," William said, "men in blue."

"Hard to feel good," Mary Grace said. "But Jephthah didn't know. Did you, Buddy?" She reached to tap him on the head, blew him a kiss.

* * *

Whether last week or last May, yesterday or another time last week. Little matter—the exact time. I can't tell my youngsters all that piles up. No more tell than explain. Forebodings. Gabriel coming, could be but the start.

Those soldiers and their visit, no more puzzling than all that had raced after I saw that Hildebrand man in our church. That was a week ago. The very one Peter said was made deacon—Benjamin's father. Dark hair and standing erect when called to the front to make comment on Scripture. Mary Grace looked at me quick when his name was announced, but never said more.

It was the annual meeting of Mennonite ministers in Virginia, planned months ago to take place at our Weavers church. I'm surprised they went ahead; we still don't hold regular church service, not nearly every Sunday. But Brother Samuel had encouraged us, despite the upheaval, to make extra effort and show forth unity. Many ministers from a distance chose not to come, but this man from Staunton was one who made it safely. He probably had a pass for travel—if Peter's right that he checks on his boys when a battle's done.

Our church building hadn't been that full in over a year. But we women had been instructed to sit farther back, so that the visiting ministers could occupy the front benches on both sides. I can't say as to Hildebrand's comments; I only heard monotone. Did the man, this deacon, know where his sons were right then? Even his Gideon who rides a fancy horse? He carried himself well and showed no malice; nor did I see animosity from Brother Samuel. He surely knows. Both of them.

When Communion proceeded for all members, a tremble suddenly seized my innards. What if this man came as messenger? His son could have asked him to convey news regarding Peter. We've heard that Early skirmished with Union men, somewhere north, near to Winchester.

But this Hildebrand's eyes never turned back to us women. If anything, he seemed to doze at times, his head down and off to the side. At the benediction I hurried to leave straightway, only nodding toward a few women. Mary Grace helped carry our babes to the door, and William got us safely home in spite of our wagon that gives concern. Soldiers guffaw at the rickety sideboards, but William says it's the two front wheels that need replacement.

That night I dreamed of meeting a stranger in the woods. I know not where—maybe near Simon's unused lime kiln. The man kept his head down, walking toward me but with a hand on his hat pulled low. He stopped directly in front, inspected his buttons at length. Of a sudden, a strong wind came, such that I crouched in a cluster of saplings and steadied my bonnet. Brown leaves whipped about in gusts; I thought I might be lifted like Mama. As suddenly as the wind picked up, all around me went silent. No birds called, no squirrels gave chase. The stranger had disappeared. Stillness wrapped about me.

When daylight came, I wondered if in truth I'd gone outside as Simon used to do. If I'd tiptoed and met a wanderer in the middle of the night. Mary Grace said nothing of my being absent from bed, but I could feel again the rustle through my bedtime braid—wind changing abruptly to quiet.

David — Shenandoah Valley, September 1864

They say 40,000 coming. Worse than Hunter. Coming—to burn. The word scorches my mouth. This Sheridan put out the order, middle of last month: wheat and hay fields north of here. Three days ago, J. M. came to tell. They targeted Clarke and Frederick counties, close to Winchester, where our Emma went with her Lutheran husband. Houses to be spared.

Abigail clings in bed. "Five children birthed and only one remains."

"We know not the end," I whisper back. "But Delilah, our Rock." I no longer go to the post office to check for a letter from our boys.

Why can people not see? Retaliation only begets more. This new Army of the Shenandoah coming with torches. Why? *Because* the South burned property in Chambersburg two months ago. And that? Retaliation for the terrible defeat the Rebels suffered at Gettysburg the summer before. Generals only know an eye for an eye. The last victor may be willing to stop the cycle, but the last defeated one cannot forget.

I was little better, all summer long; I wanted someone to pay. If authorities had tried, they could have found the culprits in Johnny's murder. Men somewhere, must still be cowering. Some say the Linville Partisans are no longer active, that some up and left. Brother Neff thought some joined other Ranger groups; others said, a Ranger unit that does not measure up is forced into the Army. Also back in summer's heat, J. M. had whispered of several items that swirled. First, that Brother Kline's warning against his person at Rogan White's in Oakland had come from the highest levels—none other than Detectives from Washington. Second, that Johnny had talked with Algernon Gray.

"Yes!" I said to the latter.

J. M. stopped at my eagerness. "You know of this? Some trouble over lambs in a pen?"

"Yes," I said again more quietly, "a lamb. But the warning—I had not known the source in Oakland."

"And you know that John named names of all the locals present, that day of the lamb."

"Oh! No, not told that. Do you think? Would he name—?"

J. M. shrugged his shoulders. "No way to know, unless Algernon says it straight out." But J. M.'s words pitched another log on the fire within me.

This speculation in the summer came while Elder Wine had closed his eyes and said, "If there is to be punishment, it will come in the next world, not at the hands of any of us." I wanted to shout back: "How can you stay calm?" Ever since Brother Kline's death, Brother Wine has known threatening messages on his own person.

A $500 reward was issued for evidence in Johnny's case, but no one stepped forward. No one claimed to have witnessed the deed. Why did authorities stay daft? I could have zeroed in on one or two suspects. For certain, the one who innocently asked regarding Johnny's plans for the day; we know that man had companions. If only couriers, they still played a part. For someone. The three young lads who found the body had named the very ones where my suspicions festered. But those boys are no more than ten; their testimony would not have held up in court.

Our *Rockingham Register* managed a few warm words. While they identified our brother as a Union man—his views seen as erroneous—to their credit, they called him "uncompromising," a man of "strictest integrity." They advised citizens to deplore the violence of seeking vengeance against "an unarmed and feeble old man." As if the victim's age had made this act wrong!

I could only go to the woods, swing my ax, and watch old stumps split apart. Beetles scurried away. *Quietness only puts more people at risk.* Would John have named—even if ordered?

Last month, while Delilah and I prepared clabber for cheese, she asked, "Why do you sulk?"

I gave one last stir through soured milk. "John treated my warnings as temptation. What has been accomplished—this martyrdom? No resolution."

She said no more, but that night before bed, she read aloud from the last chapters of Job. "'*Knowest thou the time when the wild goats of the rock bring forth? Gavest thou the goodly wings unto the peacocks? Or wings and feathers unto the ostrich?*'"

"What good is that?" I mumbled, running my hand over my nearly bald head. "Are we to expect pigs to fly? My hens, grow teeth?" She gave no response. "Only remain content, no control over what happens? Is that it? And where is Winfield keeping himself? Protecting someone?"

"'*Doth the eagle mount up at thy command and make her nest on high?*'"

"I never said so," I muttered, but my questions continued. "Is it better to count myself as nothing? Let lawlessness prevail? Bury my grievances? Am I not to stand up?"

"God accepted this Job. Gave him better standing than his friends in the end. It must not be wrong to question, but—to nurse anger?" A slight smile lifted the corners of Delilah's mouth. "The daughters—did you notice? Job's daughters were given names, but not the sons. The daughters carried forth goodness, given inheritance."

"That gives you a rope to clutch?" I asked. How can Delilah gain comfort by grabbing at flimsy strands of straw?

"I do not understand the whys and wherefores, Father. But more can be accomplished seeking after good than bemoaning evils visited upon us. Our neighbors need kindness. The Skellys, the Saylors. Sister Neff. Whether aggrieved over illness, or an infected cow."

"Those kinds of trouble are to be expected now and then," I said. "But murder?" She waited quietly. "Why should I be expected to say, 'Johnny's death may be within the providence of God's will, but not the Almighty's *plan!*' I cannot turn a blind eye to the evils of human choice, not when it includes concocting dark designs. And the malice to carry them out."

Delilah reached to put her hand on my shoulder. "I do not know. But I need your care, Father, not your slings." She grabbed my hand. I felt compelled to squeeze back. "We must not lose sight: the Negro man and woman carry the greatest burden. Our troubles, few." She held up a hand to stop me. "Remember Lila, going to find her man? Their race—intent on one Promised Land or another—yet forced to live life through the will of a master, year after year. We should stand against that! Not so? Better to sing of the Jordan also."

Her voice did not scold, but I felt scolded. I did not want to admit to her wisdom. Not when we are left adrift. I give her credit, but nothing is clear. There may be more needless suffering, when license is given to overlook.

No one stepped forward all those summer months; no one could replace Brother Kline. Only Brother Moomaw from Botetourt County journeyed any distance. Twenty years ago, when I first met him, he carried himself with vigor; now he goes about stooped. Still, he brought one piece of good news this summer: our German Baptist church building in Maryland, riddled with bullets at the Battle of Antietam and used for a while as a temporary hospital, had been repaired and made into a place of worship again. The Northern War Department had wanted to make of it a relic, but our brethren prevailed to restore it to its intended use.

But now, none of us knows what may soon pound at the door. Flames! Each congregation, more and more prone to arrive at its own understanding. Even, each family. Can that be wise? Yet how are we to consult when travel remains hazardous?

J. M. maintains connections with men in New Market and came again yesterday with more local news. My women and I were out walking corn rows, inspecting ears. How we yearn for signs of fullness—bright yellow kernels, full-sized like eager teeth.

J. M. beckoned for me to step aside with him, but I stayed firm: "We do not keep from each other. The times are such—"

His eyebrows lifted, but he came closer, speaking quietly. "You have heard—Sheridan coming?" Delilah stepped closer; Abigail stayed back but with her ear attuned. "He relies on a confidential assistant, a Meigs man, who knows the lay of the land—distances, roads, streams in our Valley." J. M.'s brow furrowed. "Retaliation may not be the only motivation for the North."

We waited.

"He accuses us—you, me, ordinary citizens and farmers—of keeping the South's soldiers alive," J. M. said. "General Grant has promised: 'Eat out Virginia clear and clean.'"

"Some truth," I said. "Worthless with guns—we accepted the South's terms: allowed to come back to farm; told to raise food for soldiers."

"And now the North contends that we farmers bear fault. Grant's latest order: Not so much as a crow to find nourishment in these parts."

"Last spring's burning was selective," Delilah said.

"True." J. M. ran his hand through his thick strawlike hair. "But that pattern may be a thing of the past. No more protection—having *favored* the North."

Delilah drew back. I turned away, looking to the distant mountains, the cradle for my fields. Our beautiful Valley—over a hundred miles. Blue Ridge Mountains in the east; the Massanutten Range close about. To the west, the Shenandoah Mountains and Alleghenies stretch far beyond. But now, helpless to defend. *Whence cometh my help?* Our Valley waits, not unlike when the warning came to Johnny. How much longer—another fulfillment?

"Just as Anna predicted long years ago," Abigail said.

I turned on her. "Woman! Your meaning?"

"Burning," she said dully. "You know of it. Rampant destruction of grain."

"How was that given to you? I never—" I am certain I never told of Anna's Armageddon dream, not even when John's body was laid out. Nothing of that sort passed my lips.

"We may not be first to know," she said quietly. "But we women have our ways."

"So it is," J. M. said, as matter-of-fact as Abigail.

I fanned myself with my straw hat, my face flushed. I sought to even my breaths. "Picked clean, you say? Not by *our* hands—not those of us who planted." My voice weakened. "Another's scourge."

Delilah interrupted and spoke like a prayer, "'*The earth is the Lord's.*'" Then like a plea. "How could anyone wantonly set fire? Our wheat given—that which sustains."

"We do not understand," J. M. said. "But word spreads also—" We looked to him. "Grant wants us to leave."

"Leave?" Abigail asked like a lost child. "Where is there to go?"

"By what means?" I added, my legs wobbly like soft cheese. "Johnny used to say we might need to go. But that was—*given choice*, to depart or not."

J. M. scuffed with his boot at a weed, stooped to yank it with a hand. "All is different now. The Confederate's General Early is credited with bringing our Valley to the North's attention. His men marched to the outskirts of the North's capital city."

"That was only a day!" I protested. "For show."

"Nonetheless, it spread panic," J. M. said. "They also went to Chambersburg with lighted torches. Remember? The man has a knack: when to cross the Potomac, when to come back safely to our Valley."

"Come back to regroup?" Delilah asked.

"Again and again," J. M. said. "All summer, it seems. Early kept moving his men around. Feds never certain of the South's whereabouts."

"But the South is weakened. Is that not so?" I asked. "No big battles to speak of, not recently."

"True also," J. M. said, "but constant cat and mouse has kept nerves on edge. Both sides use snipers, hide behind trenches."

"We have not laid one hand to harm!" I said. Black starlings flew up aflutter with my raw voice. A crow cawed in the distance. "Not you nor I."

"I only bring word," J. M. said. "Perhaps the North's intent is only a threat."

"We need," Delilah said, her voice scratchy, "to prepare."

Abigail's eyes squinted. "Some say our houses, *not* to be torched."

My rage dug in. "Elder Wine says, only the barns of widows and single women *not* to be *touched*."

J. M. shrugged. "That is how it goes." He placed a hand on my shoulder. "No one knows, David. Many voices, rumors. Some still speak of a *just* war."

"Nothing just." I turned away to spit to the next row.

"Civilians must *not* be targeted," Delilah said, "if *just*. We learned in school."

"That is the standard," J. M. added. "Discrimination is to be used, regarding the war's conduct." His cheeks puffed with air. "But—best not count on wisdom. Not for these parts."

"Nor in Atlanta," I said. "That we know."

Abigail reached to open another husk of ear, shaking her head. "Some say that folks given vouchers there—what of theirs destroyed."

Delilah's eyes blinked fast. "Those could be false reports also, Mother. Nothing to be gained from fickle promises."

"Only know for certain," J. M. said, "when whatever is going to happen, happens."

"All to be blackened," Abigail said. "Anna foresaw."

I smacked a fist into my open hand. "They cannot go everywhere! Most likely, torch farms on the main thoroughfare—where easy." I looked directly at J. M. "Your land could—"

"There is little that can stop the determined hand," he said.

Today, we have doubled our efforts: harvested anything that looks anywhere near to ready. Now beaten down from haste, my back sends twinges from lugging large sacks inside. Thankful not to carry barrels to the loft anymore, we stuffed our closet—any usable grain. No room inside for a wayfarer. Our own preservation first. Yes, it has come to that: my women and I filled every inch, even though sweet potatoes, half the usual size.

We can only beg the Lord's forgiveness, placing importance on our own heads. Delilah says she prefers nights on the day bed for the next while. The two women carried extra bedding down from the loft. A straw bed in the barn will have to do for a weary man on foot.

Come Sunday morning, I will look again on the few who venture out. The usual cluster of old men, a few faithful women, a scattering of girls and young boys. My breath will falter once more. Our singing, already as sad as our hearts: "*Jesus, lover of my soul, let me to thy bosom fly.*" I will give whatever consolation I can scrape. "*Take my yoke upon you, and learn of me . . . my yoke is easy, and my burden is light.*"

Esther — Shenandoah Valley, September 1864

How can anyone be so cruel? Drag a boy, miles on end—a man who still thought like a boy. Out shooting squirrels. Everyone knows Davy Getz wouldn't harm a soul.

Frances came to tell. Union men with fancy white stripes on their blue trousers, provoked by bushwhackers firing at night. Local men, not officially in the Southern army, but sniping from the woods, doing hit-and-run raids on supply trains.

"That's no excuse!" I said. Tying a body and dragging the boy behind a wagon through the streets? Parading him like an object of ridicule! Meant as a warning, I suppose. Not something I would ever want to tell William and Mary Grace.

"His poor parents, beside themselves," Frances said. "The father, a sexton in the Methodist church, following behind and imploring, until repulsed by other Union men."

"Mercy on us all!" I said. "How can anyone allow such? Our righteous God!"

No, I can't tell my youngsters, but the story stays burnished. These Northerners came with a General Custer—headquarters nearby in Dayton—and another general, a Sheridan, set up in Harrisonburg. That last one, said to be intent on destroying crops. Frances said we may be next. How can I help but give way to choppy breath? Right here at Dale Enterprise, some of Sheridan's men are spread out in camps. The ones on foot more polite, but cavalry men—mean through and through. They seek to frighten with their threats. The North can't leave us to starve.

But this Davy boy, deprived of full understanding and childlike, not intending a lick of harm. Outside for sport, shooting at birds and ground squirrels with an old musket. Not bothering a soul. The parents shouldn't have allowed it, what with soldiers milling about. But the way Frances told it: soldiers riled the boy, asked if he was a bushwhacker. He didn't know the word; said he was. An innocent mistake—maybe wanting to sound tough, like his brother in the Confederate Army. But at that wrongful admission, the Northerners tied and dragged him—Frances said the lad was screaming—all the way to Woodstock. Worse treatment than a bully boy ever could have delivered. Townspeople are said to have gone to this Custer fellow and begged him to release Davy. Everybody knows the boy's harmless. But Custer wouldn't hear of it. "A civilian holding a weapon is to be shot." No exceptions. No civilian worth—

Coming back, the soldiers followed orders once more; they tied Davy to a wagon again but made him *walk* the forty miles. His body already battered. People in Harrisonburg saw the spectacle; bystanders wept. No one could bring any sense. And then—no, I won't tell William and Mary Grace. The men forced Davy to dig his own grave. Shot him dead like he counted for nothing. Cast off. Right behind—close by anyhow—the Dunkards's church in Dayton. His body left uncovered overnight.

Nothing but madness! Southerners even more enraged now. No fairness on either side. Peter wouldn't do that, would he? No, not as wicked as a Union soldier, not scheming like a bushwhacker. I can't bear to think. How a man—either side—can look on another as a scrap of wood.

* * *

They came again—Union cavalry. The worst. The last ones gave a receipt for what they took; the man said to present it for reimbursement when the war's over. But this afternoon they came to kill. William saw the men first and came running. "One man on foot, another by horse."

"Stay inside!" I said. But he went out the door, halted on the porch. Mary Grace begged with her eyes to follow. Last time, we had been stuck in the shed.

I don't know what's better—to hide or make conversation. But when a third man came with a horse and wagon, I checked to make sure Miriam napped, before I ventured out. Jephthah sat on my hip; Mary Grace tagged behind. The men asked for water. I nodded to William and he drew a bucket, staying back while they slurped from the dipper. They threw their hats and bags on the ground, propped themselves around the well wall.

"Where's your man?" one of them yelled.

"Gone," I said. "Not much left, my children and I. Two babes, two youngsters."

"Mighty nice-looking stock," another one said.

"My brother and I," Mary Grace said, standing by William, "give care."

"Takes a man, do that," the one with curly hair said. "Betcha he's hiding inside. Or taking his rest at the bottom of this here well," he added.

The other men laughed loudly. I kept Jephthah's hands tightly closed.

"Those are my sheep," Mary Grace said.

The men stared, looked her up and down, my tall fourteen-year-old.

"Best have a look inside," the tall, skinny one said. "See what the woman hides."

"Nah, come on." The first one stood erect. "Work to do. Catch ya, next time, Missus."

The tall one grumbled but followed, grabbing at belongings. They went to the hog pen and commenced firing. Then to the sheep, finally the cattle. We only saw in part, but shots echoed; sounds come back around our hills, deflected. Dogs barked far off. The men cackled and egged each other on. Then all fell silent. I buried Jephthah's head in my bosom. I've heard they have large cooking spits in their camps. Jephthah squirmed, but I squeezed tighter. We all lurched when a loud boom broke our ears. Hens squawked and flew.

Finally, Miriam's cries registered. "Come back to the porch!" I said to my youngsters. "Tell me if they come to the door."

"Ma, they'll shoot everything," William said, his voice like a child's.

"Make no attempt—" I stumbled inside with Jephthah, knowing not. My tears on fire. I grabbed Miriam and pressed both my babes to me, crooning. The rocking chair creaked. Tears fell on Jephthah's brown head of hair, Miriam's black crown. I couldn't think how or what.

Suddenly, that awful quiet came again. What were they up to? I placed Miriam in the trundle bed and tiptoed out—carrying Jephthah again, but whispering to be quiet. There sat Mary Grace and William, huddled on the porch step as one twisted body, arms linked and heads buried. The soldiers stayed busy, gathering plunder, pitching bloody carcasses on their wagon.

I whirled to carry Jephthah back inside. "Stay! Your blocks."

I sat beside Mary Grace and reached my arms around both youngsters.

"Ma," Mary Grace said, her head buried in my shoulder. "Ma."

"It was his," William whispered.

"What?" I said like a command.

"His haversack," William said. His voice louder, rasping, "Peter's."

"Tell!" I straightened. "Speak to me."

"We both saw," William said over Mary Grace's sobs. "When the men put down their bags at the well. The light brown one—two straps and a big V."

"The V to strengthen straps," Mary Grace said, her voice muffled. "Peter always said."

"Now, now, bags look the same," I said, my assurance back. "Many but different."

"No, Ma," Mary Grace said. "We both—"

Of a sudden, I rose and said to my big ones, "Stay here. No. Inside, both of you. Go in! Watch the babes. Look at me." I leaned to them, their streaked faces lifted. Jephthah pounded on the window pane. "Stay inside. You must."

The men had started down our lane, their wagon creaking from its load. Hoofs and heads dangled off the side. The man on foot led our best horse, Nimble. I hurried to catch up, my ankle bending sideways on a rock. I turned back to make sure no child followed, then made haste again. The man on horseback heard me coming.

"Sir, a moment." I stopped for breath.

Nimble jerked his head at the sound of my voice. The man on the wagon came to a halt, but Nimble frisked at the leash. "What is it?" their leader said, his voice gruff.

"That's our best horse," I said. "My children and I—we take care."

"Won't shoot it, Lady," the curly haired one said. The others guffawed.

"I mean, I need—your bags. If you please— I need to see."

Each man grabbed for his haversack. One hung loosely from the saddle. "Our bags—nothing to do with you," the tall one said.

"I know. I mean—" I gulped for air. "That one—the one with the big V. Two straps. I need to see. Inside."

The man with curly hair sticking out from his cap grinned. He stretched the haversack toward me, jerked it back. "*My* bag, Lady. Found it—Fisher's Hill. Gray boy—no use for it no more. Poor sucker."

I stepped closer and stretched up my hand—drew back when his hand whipped to his holster.

"Lady, no name!" he said. "I'm telling you. Someone covered up initials. Black thread, all zig-zag. You hear? No name. Mine—"

I stared, blinded.

"You have a good day now," the man in charge said. "Go feed your children."

"Two of your girl's stupid sheep, still there," the tall one said. "A crippled cow, too. Near to half the hens."

I stepped back and looked to my house, my four babies. I staggered, blurred eyes down—not to crumble—sidestepped Nimble's fresh trail. I said nothing to my big ones. They asked nothing. I gathered Miriam and rocked her slowly, my eyes tight closed—the feel of the cold needle in my fingers again. Peter had said to stitch over.

Later, I put out cold food. I don't know if anyone—yes, Jephthah ate cheese and bread, babbled about the men. We took turns like dullards, telling him to shush.

I said nothing of remainders, but we could hear weak cries—random clucks—from the pens. No one made a move to chore. I couldn't tell either child: Go step around blood. But later, William went on his own, brought in a pittance of milk. I huddled tight with both my big ones in bed that night. Dogs barked far away; a lone howl.

David — Shenandoah Valley, October 1864

Botanicals were not the only reason I paid a visit to Hinkle's apothecary at New Market. I needed extra word; J. M. has not been back to our place. We had heard sounds of troops moving on the Pike late last month.

Solomon Hinkle had bought some of Johnny's medical instruments back at the time of the farm sale, and I had assured him I would keep to my habit of digging roots. Today he purchased two pounds of my dogwood bark, said it is in demand as a replacement for quinine and used for treating fevers. He looked surprised, though, when I said my daughter's cough had lessened from chewing on the bark of the holly root.

Back home, I'd barely unhitched Ruby and walked to the women, when Abigail started in. "What did he say?"

She and Delilah were taking turns stirring apple butter. They had started with five bushels of apples and most of the cider we had pressed earlier. I had promised to be home to help with the heavy stirring and pouring into five-gallon crocks.

Abigail squeezed my arm. "Where do things stand?"

"The Feds had success at Winchester. Fighting also at a place close to Strasburg called Fisher's Hill. Mister Hinkle said Rebels have a signal station there—a raised area in the plateau between the Massanutten on the east and Little North Mountain on the west."

"You know what I mean." Abigail tugged on my jacket. When she is insistent, there is no turning away.

"A mauling. Ferocious, in thickets and ravines," I said.

"Severe," Abigail said, her eyes filling. That quickly, she can fall to pieces.

"Severe," I repeated. "Union men attacked late in the afternoon. Surprised Rebels, such, they had to scramble on up the Valley. Chased on past here—just as the sounds had suggested—past Harrisonburg. All the way to Staunton, maybe Waynesboro."

"Still destroying?" Delilah shoved another crock to the kettle while Abigail ladled the thickened apples.

"Only fill to two-thirds," I said. "Not so heavy."

Delilah stood with hands on hips. "You have not said all."

"Railroads," I said, my head down. "Anything that can store supplies: barns, mills, smokehouses. If the North cannot burn it, they blow it up with blasting powder."

"Moving farther south?" Delilah asked.

I walked to the end of the lineup of crocks, eyed each carefully. When the kettle has lightened sufficiently, Delilah and I will be able to lift, pouring slowly to fill the last crocks. That tedious part requires bending and shuffling the feet to stay in position, taking extra care that my back not give out again.

"Answer me." Delilah had not budged.

"Mister Hinkle said the Confederates coming through looked beaten. Limping along, straining to reach the hospital at Harrisonburg. Early's unit, beaten down at Fisher's Hill, in disarray. Many taken as prisoners." I paused. "Hundreds of Feds wounded, too, but their replacements always seem to show up."

"On south?" Delilah asked again.

My women know of General Sherman's devastating acts farther south. It's commonplace after church: a small group of old men, a cluster of women, whispering. Expired news reaches us in dribbles, even what transpired last May in Georgia: farm animals and other buildings destroyed. Mills, too. Never for certain as to when, these happenings, but the news last month said that Sherman's men pressed Confederate soldiers back to Atlanta. Now, details of closer, of warnings afresh. The North as relentless as my women. Houses of the innocent, blown up. Railroad lines damaged.

I took a turn stirring, but my women stood still, going nowhere. "Word is that Sheridan has turned around," I said. "His men head north again, driving cattle and swine, even sheep, in their supply lines. Their camps said to look like butchering grounds."

"You mean . . ." Abigail began. "Gone past, and now returning?"

I willed my mouth to move. "Coming north. Helping themselves to horses."

Of a sudden, Delilah bustled about, motioning for me to help lift.

This time I stayed rooted. "There may be a wagon train taking people north. Safety."

Delilah snapped her fingers. "Come, Father. We will talk later."

We finished pouring and filling, but with more than the usual spills. "Steady!" I said sharply.

We did not have room for all the crocks, but we kept shoving, hefted bags higher, made room where there was none—our already full closet. My justification: no one is trying to escape—not through these parts. No one seeks shelter in this clogged Valley.

From the hurry and lugging, I wrenched my back. I could have known. By evening I went to our rope bed; Abigail's tea, made from Queen Anne's lace, did not provide its customary soothing. I tried the floor a spell—no better. Sharp spasms whenever I rose to stand. The long night endless, waiting for dawn. The mind's travails unceasing.

Come morning, Delilah did the few chores that remain; Abigail fixed coffee. She does not make it nearly strong enough, but I cannot say aught. It is not oat gruel. Delilah found two eggs; we ate bread and apple butter in silence. I shuffled about the house, thinking to work out kinks. I eased my body down to the big bed once more.

My women soon pulled up chairs. Abigail said, "What else from Solomon Hinkle?"

She had not combed her hair, but Delilah looked ready for the day and added, "The turning around of men. The train. All that Mister Hinkle said. You do us harm to withhold."

Not a breath of air stirred. I tried to scootch onto my side, thinking to prop on an elbow, but sank again and looked to the rafters. "'Every man for himself.' Hinkle said that about Northern soldiers. They do not know the terrain sufficiently, not even with Meigs giving direction. But Hinkle knows how our place sits back. He agreed: they cannot follow every break in the mountains—not men enough."

My women sat as stone.

"I cannot say, regarding any of our neighbors, how they fare. I did not go to Winfield. I made no effort to learn about those who have been absent from Flat Rock. My diligence wanes. I have given over—every family alone."

"We should not be unduly alarmed about our own," Delilah said. "Everyone knows, Father. When we hear marching—see excess smoke—we know, not to gather. Do not beat yourself. We all agreed to that."

I shook my head. "Johnny would be disappointed."

Abigail snapped her thumb and finger. "What else? We must know, so we can plan."

I tried to relieve pressure on my tailbone; the pain shifts like fire caught in a gust of wind. "Even if our far field of wheat, shaded from sun, should ripen in time, how will we crush grain? I do not know. The word about mills—"

"We know of mills—the North's damage. We know, we know. What is new?" Delilah bent over me to prop an extra pillow behind my back.

"The North sees no difference, this Hinkle said, whether we support the South, or Rebels took from us by force."

"J. M. said that last time!" Abigail said. "Do not be stingy. Give us new."

I put a hand under the pillow. "John F. Lewis has sheltered Union men—some of their wounded ones—in his farm buildings. Johnny used to speak of our representative in Richmond, a Union man, through and through. Remember? He had refused to sign the secession document. And when Northerners destroyed mills, John F. emptied his father's mill of grain; Samuel, a Union man also, had hoped to be spared."

Abigail inched forward on her chair. "And?" Delilah asked.

"Three of John F.'s brothers serve with the Confederacy, so the Feds damaged the man's iron furnace beyond repair. Destroyed his factory, too. Some of what he manufactured had been put to use by Rebels. The North forcibly helped themselves to munitions." I sighed. "The man should not be judged by his brothers' choices."

"The North tolerates nothing," Delilah said.

"A better man than I—that John F. But now, he faces persecution from either side; the Rebels threaten to hang him. If John F. is not safe, no one is safe," I said.

Delilah reached to calm her mother's quivering. "One thing yet, Father—the wagon train? What more of that?"

"The rumor persists. Safety for folks going north—those who desire."

"How would we know the day?" Abigail's voice a whisper.

"I would need to go to the road again," I said. "We could miss out; things change rapidly. Some in our Valley may have availed themselves already. I did not ask."

I slowly turned my head away, and we spoke no more. Delilah brought warm cloths to soothe. I have never heard what came of William E. Coffman—whether hanged—the man who piloted through mountain gaps. But for John F. Lewis, all escape routes may have closed.

That night Delilah only read one verse—the same verse as the night before: "*The Lord is nigh unto them that are of a broken heart; and saveth such as be of a contrite spirit.*"

* * *

After two more days, my back spasms relented. A straight chair worked best. My women did any necessary lifting; I am still next to useless, lest I reaggravate. Sometimes twinges return—sudden zaps when least expected. I often eat standing up, guarding against a setback. But by using my father's hickory cane, I can traverse the porch steps, walk to my walnut trees and back. A new malady, though: pressure in my ears increases. A ringing noise. Tomorrow I will walk to the grave in the pines.

Sometimes I have said more, in spite of my faint efforts to protect my women. "Rebels are helped by unofficial ones—guerrillas dressed like civilians. They attack and then blend back into the populace. Hinkle mentioned a Colonel Mosby."

"I remember that name," Delilah said.

"Some call him 'The Grey Ghost,'" I said. "He gives orders."

"How does this Mosby know the whatfor?" Abigail asked.

"Informants?" I shrugged. "The supernatural? The man's movements, mysterious. But a courier or someone connected with the trains could convey word of schedules, troop movements, contents of shipments."

"Filthy money passes back and forth, I suppose," Delilah said.

"Sheridan keeps guards at his supply lines because of these Southern disrupters," I said. "The North stays enraged; warnings increase of brutal hangings, thought to be retribution for bushwhackers and their deeds. So Solomon said."

Abigail held a handkerchief to her nose, her voice muffled. "Why does trouble fly to us?"

"We are not the only ones," Delilah was quick to say. "Far from—" She has taken to reading stories from the *Martyrs Mirror* again.

I did not mention Hinkle's other warning: "Do not go to Cootes store. A female spy resides, cloaked as a domestic servant." But I said, "Spies on both sides. Confederate detectives stay busy, arresting Unionists they suspect. Folks held locally or sent off to Richmond. Dispensed with, one way or another."

Delilah clicked with her teeth and tongue. "Anna of Freiburg's prayer must be ours: 'Keep me in thy truth.' Keep *us*."

I tapped my clenched fists against each other. "Tomorrow I will go out to the road and learn more. Hinkle's words may be old news already."

Abigail clutched my arm tightly. "You will do no such thing."

"We do not think that wise." Delilah cleared her throat to quell her own tremble. "We have the hens, the cow. As you say, we are enough back from the road. Better not to announce ourselves more than necessary."

"The cow, sickly," I reminded her. "I will be careful. Only seek word about this so-called train. Where to assemble. Slip home again."

Abigail's fingernails dug into my wrist. "Do not be lost to us like our boys."

"We have each other," Delilah said, barely above a whisper. "Do not go again."

My women have conspired. But if I abandon them for the sake of information, I leave them unprotected. I could fall by the wayside—in the clutch of evil men. Even if carrying no coins, men might beat me for traveling empty.

I tried again. "We may miss out. The wagons will likely—"

"Then we will miss out," Delilah interrupted. "*Keep us.*"

Abigail looked at me with fierce regard.

I could only shake my head. But that is how we left it. "*The Lord is nigh unto them*—" If I am to be ravaged, it will be with my wife and daughter.

Esther — Shenandoah Valley, early October 1864

We huddled on our back hillside all night. The sky would burst of a sudden, bright with flames: fire and brimstone. Orange and yellow. Dogs barking without end. Now and again a mist fell, but not nearly enough to put out fires. I hadn't thought to reach for Mama's home remedy; it gives William respite and clears his passageways. There he sat, smoke like a lid. When he lay back, his cough commenced and his breath became raspy. We had nowhere but the night sky and ground. A bed cover each, but we stayed chilled, save for our bodies tight together.

The birds had been aflutter all week. Yesterday when we stumbled to the far back, we could have been frightened wrens. We scrambled to get far from our barn gone up, our wheat inside, waiting to be threshed on the flailing floor. The late hay in stacks fared no better. All of our standing field crops, targeted. Our corn crop, not favorable, but we had hoped for another week or two—the kernels to develop. If Simon knew we'd waited, he might have laughed. Snorted, more likely. We dragged our rickety wagon to the fields for safety. Never thinking, nor believing.

Late afternoon, the men gave us thirty minutes to gather what we could. "Git your duds, Lady." They didn't ask if I had Rebel sons, if my man voted for secession. Several days before, some men had driven Mary Grace's last two sheep away.

When they threatened fire yesterday, she turned sassy. "How would you like to have someone come to your house and burn everything?" I made no effort to stop her.

"You're livin' at the wrong place, Girl," the man said. "We do things our way."

One soldier, more cordial, turned from his companion. But the rough one—"thirty minutes, Lady"—jerked open dresser drawers, yanked garments hither and yon, shouted frightful imprecations. I stood rooted. I forgot to snatch Simon's watch, Mama's brooch. The day the birds made the worst commotion, I had thought to grab the watch. But something intervened; I put it off. Only the gold, I remembered. For that, I had stayed up late, sewing pieces onto undergarments, an extra apron beneath. I wear the layers.

We'd been warned. But who could believe fully? Our apple butter stowed. Thinking—long winter nights. Only when on the hillside last night, did William remember the ball of fire falling from the sky the other summer. Yet, despite warnings, it seemed we had no time to think. What to grab first? No reason to trust the men with their thirty.

"The pie safe," I yelled to William over Miriam's cries. "Help empty and carry." We dragged it outside, helter-skelter, bumping down porch steps, but didn't go far enough. Only later, we had to shove and drag it beyond the well. One tug on the wooden sink—much too heavy. Countless trips, half running with pans and what food-makings remained; near to throwing things back in the safe, once outside. Clothes and leftover wool jammed in crannies. William loosed the last horse and poor cow to the woods. No way to know where or if they'll come back. No birds to speak of now.

How could anyone plan ahead: first this, then this? Would I tie Miriam to a chair? What would I do with Jephthah underfoot? Mary Grace thought to have him stuff wooden blocks and spools into socks.

Except for sewing the coins—in case—I hadn't thought it would be ours. Not for truth. The barn—Simon's barn. The haymow where the children played. The hay and oats we had cut—the best we could. Fodder for the torch. The men set fire to underbrush first. Rolling balls of yellow and orange. But barking, barking—as if dogs thought us unaware. William's thin voice, hacking. My mind goes back and over: how could I have forgotten his remedy?

In my haste, I carried out Mama's rocking chair. Who would want to sit now? Some of our big bags, too—dragged from the pantry. Foragers had already taken the last of the lard. Simon's watch—no! The least I could do. Poor man will never know.

"Time's up!" the rough one yelled. He must not have a woman and babes. I opened my mouth to beg, but no sound came. No mercy.

Two soldiers carried the table and dressers near the hearth, piled kitchen chairs atop. Beasts, set to feed an inferno.

"Don't look," I yelled, clutching Miriam and herding my others. "Grab an extra coat!"

The night. I don't know how or whence. How could anyone sleep? Eerie shadows. Darkness and smoke took on the battle. Jephthah finally settled beside Mary Grace. Miriam wouldn't sleep atop my bosom, my face to her nose, our tears and slobber mixed. My milk, no good. I moved her to the crook of one arm, then the other.

When the babes finally slept at the same time, Mary Grace's sniffles turned to weeping. My big girl whispered, "Ma, what will we do?"

"Child," I said. I took my arm from cradling Miriam's head and touched Mary Grace's cheeks. My fingers pressed to still their tremor. "Child, we have each other."

"My feet hurt, a pinching."

"No one to cobble," I said. "Keep your shoes on, for readiness."

But she turned away to shape her shoes into a pillow. This morning she dumped ashes from the insides.

Peter—oh, my son. No official word ever came; no letter. Never heard—not once—from that army; not direct. My boy, gone to his cause. Someone's traitor. No reason to think now: he'll walk up, like Genevieve's boy.

With all that hangs—is it daybreak or a different shade of night? Faint light in the firmament brings blackened hillsides clearer; fall colors dulled to scorching. Dogs. How can so many dogs be left? My babes cry for milk or bread. I can't let Jephthah suck, too; I have so little.

Mary Grace wanted to go look. I wouldn't let her go alone, so she turned to William. They came back, one limping, the other stumbling. They fastened tight together again, one on each side of me, my little ones squeezed between.

"The fireplace stands," Mary Grace whispered. "Legs of the cook stove, Ma, twisted like a monster."

"Ashes, Ma." William sobbed in rasps. "I couldn't stop the man."

I tightened my arms around all that I could. "No match, none of us, when a man lights a torch."

I tried to stifle their questions. "I don't know where—" Not till later, I said, "Someone will come, sometime. We don't know what, of neighbors." Our remnants scattered about. Where, the tin cups and small bucket? My voice little more than a whisper. "We have a kettle, some grease. A little cornmeal, potatoes. We will build a fire."

I must send William back to the well; Mary Grace must fetch cloths from the pie safe. Find a flat rock to clean Jephthah from his stink. Miriam—no place to put her down. Once, when up during the night, I tripped in search of a rock to squat. I heard no rips, but couldn't inspect in the dark whether the stitches held. The layers under my dress still feel weighed down. We *must* have our coins. Frances will come when she can. We must stay warm another night—

* * *

We heard the horse, fast approaching through brush, and William ran with caution, Mary Grace hobbling behind. They called for me. "It's Samuel!" I carried my babes to him as if to Simon: a man's arms to comfort. He can't go every place at once. Other women keep sole charge as well. But he rode to us on Frances's horse. "She gave strict orders," he said.

Before he escorted us, we all went to look. Smoldering ruins and rubble. The stone foundation. No sign of jars—our preservation reduced to ashes. Thin lines of smoke still curled and disappeared like ghosts. Our pie safe, singed from sparks, the rocking chair silent. Mary Grace and I stood with arms linked, each a baby on the hip. Jephthah pointed and said, "Hot, hot." William stood apart like a statue. No sign of horse or hobbled cow.

"Do you want to inspect more—the remains of barn or out-buildings?" Samuel asked. I shook my head.

He insisted I ride on the horse with Miriam in my arms; he carried my smelly Jephthah on his shoulders. Mary Grace sat behind me, balancing a half bag of flour and her shoes. William walked alongside, bundled with extra clothes. Before we set off, everyone put on another layer that had been crammed in the safe, on top of what we'd already added for last night. We trooped on Rawley Springs Turnpike to Samuel's house. He promised to retrieve what provisions remain in the pie safe. I don't see when, not with others to tend. If someone pilfers, it's theirs. A pittance.

What a sight through the Valley's haze of fog and smoke: the red brick Coffman house, standing whole! Frances fed us nearly as soon as we walked in, her girl Esther working alongside. No appetite for me, but water to guzzle. Not room enough, alongside their own. Their John and Jacob are big, compared to my William. But they put us in the parlor, a carpet to sleep on. How long and where next? My answer hasn't changed. I can't put my young ones outside. Miriam has the runny nose; Jephthah's bottom afire. If someone had an out-building to spare—half a granary. William's sneezing eases, but his watery eyes continue. He sleeps sitting against the wall; his head slips to his chest. He reminds me of Simon as never before.

I thought sleep would come—a safe warm house—the dark of night hidden by walls. But when I closed my eyes, I saw hills on fire. I couldn't still my mind. What will we do? All my big ones gone. Fitful. First on my right side, then the left. Peter! Up for the chamber pot again. Not till the next afternoon, when Mary Grace watched Jephthah, could I sleep.

Frances has most everything. This house. Lye and grease, enough soap to scrub off soot, hops for yeast. Their butter and lard gone—left sitting in the shade by mistake. Her parents lost all, but for an old log house on the north side of the road. Otherwise, they'd be here, rightfully, in the parlor. All buildings on the south side, burned. But the north side of Rawley Springs—men refrained. Not even barns. No sense to be had.

When the soldiers came here, they told Frances to remove what she wanted saved. She and her Esther worked, frantic. That part, familiar to my own. But the men changed their minds: the brick house not to be blown up.

I never thought to barter. But Frances whispered, "Samuel gave gold pieces." The men still shot his dozen sheep and one remaining hog. Butchered them in the yard—the family made to watch. Samuel's cattle driven off earlier by a squad of men in uniform. His best horse ridden away, too, just like our Nimble. Even their three-year-old colt, broken and gentle to ride, was taken.

"What did we do?" I asked. "Any of us."

Frances shook her head, lips tight.

That night, Samuel said a Union man, a higher-up by the name of Meigs, had been killed near Dayton. Maybe the start. Three Rebels, dressed as Union, had surprised him. That Meigs, said to be extra good with maps; he knew the whole Valley. That surprise attack—a dastardly trick—brought outrage and retaliation. The Union general, this Sheridan man, considered it an act of murder and blamed community folks for harboring guerrillas. Then that Custer man—the same one said to be responsible for the death of Davy Getz—ordered to burn houses within five miles of Dayton.

"Simon never mentioned a Meigs fellow," I said. "Never said anything about doing him wrong."

"Destroy all, to atone for the one," Frances said. "Not you nor I killed that Meigs man. But all of this killing—how is it *not* outright murder?"

"Houses not to be burned," I said. "They didn't ask if a Rebel boy came from mine."

"Of course not," Frances soothed.

"No different than the Rodes family long ago," Samuel said. "Their house burned, the daughter fleeing with a sister in her arms. No worthy answer as to why." He got up to add enough wood to last the night.

I still couldn't tell about the butcher knife. I spent another restless night on the floor. Murder on my mind. All of us, somebody's traitors, one way or another. Fault to go around.

The next day my milk still hadn't come back strong; Miriam cried out. I tried bits of bread with her. Mary Grace wandered around barefoot, her eyes as red as William's. As mine. All of us stay reduced. Jephthah screamed when I wiped his bottom. But we ate bread with sweet jelly. Lacking sugar, Frances had boiled her cider down until it thickened by itself.

Another blessing: my undergarments stayed tight. I offered small payment for our eats, this roof. But Frances shook her head and said not to unstitch coins just yet.

She asked her Jacob and John to take all the youngsters outside, except for Miriam. "Look for missed walnuts—all of you. The wooden basket by the door."

Samuel stayed at the table and told of more disputing stories. "Some claim the order to burn houses was stopped. Another Union officer intervened and told Custer to take able-bodied men as prisoners instead. But soldiers, already on the loose, burning. Not about to stop."

"How many houses burned?" I asked.

"Maybe twenty: Benjamin Wenger's, Abraham Blosser's house and barn." Samuel named more and counted on his fingers. He spends his days riding to check on one family or another.

"But you say our farm might have been first?"

"Or last," he said. "From Dayton west to Coakleytown and north to Dale Enterprise. Or opposite way about. Hard to say how organized—the men with torches. Some reports of running and trampling at random in ragged columns. Shavers may be the only mill left. Hard to know the whole."

"Margaret Rhodes talked the men out of burning," Frances said. "Only given fifteen minutes. Didn't you say, Samuel? But another horse, two more saddles, bridles, all her cattle and sheep, gone."

Samuel nodded. "The North trusts no one." He held his hot drink with two hands; his forehead stayed furled. "The other side, no better. Dayton citizens a hotbed. Maybe no one counts as civilians anymore. No matter whence the order comes or who carries them out, no one thought the North would stoop—houses of innocents!"

I never thought to see Samuel fighting the bitter taste. We have no church meeting tomorrow, not with soldiers milling about on meetinghouse grounds.

But then Samuel looked straight at me and said, "There's talk of wagons going north; they'll protect Union sympathizers."

I stiffened and pulled Miriam close. "Not for us." Frances's eyes stayed on me. "Put my children in the North's hands? Not with two babies." I shrank back on my chair. The room deathly quiet without the youngsters. "My parents brought me here, this Virginia land; buried close by. No wagon, no horse." I looked up of a sudden. "Where would we go?"

Samuel studied his nails, but Frances said without blinking, "It would be hard."

"My brother, too far away," I said. "Miles and miles. I don't know how. Gabriel said he'd return Simon's body when over and done." I stopped, then hurried to say, "Andrew promised to come back; Joseph, too."

* * *

William and I walked to Harrisonburg to get our pass. What Samuel said we needed. His big boy, John, came along, too. Men stood about, some in uniform. Tents for a camp. Only a few women. Some men in Dunker hats. The official told me where to put my X. I bristled. He called loudly to another when I signed my name. I wanted to spit. Thought to be dumb, a woman wearing the plain garb, alone but for a boy.

Tomorrow we'll go again—my four. Mary Grace says tomorrow will be October 8th. I think she's jumped ahead. I tell my two oldest, "We have no choice." They stumble outside; later, they sit silent through our supper. "You must eat," I say. I pick at food, give extra to Jephthah.

Frances says their John is up and down, whether to go or stay. But he has his pass. If only Frances—she could bring her Esther, a companion for Mary Grace. But Frances keeps her lips tight, except to say, "We've been spared—our barn, this house. I stay to help others. My parents."

"So far as we know, our people remain at Chambersburg," Samuel says. "Things thought to have settled down there."

"But we don't know particulars—my brother," I blurt. "No word of Joseph's whereabouts— Andrew—not heard from."

"Nobody has certainties." Samuel speaks softly and shuts his eyes.

I've become a bother. They took us in; their children made room. Mary Grace says it will be four days and five nights. I can't say.

"Do fires still burn?" I ask.

"Farther south," Samuel says, "we're led to believe. Authorities say for civilians to go north." Every other sentence of his, full of instruction. *The Potomac River.* Follow the lead.

We have no choice. I wasn't privy to any back-and-forth between Frances and Samuel, but when she makes up her mind, she shuts the door.

Last night, I asked if she'd heard aught of Genevieve. "Such a long time ago—the three of us. Would she and George pick up?"

Frances shrugged. "Hard to turn about and give allegiance to the North after ugliness."

"Hard to set aside such inner warmth. Grape jam and beating on carpets," I said.

We're going north—my four and I. Said to be many, many others. Some of our kind. Not room here; not this parlor. I can't impose with winter coming. No unused building, not to speak of, not set up with heat.

We have our pass: a small slip of paper with my name. I applied for a horse; the Union man could only promise an open wagon. Samuel offered their carriage with the partial top. It pulls shut on one side for inclement weather; two short benches and a place to sleep between.

I can't accept. "I don't know what Simon would say."

"You must," Frances says.

I grip Samuel's arm, but he looks away.

Betsey — West Virginia, October 1864

Poppa had stayed strong all summer; he did not need to keep to his Bitters. And last week Tobias helped him load the plow on the wagon, so the man at Brookside could straighten the blade. But Poppa came back, vexed by the blacksmith. His lips turned down when he said to Mother, "*Schlappichi Arrewet*."

Mother clicked her teeth. "That man again; still not straight."

"Only sharper," Poppa said.

But this week, when a stranger slept in the barn one night, Poppa called him a shifty one. Our sudden cold nights and smoke from the chimney must have beckoned this Hector to come in our lane. Poppa invited him inside for supper but did not hide his scowl. Shifty must be worse than shoddy. Hector quarreled when not allowed to bring his saddlebag inside. He had very blue eyes, but Mother called them cold. His mustache hung crooked, and his beard did not look soft and bushy like Poppa's. He stared at the shotgun that now hangs on two heavy pins fastened to a ceiling joist.

This man was not anywhere near to being like Joseph or Isaac. Ever since Tobias is fifteen, he is allowed seconds on meat, but Hector scooped up everything left in the pan. And when done eating, he burped and got up fast. Poppa held up his hand and said, "Halt." We had not said our prayer yet.

"Dash it all!" Hector said, but sat again, his top lip higher at one corner.

The next morning, he came in from the barn and pulled a fancy watch with a gold chain from an inner pocket. He took spit and wiped with his finger—his nails jaggedy—holding the watch at angles and squinting. "Used to trade in these parts—a wagon for hauling," he said.

"Long trips?" Poppa asked.

"The big Valley," he said.

"Where 'bouts?" Poppa asked.

The shifty one grinned and said, "A buckskin, but heading for Missouri."

"We hear the war came hard to Virginia," Poppa said.

"Not my problem," Hector said. Then he turned to me, closed an eye, and scrunched his mouth. "Purty face like that, you should come with me. Be my cook." My cheeks felt hot when he added, "I'll slick you up extra."

I stayed close to Mother until he left.

"He only meant to tease," she said later. "Maybe scare a bit."

But Poppa scowled again and called Hector a *Schtinker* and said his rude manners were a bad example for the little boys. Poppa likes to call us saplings and says big folks can bend us one way or another. Even with Tobias, if he does not answer fully when spoken to, Poppa looks around to all of us and says, "Do not prevaricate, not any of you."

Later when Tobias and I were sent out to see if any ears on the stalks had been missed, I asked, "What is a buckskin?"

"It means Virginia." He carried the bag as we walked up and down rows side by side.

"But that state brings us good friends," I said, "not a mischief-maker. I did not like Hector."

"Poppa might have meant worse—a *Lumpekaer*!"

"Up to no good and causing trouble?"

Tobias shrugged. "Maybe. Or a rowdy, running from the law."

"He did not help us one lick," I said. "Nothing like our friends from afar."

Tobias did not say more, because Poppa and Lydia came with another bag to help us. It was cold and windy, and my mittens were soaked already from the wet husks and stalks.

* * *

"Sei schtill!" Poppa said on the Saturday evening after Hector's overnight stay. The three little boys shrieked as Lydia and I chased them after their bath. They are allowed to run naked once a week, but sometimes they splash to get out of the tub, and we have a time settling them while putting on their sleep garments. Gideon is as fast as ever, now that his arm has healed with only a small crook.

Mother added, "Be not so loud! Your Poppa's nerves will go to the bad again."

I promised the boys we could say the ABC rhyme that Isaac taught us, if they cooperated better. "Not one extra peep," I said, a finger to my lips.

Finally, they were all dried and warm, except for wet hair. "Noah, you say the very first line in our Dutch. Then Levi, the next line in the German, the way Isaac taught. Gideon, you get to say both lines in English."

"*Aw, bay, tsay*," Noah said and clapped his hands.

I nodded to Levi. "*Die Katze sitzt im Schnee*," he said.

"ABC. The cat sits in snow," Gideon said.

"Good. Now take turns the same way with the last two lines," I said. "Remember to be mysterious, Noah."

"*Der Schnee geht weck*," he said. I held up my hand to stop him from saying more.

"*Die Katze liegt im Dreck*," Levi said and giggled.

"The snow goes away." Gideon wiggled his body like he was melting. "The cat lies in *mud*," he nearly shouted.

We all laughed, but not too loud.

Noah started again, "*Aw, bay, tsay*," but I shook my head and did my best to look stern.

Gideon said, "I miss Joseph."

"I do, too," I said. "We wish good men would come again, but we are glad they came once at least and could stay a whole week."

Our day ended happy, but the next morning when we all met for church, our bishop, Daniel, sounded extra fervent, speaking of martyrs in the Old Country. "We do not know who or where next."

I did not know the war had started bad again, but it was not until nighttime that we older children learned what was what. "Folks suffer in the Virginia state that we used to be part of—Johnny's home area," Poppa said. "We do not know the extent, but word has come that some might not have food." He shook his head slowly. "Their crops lost, destroyed in the war. We are to mourn with those who mourn."

"Mack and Muck, too?" I asked.

"Their families, most likely," Mother said. "Kin of Joseph and Isaac, too."

"All of that same Valley," Poppa said. "Remember how Isaac spoke of the beauty?"

"We never hear," I said, "whether Joseph found his brother. We barely got to meet and play games."

"Yes, we miss them," Poppa said. "So much we do not know—perhaps never will. Our crops are not the best, what with the late start, but without Isaac and Joseph—*Lord, have mercy!* Not to have grain—how our God can allow such—we may never understand. Sun and rain fall on the just and the unjust. But no sense can be seen."

"Did Hector steal from our pantry?" Lydia asked.

"Goodness, Child!" Mother said. "Whatever gave you that notion?"

Mary chimed in. "He did not always look straight. And he looked at Betsey with one eye."

Poppa and Momma looked surprised, and I blushed to hear others talk about me. I squeezed Mary to me; sometime I will tell her about winking.

"Children, you must not make up stories," Mother said.

"Hector looked long at your rifle, Poppa," Tobias said.

"I saw it, too," I added.

"We cannot say what gives a man his nature," Poppa said. "I have not walked in Hector's shoes. But your mother and I will protect you, if any of you are ever in danger. We are to be kind to people like Hector, even if they are a different sort."

"What if someone throws a lighted torch on one of our fields?" Tobias asked.

"So it is you, too?" Poppa said. "Overhearing and taken in by the times." He looked to the rafters. "Oh Lord, in your mercy."

"We have been blessed—no armies coming and going for a long time," Mother said. "Not since that dreadful start. We cannot say why the innocent are sometimes harmed."

"Can we say the prayer tonight that Joseph and Isaac taught us?" I asked. "We can pretend they say it with us."

"Of course," Poppa said. "When we pray, we can name all those who have stopped in—one stripe or another. Pray that they are safe and warm tonight. Mister, too." He hesitated, but said, "Hector, too."

"Can we say Mary Grace's name?" I asked. "Joseph has a sister who goes by both names back in Virginia."

"Of course," Poppa said again. "Many people need extra prayers right now."

"Enough to go around," Mother said, smiling.

That night we stayed downstairs for our prayers, but like always, Poppa said his usual part. "We pray for our enemies, those who mistreat us, for they do not realize what they do." When we were done, he dabbed at his eyes. I forgot and stared, but he said, "God is good."

We made other changes that night, too. We girls dressed for bed in the loft before Tobias came up to sleep on his tick. Mother only said, "We have so little room; our walls keep shrinking. When you girls get older, we will accommodate again."

* * *

The next morning, we found another visitor. Tobias and I were carrying firewood to our porch; the frosty white surprises us when it comes overnight on trees and tips of old corn stalks. But farther back in the woods we found a doe on the ground with her baby, the little one quivering to stand. Tobias ran to fetch Poppa while I stayed to keep watch. The baby stood wobbling, staring straight back at me. Sometimes an ear flickered.

But the mother was dead! Poppa thought an arrow. "Someone might have been hunting while we were gone to church yesterday, but decided not to drag the carcass out. Now the little one—an orphan."

I stopped myself from blurting Hector's name but asked, "Who did it?"

"We do not know who all walks in our woods," Poppa said.

"But the baby, how will it know to do?" I asked.

"Nature fends," he said.

How helpless we stood.

"Fetch a bit of milk and then finish your carrying," Poppa said, as quiet as a prayer.

That afternoon I went out to check. *Still there!* I did not dare get too close, but such a beautiful soft-brown. I could not see any scars. When Poppa and Tobias went to chore, they took a bigger pan to leave extra milk.

"Still beside the mother," Tobias said to me, once back, his voice soft like Poppa's had been. "But stronger legs."

"The fawn may survive on her own," Poppa said. "Most of the spots, gone off."

"For certain?" I asked.

"No, we cannot say. Some do not make it, but most will. We can only steady the young one's start; then it will run away."

"But the momma?" I asked.

"The fawn will know when ready to leave," he said. "All a part of growing. Then we will bury the momma. Perhaps near to Frank. Would you like that? There is room."

Esther — Shenandoah Valley, mid-October 1864

My sight grows fuzzy. Blurs of lines up high amidst scorched trees; Mary Grace says they're soldiers. She takes my hand to steady; it should be the other way. She keeps track of days. We're part of the train going north, stretching farther than we can see ahead or behind. I never thought to be a refugee—no home in my own Virginia! Fleeing like my men. Our mountains still cradle, but they're overtaken by wreckage. This is what Frances said General Grant had wanted: crows to carry their own provender while flying over Virginia.

When we left the Coffmans's, Frances and I lingered. I fought the sobs—her embrace. That last morning they sent their son, John, for certain. He walks with friends—sixteen and bigger, forced to dodge because of his size. I protested again, taking Samuel's carriage. He said we'll stay drier; he still has his big wagon. I promised to return the carriage as good as new. He nodded but got up from the table and went outside.

I said to Frances, "If your man retrieves the rocking chair or pie safe, give to someone who has need. The boys can make new when we come back."

She stared long, but then nodded, wordless.

To get to the starting place we five had to crowd in the carriage—Frances surprised me with extra bags stitched—one for the two big ones, one for the two little ones, and one for my lonesome. Samuel and John walked along beside us, soothing their horse with its heavy load. Once there, Samuel bid his son farewell and rode off on his horse; another visit to another family.

We were given a dusty brown horse for the journey. Mary Grace thought Nag a good name, but I insisted we call him Star. William says he's a very slow star, but no one hurries on this train. We commence a mile at best, and then stop. Someone's wagon has broken down, or there's delay on some other account. A sick horse, another man checking passes. Who would choose this train if set on mischief? The South has other interests. At times we hear cannon fire and see bright flashes of light in the hills. They say that's blasting powder.

Sometimes soldiers gallop past—perhaps an urgent message, an order for someone to do such and such. Other cavalry men—the North—ride along beside us. I don't mention Early to my children, but Frances had said his men on horses still cause trouble.

We travel in the company of these others. Strangers, most all. Some rough talkers. Most, given rickety wagons. Travelers with large families, given covered wagons. When either youngster gets off to exercise Jephthah, they stay away from the groaning—two wagons ahead with a bad smell. What if the North had stolen your wagon and you ended up riding on it again? Who gets to keep it for good? We don't want Star, except for now.

My sleep is poor. I see Peter, clutching his new haversack. No official letter ever came. I picture Simon, weeping to see ashes of his barn and house. He might never find us on this train, even if he went wagon to wagon. This is our new house. What if Gabriel brought remains and found no one home? He could bury the body and leave a marker.

They feed us gruel, morning and evening. No taste to speak of: maybe oats, mostly water. We take of it; we daresn't waste. One night, nothing but black bread. Mary Grace nibbled. Nothing like the good eats at Frances's table; she must have stowed salt somewhere. One good thing now: William's breathing goes better, out from the heavy cast of smoke. Not nearly enough food for a growing boy. He might stoop for pork—these conditions—but we know not to expect. Peter said the South had what they called cush or slosh; he thought maybe beef, maybe bacon.

My milk came better the last day at Frances's place. Now if Miriam finishes sucking or falls asleep, I let Jephthah take. I have to scold if he clamps with his teeth. William stares, then jerks away. No one needs to know. Another thing on the sly: I check my coins when no one's looking. One feels loose, but I keep tabs.

William and I take turns at the reins. Sometimes I doze from my unsound nights. Mary Grace, as strong as I, but no practice with an ornery horse. I have had to give Star a wormy apple—from what Frances sent. When near to dark, William must forage for Star. He doesn't say where, but he follows others. Sometimes they find hay.

William begs to walk beside the carriage; he tires from bouncing over ruts and wants to walk ahead with John and the big boys. I won't have it. If he got lost and couldn't find us— I can't let him out of sight, not more than necessary. John and these other youths say they'll walk all the way. They sleep in a bunch, too. We have no room.

I try to reason with William. "You'll be less hungry and thirsty if you sit the duration."

His comeback is quick. "Easier for Star if I walk."

"Walk then, but only till you know the babes are likely to wake. Or stay nearby—check back when we stop. We might have need. Help for Mary Grace with Jephthah, or taking the reins." I grab his arm. "William, don't leave us!"

He looks twice his age but skinny. "Yes, Ma." His voice dull.

When we stop at night, Jephthah says, "Uncle! Uncle's farm?"

"No, Child, not yet."

I hum a tune for Miriam in her sleep box but make up my own words, too. "*Jesus watches in the night.*" Or sometimes "*Jesus loves you in the night.*"

The third night I slept better and woke stronger to say, "It's only for a time. Not leaving Virginia for good." Mary Grace put her head on my shoulder.

Word is, we'll be required to take an oath of citizenship at Martinsburg. I'll have to decide then for sure. I don't know who to ask. Where to look for trust. Any talk of where we are, how far we've come, could be of help. I never thought to have Andrew write things down; Samuel gave William sketchy notes for parts of the way. If we mingle during long stops, I listen close and tell the big youngsters to pay attention, too. "Listen for a party bound for Chambersburg; we could latch on. Anyone going farther north."

Some think we do twenty miles a day. No one rightfully knows. But some of our kind are sure of their next step: "Going to Elkhart County." That's Indiana—the family with the elderly grandpop who has to be helped down and up again from the bucket to do his business. Those folks seem friendly; say they have kin there.

A younger woman with lazy eye and five small girls says she means to hire a hack for the last part, but doesn't say where she'll find such. I don't want to lose sight of her. Some say they'll head for Lancaster County; that's Pennsylvania but not where Chambersburg is exactly. John had said he might go there with friends, but I don't see him now to talk. Others have family in Ohio and make it sound like heaven.

William hears talk of railroad cars, but I shake my head. "Too early to know."

Yesterday, Mary Grace surprised me, her black eyes steady. "Will Joseph come looking?" she asked. "The big river."

My mind took leaps; I had no notion. "Child, he went to Maryland. I don't see how—he might have gone on to Illinois. Remember what Margaret and Frances said—"

"But he told me, working another's field somewhere, someone might spot him and recognize."

"He didn't know this would happen, or know of this train."

"He might guess and come looking. Meet us."

I stared long at starlings scavenging a burned field.

She pressed my arm.

I shook my head. "I can't promise what I don't know. Joseph—more than likely working or still fleeing—he can't come looking," I said, my lips aquiver. If only Frances had come. She would know distances, could give better answers. I grabbed my daughter's hand, held tight. "For now, we follow the wagon ahead. Our slow Star. Some ragtag stranger might show the road hence. Frances said to watch for pointers." I dared not say: we are at the mercy.

A few minutes later, Mary Grace brought it up again. "We'll have to cross somewhere."

I nodded but pinched my lips tight like hers. I never wanted to see the mighty Potomac. Not with Simon; less so now. Not after Peter's chant, "*All quiet along the Potomac—*"

The nights stay long, filled with rustlings. I use my hands for a pillow, tucked behind my head or cheek, one side or the other. Sometimes, footsteps right outside our buggy. Other times, faraway calls; men yelling in the distance. The groans are bad at night, sometimes louder than the call of owls. William and Mary Grace sleep squished. Frances gave two extra blankets for under benches. Jephthah won't stay curled in his wooden box but thrashes. His bottom, red again. I try to wedge him better in the dark, for fear he'll roll out to the ground.

One night, William slept in front, more room but subject to a sharp wind. His cheeks looked raw the next morning, and he coughed till he barked. Some folks with extra children crawl under their open wagon to sleep, searching for warmth. Other times the train keeps moving, well after dark. We never know.

On the coldest nights, soldiers build fires to give warmth until down to embers. Then we resign ourselves and trudge back to our makeshift beds. The soldiers laugh about filching logs from some poor farmer's split rail fence. Last night we stopped early, bogged down by a long stretch of deep ruts from rain. Star's breathing, loud and labored from plodding. Twice now, some of our kind have gathered at the fire to sing; John and that group of sixteen-year olds lead out. They never show weariness. Mary Grace begged, so we walked over, careful not to drag blankets in mud. Jephthah likes to sit close to the fire, his small body hunched. He throws up his arms at sudden sparks.

More soldiers crawled out of their tents again to listen. They call us all Dunkers, but it doesn't matter; we're reduced the same. Tonight, they asked for the same songs as the night before, partial to the hymn:

> When the storms of life assail, May Thy peace o'er all prevail;
> For a fortress Thou wilt be, When I can for safety flee.

The words and melody, haunting.

Last night I couldn't sing. My spirit bowed low—the long journey, Mary Grace's reminder of the river. But tonight, a woman settled on the ground beside me. Her head had the constant bob—I snatched peeks—but on she sang, her voice clear and steady. What tremor she lives with, I don't know. It hadn't claimed her courage.

My gaze wandered around the dim firelight of half-hidden faces. A soldier asked for the same verse again. He must need words, too—some solace, as nourishing as bread at Frances's house. Simon used to say the same thing happened when they sang in prison at Richmond. Guardsmen gathered round and asked for more, whether given to faith or not. Some small consolation.

> When my journey nears its close, Safely then may I repose;
> Feel Thy presence ever near, When the shades of night appear.

Something pulled inside tonight. Better to be sad and sing than sit with buried head.

> As I pass through death's dark vale, Then Thy love will me avail;
> And Thy rod and staff I'll see, To support and comfort me.

Pressing on, whate'er the path.

Maybe Peter remembered a wisp of church song when he drew his last breath. Maybe he chanced to think on home. And Simon—Gabriel didn't say if my man asked him to sing that last night. Heaven drawing nigh, gathering him in.

I must not despair. Mama's voice comes: *Your babes look to you.*

We stumble on with Star; our wagon lurches. Following whatever be ahead, not knowing. My youngsters and I. We'll do the best we can, even if it be a mighty river.

J. Fretz — Chicago, November 1864

Imagine my relief—that faint cry! A miracle! After holding Salome's hand and rubbing her feet—whatever gave comfort—we have our baby girl, born November 3rd at 8:30 p.m. We both liked the name Martha—my old flame might be amused. Such a head of dark hair. And such responsibility. To bring a little one—so tiny and helpless as to be frightening—into this world. Salome protests, but I say repeatedly: "Martha looks just like her mother." No denying those bright blue eyes.

Mary Ann has been a welcome help, scrubbing bedding and extra garments—I would have been at a loss—bringing food for the first week. Moses has moved his belongings over there for this month. Salome's milk has been slow to establish itself, but now mother and babe get along better. How I remember my mother nursing my younger siblings. By the time Susan was born, eleven years after me, the bond must have been effortless. Such a tender arrangement: the babe suckling from the mother.

While we rejoice with new life, I've been under the weather. Salome blames my declining health on overwork. I've had to limit my times of holding Martha, careful not to breathe on her directly. I rock her willow cradle and pretend to carry a tune. She holds perfectly still, eyes wide open, when I recite a psalm. But when my voice stops, she begins another crying spell. One of my favorite poems by William Blake, "*Three Things to Remember*," fits Martha's length of good humor.

> A Robin Redbreast in a cage
> Puts all Heaven in a rage.
> A skylark wounded on the wing
> Doth make a cherub cease to sing.
> He who shall hurt the little wren
> Shall never be beloved by men.

Such tender images!

But recently I've been brought up short: my disregard for Ross all these years. With our disagreements over the war's conduct, I saw him as a thorn.

In the last years, I sometimes avoided conversation or talked instead of marriage and house hunting. I hadn't known or asked much about his family; I only wanted to avoid his exuberance over blood-spilled victories. Occasionally, I stooped to pester him when things turned odious.

But the day I passed out cigars in the office—tempted to sneak a few puffs myself—Ross was unusually subdued. "Is she all right?" he asked.

"She's perfect," I said. What did he think? Me, unfit to sire?

His face looked pinched. "My Tommy—over four years now of lacking control; slow to develop use of his muscles." He gathered himself. "We'd hoped, given more time, he would be like others."

"Oh, I'm sorry," I said. "Very sorry. The outlook, you say—?"

He shook his head and turned back to his desk. I let the subject drop. Of course, Martha's first weeks give little indication of her future well-being, but I expect she'll be healthy, except for colds and such.

But before Ross left that afternoon, I shook his hand and said, "Give your wife my best regards."

I still feel like scum. Pious words from my pen, sent to folks at a distance, while mistreating a fellow human in the office. Not malicious, but allowing my frustration with those who remain enamored with war efforts to take priority. All along, Salome has tried to help me see hypocrisy, but I keep ignoring my inflated self. Now John Tillotson's words come back: "They who are in the highest places, and have the most power, have the least liberty, because they are the most observed." I'd always applied those words to Lincoln. But I have to admit: writing publicly brings scrutiny.

I looked at Martha afresh that evening: her fingers, feet, the miracle of each ear. I couldn't hide my wretchedness from Salome. She put an arm about my waist, patted my unruly cowlick, and said, "We never know what others may be saddled with, but we can seek to right our wrongs." I sought God's forgiveness also for letting lofty ideas transcend human kindness. I must walk more gently, not wound with neglect or disdain.

My life with Salome hasn't always been peaceful either. Last winter it was easier to accommodate each other—how often to use the fireplace in our room at Jacob's house. But now the bloom's off. "Too much heat isn't good for the baby," she says. I sit with extra blankets when I work late; my fingers are cold, as I dip for more ink.

But recently, a bigger row. I came home, weary as usual—constant pressure to balance the books. Just as predictably, Salome responded by saying I work too much. I lowered my head, determined not to rehash the same points. Martha wouldn't settle during our meal of leftover fried cornmeal mush with molasses; Salome was up and down with her. I left my plate and cup on the table and went upstairs to my office, the door only slightly ajar. I had to concentrate, find the best words to respond to a disputing subscriber in Ohio. Finally, Martha quieted and I put my head atop my folded arms on the desk, thinking a catnap would refresh before I started writing another article.

Not long after, I felt a hand on my shoulder. Salome worked her way onto my lap. We've shown less tenderness these weeks, except when drawn to our shared wonder at our precious infant. Salome ran her hands through my hair, patted the unruly spot again that insists on its upturn. Her hands caressed my cheeks, noting again my fine bone structure. I melted from her attention, secured a hand about her waist and rubbed her back.

"Put aside your pen tonight," she half-whispered. "You'll do just as well, aiming for a little less."

My body tightened. Her soft eyes took on the demand of her words. She knows better; I have no choice. If I don't keep at it through the night, I'll fall farther behind with *Herald of Truth.* I've pointed out before: she tends Martha all during the night. Her own sleep is interrupted. No different, my own. Of course, Salome can often nap during the day, but I've been getting by on six hours or less at night.

I've also reminded her, "I used to get up at two in the morning to take Father's produce to Philadelphia."

"You were only a boy."

"Home by ten at night, those times. I still know how to manage."

Sometimes when the lamp is still lighted in the office, Salome brings Martha to nurse close by. She knows my pattern: work awhile; lie down on the pallet to rest. When the floor boards make my bones ache, I get up and tackle work on another translation. It's pointless for Salome to try to change my habits. Overwork isn't evil.

I wish I'd never told her, though, about my father's father, John, dying at age forty-eight; his wife was left with eleven children—my father, the fourth son. That came up after Abe had been here, and we'd reminisced about folks back home. He had said something about one of grandfather's sons falling into a tanning vat and drowning.

"But that's what led Grandfather to move his family to Hilltop Township," I said. "Not all bad."

Abe persisted. "We can't deny, though, short life spans run in our family. Father was broken down at half a century."

"Pfft. That was from heavy work—stone and brick—*plus* farming," I said. "*If* you mean me, all I do is sit at a desk, push a pen, and add up numbers."

Abe let it go, but I wasn't surprised when Salome asked more when we were alone.

Some of what's hard right now is overcoming opponents of our newspaper. I don't know whether animosity spills from *what* we print, or from resistance to *any* innovation. Getting church folks to agree seems as elusive as finding national unity. After almost a year of this publishing effort, I understand why people in Virginia and Canada never went ahead with their own venture. There'd been talk years back, but folks couldn't agree how to go about it. "An *English* paper for *Mennonites?*" I should learn from my experience with Ross: don't demonize. But it's so obvious that preserving the status quo will only lead to extinction. Why can't other people see that?

I'll admit, though, I've sometimes wondered why I thought I was a good fit for newspaper work. I've even looked up Professor Fowler's advice, surprised again by some of his awkward wording. Two years ago when we met, I thought of him as fluent. But now a careless sentence stood out: "Cultivate a leisurely today enjoying frame of mind." I knew what he meant: find enjoyment every day. Simple enough, but it's possible he wrote that because he thought I worked too hard already back then. Of course, he wouldn't have known in 1862 how much this war would worsen and make everything more complicated. None of us did.

Nor did I realize a month ago the extra burden that would come from losing my best proofreader. I had expected Salome to give extra attention to Martha these first weeks. There's no argument there, and I've been careful not to complain. I reason that by the end of the year, she'll have more time and things will go more smoothly again. As long as *she*—and the baby!—stay well. Then our Sunday afternoons can be restful. I can write in my diary, too, and catch up. This stuffed-up head and nose can't be permanent.

But as for her plea that night on my lap—*aim for less!*—I spurned her advice and said, "Get some sleep before Martha wakes again." She lowered her head and swiveled away. I can't let a baby disrupt my focus.

There's no question that serious church problems demand my full attention. Earlier in the fall, we heard of terrible conditions for our people in the state of Virginia—literally a "scorched earth." John M. Brenneman had received word directly from a Mennonite bishop in Staunton; the man wrote that General Grant's policy of making the area unfit for human habitation had been fully carried out. How could an awful tactic like that possibly be justified? Those folks need their crops as much as a baby needs a mother's milk.

Around the same time, I received a letter from a Landis fellow, a complete stranger, telling of some church buildings in the Shenandoah Valley that had been destroyed. Compared with those disasters, my personal struggles looked small. Since then, we've been using *Herald of Truth* to get the word out—innocent people suffer!—even though that's a small gesture against potential starvation with winter coming on. We still aren't sure if it's *safe* for anyone to take aid to Virginia.

The national news stories present equally stark glimpses. Blame rests with General Sheridan and his orders late in September. I was shocked to read his report: over 400 wagon loads of people, a sixteen-mile-long train, was sent out of the Harrisonburg, Virginia, area alone. Worse, this man—shown with a thick, dangling mustache—made it sound like he'd done people a favor!

I had read the numbers aloud to Salome: "Four hundred fifty barns burned."

"No!" She pressed a hand to her belly, large at the time. "In that Valley? And the man takes pride?"

"We know what *one* barn means. My father would have slept in his haymow if that would have prevented evil. And listen to this: a hundred *miles* of fence destroyed. I know all too well, the work of chopping wood, placing pieces criss-crossed, to enclose *one acre*."

"But crops—" Salome reached for my arm. "Those numbers. What did you say?"

I read again, slowly. "It's staggering. One hundred thousand bushels of wheat; half that many of corn. From *one* valley." Salome knows the endless work of cutting corn stalks, storing in shocks. "How is there not national condemnation about an operation like that?"

"How can anyone sleep at night," Salome added, "after carrying a torch and running through fields? Someone else's labor, up in smoke, because of you."

"To lose all—" I couldn't repeat Sheridan's words when he was first placed in charge of the Valley Campaign: "Poverty brings prayers for peace more surely and quickly than destruction of human life."

"Any farmer understands an occasional natural disaster," Salome said. "Father suffered a hail-storm once, but this—a winter's worth of food!"

"Wanton destruction—what does Henry Ward Beecher think when he hears of this? Does the popular clergy dare call it 'the will of God'?"

"People will starve. No one deserves . . ." Salome's voice quieted but kept its insistence. "How many stayed? Does it say?"

"Nothing exact. Only 'Some refugees are finding temporary residence with relatives in Maryland and Pennsylvania.' But"—I shook my head—"no one can pretend ignorance."

"And soldiers?" she asked. "How will they fend?"

"Said to have moved on. They won't bother that valley anymore."

I *had* to put more effort into conveying the enormity of the situation. Our readers *must* know. But nothing could stop my helpless rage from building—not only the *absence* of condemnation or blame for the generals. No! President Lincoln had expressed personal *admiration* to Sheridan for his endeavors in the Shenandoah Valley and singled him out for his work at a place called Cedar Creek. How could I not re-enter the same despair that had swallowed me after seeing prisoners at Camp Douglas? Devastation dealt to one group of humans as part of an effort to make a race of people free! Was there truly no other way to achieve fairness?

Over the years I've been up and down with this president, trying to put faith in his good sense. I thought human compassion would prevail, only to draw back in utter disgust with his approved methods, especially the old saw "The end justifies the means." That may bring absolution for some, but when harming civilians becomes a *necessary* part of ending the war—anything *not to fail*, as the North defines it—why can't Lincoln see? The North's war on savagery has become savage itself. The British didn't need to kill each other when they debated whether to stop the slave trade. They stayed civilized in their disagreements. How can this be our young grand nation, sinking so low?

And here I am, looking on this child of mine—this face of beauty in a world of ugliness. Her innocence can't wipe out others' crass opportunism. I live with both.

Five days after Martha was born, President Lincoln was re-elected with almost fifty-six percent of the popular vote. The general sentiment seems to be: it wouldn't have happened if this General William Tecumseh Sherman—what a name!—hadn't conquered Atlanta with his burning campaign. Already late in the summer, Sherman had started in the deep South, with Union men destroying mill towns where cotton yarn was made for use in Confederate uniforms, blowing up houses and public buildings in Atlanta—even damaging railroad lines.

Now folks seem to agree: when Sheridan followed Sherman's example with the same destructive tactics in Virginia, those two generals all but sealed Lincoln's re-election. Most Union soldiers stayed on the side of him remaining their Commander-in-Chief. It's only a small consolation that McClellan's racist campaign mustered a meager twenty-one votes in the Electoral College. But after the acclaim over Sherman's past destruction, he and his men keep marching on, eyes set on the coast, determined to completely demoralize the South.

Knowing all this, how could I vote? My questions hadn't gone away; they were compounded by people applauding. A government's hands deemed successful, *because* bloodied? Viciously so! Revenge justified by making *every* citizen in the South sound like a bushwhacker. Civilians painted as combatants. People's eyes must have glazed over from the hard realities of war.

It reminds me again of those conflicting stories about bushwhackers when I was a lad. We had dared to wonder, too: were those seven Doane boys the guerillas themselves? Or were they incensed by people *pretending* to be authorized by the War Department in the Revolutionary War? If today's southern bushwhackers hadn't been successful—their endless havoc of destroying supplies and sniping at Sheridan's men—would more violence have been *unnecessary*? How to assign fault? How strong the need to blame someone else!

My brother Abe went to the polls, as he said he would. But I couldn't. McClellan had said he'd end the war, but I didn't trust his capacity to govern and I despised his view of Negroes. He'd likely be as indecisive leading Congress as he'd been on the battlefield. About Lincoln, I was torn, thinking him *more likely* to carry through with emancipation and pass an amendment outlawing slavery. But how could I ignore the blood shed? The endless drafts? The convenient overlooking of proportion?

But his enemies, disgusting to the end! So desperate to get Lincoln out of office, they used subterfuge to scare people into thinking Republicans had a secret plan to move beyond emancipation and support complete *integration* of the races. Many folks see allowing blacks and whites to intermarry as the worst! Stephen Douglas had used a similar tactic years ago during the debates, when he tried to frighten people by saying Lincoln favored the *intermingling* of races. The worst fear for some! I still side with Frederick Douglass's view: people of different races get along better when they have more everyday interactions.

Maybe I'll never put faith in a politician again. That wouldn't be the worst thing. Ross says I'm too much of an idealist. He thinks it's inevitable that a candidate will have followers with mixed motives and methods. But government manipulation—compromise used wrongly—still repulses me. No one should be taken advantage of: not Negroes, not civilians. I try to square my actions with what I espouse in the *Herald*: God's Kingdom is based on peaceful living. Even when Salome and I don't agree—aim for less! we still hold together because we share a larger goal.

And when Mennonites resist our newspaper, I also must maintain hope, somehow. What alternative is there? We've found enough readers to expand an issue from two pages to four. That's heartening! And when some readers warn that too much cooperation with others will lead to *everyone* being absorbed by lukewarm Protestant groups, I see that for what it is: another scare tactic. Religious folks aren't exempt from stooping to low methods.

Maybe my stubbornness is good. I must stay optimistic, even when discouraged. The words of the prophet Isaiah—what was foretold for Jesus—still inspire me: "*How beautiful upon the mountains are the feet of him that bringeth good tidings, that publisheth peace.*" That gives me courage, even when my cough lingers and I'm off to a late start with another issue.

David — Shenandoah Valley, December 1864

We stayed; now we have no recourse. Part of the remnant, walking this vale of tears. I dread the long winter nights ahead. Late yesterday afternoon I watched the sky's usual dark blue, but for a strip of swirling light near the horizon. Near dusk today, we have the reverse: stormy near the surface and lighter in the vast canopy above.

Our house was spared fire; for that we give thanks. But we have little to do: shell another ear of corn by hand, tend our thoughts. Turn the kernels once more for better drying. My cooper's tools, stolen so long ago, I hardly remember. Who would want a new barrel when they have nothing to put therein?

"If we can survive, yet a few more months—" How often dare I say that to Abigail? Not that warmer weather, by itself, will bring an end to troubles.

One time Delilah said, "When the grass grows again, we may graze like cattle."

"Not waste dandelions on wine, come spring," I replied.

Abigail says naught about my straggly beard, my long face. What is there to tease about? Sorrow is our teacher. Life does not ask: *What would you like from me today?* No, life wields the ax. *This is where you need to be brought low. You with your sufficient knowhow. Give me your sons, your leader and stickler for unity, your stumbling faith.*

The internal buffeting these months has been the hardest. Countless stories of burning that circle about and come round yet again. The pine-tar torch, an instrument of war. The *Rockingham Register* gave an accounting: thirty houses burned in that county alone. Dayton spared, but not the surrounding countryside. How many nights did families sleep outdoors? If sleep came. Some had carried day beds outside in advance. Some went back into burning houses or barns and tried to outen flames. One woman poured a full crock of milk. Others stomped on flames with their feet. Still others raked with a fury, determined to keep embers from the next shock.

It's a wonder that people can steady their minds. Sometimes the retelling brings healing for me; other times it reignites fury. One story stays stuck:

soldiers put torch to a house. But before rushing away, they warned the two sisters who were keeping watch over children that they would return later. If the women put out the fire, the soldiers would kill them and all their offspring. But worse yet, when the husband of one of the women came back from hiding his horses and heard of this threat, he was beside himself. The women had put out the fire. The man restarted the fire and burned down his own house. Stories and their variations, around and around.

Those of us at Flat Rock escaped the worst, but we fear for sufficient resources to survive the winter. Only a few have stomach to voice thoughts of beginning anew in this blackened area. My fellow ministers and our deacon headed for relatives in the north. J. M. said the wagons in General Sheridan's train arrived at New Market after dark, with rain pouring down. The next day, more folks joined the thousands already started.

For days, we had gone through a row with Delilah. "Brother and Sister Neff and their dwarf son will take you," I said.

"I belong here with you and Mother," she said.

"We need you kept safe. Your mother has spoken with Sister Neff. Go."

Delilah shook her head and returned her attention to stories from the *Martyrs Mirror.* She read aloud about Jan Jans and the basket escape through the window—her favorite of those Anabaptists, persecuted during the Reformation.

The next morning, when she admitted to poor sleep, I tried again. "Have you thought better of it?"

"It would not be better!" she argued, her countenance dark. "You must think I will eat too much," she said, her eyes cast down.

"Oh, my daughter. Never." In truth, I thought perhaps the Lord required our last child.

"You tempt me! Like what Perpetua faced."

"Perpetua?" What had our daughter read now? "Tempt you?" I looked to Abigail, but she stood wringing her hands in her aprons.

"From the third century," Delilah said. "Her father, a pagan, came to her in prison and begged her to deny she was a Christian."

"I never asked anything of the sort," burst from me.

"But to save my life, you are asking me to deny my love for you and Mother. That would be unchristian. Besides, survival is not assured, one way or another."

"Nothing of the sort! What do you make of me?" I made no effort not to glare. "Your chances of survival . . . would increase, though," I said, my words trailing.

"I will not depart to save myself." Delilah's homely face convulsed with trembling. "Perpetua would not renounce, not even for the sake of her child.

She was killed by the sword—both she and her friend Felicitas who carried an unborn child. Perpetua's slave stayed true also."

"Oh, my child," I said, rising to wrap an arm about her. "You must not read so much of terror. It may cause nightmares. Or sow unsound thought."

She did not reject my arm; nor did she seek to reciprocate. But that night Delilah told the full story to Abigail and me of a large group of Christians at a place called Carthage in North Africa. She hugged the thick book to her chest. "They were persecuted by Romans; the crowds wanted blood. Some of the martyrs were thrown before wild beasts. But an early church leader, Augustine, preached four sermons about this woman Perpetua—how she was manly as a man. How they were to look up to her for courage."

Delilah had her say; we listened. We live with a mix of fear and relief. I do not know what sense to make of suffering. But we are far better off with Delilah staying—we made that clear—even though her cough has come back with a vengeance. The bark of holly root no longer effective; only the sassafras bush offers soothing. If only we had a drop of honey! If only she did not read so much.

We could start every other sentence with the words "if only." But we are not starving. Abigail's cheeks have lost their plumpness; I picture the face of her mother when her jowls sagged at the end. But we have a portion of flour from last summer's wheat. Those with torches did not find our corn, although the yield was poor. Once a week we allow ourselves enough cornmeal for cakes. I have set up the hand mill on a barrel in my woodshed—the mortar and pestle too tiring—and we take turns grinding. My arm strength is not what it was a month ago. The meal is coarser, the cakes flatter. But for a day or two, we consider ourselves blessed to have a fresh, familiar taste.

Each of us eats one potato every day—white or sweet. A month ago, I spread them out behind the house and counted: over 500 good-sized ones. They do not keep as usual; Abigail says I handled too much. I cannot take on another troubling mystery: what makes one potato hold firm, while another rots? But I predict: our potatoes will not stay edible through March. We recall counting and dividing eggs among us two years ago, but we are not accustomed to dwelling on food to this extent. I never thought to be without. But at every meal we must eat sparingly. Only when we become certain the potatoes will spoil early, will we dare to eat more than one per day.

Our hens are a problem, too; they do not lay properly—more feisty than usual—for we have little to feed them. Scraps are rare, because I eat everyone's gristle. And with colder weather, there is little our hens can grub for. A month ago, a fox scoured the area; we lost eggs *and* hens. Someone else must have finished off that fox, for we have not had further trouble of that sort.

If someone knew how to prepare fox meat or dog, I might partake. But the thought of possum or raccoon turns my stomach. I see traps again on Winfield's land. When I hear an animal crying, I am sorely tempted. But if I release the hold, then what? I would likely be accused. All of earth's creatures have dwindled, even our squirrel population. Delilah's hands stay strong enough to twist a neck, if the three of us can avoid sharp teeth and manage to entrap. We pretend a squirrel stew is the same as a rabbit stew.

But coffee! I never thought to be deprived of my morning drink. Delilah's sassafras tea makes a poor substitute—worse than nothing, to my way of thinking. Nor can I tolerate using parched wheat. Instead, I take ripe acorns—plentiful in the woods—wash them in their shells, and let them dry until they are parched. When they open on their own—with a hard knock of encouragement—I remove the shells and roast what remains. Sometimes I sneak a little fat into the pot. How routine our thanks used to be. What strange pastimes now: tending the acorns, shelling another ear of corn, checking the acorns again, sometimes cracking a hull to break open the secret inside. The same activities as yesterday, but my women have not passed judgment.

We have little contact with the outside world. Our unreliable governance has moved from bad to worse. No full investigation into Johnny's death ever took place. The Rockingham County sheriff said he made his report to the governor. That may or may not be true. It is common to hear: the shooting was ordered by someone higher up in the military. No one seems inclined to inquire further. I have finally come to see the pointlessness—clinging to anger toward Johnny; he did what he thought best when he went into the North's territory. But there are days that I still gnaw against those who plotted or carried out murder. Oh, I know; nothing useful is accomplished by maintaining grievance against them either.

As for warfare, the North let down its guard after the days of burning, thinking themselves victorious. But true to Jubal Early's reputation—J. M. calls him "a wounded rattlesnake"—he scrounged up help from men at Petersburg, near to Richmond. Assisted by our mountain topography that still confuses newcomers, those leftover Rebels surprised the North again. Sheridan had to return from farther north and rally his Federals.

But by the middle of October—the Battle of Cedar Creek may have been a turning point—both sides wearied of our Valley. Nothing left to sustain soldiers, for one thing. The risks lessened for us to go about, as did the pilfering. But what worthy business was there to take care of anymore? Money had gone from scarce to scarcer. The Confederate currency had been worthless already long ago, when Rebel soldiers handed out bluebacks as bankrupt payment for goods taken. But a month ago, we knew without doubt: if we *were* accosted while out and about, no effort would be made to stop or punish any crimes committed.

Now it seems safe to think the war is nearly over. But it would not surprise me—this may sound strange—if we lost our exemption. Newspapers still print rumors about us, and public opinion stays heated against us. If authorities do not honor our scruples, they could force us—my women know I might have to go—into some kind of auxiliary work. I still welcome any authorities to come to Flat Rock and see for themselves: we do not harbor men with fighting power on the premises. Nor have I ever allowed anyone to join our church group solely to escape the military draft. If I ever have to give written account, Delilah will help with the wording.

I am all that is left at Flat Rock—the weakest of us ministers. Before the others departed, I was appointed to preach, even though everyone knows I lack eloquence. Sometimes my words cause women to dab at their eyes. I make stark statements: "We are all we have. Look about. Our *Gemeine* is our most precious. If we are to survive, it will be together." How often can I say that, when I am not the only one teetering from doubt? One time I counseled against selfish prayers. "We need only look to our brother and sister of the darker race; they have suffered for years." Another time I chided: "If you cannot sing, at least hum the chorus."

At the same time, our Sunday mornings have taken on a looseness; I am not strict about rules. Abigail knows that I have never wanted to close our doors to honest questions. Or new understanding. I do not know what B. F. Moomaw would say if he happened upon us, although I have some idea. Or if Brother Kline's spirit listened in—

I have come to depend on those left around me. I see no other way. J. M., our most able-bodied, has mostly refused to speak in public, but he is wise regarding business matters. Now he also reads Scripture on Sunday mornings. "The truth is," I have said, "we err to ignore the gifts among us. Would anyone here be hungry and allow a nut to remain in its shell?"

Perhaps of more consequence, I have called on Delilah, too. Would anyone let a ripe peach go to waste? At times she tugs at her throat and shakes her head. Other times, she reads aloud from her New Testament, right where she sits. No one has objected. Sometimes her voice is mournful, sometimes more of a chant. But a hush falls and people accept the blessing of hearing God's Word.

I will accept blame for any indiscretions, if reprimand is needed. Decision-making by consensus at the local level has always been allowed to some degree among us German Baptists. And ten years ago, our church body boldly opened the door for young publishers like Henry Kurtz with his periodical *Gospel Visitor*. In that same spirit—what is left to be lost?—I turn to Delilah on a Sunday morning. The times require it: no more of lesser, whether Negro or woman; no more of greater, whether white or male.

Another departure occurred recently. After reading Scripture, J. M. shared his heartfelt story. He said he needed to confess. I called it a testimony. He laid bare his sorrow at having voted for secession. "All because of fear," he said. For him the threat had been loss of land, if he did not vote in the expected way. The Garber families have been wealthy for generations—ninety years in this area. J. M. gave himself over. His abundance led to his undoing.

Ever since 1861, he has known much loss. First, he mistakenly invested in large amounts of Confederate bonds. Over two years ago, his farms were in the paths of armies; during this past year, that has accelerated in degree. Trampled fields, confiscated bushels and stock, thousands of fence rails—good oak, no less—taken for campfires and cooking. Farm equipment, too. He had invested, like others, in a threshing machine and a McCormick reaper, made far away in Chicago. At one point, a tinge of bitterness crept into his testimony. "That machinery, of no use to the Army, but they destroyed it anyway."

Yet he made clear his greatest loss; I do not know that he has forgiven himself. After the fighting at New Market last May, he sent his firstborn away. Young Martin, only fifteen and determined to be of no help to the Confederacy, was horrified also at the South using Virginia Military Institute boys. So it was that last spring, J. M. gave sufficient money for his son and an older travel mate to make escape. Ever since, he has heard nothing. "Nothing," he repeats.

I say again to Abigail that we are fortunate to know Joel and Amos made it to Iowa.

She shows little satisfaction, saying instead: "No word in over a year; we do not know if *they* have food."

"Nor do *we* know what *they* know of *our* food supply," I said.

But so long as the war continues, and with it an unreliable postal service, it seems premature to think they have disappeared for good. Sadly, that happens to some. But as I remind J. M., it does not have to be so. We should not be faint of heart. My oldest daughters married early and went their own ways; over the years, we have rarely sent or received letters. But my sons—their circumstance—I cannot forget. I have to believe they are not lost to the world.

Nevertheless, with uncertainty in the very air we breathe, as well as the accumulation of J. M.'s recital and Delilah's ongoing stories at home from *Martyrs Mirror*, my stark statements at Flat Rock became starker. Our usual time of thanksgiving for harvest was upon us when I declared: "We grew fat with ease and plenty, before the burning." Every head and every set of eyes fixed on me. Once started, I had to finish. "We failed to guard against thinking ourselves better than some. We set ourselves up for reckoning." Every head went down, even Delilah's. Women sniffled. But I said, "We can yet learn the ways of God." A man, about my age, sobbed in his hands.

When home, Abigail's assessment left no doubt. "No one needs scolding. We are still grief-stricken. *You* hold yourself above the rest of us."

"I am no better, no worse. Who else is left to speak?" I asked. "You had no problem accepting Brother Kline's words, when he preached about people being dead trees in winter, having no life in the soul."

"You were right to remind us . . ." Delilah's voice drifted off. "But we fight the bitter taste, wanting to appear blameless."

"It is not *all* our fault," Abigail said. "You called it *reckoning*."

"Perhaps not." Delilah knows how to smooth the rough places. "Father included German Baptists of much earlier years, also not prepared. The price of self-satisfaction. He did not say *only* Flat Rock, nor single out any individual."

I nodded but steadied my hands on the top of the nearest chair. In fact, I had gone back to the late eighteenth century, reminding folks of Christopher Sauer II, our preacher and printer in colonial Pennsylvania. Already then, he had called the slave trade sinful. I followed with: "Over the years some of our members have taken with ease and used the Negro to make more money. As if gold were our calling." I may have acknowledged that such behavior occurred at harvest and with every effort to pay the man himself for his services. My memory is not always the best—unsure whether I actually said this or only thought to do so.

I let go the kitchen chair and sat myself, my arms folded in reverie. I had not determined before that morning, exactly how much to say. But no one stood up to stop me, not even when I said, "We thought we could handle our choice safely. Stay quietly off to the side, only dip into taking advantage when dire conditions—the threat of rain, even snow, during harvest." Now my women pulled out chairs also and sat, arms resting on the table.

"You may criticize," I said, "but once I started, I could not seem to stop, even when my heart raced. You have heard me say before, how I had not given serious thought to warfare coming to our beloved country. Certainly not to our dear Valley. Was it wrong for me to say, 'We looked on ourselves as a blessing; we patted ourselves as giving *better* treatment?'" I reached for my cup of water, even as I had wished for a drink that morning.

Delilah added, "You also said, 'That is when surprise came. When least expected—' Is that not right? Also, I thought I heard, 'Our excess—coins stored up—turned to wanting.'"

My throat felt tight at her remembrance. "Yes, 'choice taken from us'—I said that—'when we became slaves to the powerful regarding our duty to obey.'"

Delilah's eyes stayed on me. "Something, too, about 'dried crust from our eyes.' What prompted? Did you feel seized?"

I nodded. "Doubtless said along those lines. But no, not seized. 'Wipe dried crust' is what I likely intended. Perhaps cursed—too much time to think. I recall saying, 'When the threat of bondage fell to our own person, then—then at last, we understood what it is to be free.'"

"And was it not 'tilling of land turned to bargaining'?" Delilah asked. "'Farming used as a substitute.'"

"Or *weapon*, 'used as weapon,'" Abigail added. "I thought you were going to faint, David."

"I cannot deny; it has seemed a bargain." I gripped the seat edges of my chair. "But my ideas, garbled. I should never have begun—"

"No, Father," Delilah said. "We needed to hear."

"No child whimpered," Abigail said, "even though far from usual. But you forget—we are bereft. Our world snatched from us."

"I forget? I think not. When I fully stopped speaking this morning, you, Delilah, had raised your head again and looked me in the face—your eyes startled." My lips fell to trembling again. "I do not grasp all that churns within. Forgive me if I have erred." I lifted my face full to the wooden beams. "More understanding may yet come. Break from . . . its shell. Chastisement for myself."

My women came to me and placed their hands on me. I wanted to escape—but from what? The kindness of their touch? While yet at Flat Rock, everyone had turned to kneel on the cold floor, their arms and elbows balanced on the benches where they had sat. We repeated the Lord's Prayer as is our custom. When we rose, I managed to say the usual: "We will meet again the next Lord's day, God willing."

* * *

Weeks after that turbulent Sunday, the time of our Savior's birth is upon us. The haze of smoke is long gone from our Valley, but I cannot say that full understanding has come. No snow has fallen to cover the stark nakedness of the land. But I have been pondering—yes, me—a new mystery: why do some trees hang on to their leaves so long? Is it stubbornness in my white oaks? Or do they exemplify courage that leaves on other trees lack? Brown and dried, something stays those oaks. Not that this happening is new this season, only that more dried crust needs to fall from my eyes.

What would normally be desolate or go unnoticed, brings me hope: ten shades of brown in the woods; moles and voles, given the run of the land, beneath and on top. My creek still runs clear; prairie grasses will, likely as not, poke through once more. The beauty of our natural world startles and lifts spirits, even when drab. Even when few people go about to distract, when neighbors on the Pike have lost sons and fathers, barns and crops. Little seems as it should be. Mills are gone. Yet solace can be found.

With regard to relations at home since that late November Sunday of my outburst, I have guarded my words with Abigail, unsure where she stands. Some days we seem at peace; other days sharp edges show. But it was a Wednesday when we took stock again for the colder days ahead: the potatoes, the few hens that have survived. When we counted our remaining barrels of flour—what we had milled back in late summer—Abigail clicked her teeth and said, "Seven barrels—we must guard our supply closely."

My words leaped. "What do you mean?" How could we have spent these weeks together, with our minds traveling in such opposite directions?

"Otherwise, we will not make it," she continued. "We have sacrificed enough. Our boys."

I walked away. But the next day, before I went out to do the late afternoon chores, I made my tardy reply, "We will share what we have; there are widows and orphans among us. We dare not hoard." How else could I stand in front on more Sundays and face those wasting away?

"They have brothers and uncles—their own stash," Abigail said, as firm as I.

"We have been blessed—our distance from the Pike—spared from the worst of the plundering. The same is not true for all." I looked to Delilah, mending another round of socks and stockings. She kept her head down.

Abigail stayed matter-of-fact. "We never owned excess money to start. Others may be reduced to our level now."

"You do not know!" I caught my breath to soften. "We are not to compare. But since you have—let me remind you: Sister Blough's cellar uprooted; Brother Yount told he would be shot if he tried to pursue the thief. We have known no such mental upheaval. We still have our Valley—the promise of springing again."

Abigail did not pursue the disagreement, but none of us showed much warmth the next days. Sometimes we offered silent thanks before eating. Sometimes Delilah took to the day bed, her coughing unmitigated. I do not know if anything transpired between them when I spent time outside, watching water flow around rocks in the creek, as if a mighty river had caught my attention. I passed the time by prodding a letdown of milk from our dispirited cow, staring across the way at Winfield's traps, as if I had never seen them before.

I silently emptied chamber pots and dumped excess ashes outside. Abigail did most of the cooking, while Delilah was more to straighten and keep plates clean. We weathered the strain, but our words stayed limited. One night, Delilah and I went through the motions of playing checkers. I read my Bible; she read silently from the *Martyrs Mirror*. My women baked one less loaf of bread on Saturday; Abigail patted my shoulder that evening. I looked up but did not ask regarding her touch.

When Sunday came, I proceeded as I thought best. Abigail placed no hand to stop me when I motioned to Delilah. She understood to help me half-roll a barrel of flour on its edges to the wagon; we lifted in harmony. I found small sacks and a scoop. My sermon lacked fervency, cautious not to overstep. But at the end of the service, I told any who had run low to avail themselves. No one would think to purchase flour at today's prices. It would be like baking gold coins for dough. We took home a nearly empty barrel.

We inhabited our house, but we still had little to say to one another, as if our fears and griefs were better kept separate. I am no saint. Some days I still railed at the Almighty—allowing such senseless death and deprivation among us.

But in my own self-reckoning, I became acutely aware that I *could* go see Winfield. My neighbor, doubtless, a victim, too, even if his traps continue to produce some catches. I wrestled. *Must* I go? What would I say? What if words tumbled from my internal accusations, and I asked what he knew of Johnny's death? What good would there be to see him buckle? Even if he likely would not. What benefit, my giving air to that desire? What satisfaction, to speak of the misguided courage of relying on violence? All of these questions tossed back and forth, while I pictured him modifying a Yankee gun, jamming the cylinder of a pistol, contaminating powder with oil.

One night, I dreamed I went. I stepped through the low creek bed and approached with caution. Winfield was cleaning his rifle in his work shed. From the doorway it looked to be a Springfield. He had removed the bands and forestock and gave painstaking care, rubbing and polishing wood.

Without turning to the door, he said, "Go home."

I had imagined my stealth, glowed in my courage. Like a flushed hen, I left at once, stumbling on a tree root. That might be what woke me up, thinking to catch my fall.

I have no business going to Winfield; I still want to trap him. Johnny showed forth reconciliation with Joseph Funk, but I have not achieved the proper frame of mind. Vengeance prevails within. I sit with another cup of parched acorns, pondering the rotten meat within—the core I must yet strip. Others' faults I can see so easily; my own I prefer to hide.

By the time a second December Sunday came around, Delilah had spent extra time grinding at the hand mill. We keep it inside now—our hands too blistered and the temperature too cold to work in the shed. Of her own volition, Delilah took from our corn flour to the church gathering. During that church service I asked her to read from Acts, chapter two.

I did not know what would come from my mouth in response; I do not write down points in advance like Brother Kline did. But when I stood, all I could picture were scrawny hens—pointed noses, aimless clucking and wandering about. "I have never seen one of my hens dig for a worm and pass it to another hen," I said. I waited for something more appropriate. All I could do was hearken back to what Delilah had read: "*And all that believed were together and had all things in common.*"

I said, "What people in the early church did is what we may slowly be learning from necessity. We are higher beings than our surviving hens. None of us can do this alone. What we have left, we give, even when we do not have more to spare. We can do better than the chickens."

The next week on Sunday, a few others brought from their store: plum jam, molasses, canned strawberries set out for all on the table at the back of the church building. People helped themselves as they had need, cradling in their hands for the ride home. The offering voluntary, or of little good. No one has spices—no salt or pepper, certainly not sugar. But I took from my black walnut meats, laid them on the table at the back. A few young boys filled their pockets.

I tell myself in this Christmas season, if we can keep the *Gemeine* together—if the Lord wills—

It is much too early to think of planting; I do not know if anyone has leftover seed. First, we must pass through more desolate days of cold and snow.

Jacob — Iowa, January 1865

This fractious war—will it never end? Not that soldiers surround us—only occasional reports of scattered men marching nearby—but the air, heavy with grief. Tiny caskets and women wailing. From last summer's drought with prairie fires on the loose, to this winter's cold. I should not complain; no one forces me to stay on an island with guards watching my every move. But a spirit of recklessness seems loosed in the land.

Even on The Bench, members quarrel. Our Benjamin Schrock may have said his mind too boldly—"We do not weep for them"—when some of our troublemakers moved back to Ohio. We still ended last year with sixty Amish families in our settlement; only the German Lutherans are doing more to fill up Sharon Township.

But the winnowing takes its toll. When weather permitted last fall, families boiled their clothing outdoors in a copper kettle. Our church children, the most vulnerable to this tide of scarlet fever and diphtheria. A nine-year-old Stutzman girl, a four-year-old Yoder boy—his hair as red as his father's—followed by a still younger Yoder, then a sixteen-year-old Schoettler. Two years ago, we had sporadic losses, but since last year, a veritable rash. The Brenneman boy and girl, fourteen and twelve, sad indeed. I reminded Peter: nothing about being chosen a minister guarantees protection. Not that death should be construed as punishment—only he can assess his standing.

But as troubling as it is to lose our children, sometimes they are the ones left to fend. My son Christian and his wife Elizabeth—she calls him Chris—had stayed childless all these years. What did they do but adopt three of the five Lehman children last year! Their tender hearts are to be admired, but now they live in a din of noise and sleepless nights. These orphans came about when the sick Lehman father—only thirty years old—succumbed this past summer, after his woman Magdalena had died over a year before.

With all this upheaval, our burying has changed also. For years, people were grateful to use the land Peter B. Miller had donated. But two years ago, folks started what they call family cemeteries: Schoettlers, Yost Yoder, the

Brennemans. There is no teaching prohibiting this outbreak, so we have not stood in the way. Some ministers call it a natural outcome of growth. I can only remind: we must stand clear of individualism.

I have tried to offer a steadying hand, but I am still not good at making repairs. The four brethren who came a year ago would be disappointed. My own omissions stand out; I have not visited Emanuel's burial site. Worse yet, the gate stayed broken with John P. Guengerich, my stepson. His was the only death among us last year of an elderly one, living to the ripe age of 73. Mary and I were tending kettles, deep into applesauce and cider-making from Sarah's excess of apples, when word of his demise came. I had to sit awhile on a nearby stump. My early friend and late foe—gone from this world. Even when I heard his body was weakening, I did not properly seek to mend the rift. There is no good excuse.

But compounding all these travails—the burdens of war. So long exerting its influence, we have not stayed untouched. What started as an adventure for some has finally lost its appeal. A shortage of volunteers led to my son Joseph being drafted last year. He paid his $300 to be exempt, as did five others from our church. I warned of improprieties in how that money might be spent; I have not forgotten the earnest words of that young Funk man in Indiana last spring—all that is amiss. But Joseph insisted all was clean in Iowa.

"Clean?" I asked. "You may think me infirm, but when it comes to warfare . . ."

"You want me to skedaddle?" he asked, his raised eyebrows all but mocking. "Leave my expectant woman and eight children?"

What more could I say? The Lord has blessed him with no shortage of cash, even after the expense of his brick house. He fairly boasts of foot-thick outer walls.

Stories come also that Pennsylvania stays caught in the grip of war. One of our newcomers last year, Tobias Yoder from the western part of Maryland, spoke openly of troubles in Somerset County and the Glades area. "Soldiers from both sides demanded food; Rebels helped themselves to cattle and horses," he reported. He and his wife Mary, another Hochstetler daughter of Henry and Susanna, have not been strangers to grief. Before moving here, they buried four youngsters in a field with nine other tender ones ravaged by diphtheria.

"Even before disease and death struck, though, we considered leaving," Tobias said.

"More trouble than unruly soldiers?" I asked.

"Church troubles of excess drinking and hidden sin. Some drifted to the Dunkers. Others moved physically opposite, away to Johnstown. Those had nothing good to say about Indians or Negroes. When we left, some still thought the South would win."

"My grandson Samuel has located back there in Elklick Township," I said. "I pray he remains safely removed from the rough element."

"Hard to say. I only know, a Lutheran or Reformed man, better than some of ours last year," this Tobias said.

"Let me know if you hear of new goings-on," I said, shaking my head.

Right here in Iowa, we had our own difficulty with voting last November. What is it that makes such disobedience? We ministers had advised our members to stay away from rubbing shoulders with the world, but Frederick says some went to the polls anyway. He thought a few ministers might have stepped over also.

Even if not guilty on that count, our Jacob Marner must keep a tighter hold on his family members. The scourge of rats on his land is unfortunate in the extreme, but this word of twin grandsons: the one, rightly named Jacob, while the other has been saddled with Abraham Lincoln Marner. I shudder to strap a babe for life with the broad brush of the world.

Sadder still our neighbors, the Iowa boys who have given their lives. When Frederick ventures to Richmond or Iowa City on business, he makes a point of asking about Emanuel's unit. We knew they had been sent to help in the East. But last July a local boasted: "Our 22nd Iowa Infantry helped save the day. Shipped to Washington, where that Confederate commander, Early, had his sights on our nation's capital."

In the fall, those same Iowa soldiers found themselves fighting under General Sheridan in the Shenandoah Valley, that very area from whence Mennonites and German Baptists had to flee, their crops burned out from under them. Iowa boys took part! How could they not know the consequences for farmers? Frederick claims that nearly 200 soldiers from here lost their lives in that Virginia valley; he names places called Fisher Hill and Cedar Creek. And another fellow from Amish, our Deer Creek area, was taken captive at a place called Winchester. Even a higher up in the Iowa House, our Representative Smiley Bonham from Frank Pierce—his son was wounded! So far as I know, the remaining boys still have not come back, but are said to spend the winter with a General Sherman in the state of North Carolina, awaiting their next go-round. What agony for the parents, longing to be reunited!

But now another infestation of grief has been brought to my attention. Much closer! Terrible conditions at the Rock Island Prison in Illinois—practically our backyard—directly on the other side of the Mississippi. Over the years, we have done most of our river business at Davenport, a straight ride by horseback. But when reports abounded of disease and high mortality at this prison, Frederick decided to see for himself if there was truth. Tales of murder had been bandied about. He convinced Jakob, Daniel's son, to ride with him before the snows fully set in. Of course, Jakob did not want to set aside his work; he has been pining to make another cherry cabinet ever since his father lost two trees to that wind storm. But Jakob has a tender heart for more than wood—I do not see why he cannot find a suitable wife—and agreed to make the excursion.

They came together to make report and found Mary and me picking out hazelnuts at our table. After standing at the hearth to warm hands and exchange pleasantries, Jakob wasted no time. "A dead-line." He scooped up a few nut-meats in his fingers and motioned with his other hand. "A ditch marks the line on the north, east, and west sides of the camp with a row of stakes on the south. If a prisoner strays beyond—shot dead by a sentinel."

I looked to Frederick, for Jakob can stretch things when excited.

"He does not exaggerate, Father; this prison sits on twelve acres of swampy island, mired in wickedness." The look in Frederick's eyes brought to mind the day on our long journey to Iowa, when Sarah had screamed and fainted at the sight of her box of money nearly sliding into the Mississippi.

"Five thousand men!" Jakob insisted, pounding the table. "Many my age. Not nearly enough room. Five thousand." He licked nut residue off his fingers. "Not all were reduced to skin and bones, but—" He shook his head. "Drainage problems—the look of a frozen hog pen. I would not want to smell that in summer's heat."

Mary quickly went to the other room where she keeps the flax wheel.

"A man showed us around," Frederick said. "He looked at me as if he did not believe I was a minister. Some hick farmer, I suppose he thought. He kept saying, 'Things good here. Not like Andersonville.' The man said that while looking around at eighty-some barracks—most all of them, boarded up, no air."

Jakob sat with his hands clenched on the table. "Andersonville is a prison camp the Confederates operate somewhere in Georgia. But Grandfather, that one prisoner, the Whanger man, told a very different story. 'Nothing good here,' he said. 'Food cut back last June.' I believe *him*." Jakob was up again, pacing. "You do not want to know more of how that operation looked. Those men should be up and working—not making buttons from shells."

I brushed nut shells onto a pile. "Might they need potatoes? We could send—"

Frederick's head was swiveling from left to right. "Prisoners are not allowed to receive supplies other than clothes. And those, only from family members or friends. It goes back a long time. Problems started a year ago with the first prisoners. Before that, the two sides had exchanged men, but that arrangement broke down that summer."

"Prisoners piled up on battlefields." Jakob glared at me, as if I shared blame. "Surrounded by dead horses. Think of that!"

"Little security, of course—a battlefield," Frederick said. "So they started using Rock Island. 'Get the prisoners out of sight' must have been the mindset. They had to know that camp was not ready. Had to."

Jakob stayed restless, up and down. "Almost a third as many guards as prisoners now. And listen to this: a twelve-foot-high fence." He stretched an arm way high. "Twice as tall as a man. A sentry box every hundred feet or so."

"You say you spoke with a Whanger man?" I asked.

"A prisoner from West Virginia," Jakob said. "The part that used to be Virginia. A David Whanger and his sickly brother."

"Sickness everywhere, not only overcrowding, Father. That David said almost a hundred men with smallpox, exposed everyone else. Worse than disease in a family. You can imagine."

"No, he cannot!" Jakob chewed on his thumbnail as if on a chicken bone. "No one could picture half the extent."

"Those first months, almost 700 men lost." Frederick took a turn sitting at the table and reached for Mary's nut pick.

"At the prison?" I asked.

"Right there. A new cemetery, right there. Guards died, too. Finally—" Frederick lowered his voice. "Finally, they separated sick ones from healthy."

"Anyone knows not to leave a sick calf with other cows," Jakob said. "Unless, of course, you *want* them all to die. From the sound of things, most all took sick."

"Finally, this past July, over a half year after the first prisoners came, they opened what they called a hospital. Only for the worst, Father. Someone finally thought to boil clothes when they washed 'em."

"And stopped throwing kitchen refuse on the open ground," Jakob added. "Whanger said that. Not that first fellow; no, not that 'things good' fellow." Jakob stared out the window, his lips tight, as if picturing the culprit.

"No one can live like that," I said. "Is there anything—"

"Whenever I questioned the man who showed us around," Frederick said, "he claimed they lacked money. Oh, another time he blamed colonels. Admitted, though, some higher-ups had filled out reports—'most probably' the man said—that the drainage was good." The whir of the flax wheel continued from the next room. "That same man vouched for good medical treatment; hard to believe."

"Impossible!" Jakob said. "And listen to this: when they finally built a sewer system, those in charge would not pay civilians the prevailing wage. So what did they do?" Jakob placed his hands on the table and leaned toward me, brown eyes piercing, hair awry. "Used the labor of prisoners. *Ja*, honest work for men—that much. But what do you think they paid? Ten cents a day. *Ten rotten cents.* Should have gotten over a dollar, heavy work like that. When Uncle and I showed surprise at the wages, the guard said, like a boast, 'Prisoners got full rations if they worked.' As if that made up for piddle."

"Settle yourself," Frederick said, as if chiding one of his own.

"Why has this not come to light?" I asked. "There must be some way to alleviate."

Jakob paid no heed, slouching against the dry sink. "Only way to get a full ration and not do labor like a slave? Sign up for the western service. Men my age!" He paced again but this time not so loud. "Only way out? Pass a medical test and take an oath to the Union. Called a Galvanized Yankee then, hoping to make it out. This Whanger fellow, this very one, waiting to be sent. More like wasting away," Jakob mumbled. "Go kill Indians, I reckon."

"That's President Lincoln's idea: recruit prisoners to go out West," Frederick said. "But it causes more dissension. Recruits like this Whanger are allowed to live in a better part: the Calf Pen instead of the Bull Pen. No longer considered prisoners exactly, but not organized either. Waiting. Time must drag . . ."

My men finally lost steam, and I did not mind seeing them out the door.

I slowly went to Mary. "A travesty. Inhumane on all counts. Both sides."

"Disarray," Mary muttered, "whether country or church."

I could not stomach another dispute. "You did not hear. No one starves among us. No dead-line exists."

She adjusted the spool of thread on the distaff. She knows it tears me asunder—almost three years since we held Communion. Even when I choose my words carefully, folks remain stubborn. The women . . . some of the men, weak-kneed. "Recalcitrant" says it better. The ear to listen stays distant when the spirit is unwilling.

Not fair for Mary to compare. But the truth comes closer and closer. I fear I will need to bear the brunt, much as I do not want to be seen as hard-nosed. Only God can change minds and hearts, make us fit to come together at the table.

Esther — far from home, March 1865

We're here. Mary Grace says we've been here four months. Joseph, too. Most of winter. I look at Matthias and think to call him Father. Then I catch myself. I always catch myself. Children play about; I pull Miriam to me. She smells good, but Jephthah runs away. I lost a tooth in front and don't look the best.

I don't always have things right, but Mary Grace says I'm getting better. Lena tells me what to do about the spinning. At first my elbows didn't bend right, and my fingers were stubborn.

Lena says, "Start over. Your head isn't always for the best."

But Mary Grace gives me a hug and says, "You're getting better, Ma." She's my mama, only nicer. She holds my hand and caresses when I don't know where next.

I don't mean to be a bother. I don't mean to disobey Lena. She told me to cut the beef; she wanted things done like so. Mary Grace had to wrest the knife from my hand. I couldn't think what. Such a beautiful smell. Blood oozing in little rivers.

Lena hasn't asked me to cut more. "I'm glad for your spinning," she says. "Your fingers will learn to do right."

When we came, they were surprised. Matthias looked different—spread out in his body. And their youngsters, all new. Right away Lena gave me one of her dresses—dark brown. She's shorter than me but has the wide bottom. My old dress was raggedy where I scuffed on rocks and dragged through tall weeds. Lena showed me the tub for washing my apron and undergarments. But first, Mary Grace removed the coins and put them away; she saves them for me. She helps Lena best.

This isn't Virginia, but we are here. Mary Grace and William found the way. It was hard to know. This house faces the rising sun. I lost three coins and my front tooth. I didn't mean to lose anything. Mary Grace pats my arm and says, "Of course not, Ma." One coin rolled under the dry sink, but Matthias wouldn't budge to look. I motioned to Andrew and Joseph, too, but nobody would do. At night the edge slips away from the table. The corner at the pantry comes up fast. Sometimes I bump my tin cup, and when I reach to grab, it tumbles to the floor, clankity-clank.

One time we played a game, all of us grownups. We were to think of all the people we know. Right away, I pointed to Andrew and Joseph; they are my big boys. Joseph is big like Matthias and Father. Joseph gives me hugs and says, "I missed you, Ma." My big boys came before me; Andrew made it first. He says their Streak remembered him.

Simon isn't here, nor Father. Not Mr. Baumgardner either. He was a neighbor farmer when Matthias and I were little. Lena frowns about that. She has light and dark hair. When she stands close, I see the start of chin hairs. Lena's are light, but her brows are dark like a storm.

Matthias took me to his granary; he wears two suspenders. He says my boys helped with the wheat. "The Lord is good"—out of nowhere, he said that.

"Will anybody have me?" I asked.

He gave me a bear hug. "Eat as much as you like. When the sun warms, you can sit outside and lift your face. You'll feel better. Very soon."

I shook my head. "Mama said not to worship the sun."

Matthias said, "You'll see." The floor shakes when he walks.

Lena says I'm jumpy. She says it extra when we go to their church. We use a bridge to cross over water on both sides. Now it goes better with snow and ice. I like to say, "*The Lord is my shepherd.*" I say it quiet and put my head down. I know most of the Lord's Prayer. And they sing a song I used to know in Virginia. There we had our mutual woes and burdens, too. When my boys were little, we sat beside Frances in our Virginia church. But she didn't come along. Here I don't have a sympathizing tear. Lena says to be patient.

William says the hack driver took us down to the big river. The water sloshed on the sides and Jephthah clapped. We were going to die, but I told Miriam not to scream. Pharoah pulled his sword out of his britches, but it was a butcher knife. I was very, very sorry. But now we are here. They have sunny days.

We rode a long time on a wagon train. Sometimes we were lonesome. I sang for Miriam, but the words were new. Sometimes it went, "*Jesus watches in the night.*" We saw fires—that was Virginia. Months of fires and bumpy rides; William said it was two weeks. "Winchester," he said. "We took the carriage to Winchester. You had a pass, Ma. Two days to Martinsburg."

"They burned our wagon," I said.

"We had Samuel's carriage," William said quietly. "Our bishop back—"

"I remember Frances. Then what?" I asked.

"At Martinsburg we unloaded, but they didn't want Star," Mary Grace said. "Our brown nag, too old. We loaded again and slept in the carriage another night. Some folks packed their belongings in boxes."

"Miriam had a box," I said. "Where did we do?"

"We took the oath," William said. "We watched and did as others did. We signed. You and Mary Grace and I. We drove alone and found the river. "

"And Samuel took his carriage," I said. I pressed William's arm.

He looked straight ahead, and Mary Grace shook her head. Sometimes they're that way. Mary Grace took my hand and said, "We're here now."

"And our other boy?" I asked. "Peter. Big and tall. When will he come?"

Mary Grace said, "No, Ma," and William walked out. I don't like him to bang the door. The dogs bark loud, like when we came. Matthias has two dogs; they jump on me. He and Lena have seven children; I counted once, when we sat at the table. Timothy has sandy hair and is a crybaby. We sang a song for Miriam's first birthday. I wrap a finger in her curls when she sucks.

I might have hurt Peter. I want him to come tell me, so we can be right. Mary Grace never says about the boxes.

But Joseph smiles when he sees me. "Hello, Ma. I'm glad you're here."

"How did you get here?" I ask.

"A miracle, Ma." He pats my hand. "Like all of us."

I made a new dress from pretty blue cloth. Lena helped me match the seams up right. The sleeves are extra loose, but I stay warm in this house.

Jephthah won't shut his eyes in the afternoon. He wants to chase Lena's Michael. She says they're cousins. I tell Jephthah to run outside, but Mary Grace stops him. Lena clicks her teeth. Here they have piles of snow.

* * *

Today we had more talks. Mary Grace told me about the haversack. I cried about Peter. She says soldiers came to our house. She was nice and said I don't need to remember every little thing. We had a big kitchen knife. Mary Grace said that was a long time ago. She said she and William saw the haversack by the well; it had a V and straps. I shook my head, but she said I followed the soldiers out the lane. That was before the fires. She said I told her and William that the man said zig-zag. I wish I could think better. I close my eyes to try extra hard. If I could just say better. Soldiers can make things up.

I wanted to find Miriam's box, but Mary Grace said to stay sitting. She gave me a hug and told surprises about our trip. We got here before the snow did.

"How did we know where to go?" I asked.

"Mr. Roedeker helped us," Mary Grace said. "Short and stocky with a pipe."

"Like Mama's?"

"No. Well, I don't know. He wore a dark blue and brown checked vest under his coat. A Mennonite, but snazzy. He brought us in his wagon from Hagerstown. You sat beside him in front with Miriam. He gave us water."

"Did we know this man?"

"No, Ma. He took pity. It was misty out and our hair straggly. William told him we were refugees. One time Jephthah tried to grab the man's beard. But in Chambersburg, Mr. Roedeker knew who to ask. William kept saying, 'One mile north of town.' And here we are."

"Here we are," I said. "Where do we go now?"

"This is Pennsylvania, Ma. Chambersburg."

"And this is Wednesday?"

"No, Ma, this is Tuesday—you're getting better—the second Tuesday in March."

"And are we happy or sad?"

"Happy, mostly. Uncle Matthias is very kind. He's your brother."

"I know. And we have Joseph."

"Yes, Joseph and Andrew, your big boys."

"Did we find Joseph at Hagerstown?"

"No, but Joseph was there earlier. We came after the wagon train and after the Potomac. The hack driver promised us safe passage; he knew where to cross. William watched and said you gave him plentiful coins."

Mary Grace has dark eyes, like Simon. But he's not here.

"And the hack driver took us to the Roedeker man," I said.

"No, Ma, another man between. The hack driver dumped us after we crossed the river. You were tired and fell—at the big river. A bad fall on rocks, trying to wash Jephthah's bottom. The hack driver pointed the way to Hagerstown but said he needed the carriage for a quick errand. He said to gather our belongings and said he'd be right back."

"Did we have a box for Miriam?" I asked.

"You had too much to carry, Ma. The box, the big bag from Frances. Miriam, most of the time. You held tight, but Jephthah slipped away. William chased after." Mary Grace stopped a long time. Then she said, "We were cold but we huddled awhile. Miriam cried while we waited for the carriage to come back. The big bump on your head got darker. That driver didn't come and didn't come."

"Where was I?" I asked.

"We decided to trudge, Ma; we were all together. We found a smokehouse and curled up. A makeshift of a night. Come morning, this other man found us; he was nice. He heard Miriam crying in his smokehouse. He took us inside his big house, and his wife fixed eggs. She wore a dark blue kerchief. Their children stared, but the woman cleaned you up. Your face—the scratches and bad bump. Water to rinse your mouth. She told you to spit and spit in the tin pan."

"What was his name? The man."

"He never said, but William told him where we needed to go."

"And what did I say to the nice woman?"

"I don't remember, Ma. You had trouble with garbled words. The man said we had to stay another night and sleep stretched out."

"Was it snowing?"

"No, Ma, not till here."

"Then what?"

"We did as the man said; we bedded down by their hearth. Like with Frances at their house. Miriam was better satisfied when warm. You fell asleep, but Jephthah was on the loose. William helped the man and his boy with chores. That night and all the next day—whatever the man said. The woman had her tomato soup. You liked it, and the next day we had more soup with eggs and rye bread. The eggs went down slick, and the woman fixed more. Then the man took us in his wagon to a tavern keeper. That one had a big fat cigar that made William cough, so I had to talk. The tavern man knew Mr. Roedeker."

So many men to keep straight, but Lena says the edge of the table will stay put soon. When I stand to spin, I go over who was where. I say to myself, "The hack driver. Then this Mr. Roedeker knew a tavern man." No, the other way. I start over. The in-between man first. I wish I could say better. Lena walks by and says not to babble. "Pay the threads more mind." She whispers to Mary Grace in the pantry.

When Lena is out milking, I ask Mary Grace about the coins. She says I gave plentiful. She starts to say more but stops. I pull on her arm.

"I didn't like the hack driver," she says.

"Did we sit huddled by the side of the road?"

"Yes, after Martinsburg and before the big river. After again, too. You and Miriam lay down in tall grasses. But your head hurt worse and we huddled. You saw red eyes in the woods."

I rub my forehead, but I do not like my fingers to go where the bad bump was.

Matthias says we're family. We're not to have any more want. My boys help him good.

"Mama had to do without her rocker," I tell Matthias.

"But Father made her a new one," he says. "Virginia hickory. Whatever she wanted. Always more rockers."

I shake my head. I wish I could say better about that other state. But Matthias stays kind like Father. He says the sun will warm me soon.

I wish Simon would come. I start to say so, but I catch myself.

David — Shenandoah Valley, April 1865

I was out walking along the edge of our fields, stumbling for volunteers, even a stray potato leaf poking through. It is too early to think a squash shoot could work its way. But we have had early rains; the air feels warmer, like winter has thrown off its grip. We are weak from living without, but we make effort to exercise a quiet spirit. Only one recent disagreement: whether to save the sprouting potatoes for seed.

I do not know my body—these thin arms. I could be a skinny lad again, but when I try to flex my hands and fingers, I have no strength. My bony knuckles bend slowly to secure a cup. I sleep in my day clothes so that I do not need to look upon my nakedness.

We have been aided by a scattering of spring greens: field cress and lambs quarter near the creek. A flushing of the body that rids the bowels of its prisoners. But we have nothing hardy to replenish our needs. The black walnuts, long gone. I do not give the plow blade a second glance. How would I budge it to sharpen? Three solid men are not to be found.

But as I walked that day, a commotion in the distance grew louder, such that I could no longer dismiss it. My ears stay alert to danger, like Ruby's. This sound was reminiscent of soldiers marching, but not entirely. We had been led to believe things were winding down. Now this.

A wave of weakness washed over me. How would I resist whatever marched toward me? My nostrils flared—a waft of animal? I slowly headed back to the porch, seeking safety. Out of breath and lacking the wherewithal to climb steps right then, I backed up to sit on the edge.

It might have been an hour; time has little meaning. What finally came clear: a caravan of wagons, wending their way down through the pass. I called faintly, "Delilah. Abigail." I shifted my perch toward the door, willed my lungs to expand, called again.

Delilah came and stood beside. By then, the wagons had disappeared in trees, but the clatter could not be denied. My daughter's coughing has slowed, but she uses a cane or my arm to manage steps. She went again to the door, calling for Abigail.

When we could no longer question—not drums, but heading our way—we walked halfway to the road. We stood huddled. Not strangers come to harm. No, we blubbered to see friendly faces. Eleven wagons in all. Up the Lost River from Hardy County, just as Brother Kline and I used to do in reverse when we passed through on horseback to visit mission churches. One brother said Johnny had drawn rough maps long ago—a semblance of travel directions to our farms. They knew of his passing.

To be the recipient—something of God, the miraculous. My eyes fill quickly again. The men came from as far away as Petersburg, West Virginia, even the South Fork churches in Pendleton County. Word of our plight had reached them; once enough warming and safety arrived, they determined to make passage.

These days later, trembling still catches me up. A feeble tongue remains for what cannot be described. Our unity, our *Gemeinschaft,* larger than Flat Rock.

Six milk cows, healthy—and a bull. Food from their stores: hams and bacon. Wagonloads of grain. Tears rained when the man lifted down and opened before me a bag of seed. He allowed me to cup my shaking hands, to touch and let fall through my fingers, precious seeds. Safe from mold! Ready to burst— And *six* milk cows! Our brothers gave due warning: "Exercise caution, so as not to upset your innards. Do not devour too quickly."

I cannot speak gratitude enough. Word spread to our people nearby. One neighbor to another, from New Market and Broadway, on farther south. Those who could, came dragging their weariness—bones of their former selves. Fearful, lest the largesse might have been distributed already. A local brother admitted he had been eating raw eggs. He cradled a ham to his chest like a newborn. I crooned with him.

My women and I had talked of moving West, even as strength seeped from us. Empty talk, but something to latch onto. I had named some of those very brethren who came, thinking we might find lodging along the way. Instead, they came to us. Given sustenance—food for our broken spirits. It is too much to fully take in.

Abigail promised to stretch our portion for weeks—at least three, she plotted. We do not begrudge anyone who came to avail themselves. We have known too much hunger to clutch. Our old cow, gone a month ago. No strength to dig a grave, but over two days' time we dragged the carcass with a rope to the nearest cove and covered with branches and dead grasses. The smell comes and goes with the north wind.

One brother—I cannot recall his name—looked upon our raggedness and half-whispered, "I will return another time." He squeezed me, such that my ribs hurt. These are not people who live in abundance. I have been there;

I know how they carve out a living amidst steepness, lacking the expanse of a wide valley like ours.

"Cattle and grain. I never thought—like unto a heavenly vision," I said to him. "Given seeds, we can stay, make a start."

Johnny never spoke of it, but I know now that the war was discussed at the last Annual Meeting he attended. That fateful trip, almost a year ago. People were advised not to pay bounty money—only give toward required fines or taxes. That same brother—was it Fitzer or Foster?—told me, "Our leaders made clear again: no soldier on active duty could consider himself a member of our church, unless he turned around and promised not to shed more blood."

But this same brother stunned me when he said without pause, "The *rebellion* is near its end." I flinched to hear that word; he said it like the Northerner he now is. Johnny had always been of the mind not to throw fire on public opinion, not to use imprudent language. A Southern neighbor might overhear and be offended. But this man openly—

Another change: we have no need to worry about Johnny thinking to go north for the Annual Meeting this year. No need to hurry to make plans at Flat Rock for a Love Feast either. No deacon remains to ask the three questions: "Dost thou believe, renounce, covenant?" No need that I can see, to question if we have been faithful—

* * *

Abigail has made bread again. I take tiny bites; tears spring unbidden. My mouth gums up in the chewing. A month ago we drooled to recall the dill bread that Delilah made more than a year ago. We took turns naming gratitude for what we had previously taken for granted: venison for Delilah, potato soup for Abigail! Now I will not need to beg like Lazarus. A snitch of salt on the tongue. Lard.

When the newcomers stored the sudden extravagance in my barn—extra oats and barley, too—I made my bed there several nights. My bones prone on straw, near where our Visitors and runaways had rested. A caravan, such as came, could not help but draw attention. I feared people might be accosted coming or going. I worried that my barn could become the object of others' grievances and desire. I had to pretend some semblance of safeguarding.

Then a dread seized me. I could be guilty, like the rich man. "Winfield." I spoke his name in a whisper to my women. I had claimed generosity toward anyone.

Abigail was quick. "That was not the intent of those who brought sustenance."

I grabbed the back of a chair to steady. "This sudden overflowing cannot be ours alone."

"Why must you ruin the gift?" Abigail scolded. But she bowed her head. "I am sorry."

A pall spread over our household. What is left to be done when everything unexplainable is open for examination? We had learned to dwell in scarcity, but now this abundance . . . I knew Winfield had trapped all winter, but I had never made overture concerning his welfare. Nor had I ever acted on my devious inclination to stealth about his traps. Did my avoidance of that dastardliness wipe out former lapses? I still did not want the sound of his voice, the smell of his breath.

Not until evening, when Delilah suggested, "Tomorrow is soon enough; we will sleep on it," did I find release. "We cannot rightly be judged to have excess," she added.

These days later, I have not yet cast out fear. My neighbor still haunts, as do the words: "*And forgive us our debts as we forgive our debtors.*" Another mystery to plumb—*our* trespasses, as some say . . . *those who trespass against* us. It would be easier, if we knew our brother from Hardy County would keep his promise and return soon with more goods. But I must remain open, not close the door on what is newly required.

What is needful to preach comes halting also, even when gratitude overflows. "We are allowed to make the land fruitful once more, the blackened places green," I say. "Seeds sprung from their containers, given to us." We never dreamed it would be thus, beyond our own weak efforts.

But other threats linger. This war, however faint, has not been entirely snuffed out. Some of us may be going to prison. "*Fear not, little flock . . .*" The Confederate Bureau of Conscription was abolished early in March; local officials were told to handle anything pertaining to the draft or exemptions. Ten days later all religious exemptions were canceled.

If dragged in chains—to do what?—we can only manifest humble spirits. Go in weakness. Refrain from quarrelsome display, any selfish expression. The taste of bacon once more upon our lips.

J. Fretz — Chicago, April 1865

"I told you we'd get 'em. Lee's men, outnumbered five to one, living on parched corn. Squeezed him till he had to give it up. He should have called a halt months ago."

"Three *years* ago," I mumbled, my eyes on columns of numbers, "there should have been a stoppage."

Ross thinks the South should have surrendered back in December, when Sherman gave President Lincoln a "Christmas gift"—the city of Savannah, along with 150 heavy guns.

But our war talk at the office stays limited. My desire to argue is gone. Ever since last fall when Ross told me about his boy, Tommy, I settle for general questions: "How is everyone?" I can't tell him about Martha's milestones: rolling over on her own, sleeping through the night.

Yesterday, though, my minimal approach gave way. Ross wanted to rehash the surrender, roll Lee in the mud some more. Of course, I had heard the bells ringing throughout the city. Flags had sprouted everywhere, even used as decoration on people's dresses and hats. Bonfires, processions, meetings with absurd proclamations. Thousands drinking to excess. The whole city making a fool of itself. It reminded me of the 34-gun salute and celebration after Fort Donelson, one salute for each of the thirty-four states at the time. How long ago that was! Are we any closer to being united as states now?

Ross smacked a fist into his open palm, like an exclamation point. "Lee thought he could get away to the West. Grant is *not* McClellan; he *moves*."

"And Sherman finally told the truth," I said. "'War is cruelty and you cannot refine it.'"

Ross wouldn't take my goading. "Lee tried to make it sound—finally ready to buckle under—like he wanted to secure peace. As if he could get away without surrender."

"I don't know what that would be like, admitting defeat of that magnitude." We'd heard rumors of a Peace Plan back in January, but never knew if one had actually been offered by Confederates.

"Lee was doomed from the start. Tried to put a religious face on it."

"Both sides did." I rearranged papers on my desk, lined up edges. I could picture the three books said to be on Lee's desk: *The Holy Bible, The Book of Common Prayer,* and Marcus Aurelius's *Meditations.* "Maybe both sides finally see that it's pointless to look for God on the battlefield."

Ross looked at me, straight on. "I've tried hard not to call you what I've thought."

I took that in but sidestepped. "Everyone assigns their own meaning. But few are willing to ask: After all the sacrifice and death, what was the purpose—all that misery?"

"Still can't give Grant any credit, huh? Always saying how mean he's been. Didn't you see his soft spot? He didn't make Lee's men surrender their swords. Didn't ask for their horses."

"I'm glad he didn't seek additional humiliation. But all I feel is sadness. What advancement of mankind took place? Either side."

"I thought you cared about the Negro?"

"I do. But what attitudes changed?" I absently tapped the sheets on my desk, got up slowly and excused myself.

There's no point in reviewing the meeting in Appomattox. It must have been excruciating; Lee, known as a proud man, the older of the two and taller by several inches, needing to ask Grant for a meeting. Reports say Lee wore a new uniform, buttoned to the top, a picture of cleanliness—manliness!—with his sword at his side. Fancy boots with spurs also. The look of a Christian gentleman, I suppose—if you ignore the fact that he led his men to keep Negroes enslaved.

And there sat General Grant, described as looking like a private soldier with ordinary boots, no sword, mud spots on his clothes. They talked for over two hours—old acquaintances from the Mexican War. Finally, the men shook hands; Rebels were paroled and allowed to return to their homes.

Just as stunning, news reports of the two Commanders in Chief. Jefferson Davis and his men escaped with gold on trains, like rats fleeing a sinking ship. But why did President Lincoln go to Richmond after the residents had fled? Those folks had burned anything that might be of value to the North. What went through the president's head, walking through those rubbled remains of the Southern capital? Reports make him sound like a conqueror. Why did he sit at Davis's desk?

Yet his words in Washington were moderate and conciliatory. It's said that he didn't want to give a speech, but he asked the band to play "Dixie," a song with roots in the South. Did Lincoln mean to usurp the song as a Northerner? Or did he want the song to belong to the whole country? His actions have always been a mystery.

Back in March at his second inauguration, he had showed a warmer side also, not gloating or reprimanding the South. "With malice toward none and charity for all," he said. It could have been a line from a sermon—nothing of personal satisfaction. But he blamed both sides in that speech. In only slightly more than 700 words—still the master of brevity—he sounded like a reluctant commander, having done what was necessary in a more complex war than a simple choice between good and evil. Now leaders and historians will say the war was whatever they need it to have been. The dead will become whatever we survivors make of them. Already in his Gettysburg Address, Lincoln had given them political and religious meaning.

But whatever my quarrels with Lincoln, he's made of far better cloth than those surrounding him. Vengeful Radical Republicans sicken me. Thaddeus Stevens voices no concern for the starved and blockaded South. And Andrew Johnson? We're fortunate we don't need to rely on him to bring the North and South together again. His behavior at the inauguration was disgraceful, trying to deliver a speech while drunk. His friends excused him as recovering from typhoid fever. But rattling on and on, while Lincoln sat waiting. How the president must have fidgeted, wanting to talk about binding up the nation's wounds.

I take solace that the thirteenth amendment to the Constitution has passed; it should be hard for courts to overturn the Emancipation Proclamation. But even with Lincoln's best leadership, it won't be easy to bring enemy parts together. Some want Southern leaders put on trial and imprisoned. And many Northerners—white Christians among them—still want nothing to do with dark-skinned people. They see nothing wrong with continuing to allow only white men to vote.

It will likely be even harder to overcome obstacles to peace in the South. Many clergymen still believe slavery is humane. And Southern guerillas—it's naïve to think they're going to disappear quietly and stifle thoughts of revenge. Add to that a wrecked economy with burned communities that hold huge grievances. How will they recover without resources? And these stories of Southern women—oh, my! They're said to be especially hateful toward Grant's men, calling Northern soldiers "Satan followers" because of the property destruction and pillaging they did. The truth is: women on both sides are left in very precarious positions, providing for their children without husbands, brothers, fathers.

When I go from these national problems to thinking about what Mennonites in the South face, I wonder how refugees who fled Virginia are going to be able to go back to their burned land and start over like pioneers. That Hildebrand bishop from Staunton wrote again about extreme privations for those who stayed. His son Samuel had kept out of the war by working on the railroad in the far western part of the state. But other young men from Mennonite churches joined the Confederates. Hildebrand mentioned a particularly sad case: his cousin's son, a Gideon, died of wounds from *friendly* fire *on the same day* Richmond fell. What unimaginable grief!

And me—I'm unscathed physically by war, but I have my own upheaval. It's partly my own making, but I want to blame someone else, too—the Mennonite church or anyone. I feel put upon. I didn't *seek* this latest dilemma; it's not like my desire to publish. I claim that.

But this new one—I kept it from Salome as long as I could. I still don't like to talk about it. How can she keep a positive spirit when so many developments have gone against her? Changes started with Michael Kaegy late last December. Well, I don't know where or when they started. Maybe with more Mennonites coming to Chicago. Maybe with my keeping in touch with Mennonites—even Amish—when I went to Indiana because of our newspaper. Maybe with Daniel Brenneman moving to Elkhart County last year. Many links in the chain.

As soon as I mentioned Daniel's name, Salome remembered him as a brother of John M. and recalled my story about the 3,000-pound-plus ox that I *had* to see in Pennsylvania. In a nutshell: Mennonite connections never end, and now they're coming to Chicago. Some days I feel like I've walked into a steel trap that has no exit. And that says nothing about Salome. Here's another link: Michael is a brother-in-law of Daniel Brenneman. *But* the good part: Michael's been a big help with the business end of our newspaper because of his education in Virginia.

I've always been reasonably healthy—a hard worker. I wasn't good at playing ball as a lad and I couldn't swim, but I began to plow at age twelve. By fourteen my father pronounced me to be full-grown and ready for a day of man's work. I kept up well here in Chicago, making a living as a businessman. But when I added *Herald of Truth* and took on two full-time jobs simultaneously, I began to face serious physical shortcomings. My exhaustion this past winter—one dreadful cold after the other—left me short-tempered with Salome. She wouldn't let me hold Martha for three weeks in a row, not the way I kept hacking. I took a bath in the evening with water so cold, my hair stood on end. Then I wrapped up as warm as possible and went straight to bed. But that brought little relief.

Fortunately, Salome recovered well from giving birth; she and Martha stayed well. But she couldn't add proofreading to her day's work as quickly as we had expected. I missed not having her available to discuss articles whenever I needed her. One positive thing: when I took inventory in January, the figures showed slightly over 1,200 people had paid one dollar a year for a subscription. We were thrilled about that! My goal had been 1,000 subscribers for *Herald of Truth* in a year's time. But then my string of colds settled in, and more complications.

So here was Michael in Chicago; I offered him an upstairs room. I've never felt right about it, but I couldn't see any other solution to the burden of my workload. Back then, Martha was in her third month, and Moses had moved back here also. That made five mouths for Salome to feed, one way or another. But at the same time, Michael probably helped me preserve some of my health. While I'm gone during the day, he works on the paper. But his own physical fitness is weak; he can't do heavy work and *must* get ten hours of sleep a night. He's very fond of Salome's apple butter, but she's right to call him finicky. Why can't he eat meat? He sniffs out fat from a goose when it shows up in a vegetable stew!

And this is no small thing: since Michael lives here, Daniel shows up at our place more often. And Daniel has picked up on some of Michael's ideas. He says his body feels much more *wholesome* when he eats like Michael. Frustrations got the better of Salome and me. For a while, we found private payback by making jokes about whether this or that—a blue sock, a chair—was *wholesome.* Daniel thinks he's teasing when he calls me a Philadelphia lawyer and says I talk like a book. I've not been able to see the humor.

As if all of this isn't enough extra work for Salome, the frequency of other visitors has increased also. It started with a smattering last fall and during this winter. Now, this spring, I can't dispute: they come at all hours. Some from Canada; many from Pennsylvania. We've become a stopover with increasing numbers of church people coming through Chicago.

At first Salome was good-natured: "What's one more mouth?" But finally, she faced me, her chin set. "It's too handy. I didn't come to Chicago to run a hotel." Her lips wobbled when she said, "I'm sorry; I must sound selfish."

I felt awful. I could only take her in my arms. "It's my fault; I'm so sorry. I don't know how to stop the flood." She knows I must make acquaintance with readers of the *Herald;* on that count, I shouldn't turn anyone away. But the strain of hospitality! What's worse: I enjoy visiting with people more than Salome does. But when travelers arrive at midnight, or right *before* breakfast, even I know it's too much. One man, whose name I barely recognized, knocked on our door *before* we were up. And I'm *not* a late sleeper.

There's only one small way I've accommodated Salome. I'm ashamed to say, she had to bring it up. I had forgotten or pushed it to the back in importance. Increasingly, though, she's mentioned her home folks; one evening early this month, she asked directly. "Do you remember our second agreement when we first betrothed?"

I looked up, startled. "Why, of course—" She waited; I waited. Finally, I said, "A visit back home once a year if you desire. Right?" I pressed a fist to quell the disturbance in my gut.

She nodded. "Now that the war's over, traveling should be safer. Correct?"

"Yes, I would think. In theory, yes, the trains—"

Almost that quickly, I agreed to make arrangements for her to take Martha this summer on the cars. Ever since, I pray that one of our visitors will turn into a suitable travel companion. Salome shows no hesitation about putting Martha through the rough jerking of a train. "She's five months now, and in another two months, she'll travel well in my arms."

"Not the whole trip! You must have respite, that long ride." I studied her face. "Is that planned, too?"

"No, Fretz, no." She had a twinkle in her eye, though, that made me feel no better. "Moses and Mary Ann can help you with batching. By summer, we'll have vegetables from our garden: beans and cabbage. No good reason that Michael can't do some of his own cooking."

I gulped. "You've talked with Mary Ann?"

"Your sister understands, though concerned about a travel companion, too. Estelle is too young."

All of this going on without me! But what could I say? "It would be sadder, I guess, to leave Martha here with me." In spite of myself, I laughed, for Salome couldn't stifle her giggle. "I know you pamper me: meat, potatoes, coffee, pie. I'm grateful, even when I don't say it."

"It's nice when you say it."

I felt rotten. Again.

I have to admit: another factor has contributed to my upheaval. A celebration of sorts—I turned thirty on the sixth of this month. Salome asked my preference, and I requested prairie chickens, just as she had fixed for our Christmas meal and again for our first wedding anniversary. Thirty years old! The collision of my age, the end of the war, and an uncertain future caused soul-searching. Overall, it's been easy getting ahead in this city, although right now our money market's depressed. Gold dropped from 275 to 151 in the last month and a half.

But my age— Shouldn't I know my life's work by age thirty? I had thought I was on track. From farm boy, to school teacher, to lumber merchant, to business partner, to provider for my wife and child. Then, this newspaper. But my leap into religious publishing was balanced by my insurance policy, wasn't it? I still had say, didn't I? I could read Daniel Musser's book, decide what fit and what didn't.

Apparently, God doesn't think much of bargains. A couple days after my birthday, John M. made an overnight stop on one of his travels and politely offered me a new crown of thorns. While visiting during the meal, he told the sad news of two young men of Mennonite background. These boys—Whanger by name—had been captured as Confederate soldiers by the North but had been located now in Illinois, imprisoned somewhere along the Mississippi River.

"Countless others also," John mused. "We know not the extent—our young, scattered hither and yon."

That was only the start. Later, when the two of us were alone in the parlor, he shifted in his chair and rubbed his forehead. "We cannot underestimate the reach of the publishing ministry, holding some who might otherwise have been lost," he said.

"That is our prayer," I said cautiously. I've learned the value of plural pronouns.

But as is his habit, he moved ahead with no fanfare. "Have you felt the call to preach?"

I started to laugh. "Oh my, no! I'm up to my ears, writing editorials and editing articles." I looked in vain for amusement on John M.'s face. "Well, I suppose everything I write could be called a sermon," I added. "Lincoln's inaugural address certainly carried tones of more depth than a rally cry."

"And you've said one of your ears is compromised, right?"

I tried to smile; John M. rarely makes jokes. A trap within a trap had snapped shut.

"There's a small congregation sixty miles south of Chicago that needs help; they would welcome you."

I didn't want to show disrespect, but I had to put a stop. "My calling is publishing." Didn't John appreciate the sacrifices I was making already? "Salome and I have no personal time together," I said. Surely I didn't need to spell out specific tensions.

"Relinquishment is always difficult. You are giving much, as have others. But the need is great." This short man with the wide nose spoke kindly: no splash, no apology. He sat with his hands folded, as if the unthinkable sounded reasonable.

I stirred in my chair and shook my head with a snap. "That would never work." A preaching ministry on top of everything else! The back of my neck felt sweaty.

"I only ask that you give it some thought. Take it to your heavenly Father."

I can't explain it. I felt angry—his nerve. I felt guilty—my anger. I knew the church John referred to, the small Gardner congregation in Grundy

County that meets in a frame schoolhouse. I had visited once to introduce our newspaper. Never thinking—oh, my dear wife. Not another shackle! She'll never come back from Pennsylvania.

Who wouldn't have put off telling Salome? For two days I resisted. I went to the lumberyard and pretended to work. Occasional moments of pride popped up: John trusted me. Maybe I'd known a question like this would come, ever since I first took Communion with Mennonites in Indiana. The humility of their footwashing—stooping to another—had tarnished the glow of my business success. Or maybe this is what I sensed with the white flower that replaced the brownish-orange lily buried in my dream of long ago. But wasn't it enough to go into publishing for the church? More than enough—any sensible person would know! It was far too soon for more to be required.

Finally, though, I had to tell Salome. A shadow—that look of forsakenness—crossed her face. My *put upon* became hers. I'll never forget. We talked; I said the basics. She looked lost, asked a few questions, but otherwise, said little.

But before I extinguished the lamp that night, she whispered, "You must heed the call." I held myself taut, looking from her to the lamp and back. Neither of us slept much that night.

The next day she added, over our breakfast mush, "*Test* the call." She got up from the table, came to me, and sat on my lap. She pressed the top of her head into me and said, her voice smothered, "Test it thoroughly, John. Promise me."

I looked quickly to see why she had called me by my publishing name. I could uncover nothing. I didn't want to ask directly, so I said instead, "John M. didn't ask for an immediate answer." I kept her to me.

A day of routine passed; her bright eyes stayed dull under dark brows. If Michael or Moses noticed a strain between Salome and me, neither said anything. We talked, but mostly about Martha and their trip back East in less than two months. We agreed that they would stay two months. I felt myself slipping, resigned to what remained unspoken. Acceptance seemed a natural extension—this path laid out for me. I had been writing about two Kingdoms, but I still lived in parts of both worlds. What did I have to bargain with? My growing understanding, by turns, excited and miserable. One time, Salome said, "Inevitable. We will make the best of it."

Several days later, Daniel Brenneman got wind of it. "Another step in your transition from Saul to Paul," he said. It took every ounce of Christian grace to set that aside. Pointless to ask: "Where was the bright light? When did I persecute?"

Other nights I couldn't avoid wondering: when does service become slavery? I'm not a savior. I've never wanted to be one, right? I said to Salome, "Will major parts of *your* life with me always be involuntary?"

"I can't answer that," she said. "That's why we live—to find out."

I didn't know whether to thank her for what seemed gracious. I couldn't bear the thought: she was letting me take advantage of her good nature. Her love. I found myself saying with as little fanfare as John M., "I need to go visit that church; see for myself. Many others have given their lives. This war. Some are in prison; some can't walk. Some farm with one arm."

I sent John M. a letter, saying I tentatively accepted. Later this month I'll ride the caboose of a freight train to visit. Salome won't go along; the air is too cool for Martha. Salome stays subdued; we talk of a playmate for Martha. Will I agree to whatever the church asks? Have I no spine? No freedom? Is that what Paul's call meant to him? When is the burden lifted?

Salome added further disturbance. "You can't take on more without putting something aside. If not immediately, in the next year." There was no wavering in her voice. I know that look.

From time to time during these weeks, I've thought the same. But I never said it. In front of her, though, I couldn't dismiss it. Salome has the right to some prospect of relief. I would have to say something to Beidler. A testing of sorts. My brother-in-law doesn't *own* me, but I owe him much. He gave me a start; I'm attached to his coattails, the ropes of lumber. But I put off the test, thinking the question might come up naturally. It didn't. My teeth set up a racket.

One day at work, Abe mentioned that Jacob and Mary Ann had invited him for an evening meal. I've learned not to count on Abe, but I saw advantage in having a buffer. That evening, a faint light flickered in the often-dark parlor across the street.

Salome gave me a hug, but no advice.

The two men were conversing amiably in the corner of the parlor and expressed surprise at my appearance. I wanted to be totally clear of mind, so I declined the offer of brandy and fetched a cup of water to soothe my dry throat. I should have brought a full pitcher. I slipped in and out of the kitchen without seeing Mary Ann, but I heard voices upstairs. I chose a straight chair at a distance.

I soon gave up pretense of being unrehearsed. "I've something, been thinking about—"

Abe put his drink down with a thunk. Jacob took one look at me and must have decided to hold his wise-crack about the value of my thinking.

"I'm giving consideration—nothing's final—selling my interest in the partnership." Two sets of eyes blinked rapidly, then stared at me. Jacob shifted to being Beidler, his back straight. "The lumber company," I added.

"What in tarnation!" Beidler said. Abe harrumphed and straightened also.

I gulped more water. I hadn't considered being disowned, but I saw no brotherliness. "I can't do two full-time jobs. I come home worn out, eat supper, work at writing and translating." My words came in spurts. "Past midnight often. Exhausted, ever since the baby. Michael helps, but the toll—"

I'd mentioned some tensions before to Abe; now he leaned forward cautiously, as if approaching a wounded animal. "Couldn't John M. take over?"

"He's already worn thin—oversight in his own church and many others. Older, too."

Beidler picked up a straight chair and brought it closer, as if he needed a clearer look. He sat forward, a fist pressing on his thigh. "You would give yourself to publishing, this enterprise in its infancy, when you've put in long hours for—what is it, eight years?—building your share in a lumber business? A *profitable* one." His countenance stayed unruffled, and his words came evenly but as if running across the jagged teeth of a saw. "I don't mean to disregard your—this publishing. But you're just arriving, elsewhere."

I thought I had come prepared. I looked away from his gaze, remembering John M.'s stiff back in that same parlor two years earlier—afraid for his life.

Abe scratched his arms, reached inside his sock to scratch an ankle. "Your commitment, admirable. But what about this Michael?" His voice rose. "There must be someone living in a Mennonite settlement with easier proximity . . . could take over."

"I don't know of anyone." My voice sounded weak. "Michael's not strong enough; you know that." I'd heard so often: I was the right person—business knowledge *and* words to inspire. I couldn't make myself mention the possibility of additional church responsibility. I couldn't say that my family and I might have to leave the city.

"Have you spoken with Jim?" Beidler asked. "Or have you let this . . ." His voice *never* sounds lost, but it wavered. ". . . this overly righteous *pose*—" He slumped in his chair, hands locked behind his head.

"No, not yet, haven't talked with Jim."

Abe's eyes squinted at me, like he was looking with disgust at pride on full display. He doesn't know how hard I work to fit in with Mennonites. The Amish, too! I can't help it that attention has followed.

Beidler slowly walked back to the fireplace mantel and stood with fingertips in a vest pocket. I know that stance: he's about to close a deal. Or he's grown tired of a merchant. "You'll never get rich in publishing!" he shouted, not loud enough to wake a child, but loud. "You came here to make money. I know you did."

"Yes, I did," I said quietly. "But I can't serve two masters. I'm learning." I wondered if Mary Ann might tiptoe to the door at the sound of her husband's voice; if she might be listening on the other side. Would I ever set foot in this house again?

Beidler lowered his voice. "You're not working for *the government* in the lumber business. You're not subject to any master like a *slave*." He hesitated only briefly. "You—you're your own man!" I waited for a string of oaths, but he refrained.

"Not those two kingdoms," I said. "I've tried to please the Kingdom of God *and* the kingdom of money."

He paced in front of the fireplace, his head down. "Always two worlds for you! Why must everything be at odds?" He whirled toward me. "So now, not warfare. *Money* is the enemy! Don't you know? You can make all the money you want in lumber, give half to the church, if you must." I hadn't been scolded in years, although sometimes Salome chides. "Ridiculous, Fretz! What is it—the pleasure of seeing your name, *John*, in print?" He returned abruptly to his wingback and crossed his legs, his voice reduced to a drone. "Your financial prospects are enormous; Chicago, the commercial center, apart from the eastern cities. So much money here." He uncrossed his leg and leaned forward—an icy smile. "None of that matters, huh?" He waited. "You know the war's been good for us. It's only temporary—this spring downturn of money."

"That's not it," I said quickly. "You've done much, given me a good start, Jacob."

"*Why* then? *Why*, Fretz? Or John. Whatever you want to be called."

"It does seem risky," Abe interjected. "No man leaves home to adjust to the city, as you've done, only to throw his life away." He leaned toward me; I knew it was coming. "This ambition with publishing—it's curious—when you speak of meekness. Is it fame? Father—"

I waved my hand to cut him off. "I know Father." *Definitely* no point in mentioning the church in Grundy County now. No point, either, in arguing whether *that* would be *lowly* enough. Or maybe too *elevated*! I had to extricate myself. "I thought it only fair to say what I'm *thinking* about."

Beidler nodded but had the last say, as he walked me to the door, placing a hand on my shoulder. "Don't do it, Fretz. You're very good with lumber. Jim likes you. You have a family; you don't want to start over now.

Believe me, I know what that's like. My move from Springfield to Chicago—*very* difficult." His voice caught and he looked away. When he turned back, his face a paler shade, he said, "Don't be an impulsive nineteen-year-old!"

With that, I nodded and walked out, afraid I might show weakness.

Since then, I live among Salome's "inevitable," Beidler's incredulity, Abe's spotting pride. I scan the papers—no time to read carefully, as I once did, although I've noticed there's no longer a death count given. I offer a brief nod of recognition that nature is replenishing itself around me, as Salome shares her delight in grass greening, birds singing.

I could write to John M. and tell him to look elsewhere. Would that be more of a betrayal than leaving lumber? I could surprise everyone and walk away from publishing entirely. Well, I suppose I could, in theory. Then I could go back to Sunday school work with my new free time. Would that be less fraught with ambition, Abe? Less likely to lead to overwork, Salome?

I don't think I can turn a blind eye to filthy lucre again. I've turned that corner. Nor can I call it honoring my own father to give extra income to families without fathers. That sounds like a quick way out from a deeper way in. No, I'm changed. I'm fortunate to be able to love and cherish the two who matter most.

* * *

"The worst has happened."

"No, not the worst," Salome says.

I don't have the heart to argue. Of course, there are far worse things, but more momentous? More likely to lead to awful consequences? Who will mend our nation? Not Andrew Johnson. He'll never lead people to see Negroes as deserving equal treatment. Hatred will increase. The one who could lead us has been taken. Like a flash of lightning. Why? For the love of God—why?

Last night, shortly after ten—the night of Good Friday—some misguided fool entered Ford's Theatre in Washington, where President Lincoln and his wife were enjoying a theater production—some light English comedy called *Our American Cousin*. This deranged person shot the president of the United States in the back of the head; the ball lodged in his brain. A pure act of evil. Doctors could do nothing.

Early this morning, when we heard the sound of cannons, I jerked alert. I couldn't believe the war had resumed. No, a telegraph dispatch had been delivered, and news spread throughout Chicago. Abraham Lincoln died this morning, less than ten hours after the shooting. Fifty-six years old.

A few days ago he spoke publicly about voting rights for the Negro. He'd been reminded to use caution, not expose himself to danger, as when he walked in Richmond. Now this. Black crepe hangs from doorposts.

My usual Saturday work sits untended; I can't concentrate. Salome has made no move to bake a pie. Little Martha, sucking her thumb, must wonder why the big folks aren't up to their usual busyness. We sought consolation in the Bible but sat in a daze of verses. Nothing registered. Moses and Michael went to their separate rooms. No one has appetite. What would be the use of translating? When the child napped, Salome and I retired to our bed and held each other.

It's not that we knew the man personally. Oh, long ago I heard Lincoln debate Douglas and felt excitement. I marched for him. But as time went on, I railed against him. Increasingly so. I all but gave up when he instructed Grant to carry out his hard war policy in the South. But now—a new layer of grief and anger. They say there's a manhunt, chasing this deluded one on foot. He, too, a member of the human race.

Salome says, "We're all children before the Almighty."

"Too many have turned to the god of violence. It kills us all."

She nodded but said, "We don't know how God judges."

True, it's not for me to say. But our minds are awhirl. We don't know how to think beyond—the one who could have led us—

Jacob — Iowa, May 1865

Mary calls it an aggravation: my habit, as the shades of light draw down, to say I may not live to see another morn. How can that be anything but a proper assessment? No one knows the exact moment when sleep turns to passage. Our length of days given, not determined by man.

She says I should sing and give thanks. She begins the first lines of "*Mit Lust so will ich singen,*" the words of Felix Manz, a martyr from the sixteenth century. I sing, too, with some pleasure, but she sings beyond what I can muster.

The end of life does not work on Mary as it does on me. Two months ago, it was Jacob Yoder's boys of five and ten. And now the president of our new nation! Death is natural, but when it becomes unnatural, I tremble to get up during the night—my rapid heartbeat—and light a candle. I pray for what time is left, all while tossed about.

Jakob was helping me sow oats the day word came of the good man's demise. I fell to my knees and Jakob gave comfort, his light hand on my bent back. From what little I had heard, Lincoln sounded like the one to unify us. Jakob added to my fears. "It will not go easy for the Negro; those same ones will continue their mischief."

I do not know his full meaning, but only days before, his father Daniel had brought glad tidings that Lee had surrendered to Grant. How desperate we had been for just such word: the cessation of fighting.

But now, this unwelcome news to ponder on top of the good. Jakob and I headed slowly to the house, my legs unsteady. "Some have set their teeth against any change that benefits those with dark skin," he said.

"But we have Captain Shaver's efforts," I said. "Tell again how that came about."

"Yes, this Shaver brought with him a boy—name of Bob—to our Sharon area when he returned from the front lines two years ago. The story goes that he had found the lad sitting by his mother's cold side—most likely a stray bullet. Right then Shaver's heart took a sharp turn. The forlorn boy—no known Negro family to speak of—is now a part of Shaver's family. His daughters are said to watch like sisters, making certain that good treatment is afforded by other youngsters."

"A beacon of good-will," I said.

"A worthy model," Jakob said.

We were walking past the nearly empty granary—my breathing, more regular again—past the place where Jakob had spied my cutting knife last week. Surprises come from my own hand these days! I am no stranger to misplacing things, but exactly how my knife came to be hidden under loose straw on the floor, I will likely never know. Perhaps I set it aside or bumped it when a more urgent task presented itself. I cannot give account, but I suggested we not speak of it further.

Other mysteries, too, but none greater than those within my family. I cannot choose for the women pledged in marriage to three of my sons. But the sharpest slap yet: lacking desire to come to the Communion table. I cannot force them with a whip as I would a donkey. But how can we tolerate absence? The awful message it sends to the young when adults refuse to submit to discipline. I never dreamed—voluntary withdrawal from fellowship by some of my own. Oh, my dearest Barbara. What would she say?

It happened on Easter Sunday, a day intended for rejoicing, as we remembered again how the Lord forgives our sins when we confess. But our joy turned to mourning. More grief than from this word of President Lincoln's untimely demise.

Frederick had encouraged me to go ahead and announce a Communion service. "Do not let more years pass. We must test our unity, not make guesses in the dark." We both remembered all too well, what we had heard in Indiana.

It was no secret that dissatisfaction continued to lurk in our midst. Even after my months of less harsh wordings—I had tried my best—differences remained. But now we have clarity beyond what we ever sought. The searing pain of stubbornness! I thought people would be eager to once more receive the bread and blood of life. Instead, only half the members came to our Sharon Township church meeting at the Kempf home. Sixty persons in my district—my closest neighbors!—chose not to avail themselves of the Lord's Supper. We had already announced arrangements for Communion to follow the next Sunday in the Deer Creek district at Peter Brenneman's house. Much as I shrank from full knowledge, I could not see fit to cancel.

We went forth as planned, but the results—*oh Lord, hide not your mercy.* I do not like to think of it as rebellion, but only thirty-eight of the eighty-six members in that district came to show the harmony we desperately seek.

It is mostly women members; almost three out of four chose to abstain. Frederick cautions: "We do not know the full extent of reasons, whether prideful household decoration and personal adornment, or new members coming from differing practices already established among Amish in other states." He does not think that Susanna's disagreement over her son Emanuel could have been the cause. "She could not have swayed so many others," he says. "Not by herself."

I have made a list: all the members who broke bread on either Sunday. A separate list of those not present. "Better numbers for the men," I say. "Only one in four stayed away."

Frederick nods. I cannot help adding, "Henry was there."

After the second Sunday of spurning, I could hardly lift my head to Caspar when I prepared the buggy for our return home. I jerked the reins unduly. All the way, I stayed tense with my eyes on the muddy road, but Mary's words stay burnished: "The apple-cart is upset." As if to soften, she rattled names of several women who have given birth recently.

"Some absences may have been justified," I said. "But my Joseph's Barbara—their Noah is already eight months. You call him a babe? Surely others look to her, a minister's wife. And where was Christian's Elizabeth?"

Mary could only distract. "Any of their adopted ones could have been taken with one springtime illness or another. And George's Mary—we know she has grown exceedingly, likely burdened with carrying two."

"You know as well as I. Husbands and wives are *not* to go their separate ways."

I could not settle into restfulness that afternoon. I scuffed through last year's leaves in the woods, inspecting my hazelnut trees that have leafed out. No soothing words such as: *Well done, thou good and faithful servant* came to my ears. My own clamor may have been too loud: *Take this load from me.* I knew not to curse the Lord who gives me breath, but I may face damnation, not having led the flock into willing obedience and joy in the Lord. When I turned to circle back to the house, my distress amplified: I had crushed white blooms in a patch of Dutchman's breeches. I wept over my boots, took strides to avoid further damage.

Why, why, why? The older I become, the more these matters appear at my feet. Must everything be my fault? Certainly not the way so many of our women succumb early to hardships. Mary declares that Frederick's Sarah looks even more ragged, with another birthing drawing nigh. Already last fall, Mary thought Sarah looked washed out from the summer's work. She does not deserve ill, not when her dream of two acres of orchard is bearing fruit in this Iowa land. I must tell her how grateful I am for the consolation she gave my Barbara during her last days. I do not want Frederick to be bereft when he sorely needs her help.

Already last month, questions came regarding my grandson Samuel. I pray that no dishonor took place with his marriage to Barbry Beachy from Grantsville. Along with that development, Jakob reported that his brother had been drafted! Of course, no one could have known in advance that his summons would come only a few weeks before the war ended. But to be served papers on the same day as his wedding!

If only Samuel had gone through the deacon, as is proper! How could he not recognize his error in writing directly to Barbry's father, Joel, and asking permission to marry? Whether a willful or innocent forgetting, these newly marrieds were on their way to Samuel's dwelling at the end of their day, the 19th of March, only to be stopped by a Union army officer, turning their joy to dismay. Samuel's name had been drawn eight days earlier to fill the quota for the 16th Congressional District in Pennsylvania. *Oh, Lord, look upon us.*

My stepson Daniel insists that enough people stepped forward to vouch for his son; yes, Samuel had joined the Casselman River Amish. There is that much—he had conducted himself in a manner consistent with our scruples. I could not bear to have my grandson contribute to suspicion and hatred before a draft board. But the upshot: he had to pay the $300 commutation fee—only good for that draft term—to be discharged from liability to military duty. After all this flurry and interrogation, maybe there is yet a good outcome. Jakob says that Samuel plans now to return to us with his bride. If only—surely, much of this turmoil might have been spared, had he come sooner.

I cannot overlook, though, our own upsets over weddings right here. Whenever I think we are making headway at eliminating loud jesting and dancing past midnight, something adverse rears its head. Now two more deaths of young women have necessitated more weddings this past March. What should be blessing, brings sour suspicion. In Gid Marner's case I felt pressed, for his father serves on The Bench. But when I asked Gid about his hurry to marry Lizzie, he pleaded not to be put off. That was all I could get from him.

Equally unsettling: some of our flock still use friendship with the world to make gain in temporal goods. Moses Kauffman—again! This time he ignored his blood brothers and sold 160 acres to the Enfield man and secured over fifteen dollars an acre. How often must I preach from John 15 that God has chosen followers "out *of the world*"?

With all that troubles, what alternative is there but to write another letter for next month's gathering of ministers in Ohio? My zeal with the pen comes and goes. How can I be the Lord's mouthpiece in preventing schism for the larger body, when so many members near at hand stay away? I beat upon myself—my own *unterdrückung*—until the Lord reaches through my drivel to give grace sufficient. Some of my concerns are no different—will bundling ever go away?—than what I wrote two years ago. But questions about our response to government have come to the fore. Will we be allowed to preserve our freedom of conscience? Has God been testing *us* by permitting this ordeal of war?

I try to use kindly words; I make a plea for patience among us. But at the same time, we *must* hold each other true. How my hand perspires, even in winter, to write a new part about the use of substitutes. Now that the war is over, it may be easier to shed light; people may be more willing to listen when we are not in the midst of call-ups. Over these past years, conviction has fully come: buying a substitute is contrary to the teachings of Jesus and the apostles. Even paying $300 as protection money has taken on the look of a filthy rag. Some may think I err in letting go tradition here. But that John Funk fellow—how his words lingered about our corruption of values. He helped me see: everything must be held up to the light, even past practices.

Frederick will take my letter to those gathered on the farm of this John K. Yoder. Young Jakob has rewritten my words, so my shaky handwriting will not be a barrier. Again, those who hold firm like us, plan to meet in Holmes County a few days in advance. But as usual, Frederick says he cannot be gone from home extra days. If only I had strength to work in his stead and extend his absence. But he has told me with the strictness required for a wayward child: "Do not lift one finger to plant your fields while I am gone."

How hard that man works! He has spent tedious hours with his cold chisel again this spring, breaking the last of his third 80-acre section. This part was not as heavily timbered, but he still had to use four horses to cut an eighteen-inch furrow with his breaker. He has shown more vexation than I recall in other years when coming upon grubs and roots. I know how tiring it is to need to stop and file the share and cutter every half mile. But I want to remind him: cutting slanting notches like saw teeth is not nearly as confounding as addressing waywardness among the members.

On yet another matter—this time, my own behalf—I recently sought out Benedict Miller's son, Jacob. After the customary greetings, I asked that we go to his woodworking shed where I could assess the beautiful grains lined up. I made no attempt to hide my intent: "I want solid walnut, not cherry or pine. *Verschtehscht?*" His eyes widened, but he nodded solemnly when I said, "No padding for lining, nor handles."

Without further ado, I handed him fifteen dollars; his eyebrows shot up, but he took the money silently. Right then, a deer skittered past the open door, and we stepped outside to see if more disturbance ensued. The deer calmly reached for tender tree leaves.

Inside again, I handed this Jacob the long stick I had brought along. Of course, he has his own sticks, but I laid myself down on the floor. I stretched to what is left of my full extent, my eyes closed and buffered by the surrounding fragrance of seasoned wood. "Put a notch to mark my length." I heard him rustle for his short knife and squinted to see that he did as told. I folded my hands and arms across my chest, such that he could measure my exact width, one elbow to the other. "Do as is appropriate," I said, "ten inches of head clearance and tapering from the waist down—an extra seven or eight inches beyond my feet." He marked as asked but remained wordless.

I hastened to reassure the good man, devout in every regard, "I have no plans to harm myself; I only wish to prevent delay at the time of my demise. Suit yourself whether to cut and smooth the boards in advance. But if seasoned walnut is readily available, you will make matters easier for my sons, as well as for yourself."

He said softly, "We are blessed to have a leader who seeks order in all things."

"One more thing: say nothing of this to anyone." I groaned to turn my body sideways and lift myself from the floor. I looked him in the eye. "When you hear word, only then let it be known that preparations have been underway. No hurried late-night work need take place. The sooner to deliver my poor bones to my rightful place beside Barbara."

We shook hands and he waved limply as I rode away. Ever since, I feel a greater measure of release from this world's cares. When my breath vanishes like a vapor, my sons will only need to decipher the handwriting of my will. And whatever transpires with my letter to the church body, that is in the Lord's hands. If only people will see one day that I did not mean to trample, only carry out God's precepts faithfully. *A good and faithful servant* is my heart's desire.

But for now, my most fervent prayer is to live my last days in peace, even with my grown boys' women, and if possible—all the sisters. I will rightfully continue to say what God's Word shows forth, so that I may be granted safe passage through that last great cloud of unknowing.

Betsey — West Virginia, May 1865

We did not have abundance during the winter, but Poppa was right: we had enough, even when our potatoes ran out. If we forgot and complained when the butter went all, Poppa frowned and said, "Some in Virginia are starving. A small thing for us that our cow cannot always keep up." He looked long at Tobias and said, "This war has barely ended soon enough." Sarah said her mother worried for her big boys, too; Jonas has reached fifteen and is already near to full-sized like his brother Jakie.

We are glad, too, that the big folks in our church get to keep more money. They no longer take an extra collection to send to our people in Somerset County. Nor do they need to worry about standing clear from the Army anymore. I never asked Poppa more about why he hauled, when our friend Joseph said he would not do so.

I would rather remember Isaac and Joseph for all they helped us—a year ago already. I use the railroad game to teach my sisters how to spell, but I have to remind Lydia not to give Mary tricky words like "earnest"; "easy" is hard enough. Joseph was extra good at teaching because he had gone to school for three winters in Virginia. Many nights this past winter, especially during storms, I wanted someone to come to our door because they saw our lamplight from the road. But Poppa said no one would be foolhardy enough to be out walking in the middle of a blizzard. We know we will never see Johnny again, unless we get to meet in heaven.

After our biggest snow of all—long, long days—Poppa showed us on a Sunday afternoon how to build a snow house. He called it a square igloo. Tobias and I scooped and carved high and wide with Poppa. I barely had to stoop to enter, and when the little boys woke from their naps, they bundled up and walked right inside. Gideon and Levi wanted to sleep there all night.

Poppa and I had our birthdays again in January; he said, "*Yuscht ebaut uffgwachse.*"

Mother had to correct him. "*Noch net gans.*" She put nutmeg with the cinnamon for special and called it a spice birthday cake for both of us.

Poppa kept on smiling. "Not entirely, but Betsey and Tobias are growing fast to be a woman and man."

Sometimes before I fall asleep at night, I touch my chest to see if I am changing. I cannot tell anything, but maybe when we have hot weather, I will swell.

With our warmer weather now, we do not have time to play games because everyone has helped plant extra garden and field crops. Mother says we need more food because we children are bigger and eat more beans to keep strong bones. We spaded very hard ground, and Poppa and Tobias dug out tree roots, too. Poppa can work long hours again, because he rested up all winter.

But the furrows on his forehead came back fast when he returned from Brookside one day this spring and said our president had died. He blew his nose extra when he explained to the little boys who a president is. "That man did good—on the side of making things right. Not that we are to fight or cause pain in order to get our way." His eyes blinked fast. "Sometimes bad things may have to happen for wrongs to be set right. Like for Mister to get a fair shake."

"But the cost—" Mother said.

Poppa's head swayed side to side like the pendulum on our clock. "Yes, a terrible cost—it is not God's way to seek revenge. *Mir verschtehn net ferwas.*"

Everyone wanted to know more about this Mr. Lincoln. "Did he have children?" I asked.

"Yes," Poppa said, "but I do not know how many, nor their names or ages."

"Was he old?" Mary asked.

"Not so very, Mary," Poppa said. His eyes drooped. "Unless I am old. Mother is right: sometimes bad things make more wrong than right."

"Is it cold when you die?" Lydia asked.

"A person's body, yes. The blood no longer flows," he said.

"Is it cold in heaven, like an igloo?" Mary asked.

"No, everyone is the right temperature," Poppa said. "No troubles or war in heaven."

"But will we have bodies?" Lydia asked.

"No," I said, quick as a wink. I remembered about Momma. "Bodies stay in the ground but spirits go to heaven."

"You remembered," Poppa said. He gave me a smile that made me smile back.

"Where do we get our spirits?" Mary asked.

"You ask hard questions," Poppa said, but he did not seem sad about it. "Your spirit is how you behave with others. Well, mostly. You have a kind spirit, Mary . . ." He scratched at his beard. "I do not know how to say. We are not to have a rebellious spirit. When you are older, Brother Daniel will explain better."

I wanted to ask if Momma's spirit would get to be with Poppa's in heaven, but Mother was shooing us out the door—we were late to milk the cow and do the other chores. If I had my way, I would still be little, we would have races in heaven, and Momma would catch and hug me. But since I am big, like now, I will want to introduce her to Gideon and the other little boys. We might have to hunt to find all our new friends from Virginia.

Days later, after Tobias and Jonas had been together on a Sunday afternoon, Tobias told me that a bad man had shot the president with a gun.

"Like what happened with Johnny?" I asked.

The president was inside somewhere, not riding a horse."

"What else?" I asked.

Tobias shrugged. "They put his body on a special train and took him to Illinois to bury him. Crowds waved all along the way."

I will ask Sarah if she knows more. She mostly likes to whisper what her sister tells her about finding the right man. Sarah says her brother Jakie has to have everything just so; he will not eat from a small spoon. She did not say that Jonas is persnickety that same way. Not that I am his best girl; I am too young for that. I wish Momma were here to tell me things; Mother does not have time for extras.

But last week she told me a secret when we pulled weeds in the strawberries. Of a sudden, she stood from bending over and stretched way back, so that her belly stuck out with her smock. I tried not to stare, but she must have seen me look because she came closer and said, "Betsey, you will need to take charge soon—the berries." I looked at our two long rows and frowned. But she guided my hand to her belly. "*Bol en Glennes.*" I pulled my hand away sharply.

"The *Bobbli* kicks," she said, smiling. "It is hard for me to bend low anymore. But new life is nothing for alarm, Betsey. Someday, you, too—" She hitched her skirts a little and showed me her swollen ankles.

My cheeks felt hot, but I said, "I will help." I looked again at the long rows and added, "Will Lydia help, too?" Sometimes she wiggles out of work to play with the boys. Then my alarm grew—all the new space we have dug for peas and beans! We dare not lose Mother for long.

"Yes, Lydia will pick berries, too, but say nothing to her or Mary about the baby," Mother said. "Not yet. Nor Sarah Beachy. It is not for squealing."

It will be hard not to blurt. Sarah likes to tell about her baby sister Lizzie—another Elizabeth!—cooing in her cradle. But I will keep Mother's secret with my own. If we have a baby sister, we will have even numbers: four of each. I do not know where we will put everyone, though. Maybe Gideon and Levi will both get to sleep at the far end of the loft with Tobias.

One time I asked Tobias if he liked Sarah. "For special?" he asked. I nodded, but he shook his head fast. "She is too young." But he did not make me feel silly. Ever since Joseph was here, Tobias has been nicer. But when he yawns big, he still looks at me and grins. He knows I must always be polite and cover my mouth like Mother.

On our first warm Sunday afternoon, when Poppa and Mother rested with the little boys, Tobias was allowed to ride Tom all alone to the Selders's to play stick ball with Valentine and Daniel. I said to Lydia and Mary what Poppa would say. "Do not make a rooster; we can have races."

Mother frowned, but I was quick to promise, "I will not get sweaty." I know a big girl is to hold more still for the happy changes.

Later, when we rested from running to the nearest sycamore and back—Lydia won every race, but I always caught Mary for a hug—we took turns naming all the Elizabeths in our church, then all the Christians and Peters. I remembered not to blurt anything, but I hope Mother will choose a name for the new *Bobbli* that we do not already have in our church.

Soon Lydia jumped up and wanted to go see if Gideon was awake yet to play, but I said, "Everyone tell yet what visitor you liked best during the war."

Right away, she said, "Jack! I got to brush and pet him."

Mary was slow but said, "Isaac. He was very tall and worked hard for Poppa. What about Auntie Mommie?"

"Yes, we could count her," I said. "She helped us with Gideon and Poppa. But from farther away, Joseph came, and Mack and Muck. Well, Muck worked while Mack was lame. They both sang."

"And Mister—he was nice and had a pretty hum," Lydia said.

"Johnny brought us hostas," I said.

"But not Hector," Mary said.

"No, not—" I said, "but you know what Poppa said."

Lydia was fidgeting again to go inside, but I said stronger, "Do not bother them; Mother needs her rest. The boys will come when ready. See how the sky makes a dome? How close it comes down, like touching when it meets the trees, but how high—way, way high—the sky is, when we look straight up."

It was like unto contentment, the same as when our hostas surprised us last year. The leaves had stayed tightly curled, until of a sudden they unfurled and waved. Now I know better what to expect; this spring the leaves look bigger already, like they might open into large fans that can cool us. I know to watch for thin stems, too; they shoot up and open to flower all unawares.

David — Shenandoah Valley, May 1865

We made it through Easter, but stories of resurrection seem far away. Our rejoicing a month ago with the brothers from the north has turned to lethargy. Gratitude remains—miracle seeds!—but our strength to plant only lasts a few rows at a time. I make no claim to be mirthful, but it appears we might finish planting before harvest time. Yes, the war is over—heartfelt thanks on that count, too—but we have not been blessed with another caravan. Our walk stays slow.

"Perhaps next week," Delilah says, her eyes droopy.

"We should not have counted," I say. "Too much to expect."

"Tricked into surviving a little longer," Abigail says.

"But that *is* our wish—survival," I say.

"No heart to disagree," Delilah says.

Our bodies bolstered for a time. We do not know what calamity we might have been spared. The warmer air—a blessing also, another row planted. But will we ever know sufficiency again? A *full* field of corn? When will our want match our store?

My women and I have resumed our daily pilgrimage, putting spring beauties atop the grave in the pines, restoring the marker once more. We hear stories of Southerners visiting battlefields, paying a dollar for bones. If we are one nation, Confederates should be included in the numbering of war dead by those in authority. Until proper mention is made of the total loss, it will not be forgotten. Nor forgiven.

With regard to our boys, Abigail tells me to visit Algernon Gray.

"It would not hurt to inquire," Delilah adds.

"I do not know the man personally," I say.

Abigail persists. "There must be some way to get information."

"What would I say? Ask like others: 'Please inform us if our sons are alive or dead.'"

"It would not hurt," Delilah says again. "He might know where to turn for assistance."

"That is only for learning the fate of those on battlefields," I say.

We keep to our separate thoughts until Delilah says, "Tell him we have a soldier's buttons."

I still polish the brass on occasion, but buttons are not a charm. "They do not seem remarkable, though some distressed parent might take consolation," I say. I suck idly on my lower gum—the side where I have lost two choppers. Abigail says I smack with my mouth in my sleep.

My women look at me as if they expect me to move mountains. I wave my hand to dismiss. "More time is needful." I rub a hand over my bare head. "We cannot expect the boys to jump on a train immediately. Only better postal service will bring word." I cannot resist. "Station yourselves at the end of the lane, if you must." They stare longer. "I would rather believe the boys remain safe. Rather believe such, than know," I tell them.

"I will write," Delilah says.

"We must be patient," I say, "give more time. They might have moved." I cover my mouth.

We go to separate corners of the room as if to dwell alone.

We are learning the hard way: nothing can be restored overnight. Not strength nor spirits. Our physical weakness, my heavy breathing from the least exertion, bear witness. But my restraint is nothing compared to others' resentment. No one wages war for four years, only to put it aside like a leaking barrel. Jefferson Davis has fled, they say, but what import does that carry? Slave owners have not changed their thinking. Not in ways that matter. Time will tell if good relations can be fostered, so that folks will see another race as equal. Stars in the sky may cloud over and disappear; moons wax and wane.

This much I know: killing has not solved our problems—not a president's death nor a farm lad's. Vengeance only fosters new tactics—a response to a response—spreads new problems. I thought it before; now I know it again.

Our loving God hears the pleas of the penitent, but whether God forgets the sins of a nation, I cannot say. Of the two at the top in Washington, J. M. says we lost the better leader by far. He places little faith in this Andrew Johnson, shakes his head at any thought that it will go more smoothly for our Negro brother, still considered the inferior race. "Perhaps with time. Grudgingly. But this long shadow of injustice will stay a deep blotch," he says.

Forgiveness does not come easily among those of us targeted either. Everyone has complaints. Abigail says I go round and around. No way to measure grievances: this is greater than that. We are all torn by grief. No one can say in a wink, "All is past and done." Nor does it profit to stay stuck: "I will *never* forget." Neither lays a foundation for tomorrow. I say my lines as best I know how. "*Blessed are the poor in spirit: for theirs is the kingdom of heaven.*" I put one step forward—we have seed—even when I feel little cheer. I do not see how I can go to Winfield. Or Algernon.

If Brothers Wine and Neff return—or Brother Moomaw comes—they will want a full accounting. I will tell how one of our families—with the father limited—survived the winter in their spring house, set low in the ground where no freezing could occur. I will acknowledge that two of our sisters expired, in part, because of infirmities. A child also, given over—an ankle wound that spread, causing high fever and convulsions. No manna fell from the sky, but for the one caravan. We give thanks; we have not been entirely cast aside.

But church authorities will hear of irregularities among us; my appointment may be taken from me. I will not object nor strain to hang on. What is worthy, after all? When is life's travail ever enough?

We did what was needful. We banded together, gave of what we had: a jar of cider, onions for a poultice, Delilah's balm of reading to soothe our souls. The Lord sustains. Our faces stay turned toward kindness.

But my women take it up again like a refrain. First, Delilah's "We must send again." She motions and says, "Fold one piece into an envelope. Make effort."

"We will go together in the carriage to buy a stamp." Abigail's face has the look of a jagged cut in the mountains. "All three of us. Like going to church."

I sigh. "I do not give up hope for our sons. But already two years since word came."

"I will write," Delilah says.

"What will you write?" I ask.

"That we want them to come," Abigail says. "That is enough."

"We did not like to receive so little," Delilah says. "Their first letter—"

My women will not like to hear, but I say it anyway. "What if they have moved on west?"

"Maybe that corn sheller outfit," Abigail says. "They might know. If so, where . . ."

"We do not know the address—that company," Delilah says. "Even if they know of whereabouts."

I try again. "We cannot waste a stamp. Two years is a long time not to hear."

Long minutes pass. Delilah reaches a hand to me.

I make effort to lift my eyes to hers, beseeching. "Tell the boys we are planting," I say.

"Tell them we watch and pray," Abigail says.

"Tell them we will not give up," I say.

"It is warmer now," Abigail says. "Tell them that."

"We watch for green sprouts?" Delilah suggests. "Shall I say that?"

I nod and reach my palm to Abigail. "The ground is waking. We keep watch."

J. Fretz — Chicago, May 1865

Life goes on, moving in fits and starts. We slowly recover from April 15th, try to adjust to Andrew Johnson at the helm. I was surprised at my shakenness. These past years I claimed to give primary allegiance to God. Yet at the time of the assassination, I thought, like many others, that the world had collapsed. My trust had been in a human being, although I'd known better and said otherwise.

When I told Salome I wanted to pass by Lincoln's body, she wondered why. I shrugged. "A marker perhaps. Something of me has passed away also. Grief for all that has been lost."

Lincoln wasn't *loved* by many while alive—uncouth, ungainly—but now, in a month's time, he's revered by many. How fickle! I'm no better. People gathered at depots all along the route of the "Lincoln Special" to Springfield. His body lay in state in Chicago as in other large cities. His face, worn and sagging, a sallow cast. His hair combed as if plastered to his head. A black suit, of course. No evidence of the bullet hole. Perhaps he did as much as he could.

I stood in line and waited; I meant to be early, but a large crowd had gathered already. All that Lincoln had suffered—he hated slavery; that was his Gethsemane. But he loved the Union more. His desire to reunite and reconstruct was snatched from him. Likely from us, as well. What price, to be viewed now as a martyr! What a toll for this young country to bear. Who hasn't been touched? Lives and innocence gone.

We had to wait in line a long time. Devotion to a mortal man. But in spite of the cold, I couldn't leave. I had money on me, for I'd intended to go to the bank also. I didn't want to lose my place in line. I stood with arms crossed over my chest, defying pickpockets; I pulled my overcoat tighter. I'd forgotten my woolen scarf, thinking winter had passed. My feet felt like clods. At last, the line moved inside, and we passed slowly before the casket. Afterward, I went home directly, chilled to the core, ignoring my work piled up at the office. Salome made a hot toddy for me.

With the end of war, there's been no end to bitterness. Only a fool would expect that. Long ago, Ralph Waldo Emerson thought conquering Mexico would "poison us." Now we live with evil coursing through our nation's bloodstream. Yes, a military unit of black soldiers was included in Lincoln's funeral services in Washington. The slaves are free—somewhat. It's *unlawful* for Negroes *not* to be free. How many ways can I say this? Slavery is no longer *officially* sanctioned. But it still exists, debilitates, and destroys. I do not need to go to Alabama to see. Andrew Johnson, a Southerner, is to lead us; I dismiss him with a brush of my hand. I doubt he has ever seriously questioned the right of whites to live favored lives.

Violence is still the order of the day. Not by armies, but individuals fired by hatred. How many men wish they'd been the one who killed Lincoln? Even here in Chicago, several men publicly voiced *satisfaction* at Lincoln's death, used disrespectful language to flaunt their disloyalty. Their reward? They were shot. When will people learn? An eye for an eye still won't settle differences. There's no way to redeem this war, much as people try. They only imagine some grand design from a Higher Being in these thousands of deaths.

The work of mending is needed everywhere. Moses accidentally knocked our teapot, a wedding gift from a favorite aunt of Salome's, off the table. A result of his usual haste, but we tried to reassure. I found cement to put the lip of the spout back on. It may hold for a while. But liquid doesn't pour the same. Our beautiful black pot with painted flowers, all one piece again, but tea comes out in spurts. My clumsy repairs will always show.

Different in degree, of course, from the thousands of whites in the South who resent being forced to extend human rights. Small bursts of half-hearted effort. But change of heart? Their custom of exercising third-class treatment is still seen as a right. Little thought for what the man with darker skin has endured.

Who am I to pass judgment? My own shift from rabid follower of political events to accepting the mantle of church work feels awkward. I carry no expectation that religious faith will be a resting place. Beidler keeps telling me I'm making a terrible mistake and asking, "Why would you do such a thing? Throw your life away." I'm grateful, though, that he's willing to talk. For all my exasperation with him, he doesn't fit the common saying that men only remain true if they can make money from you. His concern seems genuine; he's Jacob at heart.

Mary Ann may have interceded. I was surprised when she told me, "It's in your blood." I wouldn't have given her credit for listening or remembering. She claims that after my first trip to Indiana, I told her about our great-great-grandfather, Heinrich, and his work of writing. All I recall from that exchange is that she showed little interest in our ancestor, coming to this New World from Europe in 1717, being ordained to the ministry, even becoming a bishop. But the way she tells it, I grabbed her arm and mentioned the Sunday afternoon when I first held his book about baptism. She says I raved about that brown binding already being over a hundred years old. She admits it didn't mean anything to her. And now when I mention Heinrich's clear thinking, whether using the Dutch or German, she looks off in the distance.

So here I am—how often have I said that? Whatever my stages of conversion, I've gone from a young man with nary a care about religion, to making effort to pull a broken church back together. I search for words to reach those in the Ohio hotbed, my Northern brothers who hired substitutes. I don't understand my bereft brothers and sisters in the South who sent their sons to war. All I can do is remind folks of Jesus's words. If war breaks out again, we'll be better prepared. We must be.

My dream of printing the *Martyrs Mirror* in English hasn't gone away—more than fifty years since the German version was printed in this country. But Salome cautions me about those expectations. I've said, "If our people *read for themselves* about Anabaptists suffering for the cause of peace during the Reformation in Europe, it will go a long way to strengthen our scruples."

"A worthy goal, for sure, John. But people will interpret for themselves."

I'm miffed, but she's probably right. When I first wrote an editorial, back in January, about the use of substitutes, some readers thought my comparison extreme. I felt scorned and intentionally misunderstood—much like with Joe over a year ago, when he diverted attention by attacking me. Another reader responded with the same argument Beidler had used: my imaginary "white slave" substitute still pocketed money. But one man wrote in agreement about not putting his life above another's. I wish he would have added "whether picking cotton or toting a gun to kill a man," but he didn't.

It will take long years, but we must change how we approach government. State our beliefs about peace, first off. We can't cling to the wishful thinking that our tax money *might* be helping wounded soldiers. Who in the draft operation, North or South, with both sides known for corruption, would have cared enough to keep track of any given taxpayer's desire for a more uplifting use of resources than destruction? That's absurd.

And the Mennonites who went to war—Salome knows I toss at night for them. Will their home churches welcome them back? Will those men *want* to return? Soldiering surely changed them, whatever their religious background—fighting beside and relying on the next man. How can I speak, though, as if I know anything, when I've lost track of Andy and Phil, even Joe now? Multiply that by thousands—soldiers who don't know if they'll still connect with friends they left behind.

The Hildebrand bishop in Virginia—I've come to dread his letters. His latest shocking news: his cousin Jacob's son—not the one killed by friendly fire, but another son—was in attendance with Lee at Appomattox. The bishop gave no explanation, but the young man must have befriended Lee in some way. Perhaps a body servant. Where does that young man stand now? Does he feel disgraced with the rest of the South? Or bitter? And the church he came from—will those Mennonites receive him again? Easier if they never turned from him.

Another development startled and came to rankle: this from Mennonites in my home state, especially the eastern part, the ones who didn't go to war. I opened the *Bucks County Intelligencer* one day to see a headline: "Patriotism of the Mennonites." I pulled the paper closer, read the whole article, reread the list of resolutions. Germantown folks back home! Not even Abe, my brother, would defend this.

I ranted to Salome, "Who gave them permission? Oberholtzer? I used to admire him; he didn't separate himself as much from the world." She paused in mincing fresh green onions from our garden as I continued: "To say that Mennonites give praise to God for the success of the North's arms on land and sea—that's a terrible misunderstanding."

She came to look over my shoulder.

"And to follow that—look at this." I swatted the paper with the backs of my fingers. "A pledge to help crush 'any remaining rebellion from the South!'" I handed the paper to her. "Read it! What has happened? Caving to their neighbors?"

"You don't know who wrote," Salome said, "not for certain. Or why."

"But those words—whoever picked up the pen, chose to adopt the government's view. I believe in keeping lines of communication open, but we should speak truthfully. This writer says it's acceptable to keep white folks in charge."

"War turns folks, one way or the other. Have *you* changed?" Salome asked. Martha stirred in the other room. "That may be the truth for folks in our home community."

"But they call themselves mainstream Mennonites. That's not mainstream. Not resolutions like that! Saying the war was a *holy* war. Rejoicing over victory that involved the flow of blood and power of weapons. It says that—right?"

She handed the paper back. Martha had quieted, and Salome went back to her dicing. "Maybe it's the middle of the stream for *that* group. Who is the judge?"

"But false notions about Mennonites—someone will have to undo them! We've held back too long because we tied beliefs to compromise."

Martha's chirping—Salome calls it babbling—interrupted us long enough to bring us both to smiling. "She wants to be heard, too," I said.

"It's not easy, John. Change comes from within, not all at once. You know that. It's slower than the long time it takes me to get used to not calling you Fretz." Salome glanced toward the door. "Why don't you go for a walk? It might clear you. This latest disappointment. I'll tend Martha."

She's wearied of me again. Of course, I know there must be change from the head *and* the heart. I've said that. I can't impose from a distance. But my newspaper—

I reached for my hat and jacket like an obedient boy exiled. Why had Salome brought up the strangeness of calling me John again? When we fell in love, I was Fretz, but now she insists I'm one person, not either or. Just as quickly, Mary Ann picked it up. I was outnumbered again.

I miss going for walks with Salome. But this spring, the sidewalks in our neighborhood are too unreliable to take Martha out in the perambulator. Nor can I go for a walk after dark; I need to be able to see where the muck is. In some places the city is building elevated wooden walks to get above the mud. But not here. Jim told me about his neighbor who calls the first floor of his house the basement and has added a floor above it, lifting himself out of mud.

As usual, walking in crisp spring air calmed me. When home again, all was quiet with Martha, too, for Salome had pulled out the rag doll she made that has a hat—a diversion for Martha to take off and put on. Salome must feel she has to keep me from dangerous ideas, too—like she keeps Martha from crawling toward our stairsteps. Salome immediately asked me to put on my black broadcloth suit so she could check the knee-length coat and study whether the slight flare hung right. I sighed, but like always, it's best not to disagree when it comes to clothes.

We'd gone back and forth earlier about parting my hair. I had tried it in the middle for several days; Ross made no comment at work. But Salome said to go back to parting on the left side to hide my cowlick. As usual, she's right: there's no virtue in appearing plain, not even to align better with Mennonites. She makes choices for herself, too, when it comes to apparel. She never adds lace to a dress but wears a white shoulder neckerchief—says her neck looks long without something to soften. I couldn't admit that I'd not noticed, but in the end, we agreed that modesty is important, along with being ourselves. I'm sticking with my black bow tie, partly because it keeps my throat warm when I speak. My trimmed beard hides some of the tie anyway, if it bothers someone.

In another month I'll head for Grundy County. John M. will be there, but Salome has decided not to go that Sunday. For my first sermon there, I used the fifteenth verse from the first chapter of I Timothy—"*This is a faithful saying . . .* "—but I haven't chosen a text for my ordination sermon. It's a new discipline, choosing words to *speak*; that first time I preached, I thought and prayed—what was most important?—wrote down a few words to remember, and went where that led. Abe hasn't said whether he wants to come along, but he's stopped pelting me with questions. I can't blame him for not offering much encouragement. He followed me to Chicago, thinking I was a businessman. Now what's *he* going to do in another year?

He knows I haven't approached Jim yet about resigning. Nor have I written to Father. After I calculated more carefully, I realized I hadn't put away enough money. I might have to stay in lumber another year. If I start my own printing business, the profit from the $1,500 I invested in our lumber company will pay only a part. But the problem is more than a cash shortage. I don't know where I would set up.

Salome has a new habit, rubbing her forehead excessively before she speaks, especially when it's along the lines of "we're still barely getting a start." All my uncertainty may have dampened her spirit; I can't blame her. She's enthusiastic, though, when we talk about her trip to see family, so we stick to that, as much as possible. We don't need to decide now if she and Martha will make the weekly trip south with me to the Grundy church meetings come fall. I need Salome to come along, but I know it would be one more burden, packing extras for Martha *and* looking out for both of us.

I was surprised at how distraught Moses was when he got wind of what might come. Abe insists he didn't spill it. Moses gets along well with Beidler, so that's probably how the news traveled. Anyone can see Moses's natural affinity for business. He'll be in good hands if Beidler spirits him away from Jim.

But to me, Moses choked up. "I don't want to lose your friendship, Fretz."

I wanted to reassure him, but words didn't come easily. "It's difficult. I don't—we'll always be brothers. Wherever—" Now I wonder if Beidler jumped ahead and told Moses that I'll likely have to leave the city.

"I know a few people here now," Moses said, his weak effort at bravery.

My hand on his shoulder felt limp, and he didn't turn to face me. The worst would be if my aunt and uncle held it against me, thinking I abandoned him. It surprises me that Moses has been here a year and a half but still hasn't gone back to visit his home folks.

Why do we disappoint people? Or set ourselves up to be disappointed? Someone might say that I've betrayed those closest: Beidler, Abe, Moses. Maybe Salome, too; she might never adapt to the city. I don't know if my decisions will ever make life *easier* for her.

And here's another question that bothers. Do we ever—not just slave owners—make decisions that don't take advantage of someone? Not that we mean to inflict harm, or intentionally make choices that hurt others. But our callings shift—our desires and interests. Is it inevitable? I never dreamed when I came to Chicago that my ambition would change. Certainly not so drastically. I was sure of myself—it's hard to remember exactly—never thinking beyond the satisfaction of coins in my pocket. Well, it wasn't hard to prefer office shirts to heavy farm britches.

Lately, I've been drawn to John Greenleaf Whittier's poem about feeling hurt because of a wrong from someone he'd trusted. Not until he'd walked past a burial place, could he take a different perspective and see "*Where, pondering how all human love and hate / Find one sad level . . . / cold hands folded over a still heart*."

At first, those words seemed heartless. But they're not the end of the story or the poem. Whether life stops on a battlefield or in a parlor, our common human ending can help us connect with others, even those who see warfare differently. Maybe I can sympathize . . . a bit more with Lincoln, even though I still think he made terrible mistakes. But as Whittier found: "*Our common sorrow, like a mighty wave, / Swept all my pride away, and trembling I forgave!*"

I can't expect everyone I come across to give *me* the benefit of the doubt. Nor can I say a slave *should* forgive his master—not with the awful way he's been treated. Not if there's no remorse from the owner. But for myself, I can be less demanding, less judgmental of others. Remember how I want to be treated, and then treat Salome that way, too. It will take more than memorable words in a speech or sermon; I have to show Salome that her needs matter as much as mine.

It's like our country's motto, *E pluribus unum*, put on our seal and on some of our coins since late in the eighteenth century. "Out of many, one," or "One from many," however it's translated from the Latin. That, too, has to be more than a clever saying for a politician. I need to apply it with Beidler and Ross. ". . . *do ye even so to them*" means now, not for some later reward.

Whether an individual or a nation, we can't undo the past, can't totally forget or forgive raw griefs. Our religious beliefs divide us. So also, the color of our skin. The mud and muck of being human. But there's more of commonality in us—if we pay attention—than race or class or belief. If we—*if I*—can resolve not to let anger or resentment take over, we can live purposefully for the peace of everyone. But I won't forget the terrible battles. Deaths! Endless suffering. My mission school boys. Farmers starting over. Remembering can keep me human, kinder.

We're all in this together. Joe taught me that about war. It's true about slavery, too. Everybody's dipped in it, somewhere on Joe's tarnal chain. I'm either part of the system, or working to stop the oppression of it. It's not possible to be neutral about mistreating people. I can't let naked hatred slip into a forgotten line of a history book.

Esther — far from home, May 1865

I took Miriam to the necessary; here they call it the outhouse. We huddled in the corner, and I whispered for her not to squirm. She takes steps now. I told stories about what it's like to go to school. "We paid money for your big brothers," I said, hushed. "A dollar for each boy, each month. When they were little, but bigger than you. They sat on long benches and practiced their ciphering. They had slates." I made swirling motions in the air to show a quill pen moving for writing lessons. "When you grow big, you will sign your name."

I jumped when Lena banged on the door and said, "Is that you, Esther?" I stayed quiet and put my hand over Miriam's mouth. I don't like Lena's questions. "Are you done now?" She wants me to stay busy, but I tell her I need to think on things. Sometimes I mumble.

She called again, louder, "Esther?"

I answered "Yes," but Miriam squealed to get away. I didn't mean to cause trouble.

"Let me in," Lena said. "*Bischt du grank?*"

I wasn't one bit sick; I only wanted to be safe. Last night men came with torches; I smelled smoke, but I wasn't going to stay another night on the hill.

Soon Mary Grace came to the door. I got to my feet right away; she's my mama. Miriam jumped up and down. I unhooked the latch, and Mary Grace took Miriam in her arms. Miriam looked back at me and pointed. I held out my arms, but she buried her head in Mary Grace's shoulder. We all went inside and played with Jephthah's blocks. Mary Grace said it was a bad dream.

My boys disobeyed the day they went to Harrisburg. That's Pennsylvania, where we live now. They went with Matthias—all the big boys—to see the corpse. William and Shem, too, but not Michael and Timothy or the others. Not Jephthah. I couldn't lay a hand to stop the big ones. Mary Grace showed dark clouds, but I clutched for her to stay. I don't want her to ever leave. She says my color is good, though I've been through one fright after another.

A man killed the president, and my boys went to see the body. They said Harrisburg was the place to go see. There they have a State House. The boys saw a hearse and fancy horses. Bands played and crowds came. They said it was like a parade, but solemn. A big flag was halfway down. William looked like he'd been crying, but it might have been spring blossoms.

My big boys work for Matthias in the fields. But not Peter. Matthias says Peter has never been here. Every day but Sunday, Andrew and Joseph work; William, too, when not sneezing. Matthias smiles big. "This year we don't have to worry about soldiers; the war is over." He showed me his nice watch with big hands. I cried to tell, "I forgot to snatch Simon's."

I did some other bad things; I can't remember for sure about Samuel's carriage. A man yelled to start walking when the hack driver didn't come back. The man shooed us away from his well. Like on the wagon train, I told Jephthah we would eat by and by.

I carried Miriam, and Mary Grace slung a bag of duds over her shoulder. Then we switched. Sometimes William ran ahead with Jephthah, but I had to call loud if they ran around the bend.

Here where Matthias lives, their snow stays a long time. But Mary Grace says it's spring. I shake my head and wear Lena's shawl all day. Lena says I was a big help with spinning. She said that before. Her strawberries stay small and white, but when it's time, I can help pick. Someone else will stem. Mary Grace milks the good cow. Matthias has two, but the one has a bad bag and is ornery.

We have no more cow in Virginia, but the boys want to go back; Andrew and Joseph say so. William won't say. Joseph says he wants another chance. We don't have a place, but he smiles and nods his head. I don't remember the way. Mary Grace says we had trouble at the river. Matthias says for me to rest. He says I have a hole, deep inside. The sunshine will patch it.

When Lena finds me counting in the pantry, she says we have plenty of sacks. Sometimes I sit there on the floor and look at every shelf. Lena says not to worry and pats my arm. I still like my blue dress.

Yesterday was Tuesday again, but Mary Grace says it will soon turn to June. She says she's fifteen. Lena beams and says, "Your girl is all grown up." I don't know what to say—Mama never said aught like that to me—but I smile and touch Mary Grace's cheeks.

I like to watch robins with Miriam; we saw one singing atop a post. That means good weather. The boys say people are making plans. They say people can go by stagecoach to our Valley. I won't let Andrew and Joseph go by themselves. They don't know the way. I tell them to obey, but I always say it nice.

Andrew says, "We know what's what, Ma; we're ready."

Joseph says, "You and the others can stay here. We want you to feel better, Ma."

We sit and have a long talk. I start to say Peter will come looking. But then I catch myself. I know not to say about Simon.

"Ma, I've done it before," Andrew says. "I know the way. Joseph, too; we know near to the same. We'll build a log house on the old spot. Then we'll come back to help Matthias with harvest. After that—" he smiles great big, "we'll all go back to Virginia. You'll see, Ma."

"Not us," Lena says, quick as a jackrabbit. "No long trips for me."

"Simon wouldn't approve. He knows I never wanted to cross that river," I say. "We don't have an axe to our name."

Joseph sits on a footstool beside me and holds my hand.

"The boys can take of my extra pegs," Matthias says. "Not weigh themselves down with tools, though."

"When we moved to Virginia," I say to him, "Father brought axes, saws, wedges. Mama had pots banging in a box. And Father's great big wagon had a white—"

Andrew butts in. "We'll borrow tools when we get there. We'll write you a long letter."

"A good plan," Lena says. "People say it's safe. Your boys know what to do, Esther."

"Too many boys lost. I don't want to cry tears," I say.

"You can trust us, Ma," Joseph says. He wipes his cheek with the back of his hand. Somewhere he got his tender heart.

"I'll keep you busy all summer, Esther," Lena says. Sometimes her hair looks reddish; her chin hairs are too light to see today. "We'll have peas, then beans. We'll get your faculties back. Won't we, Mary Grace?"

"I'll stay and help Matthias and Shem," William says. "We'll work for our keep, Ma."

"What will you eat?" I ask my big boys.

"We know how to do," Joseph says. "Berries. My friend Isaac showed me. Whatnot."

Everybody nods at everyone else, like they're for sure. Mary Grace comes to my other side; she stoops her head to my shoulder. The boys promise to go see Frances.

"Samuel will vouch for our land," Andrew says.

"It's Simon's land," I say.

"We don't know how they fared—the winter," Mary Grace says. "Frances, the others."

Everyone hushes.

"It was Samuel's carriage," I say, "with a fancy top. Tell him, sorry. Very sorry."

* * *

The big boys are bustling; their bags are packed. Mary Grace gave them from my coins to put in a pouch. Matthias says the boys did good work; they know the way all the way. He says his Shem and my William will help him finish planting. "The Lord is good," he says.

Joseph carved a wooden wagon for Jephthah. Andrew tried to carve a horse, but it looks like a hog with long legs. The wagon has four bumps for wheels, but Jephthah scoots it on the floor, all the same, with his hand. He jumps up and chases Timothy.

Joseph calls to Jephthah and holds up four fingers. "Four months and we'll come get you. Mary Grace will keep track of the months. Won't you?"

Andrew catches Jephthah and twirls him around. "We'll take all of you back in a real wagon with wheels."

"Not me," Lena says.

Miriam bounces on my lap; she babbles and blows bubbles. I wipe the dribbles on her chin with my hand. I pucker my lips and give her a kiss.

Mary Grace sits beside us and motions with her arms to go around like a wheel.

I take Miriam's tiny arms and show her how. "Do like your sister," I say. "Like so. Fast."

Mary Grace claps for her and they do patty-cake. Miriam giggles.

"I remember when you were little," I say to Mary Grace, "my first girl. You had curls like Miriam but had dark black hair like—" I know to stop, but she smiles. I swivel Miriam to face me again. "Someday you'll be big like Mary Grace. Wait and see."

She holds her hands together, puckers, and blows a bubble back to me.

Author's Note—Spring 2021

Writing this trilogy, SCRUPLES ON THE LINE, has been an enriching, albeit long journey. The deaths and suffering that run through this story weigh heavily, whether in the writing or reading. I began doing research twelve years ago while I was still teaching at the University of Wisconsin - Whitewater. I knew so little when I began to read about the American Civil War; now I'm more fully aware of all I still don't know or understand. Despite the length of this full manuscript, many buried stories await discovery by someone else.

My fiction writing depends on developing characterizations. The historical record for the characters in my novels who are based on actual people, was often neither clear nor complete. For example, not all of John F. Funk's diaries from the Civil War years were available in the Mennonite Archives, housed on the Goshen College campus when I was doing research. As with all characters, I used my best judgment in the way I described his actions, dialogue, and thoughts, based on the evidence I found and on what best served the needs of the story. In writing the early chapters I knew what circumstances each character would experience by the middle of 1865. Those early characterizations of desire were intended to prepare the reader for later reversals and fulfillment.

I often asked myself: what is the range of possibility for this character? What would be believable for a thoughtful reader? Truly, human life is a puzzle, and writing about characters' lives involves figuring out the size and shape of each puzzle piece. That leads then to imagining and fitting the pieces together.

Language has been another fascinating but complex aspect of writing this trilogy. All of these characters, coming from Germanic backgrounds in the nineteenth century, learned English as immigrants but likely used Pennsylvania Dutch most of the time. This oral language of borrowing words, expressions, and spellings from surrounding languages adds a richness to my characters' vocabularies and thoughts. The examples of German and Pennsylvania Dutch in the text are intended to remind readers of this historical context.

The Civil War story also demands that these books include a sampling of the hatefulness conveyed through some of the spoken language during these years. For us today, the nineteenth century's use of the word Negro, while considered polite then, sounds foreign or offensive. My choice to use relatively few samples of harsh speech, doesn't convey the full horror of abusive and demeaning language. Members of Anabaptist groups, like those of any other affiliation, were on both sides of the giving and receiving of mocking, derogatory depictions and name-calling. I ask the reader to understand the enormity of *hatred* shown in the actions of individuals and competing governments, and to recognize how superior attitudes among people are corrosive to well-being.

For the historical record, Jacob Schwartzendruber died in 1868; his son Frederick became an Amish bishop in Iowa. John (Fretz) Funk played an important role in shaping the Mennonite church as publisher, minister, and bishop, living in Elkhart County, Indiana, for over sixty years until he died in 1930. According to Hugh Gingerich and Rachel W. Kreider's book, *Amish and Amish Mennonite Genealogies*, 1986, Lovina (Betsey in these books) Petersheim was born on January 27, 1853, but there is no record of her life or death.

What these books add up to is for the reader to consider while imagining beyond the text. My desire is that these stories of suffering and courage will be an impetus to live more justly and generously, knowing how violent language, policies, and actions touch everyone's lives, whether during times of announced war or in years of apparent peace.

Acknowledgments

As my trilogy of books comes closer to completion, many of the names of contributors and supporters in the process may be familiar but no less valued. I begin with those who have read drafts of the manuscript at various points: Marilyn Durham, Firman Gingerich, Alex Hancock, Carol Lehman, Andrea Wallpe, Brenda Smith White, and Wesley White. They encouraged me from the beginning, pulled me out of scrapes in the middle, and gave steadfast support to the conclusion. In particular, Marilyn's "big picture" advice, along with her multiple readings, have been enormously helpful.

Many other friends and professionals became resources for specific aspects, ranging from understanding specific topics, geographic areas, or historical figures: Lois Bowman, Christopher and Marti Eads, Denise Ehlen, Lois Gugel, Mary and Merlin Grieser, James Lehman, Steve Nolt, John Roth, Paul Roth, Joe Sprunger, Lisa Weaver, Joanne Yoder, Marie and Paul E. Yoder, and Suzanne Wolfe. Additional professionals provided expertise in formatting, Jodi Brown; in copyediting, Joanie Eppinga; in knowledge of Pennsylvania Dutch and German, Mark Louden; in website design, Susanne Gubanc; in creating family charts, Hannah Sandvold; and in designing maps and offering technical assistance, Jeanie and Steve Tomasko. My daughters, Alice Schermerhorn and Sarah Piper, gave technical support, publicity advice, and "yes-you-can" trust.

I'm grateful also to the many professionals, such as Matthew Wimer at Wipf and Stock Publishers, who provided skill in creating this series of books. For the errors that remain, I take responsibility.

Numerous friends helped me manage the woes of pandemic-induced isolation by bringing together groups of people for Zoom readings and conversations about Books I and II: Caitlin Bond (UpBEAT, Athens, Ohio), Gloria Gingerich, Linda and Keith Gnagey, Suzanne Marie Hitt, Clif Hostetler, Bonnie King, Kathie Kurtz, Mandy North, Dorothy Yoder Nyce, Trevor Sharping (Kalona Public Library), Pat Swartzendruber, Lisa Weaver,

Helen Yoder, June Alliman Yoder. Through these publicity efforts I've renewed and formed friendships, and kept the candle burning.

I also want to extend less traditional thanks for the many unnamed people along the way who influenced my thinking and steadied my efforts toward shining a light on the experiences of religious pacifists during the American Civil War. Some of these folks don't know of my trilogy, but they fostered curiosity, encouraged thoroughness, and advocated for creative expression. I name Alta Brenneman Keiser, a Kalona, Iowa neighbor, as an example from my childhood who shaped my outlook by making the work of podding peas while sitting around the cistern, a fun activity when interspersed with riddles and amusing oldtime sayings. I recall visiting the Amish school where Alta taught and observing a different culture of learning.

And finally, I'm grateful to my current pastor, Valerie Showalter at Madison Mennonite Church, for holding up the gift of the moral imagination as a companion in religious understanding. Her friendship also represents that of many others, from high school and college teachers who reinforced my interests in faith and action, to people in Appalachia where I lived for nineteen years, to professors and writers in graduate school who rekindled my love of literature and enlarged my world view. Indeed, many people have pointed me to the intersections of history, religion, and art, where the struggles of human rights and equality often show up in all their mess and glory.

Credits

(first words of quoted material and sources, if not identified in the text)

"All quiet along the Potomac" appears in the song first published as "The Picket Guard," and written by Ethel Lynn Eliot Beers. Available under Creative Commons Attribution-ShareAlike License.

"Blest Be" comes from the text of John Fawcett's hymn, "Blest Be the Tie that Binds," in the Mennonite *Church Hymnal.*

"*E Pluribus Unum*" is credited to Pierre Eugene du Simitiere in the context of the Seal of the United States in 1776.

"How do I love thee" begins the poem by the same name, written by Elizabeth Barrett Browning.

"If one ill treat you" and "Of such a man" begin verses in the German hymn, used with Michael Sattler's text and first published in the *Ausbund.*

Words to Charles Wesley's hymn that begins "Jesus, Lover of my Soul," are found in *Papers from the Elder John Kline Bicentennial Celebration.*

"Keep me in thy truth" comes from Anna of Freiburg's prayer in *Martyrs Mirror.*

"*Mit Lust so will ich singen*" are hymn words from Feliz Manz in the *Ausbund.*

"Oh, we'll rally round the flag" and "The Union forever, hurrah!" come from the first verse and chorus of George F. Root's song, "The Battle Cry of Freedom."

The words "Rock of Ages, cleft for me" begin A. M. Toplady's hymn, "Rock of Ages," in Mennonite *Church Hymnal.*

Versions of the prayer with the line "*Steh' uns bei*" and of the ABC rhyme are in Alta Keiser's memoir, "Lest We Forget."

"When the storms of life assail," "When my journey nears," and "As I pass through," begin hymn lines found in *Harmonia Sacra.*

Lines that begin "Where, pondering how all human love and hate" along with "Our common sorrow" are in John Greenleaf Whittier's poem titled "Forgiveness."

(first words of Scripture references, KJV, if not identified in the text)

Exod 20:13 – "Thou shalt not kill"

Job 39:1, 27 – "Knowest thou the time" and "Doth the eagle"

Ps 23:1 – "The Lord is my shepherd"

Ps 24:1 – "The earth is the Lord's"

Ps 34:18 – "The Lord is nigh unto them"

Ps 121:1 – "whence cometh my help"

Isa 52:7 – "How beautiful upon the mountains"

Matt 5:3 – "Blessed are the poor in spirit"

Matt 6:12 – "And forgive us our debts"

Matt 7:12 – "do ye even so to them"

Matt 9:30 – "See that no man know it"

Matt 11:29 – "Take my yoke upon you"

Matt 25:21 – "Well done, thou good and faithful servant"

Luke 12:32 – "Fear not, little flock"

John 15:19 – "out of the world"

Acts 2:44 – "And all that believed were together"

Glossary of Pennsylvania Dutch and German

Aber ja. - But yes.

Bischt du grank? - Are you sick?

Bobbli - baby

Bol en Glennes - A little one soon.

dappich - clumsy

Der Herold der Wahrheit - title of newspaper: *Herald of Truth*

Dieners-Versammlung - ministers' meeting

flotchety - fluttery

Gemeine - congregation

Gemeinschaft - denomination

klutzich - awkward

Kotze - vomit

Lumpekaer - mean or crooked person

milch - milk

Mir kumme aus. - We will make do.

Mir verschtehn net ferwas. - We do not understand the why.

Mit Lust so will ich singen - song title: I will delight in singing

nixnutzich - mischievous

Noch net gans. - Not quite yet.

O, nee, nee. - Oh, no, no.

Ordnung - discipline

schlappichi Arrewet - shoddy work

Schtinker - not a trustworthy person

Sei schtill! - Be quiet!

Steh' uns bei in aller Not, und verlass uns nicht im Tod. - Be with us in every difficulty and leave us not in death.

unterdrückung - stifling

Verschtehscht? - Understand?

Yuscht ebaut uffgwachse. - Just about grown.

Selected Bibliography

Ayers, Edward L. *In the Presence of Mine Enemies: The Civil War in the Heart of America 1859–1863*. W. W. Norton: New York, 2003.

Bittinger, Emmert F., ed. *Unionists and the Civil War Experience in the Shenandoah Valley* 5. Valley Research Associates: Penobscot, 2009.

Bowman, Carl F. *Brethren Society: The Cultural Transformation of a "Peculiar People."* Johns Hopkins University Press: Baltimore, 1995.

Bowman, Rufus D. "The Position of the Church of the Brethren During the Civil War." In *The Church of the Brethren and War*. 101–56. Brethren: Elgin, IL, 1944.

Brunk, Harry A. *History of the Mennonites in Virginia*. McClure: Staunton, VA, 1959.

Burdge, Edsel Jr. and Samuel L. Horst. "A Very Great Unrest in the Whole Land (Washington-Franklin Mennonites and the Civil War, 1861–1865)." In *Building on the Gospel Foundation*. Herald: Scottdale, PA, 2004.

Donald, David Herbert. *Lincoln*. Simon & Schuster: New York, 1995.

Eberly, William R., ed. *Papers from the Elder John Kline Bicentennial Celebration*. Brethren Encyclopedia, Inc.: Ambler, PA, 2002.

Faust, Drew Gilpin. *This Republic of Suffering: Death and the American Civil War*. Vintage: New York, 2008.

Funk, John F. *Diaries, 1852*, 1857–1863. Mennonite Church USA Archives, Goshen, IN.

———. Autobiography – "Early Life," "My Ancestors," etc. Mennonite Historical Library, Goshen, IN.

Gates, Helen Kolb, et al., *Bless the Lord O My Soul: A Biography of Bishop John Fretz Funk* 1835–1930, ed. John C. Wenger. Herald: Scottdale, PA, 1964.

Gingerich, Melvin. *The Mennonites in Iowa*. State Historical Society of Iowa: Iowa City, Iowa, 1939.

Goldfield, David. *America Aflame: How the Civil War Created a Nation*. Bloomsbury: New York, 2011.

Hartman, Peter S. *Reminiscences of the Civil War*. Eastern Mennonite Associated Libraries and Archives: Lancaster, PA, 1964.

Heatwole, John L. *The Burning: Sheridan's Devastation of the Shenandoah Valley*. Rockbridge: Charlottesville, VA, 1998.

———. *Shenandoah Voices: Folklore, Legends and Traditions of the Valley*. Rockbridge: Charlottesville, VA, 1995.

Hershberger, Guy F. "Mennonites in the Civil War." *Mennonite Quarterly Review* 18 (1944) 131–44.

Hildebrand, Jacob R. *A Mennonite Journal*, 1862–1865: *A Father's Account of the Civil War in the Shenandoah Valley*, ed. John R. Hildebrand. Shippensburg, Burd Street, 1996.

Horst, Samuel. *Mennonites in the Confederacy: A Study in Civil War Pacifism*. Herald: Scottdale, PA, 1967.

Lehman, James O. and Steven M. Nolt. *Mennonites, Amish, and the American Civil War*. Johns Hopkins University Press: Baltimore, 2007.

Liechty, Joseph and James O. Lehman. "From Yankee to Nonresistant: John F. Funk's Chicago Years, 1857–1865." *Mennonite Quarterly Review* 59 (1985) 203–47.

Lind, Katie Yoder. *From Hazelbrush to Cornfields*. Mennonite Historical Society of Iowa: Kalona, IA, 1994.

Longenecker, Stephen L. *Shenandoah Religion: Outsiders and the Mainstream, 1716–1865*. Baylor University Press: Waco, 2002.

McCutcheon, Marc. *The Writer's Guide to Everyday Life in the 1800s*. Writer's Digest: Cincinnati, OH, 1993.

McPherson, James M. *Battle Cry of Freedom: The Civil War Era*. Oxford University Press: New York, 1988.

Miller, Randall M. et al. *Religion and the American Civil War*. Oxford University Press: New York, 1998.

Nair, Charles E. *John Kline Among His Brethren or How He Filled His Place: A Historical Narrative*. Reprinted for "Remembering John Kline's Life: 150 Years Later" 2014.

Neff, Ray F. *Valley of the Shadow*. 2nd. ed. Rana: Terra Haute, IN, 1989.

Noll, Mark A. *The Civil War as a Theological Crisis*. University of North Carolina Press: Chapel Hill, NC, 2006.

Reschly, Steven D. *The Amish on the Iowa Prairie 1840 to 1910*. Johns Hopkins University Press: Baltimore, 2000.

Ruth, John. "Warfare: Its Evils, Our Duty, 1861–1865." In *Maintaining the Right Fellowship*, 317–42. Herald: Scottdale, PA, 1984.

Sanger, Samuel F. and Daniel Hays. *The Olive Branch of Peace and Good Will to Men: Antiwar History of the Brethren and Mennonites, During the Civil War, 1861–1865*. Brethren: Elgin, IL, 1907.

Schwartzendruber, Jacob. Personal Papers. Iowa Mennonite Museum, Kalona, Iowa.

Stout, Harry S. *Upon the Altar of the Nation: A Moral History of the American Civil War*. Viking: New York, 2006.

Yoder, Paton and Steven R. Estes, eds. *Proceedings of the Amish Ministers' Meetings 1862–1878*. Mennonite Historical Society: Goshen, IN, 1999.

Zigler, Daniel H. *History of the Brethren in Virginia*. Brethren: Elgin, IL, 1914.

www.ingramcontent.com/pod-product-compliance
Lightning Source LLC
Chambersburg PA
CBHW070822020826
48982CB00014B/253
9781666704792